# WATER
A Vic Bengston Investigation

## ALSO BY RICHARD J. SCHNEIDER

FICTION

Who Killed Porkchop?

# WATER

## A Vic Bengston Investigation

A NOVEL BY

# RICHARD J. SCHNEIDER

South Platte Publishing
Denver

South Platte Publishing
P.O. Box 372338
Denver, Colorado 80237

ISBN-10: 0985931302

ISBN-13: 978-0-9859313-0-8

EBook versions of this novel are available for Kindles, Nooks, and all other popular eBook formats at major online eBook outlets.

For more information, visit www.richardjshneider.com.

First Print Edition

The characters and events in this book are fictitious. Any similarity to real persons, living or dead, is coincidental and not intended by the author.

201271104

*In Memory of my father, Richard Roy Schneider, whose love of mysteries infected me, and Michael Ryan Golden, who taught me to just do it.*

*Afterword / Acknowledgements follow this novel.*

# WATER
A Vic Bengston Investigation

# 1

Two shadows stood nearly thigh deep in the chilly waters of the South Platte River. The silent one shoved the reluctant one.

"You can't do this to me." She stumbled forward, hands duct-taped behind her. The unyielding flow of water pushed on the backs of her legs. "Do you know who I am?"

Only the low rumbling rush of the river and the muffled sound of far off city traffic answered. Even the wind had gone to sleep. The silent one rapped the reluctant one's right elbow with something hard.

"Aw," the reluctant one grunted, then began sobbing. "Please. Please, let me go." Then a sharp poke in the back. She slogged two more steps. The silent one followed and lifted a shadowed arm toward her head. "Not here, for the love of G—"

A pop. Then a splash. Only one shadow stood against the unceasing surge of water.

The river, the constant, the blood of the plains, gently carried the other shadowy form downstream.

# 2

Mr. Otis' elevator dumped Vic Bengston into a dense network of gray cubicles, most of them empty. It was Sunday, a slow news day. It had been a year since he last dropped off a piece of public relations hype for some ungrateful client, but the city desk was still in the same place, on the far end of the vast newsroom. As he approached his target, Vic saw that the desk was under the command of someone he did not recognize. She was attractive, late twenties, and talking on a telephone headset. Her short blond hair and bright green eyes went well with her brilliant smile, which she flashed at him as she dealt with whatever was happening on the other end of the phone.

"Where? South of Riverside Cemetery. Where 49th hits Emerson. Okay." She made notes on a computer terminal as she talked. The girl looked up at Vic and jerked her head toward an empty chair on the other side of the desk. Vic sat down. "Get some art. I don't care. Shoot something. Okay, I've got someone coming. Thanks, Steve."

Phone call over, the girl trained her eyes on Vic. "You are?"

"Bengston. Vic Bengston. I'm looking for the city editor."

"Found her."

She was the same age as his daughter, Vic's youngest of four. He cleared his throat, not wanting to sound nervous, which he was.

"You're Mr. Bengston," she said, as though she were meeting her father's business partner for the first time.

"Vic."

"All right, then, Vic." She stood up, reached across the desk and offered her hand. Vic shook it. The grip was firm. "Margaret Mayer."

"Miss Mayer. A pleasure to meet you."

"Peggy, and never Peg," she said, flopping back into her charcoal gray Herman Miller Aeron office chair. She looked at him square in the face. "We heard you'd be in today. You're not quite what I expected."

"Much younger than you thought?" No answer. "Do you know what I'll be doing today?"

"Yes, I do," she said, pulling off the headset and tossing it onto the desk. "I was two years old when you resigned and went to work for Governor Jack Mack, and now you're sitting here across from me waiting for an assignment."

"Is that a problem?"

"Not yet," she said. "But the shift just started."

Vic nodded toward her terminal screen. "What's happening?"

"My police reporter's out sick, and we've got a floater in the South Platte River."

A floater, Vic thought, wondering if she scooped that term up from some cop TV show. "I assume you've got a pool car or two? I took a nostalgic ride downtown on the Number 15 bus."

"Smell like urine?"

"A little. It brought back fond memories."

"The guard downstairs can show you how to get to the garage," she said. "Now, I've already got a photog out there. Jones. Steve Jones. He'll meet you. It's up north. Take I-25 up to—"

"I heard you on the phone," Vic said. "I know where it is. Do you have a police contact."

She scrolled through the notes on her terminal screen. "Uh, let's see. Driscoll. Lieutenant Frank Driscoll."

"Chief of Detectives?" Vic said.

"You know him?"

"I read the papers."

"Well, he's the man. Do you have a cell phone?"

"I do."

"Call me with what you've got. I'll put it together." She handed him a card. "That's the direct line to the city desk. Ask for me in case I don't answer."

So much for dictating a story to the rewrite desk, Vic thought, then said, "As soon as I get the picture."

He stood up and started to negotiate the city room maze in reverse but stopped and walked back to the city desk.

"You have a notebook?" he said. Peggy looked up.

"I do," she said. "You need one too?"

Vic nodded.

She reached into a drawer on the right side of the desk, pulled out a narrow spiral bound reporter's notebook and handed it to him. "I'll show you where the supply cache is when you get back."

"Thanks," he said, turning back toward the maze.

"Have you a pen, little boy?"

Vic kept walking toward the elevator. He pulled a fountain pen from the left inside pocket of his blue blazer and held it high in the air.

"Good luck, kid," she said. "Go carve out a career for yourself."

Luck did seem to be with him, at least on Day One of his new life, Vic thought. A cop shop assignment, a big one. A floater that demanded the attention of the city's top detective meant it was a murder.

And then there was Driscoll.

For the past five years, he and Lieutenant Frank Driscoll, Chief of Detectives for the Denver Police Department, had played golf together every Saturday morning.

# 3

A "floater" in the South Platte River was something of an oxymoron. Settlers described the river as a mile wide and a foot deep. Still, there were pockets of depth here and there that might float a body. Vic wheeled the newspaper's pool car, a late model Ford Explorer, off North Washington Street onto 49th Avenue heading east. The road ended at Emerson Street and, beyond that, the South Platte River. The corner was blocked by three cop cars, lights flashing, and a van from the Denver Medical Examiner's office, so Vic pulled into a wide-open blacktop lot filled with semi-tractor trailers and parked. When he saw the yellow crime scene tape and a gathering of uniformed and suited cops down by the river, he felt a rush, that same surge he used to get when he sensed a hot story.

He shut the engine off and slid out the door. Fumbling with the keys, Vic pressed the red panic button on the key fob. All the lights on the SUV began blinking simultaneously with the blaring horn, which announced to the world that the car was being stolen. "Ah, crap." He held up the fob, squinting so he could see the unlocked padlock symbol, and pressed the button until the SUV lapsed into stony silence, lights off.

Vic turned toward the cops down by the water's edge. All of them had stopped doing whatever they were doing and stared up at him. The six-foot-four frame of Lt. Frank Driscoll towered over the others. Nearby, a man in tan pants and a dark sport coat and a woman in a gray pants suit stood guard next to an empty gurney. Probably from the Medical Examiner's office, Vic thought. The two took a break from pulling on rubber Wellingtons and stared up at him too. Vic felt his heart pound.

The road was a good fifteen feet above the riverbed. Vic side stepped down one tier, crossed the pinkish cement South Platte River Bike Trail, and then began the rest of his descent. All eyes followed him.

The fall was quick and merciful. His left foot landed on a large rock, wobbly enough to eliminate any hope of balance. Vic's other foot flew into the air and the rest of him soared along for the ride. His rump hit hard on the grassy slope and Vic tumbled the rest of the way down to the gathering of Denver's finest.

"Can I say with some level of certainty that you are the last person I thought I'd ever see here today," Driscoll said. "To what do we owe this pleasure?"

Vic scrambled to his feet, brushing himself off. "Same reason you're here."

"I don't think so," Driscoll said. "Are you on some goofy ham radio expedition?"

"No, I'm here to find out about this body."

"Some new corporate client I don't know about, Vic? A coffin company maybe?"

"No, Frank. I'm here for the *Sun*."

"Say what?"

"The *Rocky*. The *Rocky Mountain Sun*," Vic said.

"Oh, don't tell me," Driscoll said. "You've actually gone and done it. I thought you were just babbling away the other day about your rotten company and your life and needing to give meaning to what you do. I had no idea you were actually dumb enough to do this."

"I started today."

"I still don't believe it," Driscoll said.

"Believe it."

"Believe what?" asked a patrolman standing with Driscoll.

"This guy—by the way, Vic Bengston, Officer Harvey Conran," Driscoll said, nodding toward one uniformed cop. Vic and officer Conran shook hands. Officer Denise Peterson. Vic shook her hand. "Mr. Silence over here is Detective Greg Frakes." Another handshake. "Vic and I play golf on Saturdays. He helps me forget you guys, but he apparently is suffering from sunstroke. He's got a nice little public relations company, and he's tossing it all over the side to write for a rag."

"The *Rocky Mountain Sun*?" Frakes said. "Not my favorite bird cage liner."

"Yes, but now in an even conveniently smaller tabloid format," Vic said. He thought he might as well put in a pitch since he had an opening.

"You're right about that," Frakes said. "The *Times* is too big."

"The *Sun* is much easier to read at the coffee counter," Conran said.

"And what coffee counter would that be," Driscoll asked.

"That would be at Winchell's Donuts, sir." Conran grinned.

"Can we get to the business at hand?" Vic said.

Driscoll raised his eyebrows and jerked his head toward a woman's body lying face down in the water at the river's edge. Her right leg was inelegantly hung up on an old cottonwood snag. "You mean this?"

"That's what I had in mind."

"Detective?" Driscoll said to Frakes.

"Not much yet," Frakes said. "Female, probably mid to late forties. No ID on her. I didn't see any wounds, but we can't be sure about that until the ME looks at her."

"How'd you find out about it," Vic said. "Her, I mean."

"Anonymous phone call. About an hour ago. Probably a pre-paid cell phone." Driscoll paused. "That's off the record, Vic. We want to catch this guy, not tip him off."

"She hasn't been dead long," Conran said.

"We don't know that either," Frakes said to the uniform. "But it seems like she hasn't been in the water very long."

Vic reached in his coat pocket for his fountain pen. It was gone.

"Frank, do you have a pen I can borrow?" Vic asked.

"My, aren't we prepared on our first day at the new job," Driscoll said. He looked at the other cops. "Now did we all bring our guns with us today, our mace?"

"I forgot my cuffs," Conran said.

"Two demerits for you, officer," Frakes said.

Driscoll pulled a gold Cross pen from his shirt pocket. He handed it to Vic and said, "I want it back."

"I had one. Don't know where it went."

"Lost it in the tumbling exhibition, perhaps," Frakes said. "We all gave you high nines in the scoring."

Vic stared at Frakes, then took the pen from Driscoll. "Isn't this the pen that I—"

"Yes it is," Driscoll said, holding up his hand. Then he pointed at the uniforms. "Okay. Conran and Peterson, I want you to scour the area for anything. Get some help if you need it. Blanket the place."

"Clothes, shoes, purse, wallet, you name it," Frakes said. "Clark Kent's pen, maybe."

"I'd like to take a look at the body," Vic said.

"No you won't," Frakes said.

"Frank?" Vic said, appealing the decision.

"Not in this lifetime, pal," Driscoll said. "I do not want anyone near that body except my officers and those two over there." He shot a long index finger toward the medical examiner techs.

"I was supposed to meet a photographer here," Vic said. "Seen him?"

"Jones?" Driscoll said. "Here and gone. I had a little chat with him. He's empty-handed."

"You staying, Greg?" Driscoll said to Frakes. It was an order.

"Yeah, I'll call you later," Frakes said.

"Yes you will," Driscoll said. "I'm out of here, then. Keep the place tight. No one gets in. Clear?"

"Right chief," Frakes said.

"Conran," Driscoll shouted. Conran looked up from seventy-five feet away. He waived and gave a thumbs up. "Peterson!" She did the same, from a similar distance in the opposite direction. Driscoll started for the embankment. He gently grabbed Vic's left elbow and pushed him along. "Anything more I can help you with, Mr. Fourth Estate?" Driscoll said, friendly and loud enough for Frakes to hear. Then, under his breath, "Meet me at Sapp Brothers when you leave here. Don't say anything. Just nod."

Vic nodded.

At the top of the embankment, Vic stopped and turned back around to take in the scene. The techs had waded in ankle deep to examine the body. Their hands were sheathed with light blue latex gloves. Up on the bank, a sky blue tarp had been spread out, ready to accept the body once it was pulled off the snag and out of the water.

The woman lifted the victim's right leg. Her partner helped by holding the knee. The two worked efficiently, but gently, as though the victim were still a complete woman with memories, breath, and blood coursing through the body, her soul intact. Only her soul was not there and the only thing flowing was the South Platte River.

Detective Frakes stood on the bank near the techs. He asked questions and made notes. Fifty yards downstream, officer Conran combed the bank for anything that might add to the case. He seemed eager to please. Upstream, Peterson was kneeling, looking at something on the ground.

Wishing he had a set of binoculars, Vic pulled Driscoll's gold pen from his pocket and made a few more notes describing what he saw from the hill. He sketched the river, the snag, and the warehouse in the background, then the body. Something did not seem quite right, but Vic wrote it off to his imagination, stoked, he guessed, by all those hours he spent watching old mystery movies. He twisted the Cross pen closed and held it up to read the inscription on the barrel.

"Lt. Frank Driscoll. 20 Years. Your Pal, Vic"

# 4

The two-story coffee-pot sign at the intersection of Quebec Street and I-70 on Denver's north side signaled the Sapp Brothers truck stop. Like a giant stove heating up the pot, the main building housed a vast complex of showers, lounge areas, game rooms, flat screen televisions, a convenience store, a sit-down restaurant, three different fast food counters, books, DVDs, CD's, and twelve-volt appliances capable of such tasks as making a pizza, cooking hot dogs or brewing coffee, all for the benefit of long-haul truckers.

Vic walked through the store and found a small office supply cache next to a NASCAR keychain display. He pulled a ballpoint out of a Sapp Brothers coffee mug and took it up to the counter where a skinny red-haired old man rang up the sale. Then he walked through the double-wide main entrance to the restaurant. Driscoll sat on one side of a sprawling U-shaped counter, his back toward Vic.

The graying reporter slid onto a stool next to the detective. Three stools away a boisterous mountain of a man with long greasy gray hair pulled back into a ponytail jabbered incessantly to no one in particular. His head bobbed up and down just enough so the tips of his untamed salt and pepper beard dipped in and out of his coffee.

Driscoll jerked his head to the left. "Let's move down, a little further away from the font of knowledge over there." He stood up and swept his coffee mug down the counter with his right hand all the way to the wall. Vic followed. When they had resettled, Vic pulled the gold pen from his shirt pocket and set it on the counter in front of Driscoll.

"You'll want this," Vic said.

"What in hell are you going to write notes with the rest of your shift, Mr. Newspaper Boy?"

"I got this on the way in," Vic said, flashing his new forty-nine-cent ballpoint.

"Want me to loan you my notepad?"

"No. My nanny gave me one at the paper."

"And what about your pants?"

"My pants?"

"You must have torn them up sliding into home down by the river," Driscoll said.

"I'll survive. They're just a little dirty."

"You could stop at Target. Get you another pair. You need a credit card? You got money? Did you eat today?"

"How much of this do I need to take?"

A waitress appeared from nowhere.

"Coffee, sweetie?" she said to Vic, who nodded. A fresh mug flashed from behind her. It was half full by the time it hit the counter. "Menu?"

"No thanks," Vic said. She topped off Driscoll's coffee and vanished.

"You need your head examined," Driscoll said. "Nice little company you've got. Tossing that over the side, for what?"

"I missed it."

"Missed what?"

"Journalism."

"Is that what they call it these days?"

"As opposed to?"

"Uh, let's see," Driscoll said. "Muckraking? Sensationalism? Let's get a cop?"

"You forgot treason."

"That too. What do you mean you missed it?" The detective had dumped three creams and as many packets of sugar into his coffee by now. Vic drank his black.

"I missed it, for crissake!"

"You didn't miss the money," Driscoll said.

"No. I didn't miss the money."

"You're working Sundays already," Driscoll said. "That's special."

"I noticed you're working Sundays too, detective."

"I work every day. Comes with the job."

"Sundays are slow. Good time to get my sea legs."

"You're nuts," Driscoll said, then sucked down a long sip on his creamy sweet coffee.

"Look, you left the force once," Vic said.

"Three whole months," Driscoll said. "To help Eaton get his campaign security team organized. Big deal."

Eaton was Denver's first black mayor. Driscoll and Eaton grew up together on the northeast side, where life for blacks left much to be desired in a city once run by the Ku Klux Klan.

"Can we just leave it at, I wanted a change?" Vic said.

"Change? From what?"

"The corporate crap," Vic said.

"That crap put a lot of food on the table," Driscoll said. "Helped your kids with college."

"I know. I know."

"Bought your sailboat."

"Yes, I know," Vic said. He sipped his now cooled coffee. "It gets old. No real punch, like a breaking news story."

"There's got to be more to it than that," Driscoll said.

"They stopped listening to us," Vic said. "You know, everyone's a writer."

Driscoll said nothing. He nursed his coffee. Mountain man continued to jabber. Vic felt compelled to speak.

"Age," Vic said. "I think they thought Ben and I were too old. Experience didn't count for anything."

"You're too old?" Driscoll said. "I know that one. At least you're the right color."

They both laughed.

"I'm too pasty looking to have your problem," Vic said.

"I still think you're nuts," Driscoll said.

"The work didn't feed the soul, Frank."

"And writing for that rag does?"

"That rag cleared three cops from bogus brutality charges last year," Vic said. "Have you forgotten that?"

"How about the big chief's expense account records?" Driscoll said.

"Four thousand dollars for a dinner in Las Vegas?"

"Those were grant funds," Driscoll said.

"And the source of that grant?"

"DOJ," Driscoll said.

"Right out of my hip pocket," Vic said. "You pay taxes too."

"He paid it back."

"After he got caught."

"Can we change the subject?" Driscoll said, after another long slurp of his light brown liquid. "We're going to have to re-frame our relationship, you and me."

"Here. Take your pen, will you," Vic said. "I've got to call the city desk."

"Wait a minute," Driscoll said. "I've got to talk to you about that body."

"What body?" Vic said.

"Smart ass," Driscoll said. "Look, we've got an ID, but I need you to hold it for a while."

"My first day back and you want me to sit on a story? If it shows up in the *Times* and I don't have it, I'm hosed."

"I don't think anyone else has this," Driscoll said.

"You don't think?"

"I'm pretty sure."

"You're pretty sure," Vic said. "That's fine when you're judging the distance of a seven iron shot. This is a little different."

"Look, this woman is a name you know," Driscoll said. "Everyone knows it. It's going to be a zoo when this hits the street."

"Well, then, let me be the one who hits the street with it," Vic said. He just shut up and stared at the cop. The stare usually worked back when he last wrote for the *Sun*. It was like a contest with a dog.

Hours passed. Vic knew Driscoll was thinking. More hours passed.

"This is my first day," Vic said. "Give me something."

"Okay, but do not put it out on the wires," Driscoll said.

"I'll see what I can do."

"No, you won't just see what you can do. I don't want this out tonight. Okay?"

"All right, you don't want this thing, whatever this thing is, this ID, out yet. I get that, but I'm not sure how long I can hold it, if at all."

"But you will try," Driscoll said.

"So I've got to go back and play coy with my new editor," Vic said. "This could be my first and last day at the paper, but I will try."

"Jessica Swain," Driscoll said.

"No shit," Vic said.

"Yes, shit," Driscoll said.

"I can't hold this, Frank. This is the Lieutenant Governor of Colorado. She's been murdered."

"We don't know that yet," Driscoll said, sitting up straight. "We're not letting anyone, especially you media hipsters, near the crime scene right now. You got in on a fluke, buddy. Hardly anyone knows about it yet. Your photo guy happened to be riding with me on another thing when I caught the call. We kept him away. He doesn't know a thing. CBI and the state cops should be there by now. I called the governor myself."

"You can't keep a lid on this," Vic said.

"A few hours," Driscoll said. "So we can get our act together."

"Frank, everyone scans the cop frequencies," Vic said.

Driscoll pulled out his cell phone and waved it in Vic's face. "Wonderful things, cell phones. Very private. Every cop needs one. Most of us carry them now."

"Frank, she was going to run for governor," Vic said.

"She's too prone to run at the moment," he said. "Her hair's a mess, and did you see how she trashed her clothes?"

Vic stared at him.

"I'm sorry," Driscoll said. "Gallows humor. Relieves the tension."

"You'll get relieved of more than that if I ever quoted you."

Driscoll finished his sweet creamy coffee and dropped a Jackson on top of the ticket. From nowhere, the waitress swept the tab and the money off the counter.

"I'll be back with your change, sweetie," she tossed over her shoulder.

"Shower ticket number three forty-four is up," a woman's voice blasted over the PA system. "Shower ticket number three forty-four. On deck, three forty-five." Graybeard, now silent, got up and walked into the store part of the truck stop. A trucker, in for some coffee and a hot shower, Vic thought. He probably bored the snot out of the other drivers on the CB radio too.

The waitress flew back with Driscoll's change. He dropped two bucks for the tip and the two golfing buddies walked out into the late Sunday afternoon sun. Driscoll handed Vic his card with a cell phone number hand written on it.

"You can call me at that number," Driscoll said. "I've already got your cell number on my phone. I'll give you the jump on whatever I can."

"That would help," Vic said. "And how about a stroke a hole next Saturday?"

"Only if you're giving it to me," Driscoll said. He paused, and then said, "Just a few hours. That's all we need."

"I'll try. I'll try." Vic said as he headed for his pool car.

From across the parking lot, he heard Driscoll shout after him, "You're going to miss the money."

# 5

"City desk. Mayer."

"Peggy. It's Vic."

"Do you have anything?" It was more of a demand.

"Wait a second." Vic steered the SUV with his left hand while using the other to untangle a knotted hands-free cord. He plugged the jack into his phone and jammed the ear bud into his ear. "Okay, now I can drive with both hands," Vic said.

"Tell me something," Peggy said. She sounded nervous, edgy. "Anything."

"I'm sorry about the art," Vic said.

"Huh?" she said.

"No pictures."

"Jones never comes back empty handed," Peggy said. "But all I've got is a wide shot with cops standing around. I can barely see the body on the snag."

Vic had not yet met Jones, but his stock had risen a few points.

"First, we have a request from the cops, relayed to me privately by Driscoll," Vic said.

"Do you have an ID or cause of death?" Peggy said, all business.
He ignored her question.

"They want us to keep this quiet as long as possible," Vic said.
"At least until later tonight. You guys still give carbons to Grandma
as soon as it's written?"

"Carbons?" Peggy said. "Grandma?"

"Carbon copies, of your stories," Vic said. Peggy laughed.

"I know what carbon copies are, Vic," Peggy said. "My dad
showed one to me. Now, who's Grandma?

"The *Associated Press*," Vic said.

"Grandma?" Peggy said.

"Well, that's what we used to call it," Vic said, "When I was at
*UPI.*"

"You worked for Reverend Moon?" Peggy said.

"Uh, no, Peggy," Vic said. "The company that owns your paper
used to own *UPI.* Reverend Moon is *UPI*'s most recent owner."

"Whatever," she said. "Anyway, *AP*, or Grandma, gets electronic
copies, our carbons. It's part of our contract with them. But we've
got some latitude on hot stuff. Is this hot stuff?"

"Somewhat."

"And there's that other thing," she said.

"What other thing?" Vic said.

"That internet thing," she said.

"Oh, I forgot, all those tubes," he said. "Those internets."

"Yes, Vic. The internet. There's only one." The phone amplified
her exasperated sigh. "We're online twenty-four-seven. This will be
on everyone's computer screens in seconds."

"You mean you guys are filing directly into those internet
tubes?" Vic said, playing along. He had been using the internet
since before the world even knew it as the internet. "That's almost
like what we did with the wire service. Although we'd run a story
like this past the brass first."

"I'm the brass," Peggy said. "What's the delay crap for, anyway?"

"Driscoll said they need to get their ducks in a row," Vic said.

"Ducks. Schmucks. This is a newspaper. If it's that critical, we can keep it from the *AP* for a little while. What about the *Times?*"

"I think they're still out to lunch on this," Vic said. "Driscoll said we were the only news outfit to know about it, and that was by mistake because Jones was already with him. I just said I'd see what I could do about holding the story. I didn't make any promises."

"Gimme the goods," Peggy said, right out of a Bogart flick. She was right. Vic did not want to sit on the story either, for any reason, especially today, the day of his return.

"Are you going to call anyone," Vic said. "The editor maybe?"

"Not until I know who the victim is, Vic," Peggy said.

"The lieutenant governor," Vic said.

Silence for a moment, then, "No shit."

"My words exactly," Vic said.

"What the heck was she doing there?" Peggy said.

"Not much when I saw her," Vic said. "Floating mostly. Face down in the South Platte. The rest hung up on a snag."

"Before that," Peggy said. Vic imagined her eyes rolling.

"Not a clue," he said. "Driscoll said nothing either."

"Are you on your way in?" Peggy said.

"I'm about twenty minutes away." His cell phone beeped him. "Hang on." He held the phone out at arm's length so he could read the screen and watch the road at the same time. "Peggy, Driscoll's calling. I'll be there shortly." He clicked her off and Driscoll's call came through. "Bengston."

"It's me," Driscoll said. "The chief, the governor, and the DA, maybe the CBI, are going to hold a news conference at the capitol at seven."

"Well, so much for the exclusive," Vic said.

"Were you going to hold it?" Driscoll said.

"No," Vic said.

"Then you've got a head start on the rest of the jackals," Driscoll said. "Don't quote me directly, okay?"

"On the story, or the jackals thing?"

"Neither one. I don't think any of your so-called competition knows about this yet."

"The city desk knows," Vic said. "I'll call them about the news conference. How are you going to bill it?"

"Major crime announcement," Driscoll said.

"I thought you said you didn't know what happened," Vic said.

"I lied," Driscoll said.

"Now I don't feel bad about anything I've done, even dropping that ball on number three last week without taking a stroke," Vic said.

"Hands bound behind her and a hole in the back of her head. Looks like a small caliber weapon. Don't know what precisely, though."

"Execution style?" Vic said.

"I'm not going to use that phrase," Driscoll said. "But I have no control over you media bozos."

"Hands bound with what?"

"Duct tape."

"When?"

"ME techs think last night," Driscoll said. "Not solid on that, though. Governor's office said she was seen at some environmental fund-raiser Saturday evening."

"So she could have been killed early Sunday morning, right?"

"Yeah, that's right, or late Saturday night."

"Was she, uh—" Vic said.

"That's all I know, Vic, but probably not," Driscoll said. "Her clothes seemed to be intact. But I'm not totally sure about that. You cannot use my name. Sources, all right? Police sources.

Investigation sources. That crap. Not me. Seven o'clock. In the press conference room. At the statehouse."

"You'll have a full house. We're breaking the story."

"I figured you would," Driscoll said. "I've got to go."

Vic shut the phone off and tossed it onto the passenger seat, then picked it up again and called the city desk to feed Peggy the additional information for the story lead.

As the call rang, Vic hit the button that automatically dropped the driver's side window. He shouted into the wind.

"I'm back, baby!"

# 6

Vic emerged from the stairwell and stepped into the city room. He saw Peggy in an animated discussion at the city desk with Christopher Hogan, the editor and publisher of the paper.

Hogan hired Vic for this encore performance as a journalist. "I've got a good feeling about you," he told Vic, who, at the time, said, "Back at ya." It was all he could think of at the moment, stunned that he got the job in the first place.

Alan Smythe kibitzed with them as well. Vic knew it was going to be a political story as well as a crime story. Smythe was still the paper's political columnist, but when they last worked together he was a statehouse reporter like Vic. Mal Hoffman, the senior capitol reporter, sat off to the side. The vultures were already circling, Vic thought. Still, Peggy seemed to be holding her own against this tsunami of journalistic experience. At least she had the good sense to call someone.

All four looked his way, eight eyes following him as he made the perp walk across the city room. Nothing like waltzing in the door with the story of the decade on your first day back at work. Vic had not felt this nervous since he was drafted during the Vietnam War.

"I thought you were dead," said Smythe.

"Sorry to disappoint you," Vic said. "Mr. Hogan here plucked me from my cushy prison of corporate communications."

"I've never seen a flack make it back into the newsroom," Hoffman said. He was short, about five-six, stocky, and ruggedly handsome, his old horned rim glasses replaced by some narrow euro lens design.

Peggy stayed quiet. She looked a little nervous.

"We want Hoffman to take the lead on this, Vic," Hogan said.

Vic scrunched up his mouth, pondered the decision, then exhaled. "It would be hard to protest, first day and all."

"You're still untested," Hogan said. "You haven't managed a newspaper project team. What would you do?" He was right, but Vic did not like to hear it.

"And if I did protest?"

"There's no point to it," Peggy said. "You'll get the first byline, Vic, on the net and in tomorrow's paper."

"And then?"

"And then, we'll see," said Hogan. "You're out front on this, Vic, but we can't just let you run with it. It should be a team project. You know it's going to hit the fan with this one. But we realize—"

"Realize what exactly?" Vic said.

"Realize—that you seem to have some rapport with this, uh, who is the cop?" Hogan said to his city editor.

"Driscoll," Peggy said. "Chief of Detectives."

"Yes, Driscoll. I'd like you to keep working on the story, Vic. We'll coordinate it from the desk."

"I play golf with him," Vic said, delighted he would get the byline in the morning paper. Let the world know. He loved bylines, especially his.

"What's your handicap," Smythe asked.

"My age."

"Welcome to the club," said Smythe.

"At least you didn't have a little break in service," Vic said. "Try the job market sometime."

"Little?" Hoffman said. "Twenty-five years? That's a long one to come back from."

"Okay, so the honeymoon's over," Vic said. "And it shouldn't it be 'a long time from which to come back'?"

"Thank you, professor Bengston," Hoffman said.

"We don't do honeymoons anyway," Hogan said. "At least you know these two guys." He nodded toward Smythe and Hoffman. Then he smeared on a salesman's grin, rubbed his hands together, and said, "Not everyone's gone, and I don't think they'll sandbag you too badly. So, what do you say? Let's make a newspaper."

Vic understood. If he were editor, he would have done the same thing. Like with any new client, he would have to prove himself. In the corporate world it happened over and over with every new client, and it got old. Maybe if he had stayed in the newspaper business to begin with, he would be the editor by now. What was I chasing when I left in the first place, he asked himself.

"There's obviously a big political angle here," said Smythe. "Swain was a shoo-in to become Colorado's first woman governor."

While Vic enjoyed following the game of politics, he never wanted to cover it as a journalist. Campaign politics, especially the way it now played lacked real substance. It was all fine-tuned and often ugly propaganda, mostly a string of predictable talking points and promises that were never honored. He preferred the daily politics of getting things done, in government, in business, even in sports, to the hollow and dully repetitive rhetoric of the campaign trail.

"It's bigger than you think, Alan," Vic said.

"How can it be bigger than 'Lieutenant Governor Murdered'?" Smythe said.

"How about 'Lieutenant Governor Murdered Execution Style'?"

Four momentarily gaping stares.

"Like a mob hit?" Hoffman said.

"Her hands were bound and she was shot in the back of her head execution style," Vic said. "With a small caliber weapon."

"Holy Cow," Peggy said.

Vic turned to her and said, "Clean up your language, young lady."

She blushed. It could not have been that easy for her, young and female, standing there with three old farts and a forty-something editor and publisher. He pictured his daughter struggling to be tough on the outside while shivering on the inside. No different for men, he thought, we just hide it better.

"Where'd you find that out?" Hogan said, sitting down in one of the empty chairs.

"Sources close to the investigation," Vic said.

"Your golf buddy," Peggy said.

"Not for attribution," Vic said.

"Except now they've called a news conference for seven," Hogan said, pissed. "TV will have it tonight and the *Times* will have it right with us tomorrow."

"Don't forget radio," Hoffman said.

"They'll talk this one to death," said Smythe.

"When don't they?" Vic said. "They all have a firm grip on the obvious."

"We'll just have to put out the best package," Hogan said. "Okay, Mal, you write the obit. Give us plenty of her background. Alan, you work the political angle. See what this might do for next year's election."

Peggy flopped back down into her chair as Hogan barked orders.

"Vic, you do the crime story, for this cycle," Hogan continued. "Feed everything to Peggy. She'll write it. I'll help on the desk."

Peggy snapped up straight when the publisher said she would do the writing.

"Byline for Vic on this one," Hogan said. "Page one, and let's get a nice head shot of Swain from the files.

"Any other art?" Hogan said. "Crime scene?"

"Only a wide shot," Peggy said. "They kept Jones away but he got a few when they weren't looking."

"Head shot?" Vic said. "Nice phrase given the circumstances."

"Photograph," Hogan said. "Sorry."

Peggy was not sure just who was in charge at the moment, although clearly the commander in chief was on the deck. Vic kept imagining his daughter in that spot, ostensibly the city editor but surrounded by decades of seasoned experience, her boss, and a relic who once had a promising career as a journalist.

"The bulldog deadline is nine p.m.," Peggy said, telling me and reminding the others. "But we've got to get something big, and fast, for the net."

"You want to bring Arquette in to cover the news conference?" Hogan said.

"Rod Arquette?" Vic said.

"You know him?" Hogan said.

"From *UPI.*"

"What is this, a geriatric team?" Peggy said. She was grinning. "I'd like to minimize the chance of a heart attack on this story, Chris."

"He's still on your staff isn't he?" Vic said.

"Jones can handle it," Peggy said.

Vic's fatherly protectionist feelings toward her vanished in a pop. Then he said to Hogan, "I think a second photog would be good."

"I'll go with Peg on this one," Hogan said.

Vic looked at Peggy and raised his eyebrows. She shrugged. "What about calling your friends at Channel Nine? Don't you have an arrangement with them?"

Peggy said, "What for?"

"To have them break into programming and report the story, quoting a *Rocky Mountain Sun* exclusive," Vic said. "That way you get credit for beating everyone. Channel Nine still is number one in the market, isn't it?"

Hogan stood up and said, "Not a bad idea."

Still a few ideas rattling around up there, Vic thought, then said, "After we move the story on the internet, will *AP* give the *Sun* an exclusive credit?"

"I'll call Charlie Branson at home," Hogan said. Branson was the *AP* bureau chief.

Peggy ran to catch up. "Vic, Can you give me a hundred words in about five minutes?"

Vic nodded and smiled. He wanted badly to write a lead for the story before he got back on the phone to dig for more information.

Hoffman and Smythe said nothing. No more jokes. They drifted off to their respective cubicles to start with the phones. Hogan was over talking to Jones about photos.

"I need a place to, uh, sit," Vic said.

"Use the other side of the desk," Peggy said.

Vic walked around the large city desk and found a spot with a terminal about as far away from Peggy as he could get, to maintain a bit of privacy, not much, just a bit.

"How do I turn this on and log on?" Vic asked, fumbling around the back of the monitor in search of an on-off switch.

"Hit the SPACE key," Peggy said.

He did, and the screen sprung to life, demanding a log-on ID.

"Try your social security number," Peggy said. "But I doubt if you're in the system yet."

Vic typed in the nine digits that separated him from all others in the country, unless his identify had been recently stolen. "Invalid ID," the screen said.

"Invalid."

"Try this," she said. "Ready?" Vic nodded. "555-55-5555."

This time Vic got a menu screen giving him a few choices. Some security, he thought. The menu screen was fairly intuitive: new story, open story, research, email, notes, archives, log off. He selected new story, and a blank screen appeared. He wrote five paragraphs fast:

> DENVER — Lt. Gov. Jessica Swain, expected to become the next governor, was shot to death execution style Saturday night or early Sunday, police said.
>
> Her fully clothed body was found face down in the South Platte River near 49th Avenue in north Denver.
>
> Police told the *Rocky Mountain Sun* Mrs. Swain was shot in the back of the head with a small caliber weapon and that her hands were bound behind her back with duct tape.
>
> She was seen alive early Saturday evening at a fund-raising event for an environmental cause, police said.
>
> Police said Sunday they had no suspects.

He asked himself, was it too political? Nope, she was the light governor. She had already said she wanted to run for Dowd's seat. Too sensational? Naw. It was a first day lead, a crime story, and the truth. Vic did not make any changes. He liked that.

"How do I save this?" Vic asked.

"Like a PC," Peggy said. "Control-S will do it."

"That's easy."

"Not bad," Peggy said about two minutes later. Vic looked up. She was reading his first draft lead.

"Solid on all police info?"

"Like a rock."

"By the way, is there any privacy on these terminals?" Vic said. He often kept things to himself.

"When you get a permanent desk and terminal, you'll get a password," Peggy said. "We can override, but you've got a bit of security. That terminal, though, is a part of the city desk."

"So, no privacy then."

"Not a lick," Peggy said.

"So what do you think?" Vic asked.

"Well, I already said not bad."

"Not bad isn't great, or riveting."

"It's already posted in the net, with a screaming head and two photos," Peggy said.

"You didn't tweak it at all," Vic said.

"It's got that gritty crime story feel."

"Isn't that what we want?"

"Yes, that's what we want," she said.

"But not what you want," Vic said.

"Oh, sometimes the blood and guts stuff gets to me," Peggy said. "But it's a daily newspaper."

Yes, Vic thought, and I've missed it every day since I left.

7

The news conference, which Hoffman covered, provided little in the way of new facts. It was mostly about how outrageous the crime was, sad day for Colorado, the Colorado Bureau of Investigation was on the case with the Denver Police Department, no, the FBI was not yet involved in the case, our hearts go out to the family. "They were hedging all their bets," Hoffman told Vic when he returned from the statehouse. "No substance at all."

"They don't have a clue what happened, do they?" Vic said.

"Deer in the headlights," Hoffman said. "I'll go start calling legislators."

"Vic," Peggy said. "I've got Warren Cross. That's her family lawyer. Can you take a statement from him?"

Vic nodded, picked up a phone, and wedged the handset between his left shoulder and left cheek. A headset would have been nice, but Peggy seemed to have the only one.

"This is Vic Bengston."

"Warren Cross. Family attorney. I've got a short statement from the family, and, then, uh, we can't really, or don't want to answer a bunch of questions right now. I hope you understand."

"Can we contact you if something comes up?"

"I suppose," he said. Then a pause. "Yeah. Yes, call me." He gave Vic his cell number and then said, "Anyway, can you take this down, or I can fax it to you."

"If you wouldn't mind, read it to me and then fax it. We're up against another edition deadline."

Vic had no idea when the next deadline was, but he wanted the statement now.

"Okay," Cross said. "Here goes."

"Yeah, go ahead."

"This is from her husband, Jerry."

"Okay." Vic wrote "Jerry Swain" on the terminal.

"As you can imagine, this tragedy has devastated our family. The loss of Jessica is immeasurable. She truly was my soul mate and a guiding light for our two children, Wren and Robin. We are hoping law enforcement officials will solve this heinous crime quickly, so justice can be served. Please respect our privacy. The entire family is in mourning." Silence.

"That's it?" Vic said.

"Well, yes. That's it. You can understand. The whole family is shaken to the core."

Vic continued typing in notes, after the statement was read, like, "family shaken to the core."

"Oh, sure, Warren. This is horrible. I sometimes wonder how families cope with stuff like this."

"Well, they're doing the best they can," Cross said.

"How's her mother taking it?"

"She's up at the ranch. Somebody's going to get her. I think the State Patrol. But I know a doctor was with her."

"Probably to sedate her."

"Uh, yes. That's what he said."

"Her dad?" Vic said, then wrote, "Sedated. At ranch."

"Well, he's been gone for some time."

"Oh, that's right," Vic said. "When did he, uh—"

"I think it was 2002, no, 2003. The funeral was up in the mountains, at the ranch."

"Oh boy, that's tough," Vic said. "I heard there had been some threats. Anything to that?"

"I didn't even know that was out," Cross said. "But the State Patrol and the CBI said there was nothing to them."

Vic wrote the notes fast, getting the verbatim quote.

"Sure, I'll check with them. When did you last see Mrs. Swain?"

"It's been a week."

"About?"

"Oh, that's private. Attorney-client."

"Sure. You talk to the police yet?"

"Briefly. They had a couple of questions for me."

"About?"

"Sorry, can't talk about that either."

Vic nodded to get Peggy's attention, then he mouthed the word "fax", and she pointed to a number taped to the desk. To Cross, he said "Can you fax me that statement?"

"Ah, yes. If you could give me the number. I've got a bunch of calls to make." Vic reeled off the fax number used by the city desk. "Okay, I've got it," Cross said. "I have to go now."

"Thanks for the statement," Vic said. "Goodbye."

"Bye."

Vic hung up the phone. His neck was sore.

"Anything?" Peggy said.

"I got a little more out of the lawyer than out of the statement," Vic said.

"Well, write them both up, and send them to me. Nothing spectacular, I suppose."

"She was threatened," Vic said.

"Threats," she said. "That's a nice twist."

"I thought so," Vic said.

# 8

"Can I go home?"

Vic looked up from all the papers spread out before him at the city desk. He saw the clock. It was 3:12 a.m.

"Why ask me?" Vic said to the tired geeky looking kid with a silver ring in his nose.

"Aren't you the city editor?" he said.

"No, I'm the rookie," Vic said. "The city editor, I think, is in the bathroom."

"Oh, okay," the geek said. He held out a half-inch thick stack of printer paper.

"What's this?" Vic said.

"More background stories on Swain," he said.

"All right," Vic said. "I'll make sure Peggy gets them."

"Her name is Peggy?" he said.

"If you mean the city editor, yes, that's her name," Vic said. "Why don't you go home? You look tired. How long have you been here?"

"Since midnight," the geek said. Precise, Vic thought. "Friday."

"Any sleep?" Vic said.

"From 7:30 till 9:59 Saturday night," geek said.

"We'll have to dock you for that," Vic said.

"Pocket change," geek said. "I'm outta here. Thanks."

"Anytime," Vic said.

Vic waited to see if the geek skateboarded around the building, but when he re-emerged from the library with his backpack he was on foot when he headed for the elevator.

Peggy either fell asleep on her throne or the women's rooms still had couches in them, Vic thought. He shuffled through the stories left for him by the geek. One caught his eye. It was Barney Gray's analysis piece in yesterday's *Times*. Vic thought he had better read it.

# 9

## STATE'S NUMBER TWO
## NO LIGHTWEIGHT
### In-Depth Analysis
*By Barnard Gray*
*Times Staff Writer*

DENVER — "The Senate will come to order," the woman commanded, rapping the large desk before her with the giant gavel used in the Colorado State Senate. She stood six feet tall, and her brilliant blue eyes were set off by a chiseled face framed with a severe bristle cut that emphasized her salt and pepper hair.

"The chair thanks the members for their recognition," said senate President Jessica Swain. "However, the chair rules that beyond a certain number, somewhere around forty, it is no longer considered to be in the state's interest to keep too close a tab on precise ages."

Laughter and cheers rocked the Senate chamber, which had descended into disorder about fifteen minutes earlier as the majority party staff circulated among the 35 seats distributing cups of coffee and slices from a large chocolate birthday sheet cake. The cake was made in the shape of the State of Colorado, which was easy since Colorado is basically square, having been carved out of the Wild West with a straightedge and a map in Washington, D.C., during the latter part of the nineteenth century. A spiral of red, white, and blue frosting formed the message "Happy 39th"

The celebration occurred nearly four years ago, shortly before State Senator Swain resigned her Western Slope seat to run for lieutenant governor, an office often referred to as the "Light" Governor by the more cynical members of the news media. Swain, however, is anything but "light."

Today, many of the state's long-time political observers have characterized her as one of Colorado's best and most powerful lieutenant governors. What sets her apart from previous lieutenant governors is that she actually manages to wield substantial political power at the statehouse.

It is widely expected that she will easily ascend to the governor's chair once Gov. Thomas Dowd departs, which could be after only a single term. Dowd's first three years in office have been uneventful and clouded in controversy. Even some key Democratic Party leaders predict the party will pass on a Dowd nomination for a second term, opting instead for the more popular and, some say, more capable Swain.

Despite the toothless nature of her office, Swain has managed to gain a strong political foothold at the state capitol, primarily through her position as chief policy adviser to the governor. She is considered unique in Colorado history because she parlayed a largely ceremonial post devoted to ribbon-cuttings and funeral appearances into one of significant power within state government.

When the legislature is in session, roughly the first four months of each year, Swain spends most of her time in the senate lobby or even on the senate floor, following legislation, advising the governor, and even arm-twisting senate members to vote her way. As a result, Swain is credited with getting Dowd's legislative agenda advanced through the General Assembly. When she is not hovering over the state senate, or making obligatory ceremonial appearances, Swain devotes a great deal of time promoting a wide range of conservation projects in Colorado.

Swain's frequent appearances on the senate floor spurred local political pundits to dub the state senate "Swain's Chamber," much to the chagrin of the more traditional figures who run Colorado politics.

"I simply want to know what the hell is going on at the legislature," she said during a recent interview with the *Denver Times*. "Plus, I'm the governor's chief legislative adviser." And that she is.

Dowd, a fabulous glad-hander and schmoozer on the campaign trail, has turned out to be a dud as governor, some observers say, unable to make a decision and often turning to Swain for a nod one way or another. She makes her decisions swiftly and crisply.

KHOW's morning drive-time host, Preston Berry, once put it this way, "Jessica Swain is the perfect bridge between two branches of government, one foot on the senate's throat and the other on the governor's nuts." The comment drew an apology from the station and a one-week suspension for Berry, who never did apologize. Political insiders said he had it right.

A lawyer and former environmental law specialist, Swain reviews every judicial appointment, and is credited for getting two more women named to the state supreme court.

While Republicans, business leaders, and conservatives understandably view her as too far to the left, a number of Democrats, who asked not to be identified, are not happy with some of her positions either, especially her strong support of efforts to shut down irrigation wells in northeastern Colorado.

Shutting down these wells is viewed as a direct attack on Colorado's agricultural industry. The current legislative session has been marred by several explosive disputes over water rights and the use of large wells to irrigate crops in northeastern Colorado.

In a series of controversial rulings, state water courts ordered many farmers to shut off their irrigation wells at the request of the Dowd-Swain administration. The court orders, under review by the state appeals court, are based on recent hydrology studies that conclude the irrigation wells are depleting the South Platte River Basin water – the water that has turned an otherwise semi-arid region into the nation's richest farmland.

In their rulings, the water courts pointed out that the farmers were warned by state water resource officials a decade earlier that they needed to acquire water rights on the South Platte to continue using the irrigation wells. Some farmers acquired rights, but many did not.

The current legislative session already has approved several measures introduced as part of the Dowd-Swain agenda. These dealt mostly with increasing the power of the State Engineer's office, which administers Colorado's immensely complex water law, limiting the compensation to farmers for losses caused by the court-ordered shut-offs of irrigation wells, and giving the Division of Wildlife more power to keep water flowing in rivers and creeks for wildlife habitat.

Some political insiders say the governor would like the wells turned back on, at least temporarily, but he apparently has yielded to Swain's tougher position in favor of keeping the wells shut off so a basin-wide conservation plan can be developed for the entire South Platte River.

Swain has said, on several occasions, the state's agriculture lobby is far weaker than it likes to think it is. However, the most recent well shut-off order came from a Greeley judge who admitted from the bench that she had never stepped foot on a farm or ranch her entire life. Her ruling, which specifically mentioned potential harm the wells could cause to migrating ducks, geese, and sandhill cranes, drew the ire of the state's farmers and ranchers.

Agricultural interests are fighting her at every turn, including several attempts at passing legislation to reverse the well shut-off orders, but appear to be losing the battle.

Exactly how Swain manages to resolve the growing split over the water issue within her party and between the conservation and agriculture communities may well be the defining moment in her thus far meteoric political career.

# 10

"Boot Hill isn't much of a defining moment," Vic said aloud, tossing the *Times* onto the desk.

"What?" Peggy said. She had returned to the city desk while Vic was reading.

"I wish I had read this a little earlier," he said, nodding toward the Gray article.

"It's from Brand X," she said.

"That shouldn't matter," Vic said. "Barney's been around longer than I have. Plus, the water's an interesting angle. I'm surprised the yak-radio gabsters haven't run some of this into the dirt, ad nauseam."

"Like what?" Peggy said.

"Like this flap over the irrigation wells," Vic said. "It probably requires too much thinking for talk radio."

"She was one powerful lady," Peggy said.

"And it looks like she made a few enemies along the way, even in her own party," Vic said.

"I'll give it to Mal," she said.

"Mal?" Vic said.

"Hogan wants Mal on the follow-ups," Peggy said.

Vic stared at her. It made her nervous.

"Follow-up is a euphemism for take over," Vic said.

"This is your first day, Vic," she said.

He continued with the stare.

"You were on the breaking story," Peggy said. "Got the byline too."

Vic leaned back and decided to give her a break.

"I'd probably do the same thing, but it's only my first day, technically."

She seemed to relax slightly.

"Quite the coincidence," Peggy said.

"Oh?"

"Well," she said, "Swain found dead in the very same river basin where she reigned as diva in a war over water rights."

"One problem," Vic said.

"What's that?" Peggy said.

"I don't believe in coincidences."

# 11

Vic was up the rest of the night. The adrenalin would make sleep impossible. Three more reporters, two men and a woman, all of them the age of one of his kids or another, were brought in overnight to work the story. Peggy coordinated the effort from her side of the desk, but let Vic put everything together before she took over for the final rewrite and edit. When he noticed she was doing very little rewriting, he looked at the ceiling and silently screamed "Yes" to himself. He still had it.

Vic worked the main story, the crime story. He got two more reports from Driscoll, nothing much, but enough to put the rough time of death between 9:30 p.m. Saturday when Swain left a fund-raiser at a downtown hotel for the Friends of Colorado Rivers and 1:45 p.m. Sunday when the cops received the anonymous phone call.

Smythe filed a piece on the political enemies Swain had made over her increasingly strident environmental views. Hoffman wrote how the lieutenant governor muscled herself into the position of becoming the odds on favorite to succeed Dowd as governor.

"Neither one of these pieces are very flattering," Vic said.

Peggy came up for air. "Is that what you guys did in the days of old?" she said, "Flatter them?"

"No, but she was executed, Peggy. There's her family to consider too."

"Her son has been busted by cops twice up in Steamboat, both times for drugs," she said. "Her daughter's been in rehab at least once that we know of, and neither one of them has made it to twenty yet."

"So she won't get mother of the year," Vic said.

"No she won't," Peggy said. "And the public won't get a load of crap from this newspaper, either," she said. "You know, Hoffman and Smythe have been covering her for a long time, while you were out buying clients three-martini lunches."

"Little testy are we?" Vic said. "Someone needs a nap."

She sighed. "I already took one."

Vic saw that he did not have to stroke her ego, the way he often did with corporate clients, many so insecure they could not make a decision if a gun was at their head. Politics was even worse. After working one campaign, Vic swore off political communications forever. Lies were lies, private or public.

Reporting a story was the closest thing to reality he could find.

"Finally, the bulldog edition," Peggy said. A runner from the press up in north Denver whisked in and dropped a stack of papers on her desk. It was three hours late, having been held for more of the Swain story.

"They still call it the bulldog?" Vic said. "I'm surprised some advertising genius hasn't come up with some hip new name for the first edition."

"You mean branding genius?" she said. "It's all branding these days. Anyway, how could you top bulldog?" she said.

"You got me there."

Amidst the huge Page One photo of the late lieutenant governor and the blaring headline, Vic's eyes zeroed in on seven little words, "By Vic Bengston, *Rocky Mountain Sun* Staff."

# 12

By 7:30 a.m. Monday, another edition had been published updating the story. Throughout the night, Vic freshened up the website every fifteen minutes. He extracted little out of a phone call to Driscoll and another to the CBI. He sensed they were holding back.

By this time, though, Vic had written everything he had, the spent adrenaline rush now morphing into fatigue. All he wanted to do was get home and pour himself into the sack, so he could fall asleep thinking about his first newspaper byline in a long time.

Peggy finished making the day's assignments on the Swain story. Vic was not on the list.

"I've got to leave for a few hours to get some breakfast," she said.

"Do you live here?" Vic said.

"No, but I've got to work the desk today," she said. "I was just filling in yesterday."

"When do you want me back?" Vic wanted more of the Swain story.

"Go get some sleep. I'm sure you need it."

Thanks, daughter, Vic thought. Do I look that old?

"This afternoon?" Vic said.

Peggy nodded, then looked over toward the door to the city room. Another young woman was walking in. "Oh, here, you should meet Marsha before you go."

"Who's Marsha?"

"She's the Deputy City Editor."

"Any guys left on the desk?"

"Joe Bemis," Peggy said. "He's the guy I replaced yesterday. Joe covers the desk a few overnights during the week and then on the weekend."

The only word that came to mind when Vic watched Marsha Gwynn approach the city desk was "prance." Medium length black hair, about the same age as Peggy. Daughter number two, Vic thought. When they were introduced, Vic caught the 'what's going on here' look. They made it smiling through the 'call me Vic, call me Marsha' routine.

Then Vic grabbed the final edition, his notebook, truck stop ballpoint pen, made a mental note to buy a new fountain pen for the job, and headed toward the door.

"Vic!"

It was Marsha, standing behind the city desk next to Peggy, holding a phone high in the air. "For you. Wait, I'll transfer it to that desk by the door."

The line two light flashed, and the phone issued some sort of an electronic tone. Vic picked up the handset. "This is Vic."

"When do you sleep?" Driscoll said.

"This is the news biz, Frank. We never sleep."

"I'm going home now," Driscoll said. "Frakes has it covered."

"Me too. Why are you calling?"

"Do you know anything about water?" Driscoll said.

"My Dad always says fish screw in it," Vic said, "not that

politely, though. I think he was quoting W. C. Fields. My Ex filters it or buys it in plastic bottles. I sail in it. Swipe trout from it occasionally. I used to swim in it a lot. What else?"

"No, I mean water rights, and such," Driscoll said.

"A little."

"Would an agricultural water right on the South Platte from 1887 be valuable?"

"Probably," Vic said. "It sounds very old."

"You mean age matters somewhere?" Driscoll said.

"The rights to use the water from the rivers are prioritized by their age," Vic said. "If you have a really old water right and you're a farmer, you put a call on the river when you need irrigation water."

"I'm still lost here, Vic," Driscoll said. "So they don't just pump it out of the river, any old time?"

"I thought you went to law school?"

"One year only," Driscoll said. "I all of a sudden had a family on the way. Anyway, I don't remember a thing about water rights."

"Ever think about going back?" Vic said.

"Where? Law school?"

"Yeah," Vic said. "Get the degree. Run for DA."

"I thought about it," Driscoll said. "I don't know."

"Do it," Vic said. "Can't hurt."

"Right now," Driscoll said in his cop voice, "I need to know about water."

"Okay. In a nutshell. When they discovered gold out here. Well, California, then here. Anyway, when mining got going, the miners needed water to run through their sluices, and the water wasn't always where the gold or silver was."

"So they had to move it," Driscoll said.

"Yeah, sometimes a long way," Vic said. "So the lawyers got involved."

"Naturally."

"Every mine needed water, regardless of whether it had a rich lode or not."

"So the lawyers started selling water rights to every mining claim," Driscoll said.

"Pretty much," Vic said. "Like they were mineral rights. They made more money selling water than mining for gold or silver."

"That figures," Driscoll said. "And farmers and ranchers?"

"They needed water too, especially to grow food to sell to the miners," Vic said. "So the lawyers, the miners, the politicians, the farmers, ranchers, you name it, got together and devised a fairly complex system for allocating water for mining and other uses like city water supplies, crops, and keeping cattle alive."

Driscoll said, "Is that where the water courts fit in?"

"Sure," Vic said. "Colorado has a separate court system for water rights. The engineers got in on it too. They had to devise and build systems to take water from one river or creek and transport it to some other canyon."

"Where does conservation come in?"

"Whom have you been talking to?" Vic said, recalling Abbott and Costello's Who's on First routine, Driscoll playing the dumb but really savvy Costello and Vic playing the unsuspecting straight man, Abbott.

"Just answer the question," Driscoll said. "I'll fill you in later, but I've got to get my head around this thing now."

"With what, another news conference that gift wraps the story for the competition?"

"You still had a big jump on them," Driscoll said. "It was all *Rocky* on the ten o'clock news."

"BFD," Vic said. He knew Driscoll was fishing for something, but he could not figure out what. The conservation thing was a little interesting though, given what he now knew about Swain. Reenergized, Vic played along.

"Conservation," Driscoll said.

"This started up back when I covered the statehouse," Vic said.

"Pre-Civil War?" Driscoll said. Vic let it go.

"Conservation is the controversial part of this water rights set-up," Vic said. "Especially with the cities fighting farmers and ranchers to get their mitts on as much water as they can to feed the Kentucky bluegrass lawns in their sprawling suburbs."

"You mean like my house?" Driscoll said. Like many other Denver cops, Driscoll left the city long ago to raise his family in the relative safety of the suburbs and away from the gang bangers they were busting every day. Now, with the gentrification of Denver, cops could not afford a house in the city if they wanted one, and many of the gang bangers and taggers have moved to the suburbs.

"Yeah, pretty much like yours, lieutenant," Vic said. "I'll bet your water bill down there in Centennial is through the roof."

"Oh, like you care about my water bills," Driscoll said. "Tell me about conservation."

"All right, let's say a few decades ago, environmentalists pushed through legislation that let government agencies acquire water rights for the sole purpose of maintaining minimum stream flows in the rivers and creeks," Vic said.

"So the trout won't dry up and blow away?"

"More than that, Frank. Yeah, fish are a part of it, but we've got a pretty big rafting industry that uses the water. People like to see water in their river beds, especially visitors who spend stacks and stacks of tourism dollars in Colorado."

"Now you sound like the chamber," Driscoll said. "That's the old you, isn't it? The last week you?"

"Nevertheless, the wildlife folks, the environmentalists, and, I think maybe the Utes, all got this ball rolling that said maintaining stream flow was a beneficial use under the state's water law," Vic said. "Besides rafting on rocks is no fun at all."

"Why would anyone care about these stream flows out in northeastern Colorado," Driscoll said. "There's no trout or rafting out there."

"Ducks, geese, herons, migrating birds," Vic said. "They need water for their habitat, so hunters can kill them when they fly through. Not the herons, though. I think they get a free pass."

"Oh shit, birds, right. Okay, let's see if I'm getting this through my skull. Some of this stuff hurts my brain, man. Say you have a very old senior water right. That means you get the water before anyone else with a junior right on that river, correct?"

"Junior right, senior right?" Vic said. "You, young man, have been talking to some water lawyer. There's no way you came up with terms like that on your own. Again, I ask, whom have you been talking to?"

Vic glanced up at Marsha, her eyes following him like a hawk. Driscoll asked too many questions. Vic concluded the water connection was far more than an interesting little sidelight to the Swain murder.

"Later, Vic, later," Driscoll said. He sounded rushed, anxious. "It's all based on the date, right? The date of the water right."

"Essentially," Vic said. "It's actually more complicated than just the date, but if you've got an old date you're usually guaranteed water."

Driscoll said, "What if you got a water right but then changed something, like how the water was supposed to be used? What does that do to the whole set-up?"

"Oh, I think you've got to prove to the water court that the new use is the highest and best use of the water," Vic said. "I'm not too sure, really. Agriculture might still take precedence, but—"

"—but maybe not," Driscoll said.

"Maybe not," Vic said.

"And if you kept the use the same but really planned to use it for something else, or halfheartedly used it for its intended purpose?"

"You've got me there," Vic said. "I think you need a water lawyer."

Driscoll had already talked to a water lawyer, and Vic knew it. He did not want to get into the newer legislation that made it even easier to lock up water rights for conservation. But he figured Driscoll's water lawyer could tell him about that, at five hundred bucks an hour. Vic was done playing. "Frank. What's this about?"

"Oh, nothing. I was curious." Curious, my ass, Vic thought.

"Nothing?"

There was a pause. Vic let the silence run. It always worked. Then Driscoll lowered the boom. "Do not mention this, okay?"

"You held something back," Vic said.

"We always do," Driscoll said. "You cannot do anything with this. I'll arrest you."

"And charge me with what? Felony reporting? Is that a crime now?"

"I'd appreciate it, Mr. Bengston, if you wouldn't write anything about the water right thing. It's a side issue we're looking into."

"It'll cost you a few more strokes next Saturday," Vic said.

More silence. Then Driscoll said, "We heard she had a water right, one on the South Platte, an old one."

"And so?"

"And so," Driscoll said. "The story is she was going to flip it from agriculture use to conservation, to help the—"

"The damn birds, Frank. You knew about the birds, the habitat, and the conservation all along."

"I needed to confirm it, you know, get corroboration about water rights from someone, well, who knew what they were talking about."

"Like me?" Vic said. "Genius me?"

"Actually, we're waiting to talk to a wildlife conservation specialist from Colorado State," Driscoll said. "Someone who really knows what she's talking about."

"Whatever," Vic said, pleased he had a lead all to his own. "Anything else you need my counsel on?"

"One other thing," Driscoll said.

"What's that?"

"And, look I haven't even talked with this guy," Driscoll said. "But his name came up in a routine inquiry, and I wondered if you knew anything about him."

"What's the name?" Vic said.

"Gary Kendrick," Driscoll said.

Once again, Vic turned into Bud Abbott, with Lou Costello again asking the naive question.

"Can't place it right now," Vic said. "Hum a few bars."

"Okay, it's nothing, really," Driscoll said.

"How did, uh, Kendrick did you say, enter the picture?" Vic said.

"A tangent," Driscoll said. "Left field, but don't talk about it. Understood?"

"Understood," Vic said, thinking that this was starting to get interesting. They hung up.

Thirty years ago, Vic covered a complicated energy and water trial in federal district court. Western ranchers, some farmers, several environmental groups, the Mountain Utes, duck hunters, and trout fishermen sued major oil companies over water in the rivers flowing from the Continental Divide in Colorado. Ranchers wanted the water left in their valleys so they could irrigate hay meadows for cattle and horses. Farmers needed water for crops. The eco crowd wanted the water left in the creeks to provide habitat for native trout and the humpbacked chub, a hideous little prehistoric monster that interested no one except some microbiologist at

Colorado State University. The Utes felt Native Americans should have a say in western water use, the duck hunters wanted water to attract their prey, and the fishermen wanted something for their trout to swim in. The oil companies wanted the water for oil shale development.

At the time, the entire country was in a state of panic, freaked out because a few Arab countries cut off oil supplies to the United States. Long lines at gas stations triggered fear and fist fights. Oil shale promised to alleviate the problem. Billions of barrels of potential fuel were embedded in the brown rock formations beneath northwestern Colorado and parts of Utah. All the oil companies had to do was to dig up a quarter of the state, crush trillions of tons of rock, heat up the rubble with steam, fill countless valleys with the waste, and then tell the Arabs what they could do with their oil. The process, however, would consume massive amounts of electricity and most of the water available in the region. But panic over the Arab oil embargo drove the politics of the day and the oil companies won their right to use the water. Ranching and farming took the second seat followed by the environmentalists. The ruling froze out the Utes, the duck hunters, and the trout fishermen altogether.

Within a few years, the oil shale operations had gone bust. The Arabs simply walked over and turned on the oil spigots. Gas prices plummeted. Ranchers and farmers got their water back for the time being, at least until the next panic over foreign energy supplies. Trout actually grinned, and the humpbacked chub was left alone to do whatever it did in Colorado's backwaters. The ducks were nonplussed.

The big winner in the lawsuit was the brilliant young water lawyer who led the fight for the oil companies, Gary Kendrick.

# 13

Vic knew what was coming. He wanted it over with fast, so he sauntered toward the city desk. Peggy gone, Marsha now anchored the desk

"Anything from the cop?" Marsha said. She must have recognized Driscoll's voice over the phone.

"I think he's gone round the bend," Vic said. "He's probably tired like me, up all night too."

"You were giving him chapter and verse on water law. What was that all about?"

"Oh, he's got some land down on the Arkansas, near Salida. You know, he kept asking me about the water, and I told him he had to get a lawyer in on it. I don't know. He's got a well or something, not far from the river. He thinks he's a gentleman rancher, if you can believe that." Vic hoped she would.

"A Denver cop, ranching? Now there's a picture."

"Yeah, that's what I thought."

Vic also thought about Bradford Chase, poet, amateur historian, state supreme court justice, and water lawyer. Maybe he could catch him at breakfast. He also thought about Gary Kendrick.

"I'm whipped," Vic said. "I've got to go get some rack time."

Marsha laughed. "Rack time? Sleep?" Vic nodded. "Haven't heard that before. I like it though, rack time. Uh, Peggy wondered if you could come back in for a few hours this afternoon before deadline. Four? Five?"

Old clichés are new clichés, Vic thought. That might give him something else to teach all the youngsters at the paper. For now he needed a clean getaway.

"How about five?" Vic said.

"That's good, I'll let her know," Marsha said.

"Right now I've got to go see a man about a horse," he said, heading for the elevator.

"Bathrooms are the other way," Marsha said. "Back there." She nodded to her left.

Not all clichés fade with age, Vic thought.

"Oh, right," Vic said. "Is there a way out back there?"

"Keep going down the hall," Marsha said. "There's another elevator that takes you down to the parking garage. You'll need to badge your way out."

Badging out as well as badging in was rather odd, Vic thought as the building dumped him onto the sidewalk. One more way for management to track the minions who worked there, he supposed. The last time he worked for the *Sun*, the word "badge" was merely a noun. Now it's a verb too.

Vic could not recall a more electrifying twenty-four-hour period in his life, except maybe the births of his four children. No, a front page byline the first day back might even be better, he thought, such a nice way to drop back into the news business. He looked down 15th Street at the snow-capped mountains to the west, a vertical slice of beauty all framed by the buildings of downtown Denver, and thought about water.

Fed by winter snows high in the Rockies, the blood of Colorado courses through major water arteries that begin as clear trickles on the Continental Divide and finish in the Mississippi River Basin or the Pacific Ocean depending on the sheer randomness of Earth's evolution. Along the way, humans remove water from the river basins and create the wealth of food, real estate, cities, manufacturing, and electricity generation. Some of it they put back, but not all of it. The Colorado River, which carved the Grand Canyon out of rock, dries up before it hits the Pacific. Humans pollute the rivers with pesticides, mining waste, and crap from cities. Wildlife fends for itself and uses whatever is left.

Vic wondered if the last thoughts in Swain's head were about the birds and the fish before the bullet scrambled her brain.

# 14

Vic needed to walk, walk the city, walk out his knotted up insides, his tightened muscles, walk away from his old life, walk into his new one. He bolted from the *Sun* building and crossed Colfax, then the Civic Center, meandered south on Broadway past the main library building remodeled by what must have been a third grade art class, and past the Art Museum's new annex which looked as though the mother ship had wobbled out of orbit and crashed in the middle of 13th Avenue.

He crossed Broadway. At the foot of the Colorado Supreme Court Building monolith he looked at his watch. Chase should be arriving at his favorite breakfast joint, Vic thought. Then he felt old. When he last covered the statehouse, Colorado put up the money to build the new Supreme Court building and the door-stop shaped Colorado State History Building next door. Now, bureaucrats planned to tear down both structures within a year and build new ones in their place, a fine use of tax money. It was not the first building to be built and demolished during Vic's adult tenure in Denver. He witnessed the same cycle with McNichols

Sports Arena, named after a mayor while the politician was still alive and still in office. The arena's round and layered design eerily resembled the hot burger of the day, complete with the sesame seed bun, sans the seeds. Locals renamed the venue Big Mac, now only a dim memory.

Vic knew his old friend would not be in his chambers this early in the morning, but he knew where he would be. That would require the hike that Vic needed to ease the rush that consumed him in the wake of the previous day's excitement.

Broadway, like any Broadway in any city, was a mishmash of old and new buildings, terra cotta facades, cheap aluminum and glass storefronts, run-down holes in the wall, elegant furniture stores, shabby second-hand furniture stores, used book stores, coffee shops, shot and beer bars, the occasional jazz spot, a tattoo parlor, coin stores screaming that they bought gold, food joints, old movie theaters, and trendy new urban mini-complexes and bistros. He had to walk hard, had to stay downtown, had to stretch his body, smell the city, feel its thunder, dodge its cars, trucks, and buses. Vic Bengston was back.

As Vic pushed his way through the swinging glass door of Swift's Steak House, the bitter odors and dull rumblings of the city surrendered to the sweet aroma of bacon and eggs sizzling on a hot grill. He stopped at a small table to the right inside the door and snatched the *Times* sports section from an untidy pile of newspapers. He wanted to see what Woody Paige had to say about the latest foibles of the Denver Broncos, who had managed to fire one of the league's most successful veteran coaches, hire a young rookie head coach and trade the franchise quarterback to the Bears for a spotty starter. At least they were happy in Chicago.

A lone Hispanic short order cook clinked his way through the morning's breakfast orders with his stiff metal spatula, shaping and piling the home fries on one section of the cooking surface, squeegeeing liquid fat into the trough around the grill, stacking up rashers of bacon on another corner, while he deftly cooked a half dozen eggs to various levels of doneness, over easy, over hard, sunny side up, depending on the tastes of the customers. Bradford Chase sat in the last booth on the right. His head was down. Every morning the judge read both the *Times* and the *Sun* cover to cover before he sauntered up Broadway to his chambers in the Supreme Court Building.

"Where you been, Vic," said the disembodied voice from behind him. Vic spun around. Dorothea sat behind the cash register, half hidden by the plastic palm trees that occupied the front windows. She was reading a copy of the *Sun*. "This you?" she said, jabbing the paper toward him.

"That's me," Vic said. "I have returned."

"Sad, sad thing," she said. "She was gonna be governor, you know. First woman. Sad, sad thing. You see the body?"

"No, no one did. Except for the cops."

"Bet it was awful," Dorothea said. "I suppose you want your usual?" Vic nodded. "And you'll be joining the judge?" He nodded again. The old Greek woman shook her head, vibrating the reddish hair puff that encased her noggin like an NFL helmet. Vic headed toward the back of the narrow restaurant. He liked his eggs over easy so he could pierce the runny yokes and mop up the tasty golden liquid with rye toast.

"Morning, Mr. Justice," Vic said as he slid into the green vinyl booth across from him. Chase looked up from his *Rocky Mountain Sun*.

"This would be like me," he said, yanking a battered pair of drug store reading glasses off his nose and tapping the front page of the newspaper, "like me."

"Like me, what?" Vic said.

"Like me going back to work at the Public Defender's Office.

Or the Legislative Drafting Office. Something like that."

"I suppose," Vic said. "But don't you think it would be fun, doing that again, knowing what you know now?"

"Absolutely not," Chase said. "I like what I'm doing."

"Well, I didn't like what I was doing," Vic said.

"I gathered that the last time I saw you," Chase said. "I wish you would have warned me. I about fell out of my seat here when I saw this. Somehow I missed the announcement of your triumphant return to the scandalous world of tabloid journalism."

"There was no announcement," Vic said. "Yesterday was my first day back. They've already got second thoughts. I think they wanted to test me out on a few lightweight stories first before they dusted off a byline from ancient history."

"Some fluff piece," Chase said. The headline and the tight head shot of the lieutenant governor screamed up from the breakfast table.

"The police reporter was gone. I caught the story by sheer luck."

"You can only go downhill from here."

"That's what I'm afraid of," Vic said. "I'm already off the story."

"And Frick and Frack are on it, I suppose," Chase said.

"Hoffman and Smythe?" Vic said. "With both hands."

"That's about what they've got between them, one head, two hands, and a pair of asses," Chase said.

"Not your favorites?" Vic said.

"Never have been, Vic," he said. "You should have never left. No one covered stories like you did. You got into them, made them relevant."

"Well, I'm just trying to keep my head above water right now," Vic said.

"So, why are you here?" Chase said.

"Taking a walk," Vic said. "Stopped in for some chow."

Chase laughed and retrieved his reading glasses from the chasm between his all but empty white porcelain breakfast plate and his half-full non-matching coffee mug. Vic always knew him as thoughtful and intelligent, but could never picture him as a state supreme court justice. This was a guy he went with to Leo's Place after a long day at the statehouse, he drafting legislation for the crazies who were elected to represent the people and Vic trying to explain to the reading public what their lawmakers were doing with hundreds of millions in tax dollars and why. Both jobs were impossible.

"Too many coincidences," the judge said. "This terrible crime. I see your byline for the first time in a century on the front page of this incredible shrinking newspaper. Now you waltz in the door of Swift's on the very morning this story is published to interrupt my breakfast."

"You are a perceptive devil," Vic said, spreading his hands in mock surrender and shook his head. "However, we have breakfast together two or three times a month, if you'll recall."

"Enjoy," the waitress said as she slid Vic's plate of eggs, bacon, potatoes, and toast in front of him. "More coffee?"

"Keep it coming," Vic said. He unwrapped the tightly wound white paper napkin, freeing the trapped knife, fork, and spoon in a jingle as they splayed out onto the red Formica table next to his plate. "Water. I need to know about water."

"In reference to a new story, or this one?" Chase said.

"You know Frank Driscoll?" Vic said.

"State Patrol. Drove for Johnny Van during his short stint as chief exec when we were doing whatever it was we were doing way back when at the statehouse. Now a Denver cop. Top detective."

"That wasn't a haiku was it?" Vic said.

"No," the judge said. "That wasn't anything other than the English language, truncated a bit. You should know that. You're the writer."

"Last time I looked, you had three books published," Vic said. "I'm oh for three."

"Finish one," Chase said. "Two hundred words a day. It's not all that hard."

"So you say," Vic said. "Yes, Frank is the top dog downtown, and, yes, it's about the Swain killing. Driscoll called me a while ago and peppered me with questions about water rights, on the sly, not for print."

"Then if something about this case makes it up to us, I might have to recuse myself if I talk to you about it."

"A lot of 'ifs' in there," Vic said.

"Hey, we all have to lay off one case or another all the time," Chase said. "We've got enough bodies up there to cover if I have to sit this one out. Go ahead. Ask me about water."

Vic netted out his conversation with Driscoll about water rights. "I gave him everything I knew about Colorado water law, but I'm not sure I got it right," he said.

"Well, for a civilian, you were pretty darn close," Chase said. "Colorado water law is based on the concept of first in time, first in right."

"Which means the older the right the better it is," Vic said.

"Basically. We use the terms 'junior' and 'senior' rights. The older the claim on the water, the more senior the right." He took a sip of coffee and then waved off Dorothea who, with coffee pot in hand, was making a sweep of the restaurant. "Driscoll asked about an 1887 water right on the South Platte?"

"He did," Vic said.

"But he didn't put it into context," Chase said.

"How so?"

"Sounds like he didn't say who owned the right, or what was going to be done with it, except he mentioned conservation," Chase said.

"I assume it had something to do with Swain's murder," Vic said. He tore a piece of rye toast in half, broke one of the two eggs with it, wiped the bread through the yoke, and took a bite of the now yellowed portion.

"You had it right when you were talking to Driscoll," the judge said. "I think this happened when you were covering the statehouse, but the legislature passed a law that designated maintenance of stream flows as a beneficial use of water."

"For conservation."

"Mostly to protect fish populations," Chase said, "but it could be used for other conservation purposes as well."

"Such as?"

"Oh, maintaining a wet habitat for migratory birds," he said. "Hasn't been used for that yet, as far as I can recall."

"But it could, right?" Vic said.

"Sure," Chase said.

"What about rafting?" Vic said.

Chase laughed. "On the South Platte? You can walk most of the river."

"Maybe the water could be diverted to another river basin for rafting, for tourism," Vic said.

"Now there's a thought," Chase said, "but so much water is sucked over the divide to water the lawns in the cities, the conservation right could be used I to stop the diversion."

"You mean bring less water over the hill?" Vic said.

"That's right," Chase said. "Leave it where it belongs."

"Belongs?" Vic said. "Do I detect a predisposition to some vague future legal ruling?"

"Like I said, there are plenty of judges up there to handle a water case without me."

"How would I go about finding out if Swain had some plan to do something like this?" Vic said.

"Start with the Colorado Water Conservation Board," Chase said. "Under the statute, which I wrote by the way, that's the only entity that can acquire water rights to maintain minimum stream flow. The application process starts there."

"How does the board actually acquire the water rights?" Vic said.

"If the legislature feels generous, they can authorize funds to allow the board to buy or lease a water right," Chase said.

"Any other way?"

"Donation," the judge said.

"Someone can just give a water right to the board?" Vic said.

"Yup," Chase said, "And if it's a right dated 1887, it's probably worth a boatload of money."

"To whom?" Vic said.

"To farmers and ranchers, for one, or two, if you're counting," he said. "And the municipalities and housing developers. They trip all over each other to get their hands on water."

"That's plenty of competition right there," Vic said.

"Energy companies too," Chase said. "They're buying up water rights as fast as they can, in case they have to rip up the state for oil shale development, or pumping it into the ground to force out more oil and gas."

"I assume Gary Kendrick is up to his neck in this water chess game," Vic said, wondering how the judge might react to the name.

# 15

Chase placed his elbows on the table, folded his hands, and pointed both index fingers skyward to make a small church. He rested his chin on his thumbs and hid his mouth behind the steeple.

"I can't talk much about Gary Kendrick," Chase said. "He's been before me twice and no doubt will be in court again sometime in the future."

Vic saw the opening. "But you can say something."

Chase took his hands away from his face and said, "I did hear he's gotten himself involved in this campaign to get the state to issue two hundred million in water development bonds. It's in the legislature now, but it'll need voter approval so there's going to have to be a campaign and election. He's probably the brains behind that. All rumor, though."

"Nothing you say leaves here," Vic said, tapping his right temple with his index finger.

"I would hope not," Chase said.

"Could a senior water right, I mean a really senior water right, be worth killing for?" Vic said.

"Like the lieutenant governor of a state?"

Vic nodded.

"You bet it is," the judge said. "This is still the Wild West."

# 16

John Michaels knew he was destined to govern the state of Colorado. Now it looked all but certain. He had to move quickly, but he did not want it to be all that obvious. He began his political work day like any other when the legislature was in session.

He leaped to the curb from the Number 15 bus at Lafayette Street, walked south one block to Fourteenth Avenue, and then headed west toward the mountains and the gold-domed building hewn from giant blocks of white stone quarried in western Colorado near a speck of a town aptly named Marble. Denver was fresh with crisp spring mile high morning air scrubbed of dust and pollution by a rain the night before. Early sunlight filtered through the oaks, maples, and the few elms that managed to survive the Dutch elm epidemic and spilled its brilliant yellow wash across the earthen red of the early Twentieth Century buildings that dominated Capitol Hill.

He walked across the Capitol's east lawn and around the circular drive where the state government elite were permitted to park. All the parking slots were empty except for two State Patrol SUVs.

Even the slot for the other early arriver, Colorado Attorney General J.R. McInerny, was devoid of its usual junker, which surprised Michaels. McInerny was known for his five-hundred dollar cars, which he drove until they died. Then he would simply find another junker. His current jalopy was a rusty Chrysler K car, the color of which was something between white and dirty tan. Given what had happened, he expected to see the AG's car there. The governor was probably in, Michaels thought, trying to figure out which end was up.

Michaels badged himself through the lower level security door reserved mostly for those who the voters elected to run the state. That included legislators, the governor, lieutenant governor, state treasurer, attorney general, and the secretary of state, along with their staffers. State Supreme Court justices used to wander in and out of this all but hidden basement level portal, but the judges were rarely seen since they had moved into their own building a few blocks away. Before September 11th, it was a door that anyone could use. Afterwards, however, the badge swiper was added along with state troopers and metal detectors inside. Michaels had never seen the governor use the door. He made a mental note to continue using it when he became governor.

"Good morning, Mr. Leader," said trooper George Lochlear, standing tall next to the security screening line.

"George. How we doing this morning?"

"Fine, sir. What about you?"

"Just dandy," Michaels said. "Did you get Amy off to school okay?"

"We did. Ellen and I loaded the pickup and drove Amy up to Greeley on Saturday." The trooper stared out past Michaels for a moment, into the darkness of the capitol basement.

"She'll be fine, George."

"Sure she will," the trooper said. "She's got a little apartment through the summer, then she'll move into the freshman dorm in the fall. She wanted to start with summer school." Then his voice cracked. "First one out of the nest."

Michaels could not remember ever hearing the slightest hint of emotion from a state trooper assigned to the capitol. "George, you taught Amy well. Don't worry."

"She wants to teach music," he said with a note of resignation.

"Look, by the time she graduates, we'll have music programs back in the public schools. She'll be fine, George." Michaels patted the trooper on the shoulder. "I've got to hit the office."

"Papers are all there. *Times* didn't show up though. I'll bring it in when it does."

"Thanks, George."

"Mr. Leader?" Michaels stopped and turned around to look back at the trooper.

"Are you all right?" the trooper said.

"I'm all right, George," he said.

The state senate majority leader walked over to the kiosk tucked into a nook set off by two massive Roman columns. An American flag waved at him from the video screen built into the unit. Michaels poked the screen with his right index finger. The kiosk came alive.

A calm female voice spoke to him. "Welcome to the Honor Roll of Colorado's War Dead," it said. The screen displayed a white text menu over a U.S. flag. Michaels followed the on-screen commands.

He touched "By Conflict."

A list of wars, skirmishes, and foreign adventures scrolled onto the screen. He touched "Vietnam War."

"Touch the first letter of the last name," the screen commanded. He touched the "M."

"Scroll up or down the list to make your selection."

He touched the "Down" button on the screen and scrolled to

"Michaels, Jeffery." He touched "Select."

A photo and a short biographical blurb appeared on the screen. A steely-jawed Marine standing at attention, his head covered with a short light brown bristle of hair, stared out at Michaels. "Lt. Col. Jeffery Michaels, U.S.M.C. Born July 10, 1945. Killed in action February 25, 1971. Saigon, Rep. of Vietnam."

"Morning, Dad. I'll do you proud today," Michaels said quietly to the kiosk screen. "This will be an important one."

Michaels looked back and saw trooper Lochlear watching him. Both men nodded. Then the state senator turned and walked toward the capitol rotunda. He slowly and deliberately walked up the massive marble stairs that flowed up to the executive offices on the first floor and then up to the house and senate chambers on the second floor. He paused on the stairs for a moment to look straight up into the wide round expanse of the capitol dome before continuing his ascent to the first floor where he stood quietly outside the oak and stained glass doors that led into the Governor's Office. Michaels pictured himself entering that door as he went to work on the state's business. He walked leisurely to the elevator, which he took up to the legislative offices on the second floor.

Michaels' office was far less pretentious than the governor's office suite, but he liked it anyway, with its single wooden door and frosted glass window, just off a small hallway that led directly to the floor of the Colorado State Senate, where he reigned supreme. Before he went in, he stopped at the credenza just outside his office to pour a fresh cup of coffee, but there was none.

"Monday," he muttered to no one.

During the week, Michaels' administrative assistant, Anthony Napoli, set up the coffee maker before he left the office each night, setting a timer on the machine so the majority leader would always have a fresh cup first thing in the morning. That happened Monday through Thursday nights. Coffee drinkers were on their own weekends and Mondays.

Michaels pulled out the coffee fixings, inserted a new filter, ground up a batch of fair-trade organically grown Guatemalan beans in a separate grinder, dumped in the coffee, and walked down the hall to the men's room. After filling the insulated coffee urn from the sink, he returned to the coffee area, poured in the water, slipped the urn back into place, and hit the "brew" button. Then he eased over to the thick brass rotunda railing to stare down into the basement and languish in his joy at being inside the Colorado State Capitol Building. Early morning sounds indicating the statehouse was coming alive for another day of governing echoed up toward him. Behind his back, the drip system sputtered and dribbled fresh brewed coffee into the urn.

Near the end of the last legislative session, Michaels, suffering from some sort of caffeine-induced epiphany, bought a complicated new whiz-bang coffee maker for his office. The three-hundred dollar robo-brewer actually ground fresh coffee beans and then made the coffee. Cool as it seemed, this latest technological gift to coffee-addicted humanity was such a high maintenance wonder it drove his staff nuts. After weeks of complaints, Michaels said he would wash the thing out each night.

"Not each night, Mr. Leader," Napoli informed him. "Try before each pot."

So Michaels did. He had to pull out several components of the coffee maker and literally scrub them so they were clean and free of any old grounds before the thing would even make another pot. The process took about ten minutes. It was a real pain. The few times the machine was not thoroughly scrubbed between pots it boiled over, issuing a frothy lava flow of coffee grounds and hot brown water across the entire credenza. So much for the "Italiano Express Coffee Maker." It was replaced with a used Mr. Coffee picked up at the local thrift store for five bucks. The rest of the legislative session proceeded smoothly, coffee-wise. The politics remained ugly as ever.

Michaels poured himself a cup from the urn and walked into his office to read the papers.

The smaller, more colorful and redesigned *Rocky Mountain Sun* tabloid was always set on top of the pile. For the moment, he managed not to look at the headline that he knew was there. That mental compartment would remain sealed for a few more minutes as he shut down and filed away the memories of the morning's events thus far: his invigorating walk to the capitol, the bantering interchange with trooper Lochlear, his good morning moment with the ghost of his father, and the ritualistic preparation of the Monday morning coffee.

His heart racing a bit, Michaels cracked open the psychological partition he hoped would eventually deliver him to the governor's chair on the first floor. He carefully set his Colorado Rockies coffee mug on the ceramic tile coaster he always kept on the left side of his desk. Coffee steam spiraled toward the century old ceiling. Then he looked down at the front page of the *Sun*. There was one large photo, a headshot of Jessica Swain, three bold Helvetica words declaring, "Lt. Gov. Slain!" and the first paragraph of a story by Vic Bengston, a name he recalled, but a name he was surprised to see on this story.

Easing back into his overstuffed office chair, sipping the hot drink, and thinking about how this event makes his glide path to the governor's office much smoother, Michaels fought the urge to run downstairs and get a fresh bear claw to go with his coffee. Then he spoke quietly to the portrait of Colorado's first territorial governor, David Evans, hanging on the wall across from him.

"Assassinated, was more like it."

# 17

Vic still was not ready to go home. He and Chase went Dutch on their breakfast tabs. The state constitution precluded them from doing anything else. Liberal do-gooders had convinced voters to pass a state constitutional amendment that nearly made it a felony to pick up a breakfast tab for a public official. It was one of many amendments draped on the Rube Goldberg Colorado Constitution to satiate the generally unreasonable demands of one special interest group or another. The reporter and the state supreme court justice parted ways outside the breakfast joint, Vic passing on Chase's offer of a ride.

Instead, he retraced his walking route back up Broadway toward the capitol building. He wanted to wander through the statehouse where his earlier career in journalism really got started. Plus, he was curious about how the Swain murder might be affecting those who frequented the halls of power in Colorado. Vic had not been inside the statehouse for years, not since he worked for Governor Jack Mack back in the seventies and while committing daily journalism before that. He walked up Fourteenth, headed east along the south side of Civic Center Park, and waited for the crossing light at Lincoln. A brief red light stymied the morning commuter traffic hurtling toward downtown long enough for him to jog across the six lanes of pavement. After a one-block uphill hike to Sherman, Vic turned left and headed for the south entrance of the statehouse.

Crossing gates and massive concrete blocks impeded what used to be a free-flowing thoroughfare around the building. More post-9/11 security measures. The capitol circle was so free flowing during the pre-attack era, it became a prime pick up spot where older men sought relief from younger men, guaranteeing the newspapers at least one juicy scandal story a year when some judge, legislator, or a well-connected businessman got caught with his pants down, literally.

Vic pushed his way through the same heavy wooden doors he used decades earlier as a reporter, but halted at a security station inside the second set of doors leading to the basement level of the capitol. Three troopers guarded the security-screening gateway that isolated the seat of state government from the taxpayers who paid for it. Vic dumped his wallet, house keys, loose change, and a fountain pen into a small plastic tray, then rolled it down the conveyor line into the scanner's gaping mouth.

"Okay, step forward please," said the female trooper who filled out her state patrol uniform quite nicely. Vic walked through the security portal, which beeped.

"Stand over there please," she said, pointing to an area next to the large scanner.

"Raise your arms up like this," said a far less appealing male trooper, a buff Hispanic with a brutal military haircut and fully squared away uniform.

Vic complied and the cop wanded him down. No beeps. Then he waived the wand over Vic's gut. "Beep."

"Belt buckle," Vic said.

"That's fine," the trooper said. "Thank you, sir."

Vic scooped up his personal items and targeted the small cafeteria on the north side of the basement just north of the rotunda. He had a taste for another cup of coffee.

As he turned into the tight alcove where coffee, rolls, bagels, sandwiches, soft drinks, and snacks were dispensed, Vic bumped into another patron of this fine cuisine. A bear claw flew from the right hand of neatly dressed man in his late thirties or early forties. It landed on the tiny counter next to the cash register right when the cashier said, "That will be a dollar seventy-nine, Mr. Michaels."

"I'm sorry," Vic said. "I guess I swerved into the passing lane."

"No problem," Michaels said as he snatched up the sticky bear claw with a napkin in his left hand. "Five second rule. Plus, Pete here keeps this place so clean you could eat off the floor."

A picture materialized in Vic's mind, legislators on all fours licking up soup during a break in the activity on the second floor. He suppressed the laugh.

"At least let me buy the bear claw," Vic said.

"Sorry," Michaels said. "Amendment 41. I'd be thrown in jail. You'd be stuck with hours of paperwork." He looked at Vic, then said, "Don't I know you?"

"I don't think we've ever met."

"Didn't you used to be Vic Bengston?"

"Still am."

He held out his hand. "John Michaels."

"I know," Vic said, returning with a firm grip. "I recognize you from your picture in the Pink Book."

"The Pink Book doesn't print pictures. Only names, addresses, and committee assignments."

"You're right," Vic said. "Post Office?"

Michaels laughed and said, "Not yet. You were in today's paper. Page One. The assass—murder."

"Is that the prevailing theory?" Vic said. "Assassination?"

"Well, no. I don't really know. I'm not plugged into the investigation. It's just that, well, when someone like the lieutenant governor is killed, you know, deliberately, it's like an assassination. I don't like the word much, though."

"It was like an execution though," Vic said.

"The word you used," Michaels said.

"Assassination connotes a political motivation," Vic said. "Was there one?"

"Is this on the record?" Michaels said, backpedaling. "Don't say I said assassination."

"I'm too tired to say you said anything," Vic said. "But I could phone something to the desk if you have anything new to add."

"I'm devastated," the majority leader said.

"I think your press release said that," Vic said. "Or someone's did."

"You really did write that story, didn't you?" Michaels said.

"Well, yes. That's sort of how these things, these newspapers, work."

"I thought they wrote it at the desk and you guys just fed them the facts," Michaels said, sounding a bit too naive for Vic's taste. Maybe he was just making small talk, Vic thought.

"No, they let us write our own stories occasionally."

"I haven't seen your byline in the paper since I've been at the statehouse," Michaels said.

"Then how did you know who I was?" Vic said.

"Your picture was in the Denver Business Journal, last week, when you closed down your company. Also, I have a whole file of clips on some old stories about oil shale development in western Colorado. You wrote them. I put two and two together."

So this was the young fresh political mind that seemed to keep tabs on many things, Vic thought. Many issues, many stories, and many people in Colorado. Even more reason to wonder about the sincerity behind the question about how the newsroom operated. This guy knew. Vic envied the man's memory. His was failing, or at least it seemed as though it was.

"Yeah, real old stories, but I see the energy companies have paraded out oil shale again," Vic said. "All they need is about every drop of water on the Western Slope to develop the stuff."

Michaels slapped on a serious face before replying. "Managed correctly, the water end could work out," he said.

Water again, Vic thought. So he dove in.

"Was the lieutenant governor involved in some sort of a water deal?" Vic said.

The serious face morphed into a stern one, a mask of power. "I've got a meeting," Michaels said. "Already late." Then he quickly slipped the happy face back on. "Good luck with your new job, but I already told you I'm not in the loop on the investigation." He spun around and shot toward the elevator.

Like hell you're not, Vic thought.

# 18

"Vic Bengston. As I live and breathe. The man himself, back from the wilderness of corporate America."

"Dwight," Vic said. "Isn't this where we left off about a million years ago?"

Vic sat down at the small table hugging a massive marble column. He placed his coffee, now designer drip coffee, not the burnt offerings that used to be served up in the statehouse cafeteria, in front of him and across the table from former TV news reporter Dwight Anderson. The Monday edition of the *Sun* was in front of him.

"I thought this might have been your kid," Anderson said, nodding at the newspaper.

"It's me," Vic said.

"Whatever possessed you?" Anderson said.

"I don't know, Dwight," Vic said. "Got tired of shoveling corporate—"

"You missed the game," Anderson said.

He knew. Anderson was a real reporter, covering the statehouse and uncovering plenty of corruption in his investigative journalism days at Denver's CBS affiliate station, or was it ABC? Did not matter. Affable and articulate, which Vic always thought should have been enough to make it in television, Anderson lacked the glitz and glamour all the media consultants claimed drew viewers to television news. Real story content seemed to have little to do with viewership. Anderson had the look of a northern European craftsman, light hair, full lips, and a prominent nose. He was one of Denver's best reporters, print or electronic, and the station canned him because of his age, and because he did not look like a cover boy for *Gentleman's Quarterly*. Too bad for them. Anderson sued, won a hefty settlement, then went into business for himself as a public relations consultant.

"Lobbying are we?" Vic said.

"For the Teamsters, Vic, so don't cross us," he said with a jovial laugh. He offered his hand, and Vic shook it.

"I thought I'd entered an alternate universe when I read the paper this morning," he said. "When did you rejoin the ranks?"

"Yesterday was my first day," Vic said. "I caught the story on a fluke."

"I could use a fluke like that," Anderson said. "I've got a committee this morning that wants to end union representation as we know it, and I think the bastards have the votes to get this thing through."

"Have the governor veto it."

Anderson shook his head. "Our governor, our Democratic governor, has been handed his hat by the Republicans. They're the only ones who can re-elect him, and they've got him trussed up like a Christmas goose."

"What about the majority leader?" Vic said.

"Michaels?" Anderson said. "He's buttering both sides of his bread."

"Meaning?"

"Meaning, he's in bed with whoever will advance his political career," Anderson said.

"But the Dems control the senate and the house," Vic said. "That should be enough to kill the bill."

"Not when you've got your eyes on the prize."

"Governor's Mansion?"

Anderson nodded and flashed a set of teeth that the media consultants would have had ripped from his mouth and replaced with gleaming straight pearly whites anchored to the jaw bones with titanium screws.

"The unions worked their butts off to get Michaels and Dowd elected," Vic said.

"But Michaels still has to figure out a way to satisfy both parties," Anderson said. "He and his professor pal are already working on a compromise that will weaken state labor laws just enough to offend neither side."

"Whatever happened to Democratic Party positions and Republican Party positions, black and white?" Vic said.

"Went the way of truth in advertising and the fairness doctrine. Everything's gray now, one shade or another."

"I ran into Michaels, literally, as I came in," Vic said.

"I saw him in here," Anderson said. "Make sure you've still got your wallet."

"He's that bad?"

"No, but he's that crafty," Anderson said. "What did you two boys talk about after the collision?"

"The story, the newspaper, then water rights."

"Well, you know about water," Anderson said. "It runs everything in the state."

"I know," Vic said. "When I mentioned water to him, specifically the consumption of it for oil shale development, his demeanor changed."

"From detached and businesslike to what?"

"Damn near fightin' mad," Vic said. "Not quite, but awfully close."

"You must have touched a nerve," Anderson said. "Michaels is a pretty cool calculator."

"He called Swain's murder an assassination," Vic said, noticing that he was sliding easily back into the kind of gossip that generated news stories.

"Well, you guys called it an execution. That's pretty close. Anyway, isn't the murder of an elected official an assassination?"

"Not if it was an ex-spouse or a drunk friend," Vic said.

"But it was neither of those in all likelihood," Anderson said. "Wyoming militia, maybe?"

It was the old running gag among the statehouse reporters. When things slowed down, there was occasional talk about the imaginary war between Colorado and Wyoming, fostered by a tug of war over the grave of Buffalo Bill Cody, interred at a tourist site in the foothills west of Denver. Wyoming lays claim to the Wild West legend. For nearly a century, Colorado has remained ever vigilant in case Wyoming irregulars cross the border and steal the body.

"I think the cease fire's still in effect," Vic said, smiling. "I guess you could call it an assassination. It seemed like an odd word choice so soon after the killing. Then, his reaction when I asked him specifics about the water seemed a bit over the top. Although I don't really know the guy."

"He's all in for new oil shale development," Anderson said. "So are we, along with gas, oil, coal and renewables."

"Jobs?" Vic said.

"Tons of them."

"A lot of money," Vic said.

"What specifics, other than oil shale development, did Michaels react to?" Anderson asked.

Vic shook his head and said, "Better not go into that right now."

"I understand," Anderson said.

He did. The unwritten rule was that gossip went only so far between competing reporters. Reveal your hand, and you have given away your story.

"Suffice it to say, Michaels was all business when it came to water rights," Vic said.

Anderson nodded in agreement and said, "Some people would go to great lengths to control them."

After finishing their coffees with small talk, Vic continued his trek through the basement of the capitol, exiting on the north side and walking down to the bus stop on Colfax, wondering how far someone would go to advance a political agenda.

# 19

Ever since he was a kid, Bobbie Hague loved bouncing around rural Colorado in his dad's pickup. His favorite ride was the north-south run between Denver and Greeley on U.S. Highway 85, which paralleled the South Platte River as it escaped Denver and flowed into the rural parts of northeastern Colorado. The season did not matter. In the spring, like now, fields lining the highway had already started to green up as the new shoots emerged from the tilled soil. In the summer, Hague marveled at the sheer tenacity of migrant workers sweeping the fields. Bent to the Earth, they scraped out weeds and tended the crops, which by then would have turned into onions, potatoes, cabbages, soybeans, or corn. He could tell how good or bad the season would be by the height of the corn by the Fourth of July. In the fall, he watched the same itinerant workers cut, slash, and dig at the crops to harvest them for market. Expansive fields of green leaves transformed into brown dusty earth spotted with tan burlap bags stuffed with potatoes. Workers hefted the fifty-pound sacks onto flatbed trucks. In other fields, migrants boxed up thousands of white softball sized Colorado onions in crates stacked ten high on tractor-pulled trailers. He remembered working the sugar beet fields on his family's farm and on other farms in the area. Elsewhere, gigantic green, yellow, or red machines mowed down the feed corn, ground up the stalks, and tossed the separated ears into cavernous steel bins following close behind. Vegetable stands appeared every few miles along the road from mid-summer into the fall. Adjacent fields filled with parked cars from Denver as people loaded up with bushels of fresh pickling cucumbers, armloads of sweet corn, and paper sacks full of roasted green chilies. Trucks would be in from southeastern Colorado with Rocky Ford cantaloupes and from the southwest with Olathe sweet corn. All this turmoil of cultivating, weeding, growing, and harvesting turned quiet when winter returned. Fields lay dormant, brown, and flat, turned over, tilled smooth, replenishing for the next season. Leaves were off the gray winter trees. Occasionally, snow powdered the fields with a few inches of instant water, muffling the sounds of the crisp brittle winter grasses. All of nature awaited the next spring.

Each year Hague's excitement over the drive gradually withered into revulsion as paint flaked from farmhouses and barns and roof shingles shredded or vanished with each hail storm. Eventually, Hague saw only buildings abandoned and finally keeling over in decay, defeated in a futile war against the well-financed housing developments that marched northward from the city and steadily conquered thousands of acres of once productive farmland. Now, where his eyes used to drink in the gem-like blue-greens of onions and cabbages, the greens of sugar beets and potatoes, and the largesse of tall corn stalks, he saw only weeds and unkept empty fields waiting for the terra-formers to transform these old family farms into turnkey suburbs with names like East Ridge Estates, Carthage Farms, or Reunion, names dreamed up by high-paid consultants who lived and worked inside the steel and glass cages of

Manhattan. This part of the drive he did not love. This part he hated.

As Hague swung his dark gray Ford F250 off the highway a mile south of Gilcrest and raced across the wide gravel parking lot at Lil's Café, a flurry of nasty thoughts seized him. He wondered about how he would keep up the truck payments. The life insurance probably would have to go. He and Nancy might have to put off Mark's braces another year unless her folks could help. His hands tightened on the steering wheel as images of his endangered knee-high corn materialized in his mind's eye. With luck he could still save the crop and retain that rolling sea of green sweeping up the gentle rise to the west of his house and barns.

Then the image burst into the flames of drought. His equipment loan payments were late. He owed a buddy a thousand bucks for extra seed corn. The plan was to pay it off when he sold his crop to the co-op's new ethanol fuel plant. With the spike in gas prices, the Middle Eastern wars, and everyone freaking out over global warming, he thought this might be the year he would get ahead by cashing in on a corn crop that put gas in cars on the road rather than fat on cattle at the feedlot. Now the state has ordered him to shut down his irrigation wells and cut off the lifeblood to his family's survival.

Of the dozen or so vehicles parked at Lil's, most were pickups, all massive, relatively new, heavy-duty, a few rigged for horse trailers. Hague recognized Dave's truck, and Darryl's, but none of the others. Of the unrecognized trucks, Hague swore under his breath, "I hope to hell they've got irrigation water."

He slammed his transmission into "park" and jumped from the cab, thinking about that water right floating out there in legal limbo, a water right that should stay with the farmers and not be handed over to the damn environmentalists, duck hunters, and land developers.

# 20

Hague brushed past the newspaper boxes flashing their lurid execution headlines at him, begging him to buy a paper. He flung open the restaurant door and grumbled, "That bitch," but no one heard him.

"Hey, leave the door on the hinges, will ya, Bobbie," Lil said. She stood inside the entrance behind a small counter where she was ringing up an ancient couple, he stooped and bent from decades of hard farming in eastern Colorado, she with a new blond wig and now looking after her spent husband, both of them picking the remains of Lil's steak and eggs special from their teeth with Made-In-American toothpicks. Lil peered up at Hague over the top of her reading glasses. "Better not order the Wheaties today, macho man."

"God, I'm sorry, Lil. I'll watch it."

"Or, you'll buy me a new screen door," she said with a smile, then jerked her head toward the back of the café. "They're in back waitin' for you, darlin'."

Hague snatched a toothpick from a miniature milk barrel on top of the cash register and jammed it into the corner of his mouth. He walked past the counter occupied by three farmers on black vinyl and chrome spinning stools and down a narrow hallway with the kitchen on the left and the johns on the right. At the end, the passageway spit Hague into the Lil's back room where the local Rotary Club met the first Thursday of the month for their breakfast meeting and where non-smokers dined before the Democrats in the state legislature pushed through a smoking ban for all bars and restaurants in Colorado, except the lucrative casinos in Blackhawk, Golden, and Cripple Creek. The smoking ban did not sit well with the farmers and ranchers who gathered at Lil's, but the low price of her breakfast specials did, so the regulars and the help set up a smoking lounge out back with a rickety wooden picnic bench one of the boys hauled in from his farm.

Two men occupied the table in the far corner of the room. Like Hague, both of them were going for big corn crops this year. Dave Bender, who farmed east of Fort Lupton on a six-hundred-forty acre place that came from his wife's side of the family, waved his green John Deere cap high in the air. Darryl Winston farmed along the South Platte River a few miles away, north of Gilcrest, not far from Hague's section.

"Fellas," Hague said as he pulled out the remaining chair and sat with a note of exasperation.

"You heard, then?" said Winston.

"Sure I heard," Hague said. "Molly called me on the radio. She read me the story."

Bender looked at Hague, then sucked in a deep breath.

"What's the matter with you?" Hague said, exchanging a glance with Winston.

"Nothing," Bender said. "Nothing. I'm all right. What do you think this will do to the lawsuit?"

"Slow it down a lot," Hague said, grinning while he poured hot dark coffee from the brown and black plastic flip-top urn on the table into an empty white porcelain mug. "It's going to slow things down an awful lot, Dave. But it's going to make life a whole lot easier for all of us."

"We've got to get those wells turned back on," Winston said. "I may have to go back to growing pot if I can't water my damn fields."

"With that bitch dead, we've got a real shot at that water right," Hague said. "At least that's what Gary thinks."

"You met with him already?" asked Bender.

"This morning, bright and ugly," Hague said. "I met him for breakfast down in Denver."

"Better you than me," Bender said, spitting out a few shreds of scrambled eggs. "I can't stand the sight of the guy."

"Cool your jets, Dave," Hague said. "Kendrick's our only hope on this thing. You don't have to meet with him anyway."

"That's good. I'd kick his ass."

"Dave! Let me deal with Kendrick, okay?"

Bender nodded and returned to his breakfast.

"What'd he say this morning?" Winston said.

"First of all, and not many of you knew this, she didn't own the damn water right. Second, the duck hunters only had a letter of intent from her saying that she would donate the water right to them once she gained title to it, if she could."

"You're kidding," Bender said. He leaned back and ran his right hand through his shaggy brown hair. "I thought she owned it. Hell, that's what the lawyer said last month. God damn it!"

"Calm down, Dave," Hague said, reaching out and clamping down on Bender's left arm. "Apparently, she didn't own the thing. That's pretty typical of her kind. More money than they know what to do with, but they always seem to think they can do whatever the hell they want to."

"Christ! That means—"

Hague cut him off. "That means nothing, you hear? You got that?"

Flushed with rage, Bender nodded and returned to his eggs.

"She sure as hell didn't get her way this time," said Winston. He reached for his cigarettes in his shirt pocket, pulled the pack halfway out and then let it slide back in. He would have to wait until they went outside. "Now what?"

"Gary thinks we can buy it," Hague said.

"Right, when my last two pigs fly," Bender said.

"Two?" Winston said. "When did you double your herd?"

"Shut up," Bender said.

"Gary was dead serious," Hague said. "He said that because she didn't have any shot at a clear title, we can tie this thing up for years in the court."

"How's that going to help us?" Winston said. "Dave says the suit hasn't even been filed."

"Well, first off, the water right won't convert," Hague said. "It'll stay agricultural. That's critical for us. Second, the family that owns it is desperate to sell. They haven't been farming for years. The old man opened an insurance agency in Fort Morgan, and he's about broke."

"And third?" Bender said.

"And third, we're going to buy the right," Hague said, smiling.

"With what," Winston said, "your good looks?"

"No. We've already got the money lined up. It's a private source. Interest-free. Our little ditch company will own and manage the water right. We'll sell extra shares to all the other guys along the river. If we default on the payments, and that's going to be hard to do if prices stay up, the right goes into a trust to benefit agriculture, nothing else."

"What trust?" Winston said.

"Gary set it up," Hague said.

"You did all this with Gary over breakfast?" Bender said, leaning forward.

"No, we've been working on it for about two months, ever since we discovered she didn't have clear title," Hague said. Bender and Winston exchanged glances. Bender refilled his coffee from the carafe and Winston made another aborted grab for his cigarettes. Silence filled Lil's Back Room.

"Look, you guys told me to see if Gary could take care of this," Hague said. "'You're the one with the big agricultural economics degree from CSU,' you said. 'See if you can save our,' what was the term you used?"

"Sorry asses," Bender said as he tore open a sugar packet and dumped the white crystals into Lil's hot, dark liquid. "You could have said something."

"I am saying something, right now," Hague said, his face flushed with frustration.

"Hold on there, Dave" said Winston. "You wanted Bobbie to check out the possibilities. There's no reason to get pissed."

"It's almost too much to take in, all at once," Bender said. "Especially after, well, after what happened."

"No more talk about that, ever," Hague said. "Time to move on."

Bender dug into his sausage.

"Who's this investor anyway?" Winston said.

"Can't say," Hague said.

Bender looked up and said, "Then, why's he doing it?"

"He hates tree huggers and duck hunters. He likes farmers and ranchers. Isn't that enough?"

"Okay, okay," Bender said. "But we're talking about, what, a couple of million dollars?"

"Two point three million," Hague said. "Sweetened the pot a little, to 'incentivize' the family, as Gary put it."

"Bobbie?" It was Winston, calling his name quietly.

"What?"

"How does, uh, this, uh, this weekend stuff," Winston said. "How does it fit in?"

Bender looked down at his plate.

Hague smiled. "I told you. No more talk about that. But it makes things a whole lot easier."

# 21

Gary Kendrick strutted into the Castle Rock campaign office of "Coloradans for Sensible Water Policy". The desks were empty.

"Where is everyone?" Kendrick hollered, grinning ear to ear. "Out celebrating?"

Nathan's head popped out of the small kitchen in the back of the office. "Back here, Boss."

Kendrick walked through the narrow work space and into the kitchen, which served as a break room for the small campaign staff.

"I'm not the Boss, Nathan," Kendrick said. "On paper, in public, or in the open air here." He swept his right arm, Vanna White style. "Please stop calling me that."

"All right," Nathan said, returning to his seat on the far side of a table that occupied much of the tiny space.

"You haven't heard about Jessica Swain then, I take it," said Sharla Santos, the diminutive blonde titan who was running the ballot issue campaign to convince voters they need to issue two-hundred million dollars in bonds to build new reservoirs in eastern Colorado.

"Heard about it?" Kendrick said. "I've already been dancing on her grave."

Nathan and Sharla stared blankly at the stocky man who had been their meal ticket for the past six months.

"What do you mean?" Nathan said.

"I mean we've sealed the deal," Kendrick said. "With her out of the way, we've been handed this campaign on a silver platter."

"Gary," Sharla said, lighting a cigarette. "A little compassion, please."

"I wish you wouldn't do that in here," Kendrick said.

"Look, you want me to work the hours I'm working for the next god knows how many years and, what, you expect me to turn into little Miss Candyass? I'm sorry, Gary, you take the firm as it is or you can go—"

"Cool it, Sharla. Take it easy. Here, sit down."

Kendrick stood behind her chair and repositioned it for her as she flopped back down with a burst of smoke exploding from her mouth and nostrils. He gently massaged her shoulders. "The timing of this was perfect."

Nathan stood up and looked out the kitchen door again into the empty campaign office. "You're a little too giddy over this."

"There's no one out there," Kendrick said. "I locked the door. We're all going out to lunch. The Broadmoor. To celebrate."

"No frigging way," Sharla seethed through another ashen gray cloud. "Maybe in a month. But not now. We had a public debate with her a week ago. We can't go off on a celebratory toot after she's been murdered. I've already started working on a statement. We've got to issue one."

"Yes, frigging way," Kendrick said. "The new chef over there is top drawer, and we're going. That's an order." He pulled a small silver digital recorder from his coat pocket. "I've got the statement right here. All drippy and gooey."

"Let me transcribe it," Sharla said. She grabbed the recorder and handed it to Nathan who walked out into the front room of the campaign office.

"When are you going to see Gene?" Kendrick said.

"Tonight, at the home builders association awards dinner. He's going to emcee."

"Okay. Well, tell our, or your, esteemed campaign chairman to issue this as written. If he wants to change it, he's got to call me, understand?"

"Sure. Sure, Gary," Sharla said. "Your words are gold."

"No," Kendrick said. "Never forget. Water is gold."

# 22

Mr. Leader?”

"Yes, Tony, come on in," Michaels said. "Sit down."

The tall lanky aide ambled across the room and sat in one of two chairs opposite the business side of the massive century-old oak desk. Michaels never let more than two people sit across from him. He knew he could always handle two who were against him. Any more than that and it was asymmetrical warfare in his mind. If he faced more than two opponents, Michaels always moved the discussion to his conference room, where he always sat at the head of the table with at least one of his supporters on either side. He never chaired a meeting at a round table. In fact, the only round table in the statehouse was the poker table in the press room up on the third floor. Anthony Napoli was a graduate student in political science from the University of Denver, Michaels' alma mater.

"You look like crap," Michaels said.

"I was up all night," Napoli said. "This is awful, just awful."

"Learn to pace yourself, Tony. Grab those emotions. There's a state to run."

"She was your friend, wasn't she?" Napoli said.

"She was a political ally," Michaels said. "I called the family and asked what I could do. Talked to the governor. He's a mess. Calmed him down. Called all the leaders, both parties. Covered all the bases. Went to bed, oh about eleven. I made some notes on what to say this morning."

Michaels was stoked for battle. He wondered if this was what it was like for his dad.

"I don't know how you do it," Napoli said. He shook his head, then stood up. "Okay, what do we need to do?"

"Well, for starters, call Senator Lujak and cancel our meeting on the well bill. Make sure you stress that we're still okay with turning the wells back on, but stall it until we get through the next several days. There's no rush now anyway."

Napoli scrunched his brow. "Those farmers out there aren't going to like this. There's not much more time left in the session."

"Those farmers had ten years to get their shit in a pile, Tony, and if they want me on their side they're going to have to wait a little longer."

Michaels scanned his calendar and reworked his week's schedule in about two minutes. Napoli made notes on a thin pile of note cards.

"Better cancel the entire afternoon schedule," Michaels said. Then, looking out his west-facing window at the Denver skyline pasted up against the Rocky Mountains. "I don't think we'll conduct any business today. Get a hold of all the committee chairs right away and make sure they reschedule their committee hearings. One day's enough. Tell the clerks right away and have them cover our backs. We'll gavel in at ten. I'll make a few comments and open things up. I'm sure members will want to speak, but we can't let this turn into a political debate over gun control. I'm thinking out loud here, Tony, so bear with me. We'll do a moment of silence.

I'll let them talk but ask them to be brief and to the point. No, better not say 'to the point'. That sounds a little too businesslike. I'll say I'd like to adjourn by eleven. We'll adjust the calendars and pick things up on Tuesday. We need to take time to reflect on what has happened. Yes, I'll say that. We need to take time to reflect on, on this tragedy. That's how I'll put it."

Napoli fought his desire to nod off.

Michaels looked as perky as a freshly washed and waxed British racing green sports car.

# 23

Vic closed the thick book and set it on the wide flat armrest of his oak mission style easy chair. It was Len Deighton's three-book series *Game, Set* and *Match*, chronicling the exploits of British spy Bernard Samson whose attractive wife, Fiona, happened to be a double agent. Vic thought reading a bit about Bernard's exploits might ease him into sleep.

Instead, his thoughts drifted from Bernard's fictional world to his own real world. He slumped down and stretched out his legs, letting his head fall back onto the soft pillow backrest. As sleep crept over him, Vic wondered why he left journalism in the first place, especially with four kids and a wife to support. He remembered being bored with covering another session of the legislature. That seemed silly, but it was enough to make him leave the paper, especially after the offer from the governor to help start up a state energy conservation office. Then came the freelancing, forming the public relations firm, followed by years of holding corporate hands. Today, he felt free again.

About four hours later, his cell phone jolted him back to

consciousness. He fumbled for the phone and flipped it open.

"Yeah. Bengston."

"Vic, it's Peggy."

"I'll buy that."

"Did Marsha tell you when to come back in?"

"Around five, six," Vic said. "What time is it?"

"Three-thirty," Peggy said. "Make it five, would you? I've got an assignment for you."

"And what would that be," Vic said. "Hello? Peggy? Peg?"

She was gone.

# 24

"Surely you jest," Vic said.

"No, Vic, I do not—jest," Peggy said, determined to lay down an order that stuck early on and establish her authority.

"From a page oner on the murder of the Lieutenant Governor to the rubber chicken circuit?"

Was he asking too much? He knew he would have to prove himself all over again. Experience and longevity was one thing, but coming back after a quarter of a century, that was something else, especially when both papers in town were furiously trying to buy out the old-timers to cut labor costs. Maybe it was the special deal he cut with Hogan, a one-year "we'll see how it works out" contract outside the bounds of the regular Guild package. Vic was named "assistant managing editor for special projects" and then assigned to the city desk as a regular reporter. "Some special project."

"Vic, come on. It's not personal," she said. "We need someone to check in over there just to see what's what with the home builders and the water bond campaign. And—"

"And?"

"And stop sulking."

That hurt, but he knew she was right. Still, he had to maintain some semblance of independence from the Man, or Woman in this case. He did not have all that long to make a mark and reestablish his bone fides in the region's journalism game, or what was left of it. On his good days, Vic knew he could do it. On his bad days, he thought he was nuts.

"You can walk there," she said. "It's right down the street."

"Okay," Vic said, knowing that it was personal. "Anything in particular that you're looking for, besides the obvious?"

"Which would be?"

"Number one, Gene Currington, former White House advisor, might say something prescient, and number two, how do the home builders think the water project bond issue campaign is shaping up?"

"You might see what they have to say about the death of the lieutenant governor," Peggy said.

"Oh, you mean that little crime story I caught the other day when the regular cop reporter got his thing caught in his fly and wasn't able to make it out to the crime scene?"

"Dammit, Vic, he was sick, and you know that." Peggy even looked like his daughter when she got mad. Vic grinned.

"Okay, Boss," Vic said on his way down to the elevator. "I'll get you a yarn."

"And stop calling me Shirley," Vic heard her say as the elevator door closed.

# 25

Eugene Currington stood in front of his bathroom mirror adjusting his black bow tie. He stepped back and considered what he saw. Not bad, he thought, for 63. The taut athletic build remained, the piercing eyes, the wry friendly smile. The hairline dropped back too far. That was annoying. Still, he could pass for a decade younger. The bags beneath his eyes were nearly gone, the benefit of his return to Denver from Washington, D.C., a year earlier, and his return to serious rock climbing. He knew he had stayed in D.C. too long. Natalie wanted to leave earlier as well. All the grandkids were back in Colorado, and she hated the Georgetown party set.

"Gene, we're going to be late," Natalie called up the stairs.

"On my way, baby," Currington shouted back, tweeking his comber bun.

This was going to be the kind of party Natalie savored, an elite crowd, but a local elite crowd. She felt more comfortable in the small world of Denver. Washington overwhelmed her. It didn't bother Currington. Two years running the Department of Housing and Urban Development for young Bush, as the insiders called him, followed by two more advising the president from inside the White House was a nice warm-up for something bigger, maybe the vice presidency, he admitted to friends. "But it would have destroyed my family," he told one confident over a micro-brew. "And finished off my real estate development business." He loved Republican politics and how the party was challenging the entrenched Democratic intransigents, but he cared less and less for the way the right wing of the party and its Johnnie-come-lately Tea Party cohorts were doing it.

Still, he knew Natalie was happy back here. That made home life a little more bearable. Just as well, he thought, since her brother had about run his development company into the toilet. The financial nosedive was so steep, Currington wasn't sure if he could pull it out, and he didn't relish the thought of retiring with Natalie in some trailer park on his government pension and a few dribbles from Social Security. Tonight's dinner could be a make it or break it night for his company and the development, which was so nice even he wanted to retire there, assuming he could still afford to build a house in it.

"Gene?" came Natalie's coy reminder.

Another glance in the mirror. "Coming, baby, coming."

# 26

When Currington pulled his light metal gray Mercedes CL550 into the drive-up circle of the downtown Denver Sheraton, he saw two quick camera flashes. "I'm not that much of a celebrity," he said to Natalie.

"Don't flatter yourself, Tiger, there's a fellow over there taking snapshots of the attendees as they arrive, probably from the home builder's PR firm," she said.

The use of the term Tiger indicated Natalie had definitely had begun to soften from her bitter years in Washington. It was a term of endearment, one that Natalie generally used only during times of intimacy. More and more, Currington knew his decision to leave Washington was the correct one. He also knew Natalie was right about the photographer. The local media would not give the time of day to the annual awards dinner of the Colorado Home Builders Association. But, Currington thought, both newspapers did have gossip columnists who sought out movers and shakers for tiny morsels to drop into their lightweight coverage of Denver's mini social circuit. A tidbit about his planned retirement community certainly would not hurt.

"I doubt if there will be any press at this thing," Currington said. "It's only an awards banquet. Though, you never know. After all, I was somebody not too long ago."

"You're still somebody," Natalie said, rubbing the inside of his thigh.

"You get out, baby," he said, kissing her lightly on the cheek. "Look for Don and Sonja. I'll go park in the garage."

"All I want you to do is build your damn houses, Gene," Natalie said, squeezing his hand.

He looked deep into her stunning light blue eyes. "All for you, my love, our kids and their kids. For all of you."

If she only knew, he thought, that they were standing on the brink of an abyss.

# 27

It had been a while since Vic had visited downtown Denver's Sheraton Hotel. The last time he was there it wasn't even the Sheraton. It was the Adams Mark and before that the Hilton. No matter the brand, the hotel was an iconic downtown anchor near the southwest end of the Sixteenth Street Mall. Vic covered many events in the building and finished many nights in its lounges back when he drank.

He liked to get to his appointments early. The dinner did not start for another hour. Vic walked past a line of cars spiraling into the hotel's covered circular driveway and pointed his finger and thumb like a gun at Bob Scott, a former *AP* photographer who went freelance years ago. Scott nodded back and kept on firing his digital single lens reflex. He was on assignment for one of his clients, probably the home builders association, Vic thought.

He entered the main hotel lobby through the oversized glass revolving door that spun automatically as he approached the portal. Vic hated these things and had to stutter step to get in sync with it, preferring instead the human-powered revolving doors of his college days in Chicago.

Despite the name changes, the hotel interior remained much the same, late Twentieth Century Hotel Lobby Gaudy. Vic grabbed a coffee from the Starbucks barista strategically positioned in the central traffic area and sat down in one the overstuffed chairs at the top of the wide escalator that transported visitors between the main lobby and the downstairs conference center.

Vic sipped his hot coffee and leafed through a *Time* magazine he grabbed from the city room before walking over to the hotel. The anemic news weekly looked like a comic book struggling to appeal to a younger set and not doing a very good job at it. Bodies flowed up and down the escalator. On the up side, the top of a head or a hat appeared first, then a face, then a whole person, usually carrying a bag, a purse, or a briefcase. On the down side, it was all backs of heads and butts, nothing all that appealing either.

But after ten minutes, following the top of the head, a familiar face appeared on the way up as Eugene Currington glided up the escalator, walked over towards him, and sat down two chairs away. Currington did not recognize Vic. The two had met many times decades earlier when Vic last worked for the *Sun* and a few times, later, when Vic's PR firm handled a few sales tax bond elections in western Colorado. Currington was already heavily involved with the homebuilder's association before he headed off to Washington. Currington did not seem to recognize Vic. Has age changed me that much, he wondered, and decided to break the ice himself. But as he made his move, Currington's cell phone rang. Vic turned his attention back to his coffee and magazine, and eavesdropped.

"I've been trying to get you all day," Currington said.

Vic heard garbled chatter from the cell phone.

"Are you kidding?" Currington said. "The notes are due in two months."

Chatter.

"You can secure the right that fast?"

Chatter.

"I know, but it won't be pretty. I've already missed one payment. This is an extension. You know, we need that water desparately for the annexation."

Chatter.

"I got your notes from Sharla," Currington said. "They're fine."

Chatter.

"Yes," he said, annoyed. "I'll read it as written."

Chatter.

"At the Ranch? I think so. What time?"

Chatter.

"Why so late?"

Chatter.

"Give me a break. Will Michaels be there?"

Chatter.

"Are you sure about this, Gary?"

Chatter.

"Well, I worry about Rosenthal."

Chatter.

"No. I don't want you at the campaign headquarters any more. Just call in on your cell."

Chatter.

"Fine. I'll see you Saturday night. Eleven-thirty."

Currington closed his phone and slipped it into his inside jacket pocket.

Thinking that at the very least, Currington had the right to know he was sitting next to a reporter. Vic leaned over and said, "Gene?"

Currington turned toward him. "You look familiar."

"Vic Bengston."

"Vic, yes," he said, half smiling. He reached out his hand. They shook. "It's been a few years. How are your kids and, Erin?"

"Kids are grown, doing well," Vic said, astonished that Currington remembered his ex-wife's name. "Erin and I divorced but we stay friends. Two grandsons."

"I've got five grandchildren. The three girls are all doing great. Natalie and I celebrated our fortieth last month."

A disappointing thought about his own collapsed marriage seized Vic's heart. He and Erin would have been close behind in the anniversary sweepstakes. "We're an odd generation," Vic said. "Divorces, remaining friends, mixed marriages, latch-key kids, fleeing from our parents, and many staying together, like you. I'm glad your kids did well."

"What are you doing these days?" Currington said. Small talk.

"Funny you should ask," Vic said. "I'm here to cover your speech."

Currington gave Vic a puzzled look, but recovered quickly. "For whom?"

"The *Sun*."

"I thought you left the news business," Currington said.

"For a long time," Vic said. "I just got back."

"Oh wait a minute," Currington said, leaning back, a glint of recognition flashing across his face, then a wrinkled brow of concern. "That was your story in the paper this morning?"

"First day back on the job. Beginners luck."

"Luck?" Currington said. "That's an odd word for it."

"The cop reporter called in sick. Not so lucky for the lieutenant governor, though."

"No," Currington said, pausing, then delivering a robot-like message. "That was a tragedy." He reached into his briefcase, pulled out some papers, and handed them to Vic. "Here. This might help. It's an extra copy of my remarks. I plan to stick to the speech, as written."

"Thanks, Gene," Vic said. The gesture seemed odd.

"I'll be talking about the water initiative, the need to develop water responsibly for the growth of the state, you know the drill," Currington said. The robot again.

"It was the same story thirty years ago," Vic said.

"Only now, we really need the Front Range water storage," Currington said, "so the cities can keep pace with growth. This place is booming."

"The Sierra Club disagrees."

"They've become radicals," Currington said, flipping on that wry half smile with the dimpled cheek. "They used to be reasonable."

Vic decided to lob one in from left field.

"Speaking of water, Gene, do you know anything about a senior water right on the South Platte that might be in play? Legally, I mean."

Something unsettling passed over Currington's stolid face, a shadow of uncertainty, of fear, something. It was there, and then it vanished as the tough Washington cabinet level bearing took control again. "Real estate development, I know," he said. "Water law I leave to the experts."

"Like Gary Kendrick?"

This time Currington didn't flinch or miss a beat. "I know him by reputation only."

"Who's advising the water bond campaign?"

"Oh, a couple of water lawyers who are volunteering their services."

"But not Kendrick?"

"No. Uh. Lance Morgan from Boulder. He's, uh, a lawyer and a water engineer too. Um, the other one is, let's see, Jim, Jim Hennessy from Littleton. He's a lawyer too. No engineering degree though. How did Kendrick get into this?"

"His name came up in a conversation," Vic said. "Someone was speculating."

"Clearly," Currington said, pulling himself upright and extending his right hand. "I've got to get in there."

They shook hands again. "It was good to see you, Gene."

"You too," he said, then flashed a grin and nodded toward Vic's coffee. "Finish that. You'll need it to stay awake for the speech." Then he walked over to the escalator and descended back into the lower level of the hotel.

Currington was right. The speech was a non-event, at least as far as the desk was concerned. They slotted it deep inside the paper and gave it about six inches, no byline. Currington's pitch was simple and basic. Home builders needed to hit the streets and put up some real media money to get the water development bond issue passed. Colorado needed new reservoirs to store the water to which it was legally entitled, rather than let it leak out of the state via one of its five river basins originating in the high country. Currington set the home builders straight. No water meant no growth and no business.

Vic worked the desk with Peggy until midnight. She never slept. He turned three news releases into filler copy, juggled phones to put together the details on a police chase that lasted all of five minutes, dressed up three obituaries, and then wrote something he thought he would never ever write again in his lifetime, the Pet of the Week photo cutline.

# 28

Vic took Tuesday off. He did not have much choice. Hogan insisted, thinking the rest would be good.

It was. Vic spent the morning planting his garden to get it ready for another season of pesticide-free vegetables. He devoted the afternoon to a ham radio project, an all-band, all-mode short wave transceiver he was building. It was a kit that utilized the latest electronic technology. One day, he pledged, he would build a radio entirely from scratch, using only a schematic and a pile of electronic components. For now, the kits worked fine. He was already working with Devon, his oldest grandson, on an AM radio kit, teaching the boy the fine points of soldering technique and opening him up to the world of radio communications that so fascinated Vic, provided, of course, that the boy picked up the family's recessive nerd gene.

The day should have been enjoyable, but it was not. An unwanted guest incessantly interrupted his thoughts. Gene Currington. His speech the night before at the awards dinner told Vic nothing he did not already know. Home builders, land developers, and municipalities all want water, and they do not really care how they get it or where it comes from. Nothing new there.

It was the phone call that bugged him. Currington seemed nervous. Was that because of the upcoming speech? Or was it the fact that Vic worked for the *Sun*? He was sure the Gary that Currington spoke to on the phone was Kendrick, but why play dumb when he mentioned the name?

Vic carried his doubts about Currington with him into the sanctity of the shower and washed them away with hot water and aloe soap. As garden soil and puzzling thoughts swirled down the drain, Vic looked ahead to the evening "political" poker game, a monthly ritual that he knew would add to his new life as a journalist, that is if the other players let him stay now that he had rejoined the unpopular world of newspaper scribes.

# 29

Vic stood on the north Denver sidewalk taking in the early evening sun, languishing in his favorite part of the day before going inside. A few birds issued their final dispatches before they lapsed into quiet slumber as the daylight gradually waned. The modest brick house was owned by one of his graduate school professors. It was an odd but functional structure built in the fifties. The house was somewhat hidden behind two massive garage doors facing the street. Vic climbed the concrete steps to the left of the garage and let himself in. From the front door he could see straight through the narrow living room, galley style kitchen, and the dining room, an efficient shotgun design that reminded him of a custom built rail car, or maybe a large sailboat. Muffled voices drifted up from the basement where the poker game was already underway. He opened the fridge and set his six-pack of Beck's non-alcoholic beer on the counter. Rolls, condiments, clean plates, and napkins were set out for the food break, which usually occurred about eight-thirty or nine. He took two bottles of his Beck's out of the cardboard carrier and squeezed the rest into the refrigerator, the main shelf of which was layered with packages of fresh deli cold cuts and sliced cheeses. As he opened the basement door, the sounds from down below became crisper, even intelligible. Eric Clapton played quietly on the boom box. Poker chips bounced off the round plastic table. Cards shuffled. Owen Kane laughed and called into the air, "That must be Bengston, just in time for the food."

"Sorry I'm late," Vic said as he crammed one of his beers into the basement ice chest and opened the other one to drink. "I timed it for the food anyway."

Vic handed a twenty to one of the players, Stew Hansen, a serious gambler who managed the chips and the cards for the group. Hansen set several stacks of twenty-five cent, fifty cent, and dollar chip denominations on the table next to Vic's bill, which was then snapped up and tossed into the poker chip case.

Chairs were adjusted, and Vic settled in between Kane on the left and Ray Albrecht on the right. He set his beer down on one of several small white plastic occasional tables located around the larger card table. The small tables were for drinks and snacks, both of which were barred from the playing surface. House rules. Vic dipped into an open bag and retrieved a couple of nacho-flavored corn chips. He crunched on them and took a swig of his beer.

"Still drinking that non-alcoholic crap," Kane said.

"Of course," Vic said. "At least for the past twenty years or so. This one tastes pretty good, though. The American made NA beers stink."

"You get all the carbs but no buzz," Hansen said.

"No hangover either," Vic said. "There is a little alcohol in this stuff, though, so if I drink fifty of these things, take my keys away, please."

"That's what friends are for," Kane said.

They played three hands of low Chicago, a variation of seven-card stud, but the player with the low spade in the hole splits the pot with the winning hand. Vic lost big on the first hand, losing the pot split to the ace of spades, which beat his deuce. He folded early on the second hand and moved back to even on the third with a heart flush.

Finally, Kane said, "Are you going to make us beg?"

"What?" Vic said, feigning bewilderment.

"God dammit," Kane said. "You wander back into journalism after a million years and the first day you're on the front page with a story that rivals OJ's acquittal."

"Give us the lowdown," Albrecht said as he organized his chips. He worked for a defense contractor, something to do with space, the kind surrounding Earth.

"About all I know was in the paper," Vic said.

"What was it like down there by the river?" Albrecht asked. "The body. Was it gruesome?"

"Cops kept me away," Vic said. "She was all caught up in a snag, clothes all muddy. I could see that. It was in the story."

"Not very dignified for the lieutenant governor," said Jim Jackson, a politically connected lawyer. "But Democrats were always more informal than Republicans."

"Cut her a little slack, Jim," Kane said. "The lady was murdered."

"I'm sorry," Jackson said. "Sometimes I can't help myself. For the record, though, she wasn't well thought of, even within the party."

"How in hell did you pull that story on your first day?" Kane said. "I still want an answer."

"The cop shop was empty," Vic said. "The reporter called in sick. I was the only one they could send."

"A rookie," Kane said. He laughed. "They sent a rookie."

"In fairness to them, they didn't know who the victim was."

"How did you find out?" Albrecht said.

"Driscoll told me."

"Frank Driscoll?" Kane said.

"Yeah. You know him?"

"I know a lot of cops," Kane said. "At least the ones who have arrested me at one demonstration or another."

"Driscoll pulled me aside and had me meet him at a coffee shop to tell me."

"They sat on it?" Kane said.

"They tried to, for a while. They wanted to get their you-know-what in a pile."

"Who's Driscoll?" Hansen said.

"Chief of Detectives," Vic said.

"You know him too?" Kane said to Vic.

"We play golf every Saturday at Kennedy."

"I don't believe it," Kane said. "How many coincidences do we have going here?"

"Way too many," Vic said, "but they came in handy."

"Now what?" Kane said.

"Now nothing," Vic said. "They pulled me off the story. I'm rewriting news releases on the desk and covering rubber chicken affairs."

"Befitting of your talent, Bengston," Jackson said.

"Payback for all those press releases you dumped on them over the years," Hansen said.

"Let's go upstairs and eat while Vic finishes this up," Kane said.

They were all hungry and the cold cuts were the second highlight of the poker game. The first highlight was the political discussion before the card game, which Vic missed this time because of his tardiness. Politics, in one form or another, connected everyone to the monthly game. Vic was a former graduate school student of Kane's, as was Hansen, the token conservative in the largely liberal group. Jackson was an old friend of the professor. Albrecht lived up the street and knew Kane from neighborhood political activities. Other players who drifted in and out of the monthly game included more former students of Kane's, another politically active Denver lawyer, a former state legislator, and a city council member. Not everyone showed up for every game, but there were always enough for entertaining pre-game political gossip.

The third highlight of the monthly gathering was poker, although political banter usually continued throughout the game.

"I wondered what happened when I saw Hoffman's byline on the story today," Kane said. "The big boys sharpened their knives."

"It was my first day," Vic said. "Still, I wanted to stay on the story."

"Not a bad start, though," Albrecht said.

"Can't complain about that," Vic said. "Owen, I've got a question for you.".

Kane's usually grinning mouth was stuffed full of rare roast beef, rye bread, mustard, and a little lettuce. He waved on the question with his left hand.

"Do you know anyone named Rosenthal?"

Still chewing, Kane raised his eyebrows and nodded a couple of times. Vic looked at the other card players. They showed no signs of recognition.

"The law professor," Jackson said. "University of Denver."

Kane's nodding sharpened. He washed down the remains of the sandwich bite with a slug of beer. "Randal Rosenthal. That's right. He's over at DU."

"So, nothing to do with water law, or anything like that?" Vic said.

"I was on a panel with him once at a public policy conference over at DU," Kane said. "I think he teaches election law and public policy."

"Fancies himself as a bit of a kingmaker in the Democratic Party," Jackson said.

"That's right," Kane said. "He runs occasional seminars on election law, among other things."

Vic said, "Does a place called The Ranch tie into Rosenthal?"

"That's his home, up near Platteville," Kane said. "I've been up there a few times. He holds little political gatherings there, and public policy discussions."

"Like a conference center?" Vic said.

"More like a glorified garage," Kane said, laughing, "sitting in the middle of a ranchette. He's got a couple of horses, a nice house, a cow or two, and then the conference center." Kane held up air quotes with both hands when he said "conference center."

"Where did you run across him?" Jackson said.

"Oh, his name came up in a conversation with someone," Vic said.

"At the statehouse?" Kane said.

"No, somewhere else," Vic said. "Does he have his fingers in the pie up there too?"

"Yes he does," Kane said, "And some Democrats aren't too happy with him."

"Why's that?" Vic said.

"He's pushing one of his protégés for governor," Kane said.

"John Michaels," Jackson said. "A lot of Democrats are behind him, Owen."

Vic said, "The majority leader?"

"Heir to the throne," Kane said.

"Or so Rosenthal thinks," Jackson said.

Vic played dumb and said, "Throne?"

"The governor's seat," Jackson said. "But he needs to be appointed lieutenant governor first."

"So you don't think Dowd's going to run for re-election?" Kane said.

"Hell no," Jackson said. "The party's had it with him, plus he can't win. Michaels is the logical choice."

"I can't believe they'd name him lieutenant governor," Kane said. "They've got to appoint a woman."

"To stay politically correct, right?" said Hansen, wiping mustard off his cheek with a napkin.

"Well, half of the electorate is female, Stew," Kane said. "There are plenty of women who could fill the post."

"Michaels' numbers are off the charts, Owen," Jackson said. "He's a very popular guy. They love him on the western slope. He's the logical choice."

"What about the water well bill for the farmers?" Kane said. "He's got to push that through the legislature. Otherwise he'll lose all their votes."

"No, he doesn't," Jackson said. "Farmers aren't as strong as they used to be. The western slope doesn't give a shit about agricultural water over here, except how much is siphoned over the divide, away from them. The Front Range cities and the developers are doing everything they can to get their hands on more of that water flowing down the South Platte."

"And screw the farmers?" Vic said.

"Basically, yes," Jackson said. "That bill will never see the light of day."

"Can I quote you on that?" Vic said.

"No you may not," Jackson said. "What's said here never leaves here."

Everyone laughed and headed back downstairs for more poker. Vic finished the night down thirteen bucks, but well ahead in the information department.

# 30

Hal Simpson nosed the snow-white State of Colorado pickup truck up to the locked steel gate that barricaded the gravel driveway leading to Bobbie Hague's farm. He sighed at the sight of the sign hanging on the gate and shook his head as he threw the transmission into Park.

"No Trespassing," the dark red machine print letters blared. The hand-written addendum narrowed the field, "Especially State Water Engineers."

"Dammit," Simpson said, thinking this was not what he signed up for twenty years ago when he walked out of Colorado State University with his degree in hydrological engineering. He picked up the court order from the passenger seat and stepped out of the truck. The two Weld County sheriff deputies accompanying him double timed it from their patrol car and caught up with him at the gate.

"Third one like this I've seen this week," Simpson said to the deputies. "I've asked the governor to get involved in this, to mediate or something, but the bastard won't lift a finger."

"I don't like doin' this either," deputy Jake Gonzales said. "Somehow it doesn't seem right."

"It's a lawful court order, Jake," said his boss, chief deputy Pete Chandler.

"Yeah, I know, I know. But judges can be wrong sometimes," Gonzales said. "This is wrong. Damn wrong."

"Not for us to decide," Chandler said. "Right or wrong, we've got to help Mr. Simpson enforce this order. Get the binocs out of the trunk, would ya?"

Gonzales complied. He had to. He wanted no blemish on his record.

Jake Gonzales was on the way up, two years on the job and already planning to become the first Hispanic sheriff in Weld County history. It would be an honor to his family, born from migrant laborers who broke their bodies to work the region's agricultural fields, and it would be a statement of sorts to the white community, which dominated county business, agriculture, politics, and police.

Gonzales opened the trunk of the patrol car and grabbed the binoculars. He left the heavy duty bolt cutter untouched. Then he walked back over to the gate and put the binoculars up to his eyes. Bobbie Hague sat in a rocking chair on the front porch of the house, barely a quarter of a mile away.

"He's on the porch, sittin'," Gonzales said. "He's got a long gun on his lap. Can't tell if it's a rifle or a shotgun. I know he's got a Winchester Model 70, shoots a three-oh-eight."

"How do you know that?" Chandler said.

"We hunt together each fall," Gonzales said. "I gave him the gun when he got his Ag degree. We're old friends, remember?"

"Yes, I remember," Chandler said.

Gonzales kept the binoculars on Bender. "There's the scope," the deputy said. "It's the rifle."

"Aw, Christ," Simpson said. "This is ridiculous." After a moment of staring toward the house, he pulled out his cell phone and said, "Lemme try to call him again."

"I should do that," Chandler said.

"Well, I know," Simpson said, cell phone already plastered to his right ear. "Maybe I can talk some sense into him."

"Someone's coming out the door," Gonzales said. "His wife. Jackie. Looks like she's got a phone. Yeah, she's handing it to him."

"Hello," Simpson said into the cell phone. "Mr. Hague? Yes. There are two here now. Their names?" Chandler gently punched Simpson in the upper arm. Simpson looked at the deputy, who shook his head no. Simpson put his hand over the phone and said to Gonzales, "Well, he already knows it's you. Why all the secrecy?"

"Aw, that's just the way these guys want it," Gonzales said, jerking his head toward Chandler. "I went to high school with him and Jackie."

"Give me a minute, Mr. Hague. I'll call you back." Simpson slammed his phone shut and, nodding toward Gonzales, said to Chandler, "He knows him. Can't that ease things a bit?"

"We can't do it that way, sir," Chandler said. "We're here to get you on this land so you can shut off his wells and put locks on them. We're not here to negotiate the court order. That has already been done in Greeley."

"And if he doesn't let us on his land?" Simpson said. "McGregor and Whiteside just let us through. This guy looks pretty stubborn. It's not worth anyone getting hurt over. I know we've got to get this under control. It's only water for God's sake."

"If he doesn't open up and let us onto the property, I've got to pull the bolt cutters out of my trunk, cut the lock, and enter the premises," Chandler said. "That's the way it's done."

"Aw hell," Simpson said directly to Chandler. "You wait here. I'm still the state water engineer, and if need be I'll withdraw the complaint, so we can attack this from another angle."

"Hey, it's your frigging job," Chandler said. "I'm just doing mine."

"Stay right here," Simpson said. He walked behind his pickup, out of earshot of the two deputies, and dialed the governor's office.

Gonzales looked at Chandler, then at Simpson. The engineer's head bobs and hand gestures signaled a heated phone conversation with someone. Gonzales turned back around and put the binoculars back up to his eyes to see what Hague was doing. The farmer, his boyhood friend, sat there on his shaded porch, rocking back and forth with the gun across his lap. He was not on the phone anymore, so Simpson was not talking to him. Gonzales wondered whom the water engineer called. Hague looked as though he had put on a few pounds since they hunted last fall out near the town of Craig. The two played high school football together when Greeley won the state five-A championship. They shared lockers, and Hague took a lot of crap for that. Both graduated from Colorado State. Gonzales was Hague's best man when he and Jackie were married. A few months after college, they began that long glide path that friends all too often take as they build their individual lives and drift apart. At least they kept the hunting trips, Gonzales thought.

Hague squirmed around in his chair and stretched his legs. He raised the gun and twisted his shoulders. Gonzales saw a thickness in the stock that ran a third of the way up the barrel.

"Looks like a shotgun," Gonzales said to Chandler. "Probably a twelve gauge."

The chief deputy unclipped his sidearm. So did Gonzales.

# 31

His phone call finished, Simpson walked back over to Chandler. "Hold it a minute."

"What's going on?" Chandler snapped.

"You're going to get a call shortly, probably from the sheriff, telling you to back off," Simpson said. Then, to Gonzales, he said, "Hauge might talk to you, but I need to talk to him too."

Chandler spun around and marched back to the patrol car. His phone went off. Gonzales and Simpson could only make out bits and pieces of the conversation. It did not sound pleasant. They clearly heard the "Yes sir!" as Chandler slapped his phone shut. He stood by the patrol car and shouted up to Gonzales and Simpson. "Okay, the dogs are back in the pen. Call him back up. See what you can do, but I can guarantee you we'll eventually wind up right back where we are now."

Gonzales looked at Simpson and said, "You want me to call?"

"Go ahead, try," Simpson said, handing him the phone. "Hit redial."

Gonzales dialed the phone. Hague picked up his phone.

"Bobbie, it's me, Jake. Yeah, I know, man, but this isn't cool. Not at all." Gonzales listened for a few minutes, nodded occasionally, said "I know" a few times and, only once, wiped a tear from his left eye. "Look, we don't want it to go down like this, man. Think of Jackie and the kids." More listening. This time Gonzales looked up at Simpson and nodded. "Okay, here he is. You two talk, and put that damn gun away." The deputy handed the phone to Simpson.

"Mr. Hague, we're going to hold off on this. Wait a minute, wait a minute, please. We're going to hold off, but only a week. One week. I know you need water, but this has been going on for too long. I know that. You're not the only one. We need to look at the health of the river, the overall—well, well, they've all complied. No, not everyone. You know that. We've got some people working on this, but it's not easy. You boys need that water right. That's the way it works out here—I know you've been there a long time. It's the legality of the thing."

Gonzales turned and walked over to Chandler. "The legality of the thing," Gonzales repeated.

"What?" Chandler said.

"Aw, legalities. We're back into the legal mumbo jumbo. That's not going to feed his family."

"Didn't he have time to work this out?" Chandler said. "We've got the court order, Jake."

"Screw the court order," Gonzales said. "This guy's fighting for his life, his whole family's life. Look at that corn over there. It's two feet tall, and now it won't get one inch taller. Legality. Legality. Hell, my old man worked for his old man."

"So what?" Chandler said.

"Legality. That's all they talk about, legality. Back then the legality sure as hell was not in our favor," Gonzales said. "Plenty of farmers and ranchers out here stiffed us half the time."

"What do you mean, stiffed you?"

"No, no, my pop," Gonzales said. "He told me about it. Short pay. Crappy housing. They'd run us off if we got out of line. They even tried to deport him."

"To Mexico?"

"Yeah," Gonzales said. Then he laughed, "Hell, he was born in Commerce City!"

"That doesn't solve this problem," Chandler said, gesturing back at Simpson and then the farmhouse.

"I gotta talk to the boss about this," Gonzales said. "This guy, Bobbie Hague, who we're gonna shut down, maybe make him lose his farm. This guy's pop gave my pop respect. He paid good money. He gave him decent housing. See that cottage up there next to the house?" Chandler nodded. "I was born there. My pop made enough to buy our place, or the first part of it." Gonzales looked at the ground and shook his head. "I gotta talk to the boss about this."

"Two two five," the radio barked. Chandler reached in the window and grabbed the microphone. "Chandler."

"Looks like you're done there. Court order's lifted. Unless there's a safety issue."

Chandler looked back toward the house. The phone conversation had ended. Hague was walking down toward the gate. No long gun.

Chandler said to the microphone, "I'll have to check that out. Looks okay. But I need to check. Hague's walking down to the gate, unarmed." He put the microphone down and said to Gonzales, "Can you go over there and do your damn job?"

Gonzales took a deep breath. "Yeah. I'll make sure it's clear."

"Thank you, deputy."

Gonzales turned and walked back over toward the entrance to the farm. The two former high school classmates reached the locked gate at the same time, Hague on his farm, Gonzales outside of it. Simpson reached out with his right hand.

Chandler stuck the upper part of his body into the patrol car window so he could hang the mike on its dashboard hook. He glanced up to look through the windshield toward the three men at the gate. The scene had changed.

Simpson was down on his knees. Hague stood over him from the other side of the gate, holding a handgun with both hands. It was pointed directly at Simpson's face. Hague was shouting something. Gonzales stood six feet away in a classic standing shooting pose, not quite squared up with Hague, both his arms up and locked, his Glock trained dead center on Hague's chest. Chandler heard muffled shouts as he pushed back from inside the car, knocking off his sunglasses. As the chief deputy fumbled for his gun, Chandler watched his deputy. Gonzales' hands jerked once. "Pow!" Then again. "Pow!" Hague spun like a top.

Chandler pulled his gun and ran for the gate, but it was all over. Gonzales had jumped the fence and stood over Hague's crumpled body. His gun was still drawn and pointed at the farmer, who groaned and rolled over on his side.

Hague's wife ran from the farmhouse door, the back of her left hand over her mouth. As he sprinted toward the gate, Chandler kept his gun up and pointed in the general direction of the downed farmer. Simpson froze, kneeling, prayer like.

"Jake," Chandler shouted.

"I'm okay!" Gonzales stepped on Hague's motionless right hand with one foot and kicked what looked like an old revolver away with his other foot. Simpson sobbed. Chandler knew Simpson was all right. The sounds told him both the shots came from Gonzales' gun.

"Watch the wife," Chandler shouted.

The sobbing and shaking water engineer rolled forward onto his hands and knees and cried, "I can't believe this."

"Believe it," Chandler said, reaching down to pull the water engineer up the rest of the way. Simpson's pants were wet from his crotch almost down to his knees. "Are you all right?"

"I think so," Simpson said.

"Hague's not," Gonzales said, kneeling down, the first two fingers of his left hand feeling for a pulse on the farmer's neck. "Watch Jackie, Pete."

Simpson collected himself. "Is he dead?"

"Not yet," Gonzales said. "There's a first aid kit in my back seat. Go get it Simpson, and quit your damn crying."

Then the deputy shouted at his boss, "Chandler, get us a chopper will you? Now!"

Chandler ran over to the patrol car. He missed the rear door handle the first time he swiped for it, then got it on the second try, flinging the door open so hard that it sprung itself shut again. The chief deputy took a deep breath, opened the door, slid into the seat, and radioed for an air lift.

Gonzales turned toward his car and saw Simpson rummaging through the trunk. "Hurry up, damn it." He turned back to Hague who was spewing blood from his upper arm. Gonzales knew he would have to answer for this, one way or the other. The shot he took was at the shoulder, not the middle of the chest. The best he could hope for was remedial training on the use of deadly force. The worst? Right now, he did not care.

The bullet caught an artery, and Gonzales' old friend might simply bleed to death in his driveway. The deputy shoved his thumb up into Hague's armpit and squeezed as hard as he could while holstering his gun.

Gonzales looked up and saw Jackie running down from the house. She stumbled and fell, then pulled herself up, crying, screaming, and flailing down the dusty gravel driveway.

"What do you need?" Simpson was at the deputy's side with the white plastic case emblazoned with a large red cross.

"There's a tourniquet setup in there. It's orange. Open the strap, and give it to me."

Simpson fumbled through the box, found the tourniquet, and unwrapped it.

"Here," Gonzales said, holding one end of the open strap. "Wrap that underneath his arm. Okay, now back through this buckle. Get it as tight as you can. Yeah, that's good."

Gonzales twisted a small attached handle until the bleeding seemed to stop. He secured the handle in place with a small Velcro strap.

"Give me your hand." Simpson held out his right hand, and Gonzales placed it over the tourniquet handle. "Just hold it there. Don't let go. It should be okay, but watch for bleeding."

By now Jackie had made it to the three men. Her dress was ripped in the front. Blood trickled down her right leg from the scraping fall in the driveway.

"You killed him, you bastard, you killed him." She pounded on the deputy's chest. He stopped her by grabbing her wrists.

"He's wounded, Jackie. Stop it. I've got to get him out of here. Just stop it. Stop it!" He squeezed as hard as he could on her wrists and pushed her back.

"All he wants to do is farm," she screamed through dusty lips. "We need the water. For the corn."

"Jackie," Gonzales said. Holding her at arm's length, he shouted into her face. "Jackie, stop!" Her struggling ceased. "I've got to take care of Bobbie." He slowly let go of her wrists. She dropped her arms to her side, then collapsed on her bloodied knees next to her husband and Simpson, her sobs convulsing like the end of a child's uncontrolled crying jag.

Chandler had the microphone up to his mouth.

"Two two five."

"Go ahead two two five."

"Shots fired. I have one wounded male civilian. Looks like an artery. Upper arm. We've got a tourniquet on it. Scene is secure, but we need a chopper ASAP at the Hague farm."

"Any deputies hurt?"

"Negative. Just get the chopper out here."

"We're sending a backup unit two two five. Are you secure?"

"I said we're secure, damn it," Chandler screamed. "Get a chopper here fast."

"All right officer. One's coming from—looks like Flight for Life St. Anthony's. We've got your GPS ten-seven."

"Roger."

"We'll keep this channel clear, deputy."

"Okay, that's a roger," Chandler said, anxious to get off the radio. He tossed the microphone down on the floor and pulled himself from the patrol car. He reached back in for a bottle of Eldorado Springs water, then jogged back over to Gonzales, Simpson, and the Hagues.

Bobbie Hague was conscious and looking up at Gonzales.

"What the hell?" Hague said.

"You pulled a gun on me, you asshole," Gonzales said. "Just lay there and shut up."

Hague's wife had stopped crying. The hot dry sun had baked the salty tears and dust into an odd looking mask on her face. She was now holding her hand over the tourniquet, cradling her husband's head in her lap.

Simpson looked up, pale and ghostlike.

"I think the bleeding stopped, but I'm not sure," he said. "I can't look at the blood."

"Oh, God, Jackie," Hague said. He rolled toward his crippled arm.

"Don't move, Bobbie," she said, her family command returning to her. "Lay still." She looked up at Gonzales. "I'll sue your ass, you bastard."

"No you're not, Jackie," Gonzales said. "You're gonna thank me he's not dead."

Chandler handed her the water bottle. "Small sips," he said.

Jackie held the bottle to Hague's lips. He swallowed once and moaned again.

"Relax, Bobbie," Gonzales said. "You're in shock now. Try not to move. I've got a chopper coming for you."

Gonzales walked back to the patrol car and opened the trunk. He pulled a gray military wool blanket from its deep recesses and then walked back over to the fallen farmer.

"Look out," Gonzales said. He snapped the blanket open in the air and let it fall on Hague. "He needs this. I know it's hot, but he needs this over him. Shade his face too."

"Call Kendrick," Hague said to Jackie.

Gonzales heard him. "Who's Kendrick?"

"My priest," Hague said. Then he passed out.

# 32

"How's this?" Vic said, hitting the computer key that sent the story to the city desk.

"Give me a sec," Peggy said, pulling Vic's story up onto her screen:

> MILLIKEN — A Weld County sheriff's deputy shot and wounded a local farmer Tuesday in a dispute over an order to shut off illegal irrigation wells.
>
> Bobbie Hague, 41, of Weld County, was airlifted to Poudre Valley Health System in Fort Collins in serious condition, according to a spokesman for the Weld County Sheriff's Department.
>
> Deputies were attempting to serve a court order to shut off Hague's irrigation wells when the shooting occurred, the spokesman said.
>
> Weld County District Judge Emma Sorenson issued the order at the request of state water

engineer Hal Simpson, who was involved in the confrontation that led up to the shooting, the sheriff's spokesman said.

Simpson's office confirmed that the state was trying to shut down three irrigation wells on the Hague farm, located south of Milliken, because they adversely affected water rights in the South Platte River.

The sheriff's spokesman said Hague threatened Simpson and two deputies first with a shotgun and then with a handgun before the shooting.

The department confirmed that chief deputy Peter Chandler and Deputy Jacob Gonzales were with Simpson at the Hague farm.

No one else was injured, according to the spokesman, who also said Gonzales was placed on immediate administrative leave pending an investigation into the shooting.

"You seem to be getting the hang of this, kid," Peggy said. "Just the right length for the net." She hit a few more keys and the story was gone. In a second, the paper's website popped up displaying Vic's story as it appeared on the internet for all to see.

"I forgot. Did you want a byline?"

"Do I want a byline? Let me think. Should I flash my persona across the pages of this noble rag, or remain its humble unnamed servant, working in the dark, digging for the truth, seeking—"

"Never mind," she said, rolling her eyes. "I get the point." More plapping sounds flowed from her keyboard. "Now look," she said.

Vic pulled the story up on his screen. The web page news item was flanked by flashing ads, one for the world's largest used car lot on the west side, another for an upcoming cancer run in City Park, and a third with a gleaming model's smile hawking a fifty-grand dental implant job. Peggy had added Vic's byline and a headline, "Farmer shot in well dispute."

"There, you're famous."

"I'm beside myself," Vic said.

"Maybe you should look into this water thing," Peggy said, hitting the "should" a little harder. Vic had already mentioned developing some features on the plight of Colorado farmers in the wake of the recent drought and the cascading well shut-off orders.

"Lucy, haven't I been telling you this," Vic said in a terrible Cuban accent.

Peggy sipped her coffee and said, "Just as a feature," hitting the "just" harder this time.

"Yes, as a feature," Vic said.

Vic called the sheriff's office again. They had nothing to add to their original statement on the shooting. Poudre Valley Health still did not have Bobbie Hague listed as a patient let alone an updated condition. The governor had already gagged the state water engineer's office, so he got nothing there. He decided to make another round of calls in an hour while he put more thought into the feature assignment, which was a convenient way to turn over a few more rocks in the Swain murder investigation. Cops had nothing. Vic figured his nosing around could not hurt.

# 33

John Michaels, boy wonder, one of the youngest senate majority leaders in state history, family man, Colorado native, Democrat, picked up the phone and dialed his political mentor and election law professor at the University of Denver. He considered waiting until after the funeral, but the more he thought about it the more he realized he would go nuts delaying the inevitable. Strike while the iron is hot, his grandfather always said, and he was right.

Michaels' grandfather, Arnold, had amassed a nice little family nest egg in real estate by buying up a handful of foreclosed factories and warehouses in the late thirties. He leased out the buildings for war goods manufacturing at the start of World War Two and made a bundle. He bootstrapped his wartime cash flow into more commercial properties during the post war boom. When Michaels' father, Arnold's only son, was killed in Viet Nam, the old man converted the entire real estate operation into a trust for the grandchildren

Michaels and his brother, Jeremy, never had to worry about where the next meal came from let alone which university they wanted to attend. Jeremy left the state for school, Stanford then Harvard Law, returning to set up a lucrative corporate law practice in Denver. Michaels always knew what he wanted to do when he grew up, and he knew he had to remain in Colorado to do it. He did his undergraduate degree in political science at the University of Colorado in Boulder followed by the University of Denver for law school.

"You can go to any law school you want," his grandfather told him his senior year in college. "Why not get away? Experience another place. You can always come back."

But Michaels would have none of that, explaining that he planned to get elected to the state senate and, eventually, become the state's governor. He did not want to miss one political development that occurred in Colorado. He and his grandfather settled on the University of Denver Law School.

"Professor Rosenthal's office."

"Hi Beverly, this is John. Is he in?"

"John, how are you holding up?" Beverly said, threading in a note of empathy. "It's been a rough two days."

"Oh, I'm fine. It's getting a little more chaotic. You know, after the initial shock. All of the leadership, well, the Democrats, met last night to strategize. The CBI came in, but they didn't have all that much. I guess we're okay. We're all right."

"I'm glad. God, we've been wracked back and forth. I mean, we couldn't believe it at first. You know she endowed a chair over at DU, the one for environmental studies. Anyway, hang in there, and if there's anything we can do, let us know. I mean it. You're family."

"I know, and I appreciate it," Michaels said. "I do."

"Randal went down for some coffee. Wait, he's walking back in. Here he comes. It's John. Okay, he'll take this in his office. I'll put you on hold. Just a minute, John."

"Thanks," Michaels said to the click on the phone line.

In a few seconds, Randal Rosenthal, professor, lawyer, all business, jumped on the line. "John, are you at your office? How are things over there?"

"It's still pretty quiet. No one's around. We haven't even started up committee hearings yet. Things will get back to normal next week."

"Has the leadership met?"

"Last night," Michaels said. "We also met briefly with the governor. Norm said his people were already going through Jessica's projects to figure out the transitions."

"Did he mention specifics?" Rosenthal said.

"No. That's why I'm calling," Michaels said. "I want your thoughts on this."

"You've already made up your mind, haven't you? I can hear it."

"Randal, there are two more years on her term. That's too long for anyone—"

"Wait," Rosenthal interrupted. "Let's go over this in person. Not on the phone."

"You've been thinking about this too, haven't you?" Michaels said.

"Yes I have. I was about to call you anyway. Why don't you come out to the ranch Saturday night? Janine's been smoking some of that brisket you love."

"From your herd?"

"If you can call two cows a herd, but yes, grass fed, no drugs or hormones at all."

Not on the phone, Michaels thought. Something was up. He could feel it. "All right. That sounds good."

"Around seven then?" Rosenthal said.

"Sure."

"Just us boys," Rosenthal said and hung up.

# 34

"You're joking," Nelson said.

He stared at Vic, who could not tell whether it was a question or a statement of fact.

"I'm serious about this, Nelson," Vic said. "I'm going to do it with or without your help."

"Eavesdropping can get you arrested," said Nelson, chewing on the left inside cheek, an indicator that Vic knew betrayed hesitation or uncertainty. He wondered if he did that when he was a CIA spook. Maybe that was why Nelson never played poker.

"I'm not going to record anything," Vic said. "I just want to see who's there."

"Trespassing?"

"Okay," Vic said. "Misdemeanor. A hand-slap and a fine."

"What about your job?"

"What about it? Hell, I'm on probation already because I'm fifty-nine years old. If that isn't against the law, nothing is."

"They'll can you," Nelson said.

"Look, I want to see who's getting together at this late night political soiree," Vic said.

"I'd sooner take your fat ass climbing again," Nelson said.

"No you wouldn't," Vic said. "I'm still way over my fighting weight."

Longtime friend and backpacking partner, Nelson was three years Vic's senior but looked at least ten years younger and still climbed sheer rock walls for the challenge. He once dragged Vic up a rock face in Eldorado Canyon south of Boulder. Rock climbing basics were fairly simple, if you were the right weight for your height, limber, and in relatively good shape. Vic checked none of the above. He got in trouble and Nelson pulled him through it.

"You know this is crazy," Nelson said.

"I'm a wild and crazy guy," Vic said, shimmying like Akroyd and Martin in the old Saturday Night Live skit.

Nelson shook his head.

# 35

"Can't you just drive by the place with me and point out how I might position myself to determine who shows for this meeting," Vic said.

"Oh, I don't know," Nelson said. "Maybe, because if you screw up and get caught, there could be a conspiracy charge added on."

They went back and forth, Nelson advancing various legal theories on how they could be brought up on felony charges if they were caught eavesdropping, and Vic reiterating he only wanted to see who showed up for the meeting. Nelson wondered how that could be accomplished at night without using obvious and illegal eavesdropping equipment. Vic countered that he could jot down license plate numbers. Nelson did not think the unwashed public had legal access to the state's license plate computer, but Vic assured him he could work it out with his golf buddy. When Nelson puzzled over how Vic could actually enjoy that boring, expensive, and time-consuming game, Vic pointed out it was quite a bit safer than clinging from rock walls a hundred feet above some rocky creek bed. Then Nelson blurted out that he had a buddy with a high quality night scope, exactly what was required for the mission. Grinning, Vic thought to himself that he had not really lost his touch. It took less than ten minutes for Nelson to cave.

"You're worse than anything we ever encountered in the jungles," Nelson said as they parted. "It's too bad you weren't over there with us."

"I'd be dead now," said Vic.

"In all likelihood."

# 36

The night scope looked like a pair of binoculars on steroids.

"Smaller than I thought it would be," Vic said. He picked up the black device. "Lighter too."

"One point two kilos," Nelson said.

"What's that in human?" Vic said.

"Two and a half pounds."

Nelson ran through a few operational details, which were minimal. Digital focus, all electronic, turned off automatically to conserve power. Point and watch.

"Put it in a small daypack and use the lens caps," Nelson said. "Here are two extra batteries, but you won't need them. It'll last fifty hours on a fresh set."

"How much is this thing worth?" Vic said.

"You don't want to know," Nelson said.

"I do want to know," Vic said.

"You can get the civilian version for about five grand, probably from Cabela's," Nelson said.

"The civilian version?" Vic said.

"This is mil spec, latest generation of electronics," Nelson said.

"Double the cost of the version for the unwashed plebian deer hunter?" Vic said.

Nelson shrugged.

"Triple?"

He shrugged again.

"Where did you get it?"

This time Nelson stared at him and smiled.

Nelson convinced Vic to dress in all black. That meant a trip to REI or to the "tactical clothier" Nelson recommended to drop a couple hundred bucks on pants and a top.

"I draw the line at smearing the Rambo crap on my face," Vic said.

"Then you'll the one little white speck moving around out there in the weeds if anyone happens to shine a light toward you," Nelson said. "What about a ski mask?"

"Oh, that'll go over big if I get caught," Vic said.

"I'm just saying."

"I know, I know," Vic said.

"Let's go over the map again," Nelson said. "Better yet, let's Google it."

Nelson hit the space bar on his computer keyboard bringing the dark twenty-inch LCD screen to life.

"What's the address of this place?" Nelson said.

Vic flipped through the pages in his notebook.

"No Address, but an intersection. A little east of County Road 33 and County Road 32. By Platteville."

"Weld County?" Nelson said.

"Yes," Vic said.

"That's close enough," Nelson said. He plapped on his keyboard.

A satellite image of the area appeared on the screen.

"Can you spot the place?" Nelson said.

"Pull back a bit," Vic said.

Nelson clicked on a minus sign near the map key and the image jumped backward and a little higher so it showed more of the area. Vic peered at the image. He pointed to one of the farms.

"I think that's it," Vic said.

Nelson clicked on the plus sign and zoomed in.

"Right there," Vic said. "I drove by it yesterday. There's the parking lot, the small garage, house. That's the conference center."

"Looks like a barn," Nelson said.

"It is a barn, just tricked out," Vic said.

Nelson hit Command-Print, then Enter. A laser printer woke up and spit out a hard copy.

"Burglars must love Google Maps," Vic said.

Nelson also printed out a map of the area around Rosenthal's ranch. Vic had to memorize the whole layout since Nelson insisted that he not take any map or photo, especially showing the Double-R property, in case he got caught. Nelson pointed out an irrigation canal that ran near the eastern boundary of the Double-R. They also found a fairly remote area where Vic could park his car. From there he could hike along the canal about two miles to get to Rosenthal's ranch. The path had him edging along the property line for about a half mile, crossing the road, and finally settling into a small clump of bushes growing out of a dry stream bed.

"Looks like you can lie down right there and pull a good view of the whole area," Nelson said. "You can't go over this stuff in your head too many times. Take the map and photo home. Run the course backwards and forwards over and over and over. Then tear them up and flush them down the toilet. Don't shred them."

"I can't just light them on fire with my Zippo and toss them into the wastebasket, like in the movies?" Vic said.

"You'd probably burn your house down," Nelson said. "Flush it.

Toilets are wonderful things."

"I'd feel better with some kind of a map with me," Vic said.

"Look, the map has too much detail of Rosenthal's place. You don't want that. Take a small notebook and make some notes in it like you've been looking for owls at least a half a dozen other nights in the area. Google the area on your computer and start writing down nearby place names, like you've been there before. They need to make sense though. You know, you were observing from here, like a road, into this little stand of trees over here. Things like that."

"So I'm a bird-watcher."

"I think the correct term is birder," Nelson said, "But yes. It's a fairly simple cover."

"You had to do all this sort of stuff before you crept off into the jungle?"

"No, we just took guns," Nelson said.

"Yeah, but you didn't fit in too well with the native population. At least I could pass for someone going to that meeting."

"Dressed all in black, with a night scope?"

"Point taken," Vic said.

"Regardless of what you're wearing, I don't think you want to get caught by these folks," Nelson said.

"They're only politicians," Vic said.

"They run the government," Nelson said.

"I'm not going there," Vic said. He did not have time to debate Nelson's distrust of all things bureaucratic.

"Make sure you wear some good boots," Nelson said.

"I've got those lightweight hiking boots," Vic said.

Nelson remembered them, from their hikes. Leather and nylon. Gore-Tex lined. "The ones you took back?"

"Well, the replacements," Vic said.

"What kind of shape are they in?" Nelson said.

"Like new," Vic said. "Not like the first pair."

Vic wore the first pair for eight years before he took them back. The seam between the leather and the nylon was in the wrong place, running lengthwise along the outside edge of his left foot where all the pressure would be while hiking. Eventually, his left foot broke through the seam. It was a design flaw, Vic argued. The store agreed and gave him a newer, improved version of the same boot. At the time, returning a pair of hiking boots after beating the crap out of them for eight years gave Vic the lead in their informal "returned item" battle. Nelson regained the lead sometime later in a clever novelty move when he returned a used toothbrush for a full refund.

# 37

The Double-R Ranch was not really a ranch, even though Randal Rosenthal fancied it as such. It was a typical Front Range Colorado horse property only slightly bigger.

The Rosenthal homestead covered a few hundred acres of irrigated pasture, horse pens, a riding barn, a corral, a few small outbuildings, and a sprawling two-story house that appeared to be a carbon copy of South Fork. Two cows roamed the pasture. The Double-R was an old sugar beet farm picked up for a song when the local sugar beet market collapsed. It sat east of Platteville, about twenty miles north of Denver. Rosenthal was not the horseman.

The Double-R was an indulgence for his wife and two daughters, all three of whom enthusiastically embraced the equine set, chiefly the rodeo and show-horse branches. While the women were barrel racing, training a cutting horse, or exercising a grand champion American saddle bred, Professor Rosenthal was building the Western States Policy Research Institute at the University of Denver. The Institute was a moderate to liberal think tank cited and used by Democratic politicians when they needed something to counter loud policy arguments trumpeted by conservatives.

Michaels navigated his Toyota Highlander Hybrid SUV beneath the rustic Double-R Ranch arch hewn from the trunks of three Colorado lodge pole pines. He parked next to the single lamp post at the edge of the parking area, stepped onto the pea gravel, and headed straight for the conference center, where Rosenthal maintained a small office. He ignored the tall east-facing wooden barn doors that served as the main entrance to the center and instead entered through a single door set far back on the north side. As he stepped from the warmth of the yellow early evening sunlight into the near darkness of the conference center, Michaels called out, "Randal?"

"In here," Rosenthal shouted from somewhere in the interior darkness. "The bar."

Michaels wound his way in the dim light through a tight kitchen past the stainless steel shelves, counters, cooking tops, freezer, and refrigerator before another door delivered him to the bar-end of a small dining room. Rosenthal occupied a center stool. Piles of papers spread out before him on the polished drinking surface. The professor sipped on a bottle of beer and strained to see in the day's waning light that made its way through the bank of windows lining the north wall.

"John, so good to see you," Rosenthal said, peering over the tops of the half-rim reading glasses he always wore. "Grab yourself a cold one."

"I'm surprised you can tell it's me," Michaels said as he stepped behind the bar and fished a Fat Tire out of a small refrigerator. "You'll go blind in this light."

"This time of day, you're right. But it's quiet out here when nothing's going on."

"There is this invention, Randal, this amazing thing called the electric light bulb," Michaels said and laughed as he poured his

Colorado microbrew into a glass. "When's the next big shindig?"

Rosenthal hesitated, then said, "Well, tonight actually. Coloradans for Sensible Water Policy."

"Kendrick's group?" Michaels said.

"No, Currington's group. We don't talk about Kendrick. A strategy session. You need to be here."

Rosenthal took off his glasses and tossed them onto the splattering of papers on the bar. Removing the glasses meant something serious was not far behind. Michaels had taken enough seminars from the man to have that tell memorized.

"I'm not sure if I should be," Michaels said.

"You have no choice in the matter," Rosenthal said. "Closed meeting. Starts at eleven-thirty."

Michaels suddenly felt out of the loop, or at least out of this loop, the one that involved Currington's organization, which was formed only a few months ago to help shove major water development proposals through the legislature and now to push a statewide campaign to approve the two-hundred million dollar water bond issue.

"Are you sure about this?"

"I know you're worried, John, but if you want to move on, move up, it's time for some realpolitik," Rosenthal said.

Michaels sensed a mini lecture coming, the kind that often clawed its way into the advanced public policy seminars Rosenthal refereed with graduate students and law students.

"I can't do anything illegal," Michaels said.

"There's nothing illegal about a strategy session," the professor said, pulling a gulp from his beer bottle. "We're talking about reality. We're talking about the future of Colorado. We're talking about your future, John. I know you like to talk about that."

Michaels did like to talk about his future, which was why he was standing in Rosenthal's conference center in the first place and why he called his mentor so soon after Swain's murder. It was also why he was willing to step over a woman's dead and still cooling body in his quest to sit at the helm of his native state, to command state budgets from the executive branch, to shape state courts through judicial appointments, and to influence water policy from beneath the gold dome sitting smack in the middle of Denver.

"How would it look if I publicly threw in with Kendrick, Currington, and that gang?" Michaels said. "Damn it, Randal, Kendrick runs the water show, you know that."

"Yes, but the public doesn't know that," Rosenthal said. "And they needn't. That has to stay quiet. Anyway, John, they need to know where you'll stand when the crucial issues come before you."

"As lieutenant governor?" Michaels said.

"No. As governor. And while you are lieutenant governor, as the strong persuader that you are, just like your predecessor. Jessie set the precedent, John. Now you have an open field to follow her lead and continue to make yourself a presence on the state senate floor, this time as a member of the executive branch."

"That was the one thing I admired about her," Michaels said. "I didn't agree with her, but, well, it's too bad she had to—"

Randal held up his hand. "John, stop. We don't talk about the past. It's done. We must look forward."

Michaels was the law student again, recalling the heated debates he had with Randal in class or in local campus pubs and the man's annoying habit of cutting off his opponent in mid-sentence. "Well, I did want to talk to you about my replacement in the senate."

"That's taken care of," Rosenthal said with a note of finality that startled even Michaels.

All Michaels managed to muster in response was, "Oh?"

"Dowd will appoint you lieutenant governor next week and drop Joe Rohlas into your old senate seat."

"The crazy car salesman? And nobody talked to me about this?

I'm the bloody senate majority leader. Why Rohlas? I had a whole list of my own people."

"John, you're missing the big picture. Don't worry about your old senate seat. It's history. You're going to be the lieutenant governor and then the governor. Rohlas is with us one hundred per cent. He knows a good deal when he sees one. That's all that's important. We all must be sure that you are with us too."

"Well, you know where I come out on all this, Randal," Michaels said.

"That's fine," Rosenthal said. "All I want is for you to make sure Kendrick and Currington understand clearly where you are on the water issue. In favor of the bond issue. In favor of shutting down the wells. In favor of growth. Right?"

Michaels nodded. "But I have to be nuanced. The farmers need a bone tossed to them. So does the eco crowd, and you know how noisy they can be."

"That's fine. Bone tossing is our long suit, especially for Democrats. That will all be looked after. I know you're with us, John. I wanted to reinforce that point before our meeting later tonight. Anyway, we don't want to go through this all over again." He chugged down the last of his beer and slammed the empty bottle on the bar next to his reading glasses. "Now let's go get some dinner. Janine's been working all day on this. All for you. She loves you like a son, John."

The soon-to-be former majority leader of the Colorado State Senate and soon-to-be lieutenant governor took a gulp of his beer. He set his half-empty bottle down on the bar as well, but quietly. Mentor and protégé walked from the conference center into the blackness of the night and up to the Double-R ranch house.

He did not want to go through all what again, Michaels wondered. Arranging vacancy appointments, or killing a lieutenant governor?

# 38

Vic decided on steak and eggs. He tried to watch what he ate, cutting back a bit on the red meat, at the instigation of his ex-wife, and beefing up on the veggies, fruit, and whole grains. Special occasions called for comfort food. Driving over to Platteville to spy on a meeting of some political wheeler-dealers at Rosenthal's Double-R Ranch was a special occasion. Lil's was closed, so he drove up to Fort Lupton to eat at the Branding Iron, a classic country restaurant that had commanded the same northeast corner of U.S. Highway 85 and State Highway 52, Fort Lupton's main drag, forever. When he and his folks took a ride through farm country, or what was left of it along Colorado's Front Range, they often stopped at the Branding Iron for lunch or an early dinner before heading back to Denver. His V8 Jeep Grand Cherokee Laredo got him there quickly, guzzling gas all the way.

The vinyl covered booth offered more privacy to review the photo and map of his "target," as Nelson called it. Vic had pre-marked different night bird sightings on the map Nelson told him to flush down the toilet. His notebook was blank.

Out the window, yellows, oranges, and deep blues of sunset played across the Continental Divide. In front of him, whites, reds, and browns covered his plate. With the corner of a piece of rye toast, Vic broke the over-easy eggs. He mopped up some of the yellow delight for the first bite of his comfort meal, hoping it would remain in his stomach during this "insane undertaking," as Nelson had described Vic's nighttime foray.

# 39

Irrigation canal maintenance roads do not make the best hiking trails. Mostly ruts of dried mud, the roads were barely manageable by a four-wheel drive pickup.

Vic had hoped for a trail like the one that ran alongside the Highline Canal, which snakes its way from a diversion on the South Platte River in the foothills, through the Denver metro area, and into an irrigation reservoir northeast of the city. The Highline's agricultural use ceased long ago once the Denver Water Board bought it and converted the water to residential use for washing cars, flushing toilets, filling water glasses, taking hot showers, and sprinkling sprawling lawns of Kentucky bluegrass that had no business being in the high plains semi-arid climate zone in the first place. Denver morphed the canal into a ribbon park with smooth paths for horseback riders, walkers, joggers, and bicyclists, many of whom thought food came from the supermarket rather than farmlands dependent on irrigation water the Highline once bore.

The canal Vic stood next to in the darkness was far from a bridal path. It was a working irrigation ditch, delivering vital water to farms and ranches northeast of Denver. He wondered if the water in this canal one day would be converted to a "higher use" like filling swimming pools or sprinkling lawns in the suburbs.

When Vic got to the point where he was to depart from the maintenance road, he realized he had to cross the fifteen-foot wide canal, which was filled with water, moving water, cold moving water. Nelson missed that one, Vic thought as he readjusted his pack and stepped sideways down the steep inner slope of the irrigation ditch. His foot landed on something that gave way. In a blink, the frigid water swallowed him up and thrust him downstream. Completely disoriented, suddenly very cold, Vic clawed at the sheer canal wall until his head bobbed back up into the dark night. Heart pounding, gasping for air, and coughing, he steadied himself with both his hands enough to keep his head above water. Numbness in his legs told him hypothermia might render them useless in a few minutes. The South Platte River's near-freezing water, which had left Colorado's high country earlier in the day, before being diverted into the irrigation canal, gradually sapped the warm life from Vic's body.

Everyone else he knew was at home with their families, watching a movie or football game, cleaning up from dinner, figuring out the next day's transportation plans, how a daughter would get to soccer practice, or how a son would get home from piano lessons. Vic's family would be doing the same, his three sons, daughters in law, his grandchildren, his daughter, her fiance, his ex-wife, his mother, father. All of them were living their relatively normal lives while their friend, father, ex-husband, grandpa, and fifty-nine-year-old son was awash in a Weld County irrigation canal in the middle of the night. Vic felt as though he were on some midnight high school caper that had gone horribly wrong. "What am I doing?" he said to the dark uncaring sky. Then Vic smashed into something hard.

The relentless flow of the canal flattened him against an

unforgiving surface that felt like a steel gate used to divert some of the water into a nearby farm field. Vic could hear water gushing through an opening to his left, the flow tugging at him from the same direction. Visions of being siphoned down into some dark water-filled pit sparked the strength to hold on tighter and tighter for his life.

Tingling legs told him to get the hell out while he still had some strength left, so he reached up into the darkness with his right hand and found something strong and solid. It felt like a threaded bolt sticking out of concrete. He pulled hard and reached over the top of the gate with his left land. Managing a toehold on the canal wall with his right foot, Vic awkwardly struggled up from the water and flopped his numb torso over the top of the diversion gate. He lay there out of breath, chest heaving, heart pounding, body freezing, and listening to the rushing water delivering its life-giving wetness to some farmer's crop.

Reaching out blindly to his left, Vic's hand struck a large metal wheel, probably the controller for the diverter gate. He grasped it with cold stiffening fingers and pulled his legs all the way out of the water. Crouching on top of the concrete and steel diversion wall, he leaped into the darkness over the remaining few feet of canal wall, grateful he did not crash into some undetected barrier, and scrambled through the dirt and weeds back onto the maintenance trail.

Vic threw off his pack and stripped. Naked and shivering in the night air, he wrung all the water he could from the synthetic clothing, then put everything back on. He swung the small backpack over his right shoulder and began jogging back toward his car, illuminating the path with a small flashlight and hoping the run would warm his frigid body. No longer caring who saw him, he lost all interest in the secret meeting. All he wanted to do was get warm. And not have a heart attack.

# 40

After a quarter of a mile, he stopped and flashed the light on his watch. It was 10:15 p.m. It took another twenty minutes to get to the car. He started it up and turned on the heater. The dry clothes were in the way-back so he walked around and flipped up the rear hatch. Once again, he did not care about the new source of light, this time from the dome inside his Jeep. Vic desperately wanted to get warm. The dry underwear and socks were ecstasy, the soft blue jeans and black Crystal Lake Tigers sweatshirt from his 35th high school reunion, heaven. The joy evaporated when he tugged on his cold and damp hiking boots.

Glad the you-don't-want-to-know-the-price night scope was waterproof, Vic wiped it off, flipped the switch, and put it up to his eyes. The night landscape appeared in varying shades of green. He tossed the soaked backpack into the back of his Jeep and set the scope on the passenger seat. He checked the time again. 11:10 p.m. The plan was to be in place by 11:30 p.m. With no time to walk back to Rosenthal's, Vic improvised and decided to drive.

He headed down to the main road and turned right toward the

Double-R. In a few minutes, he passed a small building and a parking lot illuminated by a single light on a twenty-foot pole near the entryway to Rosenthal's ranch. An SUV was parked in the lot right beneath the light. A half-mile further on, he turned into the entrance to a farm field, parked, got out and opened the hood, feigning a disabled car in case anyone driving by got nosy about the vehicle. With the night scope hung around his neck, Vic walked briskly back up the road toward the Double-R, watching for traffic in both directions. He poked around across the road from Rosenthal's parking lot and found the small clump of bushes that Nelson had pointed out on the satellite photo. Vic settled in behind them and found a position that offered a good view of the Double-R Ranch.

Vic spoke to himself. "Why didn't I do this in the first place?"

# 41

Kane was right. It was not much of a ranch. Vic propped the scope on a log and pointed it across the road at the gravel parking area occupied by the lone vehicle. The small building on the left edge of the lot appeared to be a two-car garage set back about twenty feet from the road. A larger building on the far side of the parking lot must be the conference center, he thought. Far off to the right, seventy-five yards or so, Vic made out house lights but nothing more. If there were corrals or fences in between, the darkness hid them. He adjusted the night scope and scanned the big building. The heavy barn doors on the end facing him looked closed, locked, and dark. But along the north wall facing the house, Vic could see three dimly lit windows and a single door down on the far end. A concrete walkway led from that door out toward the house. A branch split off the main walkway and ran down to the parking lot, ending in the splash of light puddled at the foot of the single lamp post.

About ten minutes after Vic had settled in, he heard a door slam. Pointing the night scope up toward the house, he began tracking two figures walking leisurely down the pathway toward the conference center. They were talking, but were too far away to be heard. Eyeglasses framed the older man's face, and a bow tie guarded his throat. Rosenthal, Vic assumed. The spring in the other man's step told him it was the much younger John Michaels, senate majority leader. Both men disappeared into a blinding flash of light when Rosenthal opened the side door to the conference center. By the time the automatic gain control knocked down the brightness, all the night scope picked up was the door being pulled shut.

Something small but sufficiently creepy crawled up his right leg. Vic jumped up and battered the inside of his thigh, shook his pants, and even considered pulling them off. But he thought better of it considering he had already stripped down once.

A car engine up the road settled him down. Vic returned to his prone position as vehicle lights broke the dark night about a mile off to the south, the direction of Denver. As the headlamps came closer, Vic made out the rounded profile of a medium sized sedan. It slowed as it neared the Ranch and pulled in next to the SUV, sharing the pool of illumination. The car was nondescript and dark. It could have been black or a dark blue or green. As the driver stepped out, Vic saw the unmistakable profile of Eugene Currington. He smoothed out his jacket and marched up the pathway. The sedan chirped and flashed its lights as the land developer disappeared and let himself into the conference center.

A few minutes later, another car glided in silently from the right, the north. Vic had not heard it come down the road. Electric or hybrid, he figured. The tires crunched and popped on the gravel as it eased in next to Currington's dark sedan. One man got out. The night scope revealed a large nose but not much else. He wore a dark flat cap turned backwards, the way chopper riders wear them. When the scope caught a slight reflection on the hat, Vic thought it might be made of leather. In a minute, chopper hat guy also was gone, swallowed by Rosenthal's conference center. He guessed it was Kendrick. Again he flashed his small light on his wristwatch. It was 11:40 p.m.

Vic could just make out the license plate numbers. He groped for a pencil stub and something to write on, having destroyed his small spiral notebook during his Olympic swim down the canal. All he had on him was an old piece of trash in his back pocket, a corner of cardboard from something. He hated to write on cardboard, but it was all he had, and he knew he would never be able to memorize the information. Scribbling down the plate numbers, Vic hoped Driscoll would run them for him. No guarantee, but worth a try, he thought.

Vic wondered if he should move down closer to improve his chance of hearing something, anything that might clarify the story, assuming there was a story here. There had to be a story, he thought. Something had to be up. As he stood up, another pair of headlights pierced the night about a mile to the south. He crouched back down again to let the vehicle pass. Only it did not pass. A distant rattling of a diesel truck engine broke the silence. The truck stopped somewhere in that mile and turned off its engine and lights.

As the momentarily suppressed sounds of crickets and frogs rose back up to their normal mating frenzy, Vic heard the quiet opening of a vehicle door, a dinging of a door-open alarm and then the careful closing of the same door with a single snap. He flattened down even more behind his log perch in the bushes as he heard footsteps in the gravel along the side of the road. The driver was headed for the Double-R.

# 42

Vic gently edged the night scope in the direction of the walker, still far away, a dark vertical shadow moving slowly toward the Rosenthal ranch. Black clothing. Boots. Covered face and head, suggestive of a ski mask and hoodie, or both. Average height, maybe as tall as Vic, slender, carrying nothing that looked like a camera or gun, the walker crossed the road and vanished behind the garage. Vic turned the night scope back to the conference center to see if the mystery guest emerged from the other side either to attend the gathering or possibly to do the same thing he was trying to do, eavesdrop on the meeting. No one emerged from the shadows. A lot of interest in this meeting, Vic thought, now knowing he had to remain dead quiet while observer number two lurked somewhere in the darkness barely twenty yards away. He checked his cell phone to make sure it was set on vibrate only, but it was dead, dark, and waterlogged.

# 43

It was not long before the side door burst open, and two men spilled onto the pathway. Acute, quick hand gestures accompanied the heated conversation, none of which Vic could make out. It was Michaels and chopper hat guy. As they moved toward the parking lot, Vic caught a glimpse of the mystery walker easing back around from the rear of the garage. Michaels and chopper hat strode through the pool of light and crunched across the parking lot toward Vic. They stopped at the roadside. Off to the left, the mystery walker froze in a shadow at the edge of the garage and watched, just as Vic was doing.

But now Vic could hear the conversation.

"Look, I've already talked with Lujak about the bill, and he's agreed to kill it next week," chopper hat guy said as he lit a cigarette. "He's on board."

"Are you sure?" Michaels said.

"Yes, I'm sure. He'll put up a fuss when they kill the bill, but that's just for show. We'll have him run an interim study on agricultural wells, and that'll keep the farmers in our corner through the bond election."

"I don't know about those farmers," Michaels said. "Some of them are loose cannons."

"Don't even think about them, John," chopper hat guy said. "I track that part of the equation. You'll need to keep your cool up at the statehouse."

"You're sure Lujak is with us?"

Chopper hat guy laughed, "This guy wants to be Ag director so bad he pees on his cowboy boots every time we talk about it. I'll work him and keep stalling the farmers. Water law takes time, I tell them. Trust me, I tell them. I'm Mr. Water Law, I tell them. God, they're a clueless lot."

Mr. Water Law, Vic thought. Gary Kendrick, chopper hat and all.

"We've got to get through the fall elections and get the bond issue passed," Michaels said. "Is the campaign as well heeled as Currington says it is?"

"I took the whole retainer I got from the farmers and dumped it into the bond issue campaign warchest," Kendrick said.

"Isn't that illegal?" Michaels asked, sounding a bit naive to Vic.

"Who the hell cares?" Kendrick said. "The way I did it, they'll never find out anyway."

"And the governor is in on this?" Michaels said.

"Dowd's in on everything, John," Kendrick said.

"Everything?" Michaels said.

"Everything," Kendrick said.

Michaels emitted an odd-sounding shudder.

"Calm down and just focus on your job, will you?" Kendrick said.

"What about the water right filing?" Michaels said. "Have you done anything with it?"

"Just enough to make it look like I'm really working for the farmers," Kendrick said. "Currington's worked the deal with the bank. All financed through Ferguson. I've got our own little lawyer to front the water right transfer. Fresh out of law school. Paid him a big fee. He's ready to go, now that Swain's out of the way."

"That's what bothers me," Michaels said.

"What?" Kendrick said, pulling off his hat, slapping it on his leg, then returning it to his head.

"Those farmers bother me, especially Bender and Hague," Michaels said. "There's already been the one shooting."

"Which shooting?" Kendrick said.

"The farmer," Michaels said. "Hague. Which one did you think I meant?"

"That was a deputy sheriff who plugged Hague," Kendrick said. "I won't talk about the other one, ever. Understand?"

Michaels said nothing.

"Come on boys. Time's a-wastin'" It was Rosenthal, sticking his head out the conference center door. "Two more items to cover." Kendrick flicked his cigarette into a sputtering arch that exploded in sparks on the pavement. He and Michaels walked back into the building.

Vic nudged the night scope to the left. The mystery visitor was gone. A few minutes later, the diesel engine rattled to life down the road, and as the heavy rubber tires crunched the gravel, he centered the night scope on the vehicle and watched it pull away in a blaze of blinding lights on the road ahead of it. He noticed only one taillight blazing, the one on the passenger side.

Rolling over on his back, Vic stared at the night sky for a while. Clouds obscured everything out there in space. Like camping in the thin chilly mountain air, Vic thought he dozed off for a few minutes, but was not quite sure. He hoped he had not snored. These nagging thoughts dimmed when the side door opened again, and all four men emerged from the conference center. Rosenthal reached back inside and switched off the lights including the single lamp over the parking lot. The door slammed in the darkness, and the men walked off in silence, Rosenthal to his house, the other three to their cars. They said nothing as they got into their vehicles and drove off into the night. Vic waited another fifteen minutes before he made his way back to his Jeep.

On the way home, Vic wondered about Michaels, whose surprise over Kendrick's legislative conspiracy and related matters seemed genuine. No way was this guy a murderer, Vic thought. A political opportunist, but no assassin. Kendrick was another matter, though. Vic saw this guy playing everyone off against each other, unethical at best, a murderer at worst.

# 44

Under water, paralyzed, struggling to breathe, frozen hands and arms struggling to turn a rusty iron wheel, Vic woke up in a cold sweat. He wanted to scream. An off-white bedroom ceiling stared down at him, not cold water. Baker the dog emitted the squeaky sounds as his claws tap-danced in the hallway. Instead of submitting to the cold dark water death of his dream, Vic pivoted out of bed and padded toward the back door to let the dog out.

As Baker sprang toward the side fence to find his pal Oscar who lived next door, Vic barefooted his way down the sidewalk that ran alongside his house to the front yard where the morning papers might be found, depending on where they landed after the toss from the street.

"Nice jammies, Vic." His next-door neighbor and Oscar's owner was out working in her yard. "Call in sick?"

"Slept in, Lorna," Vic said. "I'm going to search for my newspapers."

"Good luck," she said. "I've still got two up on my roof."

On the way into the front yard, Vic grabbed his emergency key from the nail on the fence post inside the side gate. Miraculously, both the *Sun* and the *Times* made the front porch. He grabbed them and let himself in the front door. With toast and coffee, he scanned the papers. Nothing big. After a quick shower, Vic tossed on some clothes, got Baker settled inside for the day and headed downtown, driving because he was so late. In the car, his thoughts about the night before were interrupted only by the throbbing pain in his right shoulder and left knee. Parking cost him ten bucks. He hated that.

Vic went straight to his city room cubicle. He wanted to write up his notes from the night scope mission on his laptop, not on the paper's word processing system. Even though he still felt like he was in a goldfish bowl, the built-in desk was starting to look like his, helped along with photos of the kids, the grandkids, an empty coffee cup, a few books, stacks of paper, and the instant weather indicator his daughter had made for him when she was in grade school. It consisted of a thin wooden dowel inserted at an angle into a plywood base. A small stone hung suspended on a thread attached to the end of the dowel. If there was a shadow below the stone, it was sunny. No shadow, it was cloudy. If the stone was wet, it was raining, and if it moved around there was a wind. Worked every time.

A pink post-it note occupied the upper right hand corner of his terminal screen. The message read, "Gil called about the river thing. Wouldn't leave a phone number–Jen."

Jennifer was not at her desk in the neighboring cubicle. The only story he had written that involved a river was the murder story, on his first day back. Since then, he had not written anything about the South Platte, any other river, or the murdered lieutenant governor, whose gruesome story had been taken over by the city desk, the police reporter, and the statehouse crew. Cops had no leads, no clues, and no suspects. In the four rounds of golf he had played with Frank Driscoll since the killing, Vic pried out nothing new about the crime. Now "Gil" calls with something about the river, whoever Gil is, Vic thought. He picked up his phone and pressed the button labeled "city desk."

"Nice that you could join us today," Peggy said.

"I sent you a text message," Vic said.

"Where's the note from your Mom?"

"Peggy, do you know where Jennifer is?"

"I sent her down to council," Peggy said.

"That could take forever," Vic said.

"It will," Peggy said. "They're rezoning the property around two of the mayor's bars."

"The ones in his blind trust?"

"Blind, my ass," she said.

"So cynical are thee," Vic said. "Who's going to make hay in this one?"

"Councilman Charlie Tanner, wants to be mayor so bad, I swear."

"You swear? No way."

"Way, and deal with it," Peggy said. "What do you want with Jennifer?"

"She left me a message," Vic said. "A little vague."

"Here's her cell. Can't guarantee she'll answer, but if it's from the paper she probably will. Ready."

"Go ahead." Vic wrote down the number, said thanks, and hung up the phone to dial Jennifer when a call came into his second line. He hit the button.

"Vic Bengston."

"This is Gil." It was a deep gravelly voice.

"Gil. How are you?"

"I'm fine."

"Who are you?" Vic said.

"I want justice to be done," Gil said.

"I want my mortgage paid off," Vic said.

"I'm not kidding, Mr. Bengston."

"Neither am I, Mr., uh, Gil."

"I need to meet you," Gil said.

"Come on down to the paper," Vic said.

Gil laughed. Then he coughed.

Vic said, "Are you okay?"

After more spasms, "Yeah, I think I'll make it."

"Gil. Do you have a last name?"

"It doesn't matter. I need to meet with you and not at that rotten paper. Sides, I can't drive down there."

Vic did not want to let this guy know that a suggested meeting with an unknown character about "that river thing" made him nervous. But, compelled to prove himself in the city room, he heard himself say, "Where then?"

"Do you know the old Great Western sugar beet plant in Brighton?"

"Along Eighty-Five," Vic said. "You can't miss it."

"Oh, there's a lot of us who miss it, Mr. Bengston. That plant there put a lot of food on a lot of tables."

"I mean it's easy to spot."

"I know what you mean," Gil said. "No, you don't know what I mean. That's why I want to meet you."

"Can you tell me anything over—"

"Nothing on the phone. Nothing."

"All right," Vic said, sensing he was talking to a farmer or rancher, retired maybe. Seemed safe enough. "When?"

"Tomorrow morning."

"Let me check my calendar."

"Six o'clock."

"I'm still in bed at six."

"Six," Gil said, and then he started gagging again. After a half a minute of this, he said, "I've got to tell you something face to face. It'll make you cry."

"How long will this take?" Vic said.

"Not long," he said.

"I'll bring a photographer," Vic said.

"Like hell you will. You just bring yourself. Anyone else and forget about it."

"Okay," Vic said. "Any particular side of the place? It's pretty big."

Gil had composed himself. "Southeast. There's a small parking lot, right off the road. Six o'clock."

"I'll be there." Vic heard coughing as Gil hung up the phone.

# 45

"You don't know who he is, and you don't know what he has to show you," Peggy said.

She was standing. Vic decided to take his medicine sitting down, so he slid into her chair. "And he wants to meet at six in the morning."

"In Brighton," Peggy said. "By the old plant. Next, you're going to tell me you've got a hunch."

"Well, yeah, I do," Vic said, wondering if Peggy played everything safe now that she was a city editor.

"I don't know if I can spare you," Peggy said. "Marsha needs help with night-side. We're already down one with the cutback."

"So I've gone from disposable to indispensable," Vic said, rubbing his sore shoulder.

"You're good on the desk, Vic," Peggy said. She paused for a moment. "Okay, Marsha owns you until midnight. You'll just have to sleep fast."

"What else is new?" Vic said. "I thought the contract said eight hours between shifts."

Peggy and Vic traded spots. "Vic, you forget. You're not a regular reporter, remember? Hogan made you an assistant managing editor so he could hire you outside the guild contract."

"Just testing," Vic said. "As an assistant managing editor, doesn't that mean I'm your boss?"

"No. Check with Hogan. It means you're our slave." She let a good looking grin slip out then turned serious again. "You have no idea what Gil was talking about?"

"Sounds like my feature story on farming and the drought," Vic said.

His gut said otherwise.

# 46

Vic had worked the city desk with Marsha until about 1:30 a.m. when the supply of overnight rewrites, news releases, and obits dried up. Nothing was happening, and the news hole for the *Rocky* was so small these days, Vic knew he could almost sneeze out an edition.

He hit his front door at two in the morning, let Baker out to pee, stripped, collapsed into bed, got back up to let Baker back in, then back into bed. Sleep arrived at three. The alarm went off at five. Clothes tossed back on, water splashed on face, he grabbed the little digital recorder, notebook, and pen, jumped into the car, jumped out of the car, ran back into the house, patted Baker who danced like Vic had been gone for a year, filled the dog's food and water dishes, relocked the front door, jumped back into the car, and raced out the driveway. Vic settled for coffee and sinker from the Dunkin Donut shop run by the Arab guy who called him "boss." The doughnutista called everyone "boss". Both he and his helper worked hard and stayed open all night while the Starbucks baristas were still getting their beauty sleep.

The trip to Brighton took half a sixteen-ounce cup of coffee, two plain old fashioned doughnuts, a couple of gallons of gas in his Jeep, and big bucks for the starving oil companies. Vic took the old roads up to meet Gil. A few of them took him past what could still be called farms, but they were rapidly disappearing as the Denver metropolitan area oozed its way up and down the Front Range and eastward out onto the plains.

Vic quickly pierced Brighton's outer reaches, comprised mostly of newly annexed developments of putty-colored townhouses and single-family homes. The instant neighborhoods came ready-made with their own shopping centers anchored by big box stores, the usual chain restaurant suspects, car washes, gas stations, and a full battalion of Starbucks coffee shops that delivered four dollar lattes through drive-up windows to the ever-fattening suburbanites, many of whom merely slept in Brighton and drove thirty or forty miles north, south, or west to work at the universities, colleges, government offices, businesses, and burgeoning high-tech industry campuses in the region. The plains to the east were still barren except for ranches, farms, and prime development land.

It was 5:45 a.m. when he rolled slowly past the Adams County Courthouse, the county administrative offices, and the sheriff's department in the older part of town where big old frame or brick houses with sprawling yards and massive hardwood trees glimmered in the early morning sun. Vic almost moved to Brighton to pursue the life of a writer, husband, father, and vegetable gardener. But that was a century ago, and now he was alone, divorced, the kids all grown, and fighting weeds in the small vegetable plot he tended in his east Denver back yard.

At the main drag, the spacious old neighborhoods gave way to a well-worn downtown of Colorado brick facades built in the twenties, thirties, and forties. Each building strained to keep up the fiction that this was still a quaint old Main Street. The bank commanded its traditional spot on the first corner. A few taverns and one cafe enticed passersby midway down the block with happy hour and lunch specials, anything to divert attention away from the empty department store, missing hardware store, vanished five and dime, closed up Sears catalog outlet, and AWOL druggist. Many storefront windows labeled themselves "For Lease" and "Available". Others proclaimed "Carniceria" and "Taqueria" in bright green, red, and yellow lettering, while still more offered antiques and collectibles, day labor for farm fields or housing developments, used furniture, payday loans, and bus service to El Paso, Texas.

At the end of Main Street, Vic turned east into a neighborhood of tiny frame houses occupied mostly by Latino residents, many of them legal or illegal Mexican immigrants. Children were already up and outside playing. Men were loading hand tools and large orange, blue, and red cylindrical water coolers onto their trucks. At a stop sign, Vic watched a nice looking thirty-something woman with long black hair as she emerged from her small blue and white trim frame house with a matching small blue and white cooler probably filled with food. She handed it to her man standing next to a late seventies Dodge pickup truck and kissed him on the cheek. She headed back up the sidewalk, and the man turned back to his truck, tossing in a rake and two hoes as he readied himself for what probably would be a hot backbreaking day in some nearby onion or cabbage field.

Vic drove around the block and headed toward the northwestern edge of town where the dormant red brick sugar beet factory dominated the landscape. The main building was flanked by tall silos, bins, and other rundown structures, all connected by a series of rusty conveyor belts designed to move the softball-sized sugar beets from harvest truck into temporary storage and then into the factory for processing into sugar. Sugar beets ruled Brighton when much of the country's sugar was derived from the large root plant that looked like a radish on steroids. But one day farmers awoke to massive amounts of low-priced sugar flooding the markets from foreign countries where labor was as cheap as dirt, cheaper in some cases. In a few years, the Brighton sugar beet industry had all but disappeared, and this immense processing operation was abandoned along with the farmers who cultivated the beets that fed it and the several hundred Brighton residents who worked at the plant. Now, part of the property was used to store and sell used farm machinery, heavy equipment, and recreational vehicles.

Vic rolled to a slow stop on the dirt path leading to a grown-over parking lot near the southeast corner of the factory. He could see a shiny black long bed pickup truck parked up near the building. A man leaning against the tailgate removed his straw-colored cowboy hat and waved it a few times. Snow white hair covered the exposed head. Vic continued down the path. As he got closer, he saw the man adjust a backpack or something slung over his shoulder. Heart thumping, Vic looked for a gun but saw nothing. He parked the Jeep fifteen yards from the truck and started on foot toward the man, now clearly an old man.

# 47

"Gil?" Vic shouted.

"You must be Bengston," he shouted back. Then he convulsed into a coughing fit.

The thing on his shoulder was a portable oxygen machine. A thin plastic hose ran from it up to the back of Gil's head and around both sides of his cheeks. A small cannula snugged into his nose. Vic could hear the low whooshing sound of the oxygen pump. Gil appeared to be sneaking a smoke. The closer Vic got to the man the smaller he seemed. Each step added a decade to Gil's age. Within arm's reach, Vic extended his hand. "I'm Vic Bengston."

"Mr. Bengston," said the deep voice, the one from the phone. "I'm Gil Johansson." He held out his right hand, and Vic shook it. The mitt was rough and calloused, grip like a vice.

"So what about the river?" Vic said.

"I read the papers, Mr. Bengston," Gil said.

"Vic."

"Vic," Gil said. "You wrote the first story."

Vic played dumb. "First story, about what? Rivers? I've written a lot of—"

"Not in thirty years you haven't. What have you been doing down there? Rewriting press releases?"

Gil pretty much had the newspaper business figured out.

"What the hell are you talking about?"

"I'm talking about what you used to do at that paper. You used to come out here, and you'd write stories about the water. You wrote the first ones about the wells." He took a drag on his cigarette and then started coughing.

"That was a long time ago," Vic said. "You need a drink of water, or something?"

Gil shook his head. The coughing ceased when he got on top of his labored breathing. With bloodshot eyes he gazed at Vic. "I don't, but the crops do. The farmers need it. She was going to end it for us all, at least up here."

"Who was?" Vic said.

"That goddamn lieutenant governor!"

"Jessica Swain?"

"The one you found in the river," Gil said.

"I didn't find her," Vic said.

"You know what I mean. You wrote about her. First. When you came back."

"I just happened to catch the story," Vic said. "The police reporter was sick."

"Look, why don't you wake up?" Gil said while he deftly pinched out his half-smoked cigarette, pulled out his wallet, and slipped it in with the bills. He shook his head. "The wife. She thinks I've quit."

"Wake up to what, Gil?" Vic said.

"Those stories you wrote," Gil said. "Way back when. It's all about the water. The wells. Still is."

"You mean the lieutenant governor's murder?" Vic said.

"You're damn right," Gil said. "She was going to end it."

"End what?"

"The wells," Gil said.

"The irrigation wells?" Vic said.

Gil turned toward the shuttered beet factory. "Those irrigation wells made this place hum like a huge machine. We grew beets with that water. That water created jobs right here. I grew beets. My brother worked in the plant. He's dead now." Gil aimed his wrinkled cowboy hat toward the building. "Raised his family. Sent his son to college. All with the beets, the water, and the sun. We added the labor." A clear trail of wetness cascaded down Gil's right cheek.

"You know, Gil," Vic said. "The cheap sugar tanked the sugar beet business."

"The water made it run when the market was good," Gil said. "When the beets went away, we moved the water to other crops. Onions. Corn. Cabbage. But without the water, we're finished."

"How was Swain going to shut you down?"

"That, Mr. Bengston," Gil said. "Er, Vic. I don't really know."

"Well, you must know something," Vic said. "Why did you call me up here?

"It's just what I've heard. At lunch counters, dinner counters really, folks talking."

Gil seemed reluctant to provide details but not reluctant enough to set up a meeting with a reporter.

"What exactly have you heard?" Vic said. "Is it about shutting off the wells? What the state engineer did?"

"No, we'll get those turned back on. Lujak's already working on that. Legislature will back us farmers, but, uh—"

"What?" Vic said.

"Something about a water right on the South Platte," Gil said.

"Senior. An old one. Might be the Jacobson homestead down to Fort Morgan. Don't really know, but people's talkin' about it. That's all. Talk. I've heard it a number of times. Not sure what. But I've heard enough to know it's more than just jaw-bonin'."

"Is there anybody else I could talk to about it?" Vic said, deciding not to mention Senator Lujak's plan to toss the farmers overboard.

"Can't you look into water rights? You know, on the internet? Google it?"

Vic was surprised that this ancient farmer knew so much about the world wide web. "It helps to have some specifics, Gil, some place to start. Look, you obviously know the people you heard this from. Who are they? Who were they talking about?"

"Nope. Can't. I've got a son-in-law, my daughter, their two kids working my old place. It's theirs now. I worry about them, especially since this thing happened."

"The murder?"

"Yeah. That. Ever since it happened, we've been pretty nervous. There's people involved that — well, let me say, you don't want to mess with them. I don't want my family hurt no more. They need that water, and these people can just come and take it." He pulled out his wallet again and fished out the butt. He teased it with his thumb and forefinger, rounding the flat cigarette stub up to make it easier to smoke. Gil snapped open a Zippo and lit up. He coughed after the first drag, then steadied his breathing.

"A name. Something."

"I can't," Gil said. "I've got the wife to think about too." He looked up toward the east, squinted with the sun in his eyes, something he had probably done thousands of times before as he worked his fields along the South Platte River basin. "Anyway, I've got to go. Supposed to meet some boys for breakfast. The wife, she keeps pretty close tabs on my time." He lifted up his oxygen hose.

"She worries about me."

"Where's your farm?"

"Told you, it's my daughter's now, and son-in-law's." He pointed toward the north-south road to the east of them. "Take Main Street there. Stay on it. Run up north to Fort Lupton, five miles or so. You'll see a few storage garages on the left, but you turn right on County Road 12. Out east a mile or so, that's the farm. Past Road 29, turn right into the drive. Little white frame house, nothing special. Silo's got the top knocked off her. One barn's an old Quonset hut I got cheap after the war. All planted in corn. The sign still says Johansson Farm. There's a big new barn, too, a real big one. Dave built that."

"Dave?"

"Bender. Dave Bender. My son-in-law."

"Do you still live out there?"

"No. No. Just the kids and the grandkids are on the farm. No. The wife and I live in a little box in town, here in Brighton. Retirement village they call it. Boring as hell." Gil took a final drag and ground the remaining ash, tobacco, and paper into the dirt. He reached up and opened the driver's side door of his pickup.

"You know where to reach me," Vic said. "If you change your mind, about the name I mean."

"Sure," he said. He hacked once, spit, then pulled himself up into the cab of his pickup, probably the only remaining hard evidence of his former life on the land. He cranked over the diesel and slowly rolled down the path back toward the road.

Vic did the same, thinking he might stop somewhere for coffee, maybe breakfast. Looking down the path, he could see that Gil had turned onto the shoulder of the paved road and stopped. Vic pulled up behind him. Gil waved him up. Not wanting to stop halfway into the southbound lane, Vic threw the Jeep into park, got out and walked up to Gil's open passenger side window. The old farmer looked straight ahead down the road. Then he turned toward Vic and said, "Gary Kendrick."

"The water lawyer?"

Gil nodded, rolled up his window and headed toward town.

# 48

Vic considered following him but then thought better of it. Gil would have easily spotted him on the mostly flat occasionally rolling land to the east. Since he was only a few miles south of Fort Lupton, he decided to hit the Branding Iron where he knew he would get a good breakfast along with a fresh pot of coffee.

At 7:15 in the morning only the serious people were in the restaurant. The parking lot was dotted mostly with pickups. Inside, six of the booths were taken, all men. Two booths were filled with Latino work crews, both involved in heated but friendly conversations in Spanish. White guys occupied the other booths. English only there. One group wore hard hats and orange vests. Vic figured they were tied to the big Xcel Energy truck outside. What the rest of the breakfast crowd did for work was a toss-up, except for the three old boys sheathed in overalls and anchoring one end of the counter. Farmers all the way. Vic landed next to them, but with a one-stool buffer zone.

"Coffee, hon?" said a girl barely out of high school, if that.

"Sure," Vic said.

She had the coffee with her. All she did was flip the cup in front of Vic right side up and splashed in the hot brown liquid. "Know what you want?"

"Two eggs over easy," Vic said. "Bacon. Wheat, no, rye toast."

"Hash browns?"

"Okay."

"Be right back." She swept away and vanished around the corner.

Vic got up and walked outside to buy a newspaper from one of the boxes. He selected the Brighton Blade. Smaller dailies were growing these days, unlike the suffocating metro dailies. Local news, especially the police reports and classified ads, always interested him, always told him what was going on right down the street.

Vic settled back down on his stool about the same time the waitress returned with his breakfast. The farmers to his right were not saying much. Occasionally, Vic overheard "seed corn," "auction", "better deal on a used tractor", and then "water" followed by "wells."

"I think I'd shoot 'em first," Middleman said. "I don't know how they can do that."

"They did it to Dave now too," the one on the far right said. "Damned if the state didn't send a copy of the shut-off order to the bank and Ben Ferguson called Dave's note."

"That's downright nasty," the one on the left said, shaking his head.

"I think he was on thin ice anyway," Middleman said. "He almost defaulted two years ago when he had water."

"That's a big word for you, Henry, defaulted," Righty said. All three laughed. "Hell, we all nearly went under two years ago with that damn drought. But calling his note just because of that shut-off order, well there's somethin' downright wrong with that."

"It's Fort Lupton," Lefty said. "And Ferguson's bank."

Middleman said, "What do you mean?"

"Town's dyin' to get that land," Lefty said. "Put up some big retirement development."

"Ben would do that?" Middleman said, shaking his head. "For Fort Lupton?"

"Sure he would," Lefty said. "Damn sight more money in land developments than rolling over our notes year after year. His bank's got the financing."

"You're not thinking about cashing in are you?" Middleman said.

"Thought about it," Lefty said. "More than once."

"Like I said, I think I'd shoot 'em first," Middleman said. "They want the water."

Vic had finished most of his breakfast. He took a sip of the new luke warm coffee and turned toward the farmers. After taking a deep breath, Vic said, "Excuse me, but do any of you guys know Gil Johansson?"

Suddenly, the three hulking farmers turned into silent, uncomfortable middle schoolers caught smoking in the bathroom.

Finally, Righty said, "Who the hell are you?" All that was missing was the word "pilgrim" tacked onto the end of the question.

"Just someone who met Gil and was wondering about him, wondering if you might know him," Vic said to the three stone faces.

"Yeah, we know him," said Middleman. "You're not from the bank are you?

"Or one of them land developers," said Lefty.

"No. No. I'm. Well, I'm a reporter."

"Who for?" Righty said, leaning forward so he could see Vic's face, then nodded to the girl for more coffee. She flew down the line filling all the cups. Vic held his out to her. She hit it with deadly accuracy.

"The *Rocky Mountain Sun.*"

"Oh gawd," Righty said, leaning back and shaking his head.

"Anti-agriculture," said Middleman. Lefty turned back to his coffee.

"Well, I'm not anti-agriculture," Vic said.

"Your paper sure is," Lefty said, not even looking at Vic. "Up here to write our obituaries?

"No, I'm thinking about doing a story on farming and maybe how you guys are holding up against all this development pressure." Vic made it up as he went along.

Middleman ripped open a sugar packet, dumped it into his coffee, and said, "Now that'll be the day. Anyways, how interested are you? Really?"

"That paper don't print nothing that makes the farmer look good," Lefty said. "All they want is ads for those developments. Retirement communities."

"What do you want with Gil?" It was Middleman again, now pouring in half-and-half and stirring with a thin wooden stick.

"Like I said, I met him recently and was curious about, well, where he farmed, what he farmed, you know," Vic said.

"Gil ran the Association," Righty said.

"Association?" Vic said.

"Sugar beets," he said. "We had an association. Northern Colorado Sugar Beet Growers Association. About a dozen of us beet growers, we formed up this group, and we bought us a truck."

"Lots of trucks," Lefty said. Middleman was now blowing on his coffee, then sucking it in through his lips.

"We started with one," said Righty. "Fred here had a small front loader. We used the trucks to get our beets over to the plant. Well, that was a godsend for us. Let's see, I think we wound up with about a dozen trucks in the end."

Vic waved the girl on for one more coffee refill. "The end?"

"Henry over here," Righty said, nodding toward Middleman, "drove in a load of beets, and the foreman said he couldn't accept them. Plant was closed down."

"Laid off two-hundred-fifty people," Lefty said. "The wife was one of them, and my son. Good jobs."

Vic said, "What happened to your crop?"

"They kept a plant open in Cheyenne," said Middleman. "Had to truck the beets over to the rail. Now that wasn't too far. A mile or two. But they only gave us half what we were getting at the plant. Transportation costs, they told us."

"My ass," said Lefty. "We had a lot in the ground that year. I barely made expenses. That half was our whole profit."

"You made your expenses, though," Vic said. They paused and looked at him. Something told him that was the wrong thing to say.

"Lemme give you the Economics one-oh-one there of farming, uh, what'd you say your name was," Righty said.

"Vic."

"Vic. Okay, Vic. Yeah, it's always nice to make back what you put in. But the profits, Vic, the profits let you plan ahead a little, help buy seed, fertilizer, equipment—you name it, for the next season. Maybe there's a little left to take your family on a vacation."

"Disneyland," Middleman said. "No Disneyland that year."

"You guys have gone through that before," Vic said. "Like crop failures. Don't you have insurance for stuff like that?"

"Natural disasters, maybe," said Middleman. He sipped his cooling coffee. "But this weren't no natural disaster. It was the market. The so-called free market. No written contracts. No guaranteed price. No recourse, the plant said."

"It was a handshake deal," Righty said.

"Only we forgot to count our fingers," said Lefty, holding up a right hand with its pinky missing. Middleman all but blew cream-colored coffee out his nose laughing.

"Settle down, boys, or I'll have to call the sheriff," the high school girl said. "You done with that, hon?" Righty nodded, and she took his plate. He nudged his coffee cup an inch, and she obliged by filling it up. She topped off the rest of the half empty cups, finally Vic's, and scurried over to refill cups for a boisterous work crew.

"You want to know about Gil?" Middleman said. Vic nodded.

"Gil helped us all out," Middleman said. "He had some money put away."

"I still think it was everything he had," Righty said.

"No matter," Middleman said. "That man took care of the entire Association. He sold off, I think, seven or so of the trucks. Kept three or four and actually made some money hauling onions. He split that with us. Wasn't for him, we never would have got our crops in the ground that next year."

"Onions mostly," Lefty said. "Although I had some good luck with spinach."

"Me too," said Middleman. "And soybeans."

Vic said, "And Gil?"

"Gil had four farms," Righty said. "He didn't make it. Some scumbag low-ball trucking company came in from Kansas and sucked up most of the crop transport business. Gil lost the trucks. Then he planted everything in corn."

"Big mistake," Middleman said. "Five years too soon. Corn prices went into the toilet."

"We helped where we could, but we were still razor thin at the bank," Righty said. "Gil wound up selling three of the farms to pay off the fourth one. That one he gave to his daughter and her husband, Dave."

"And now they're in a fix," said Lefty.

"Gil's not too happy about that," said Middleman.

"I thought it was paid for," said Vic.

"Well, Dave bought that old combine, and then the new Deere tractor," Middleman said. "A hundred and fifty thousand for a tractor. Can you believe that?"

"There's four older ones, just as good, parked right across from the old beet plant," said Lefty. "Could a got one of those for, what? Fifty?" No one answered.

"Said he wanted one that was reliable, for the corn," Righty said. "Corn about killed his wife's daddy, and now he goes back into corn. Course, the prices are way up now."

"Ethanol?" Vic said.

"You bet," Middleman said. "Them wars and those gas prices. That's about all it takes."

"Global warming," Vic said.

"Oh gawd," Righty said. "Don't start with that now. It's right out there." He pointed out the window at a new gas station. "Those pump prices. That's all it is. All they're doin' is puttin' our money into their pockets."

"Corn is king again," Middleman said. "And it ain't for the breakfast table or taco shells. Dave's really bankin' on that. Hell, we all are."

"Then he put all that money into the new barn at Gil's old place," said Lefty. "He didn't really need to do that."

Righty said, "What about the pumps?"

The girl appeared and snapped up Vic's empty plate.

"Pumps?" Vic said.

"Dave's got three irrigation wells," Lefty said. "Had 'em all cleaned up and installed brand new pumps. About twenty thousand apiece?"

"For one pump?" Vic said, setting his coffee cup on the counter.

"With all the wiring," Lefty said. "And new well linings. Sure. Then he got three brand spankin' new pivot irrigators from Jim Behrens up there at Valley Irrigation."

"Dave was really countin' on this energy thing," Middleman said.

Righty drained his coffee cup. "Well, don't tell me you're not." Then, to Vic, "You know Dale Rau and his dad? Over east a Greeley?" Vic shook his head. "Well, they're buildin' three ethanol plants, and they're buyin' all the corn we can get to 'em for real money."

"And they've got the water up there to make the stuff," said Middleman.

"So what's the problem?" Vic said. "Dave's growing corn. The price is way up, because it looks like there's a market."

"Well that damn judge shut his wells off," Lefty said. His three-finger-one-thumb hand nearly spilled his coffee. "His corn is dying."

"Oh hell, it's gone, Fred," said Middleman. "It's been three weeks. Drove by there the other day. Sad sight. Sad. No way that crop's comin' back."

"Then Ferguson and the bank jumped all over it," Righty said. "Fort Lupton wants to annex that land and build houses. Farmers hold no sway anymore. Not 'round here at least."

"So Gil's pretty worried about his son's farm," Vic said.

"Son-in-law," Middleman said. "He's worried about his daughter. That's his only kid. Farm's in her name too."

"Oh, and he dotes on those grandkids of his too," Righty said. "He loves those two girls."

"Who wouldn't?" Middleman said.

"He mentioned something about a bill in the legislature to get the wells turned back on," Vic said.

"Lujak's bill," said Righty.

"That won't help Dave," Middleman said. "Too late. Imagine. Losing your father-in-law's last farm." He shook his head and then sipped some coffee.

"The bill might give Gil some leverage at the bank," Lefty said.

"Aw, they won't listen to us," Righty said.

"You might be surprised," Middleman said. Righty shook his head.

The bill won't help anyone if it's killed in committee, Vic thought. "He said something about a senior water right, on the South Platte."

Middleman said, "Who, Gil?"

Vic nodded.

There was a short, awkward silence. Then Middleman said, "Don't know about that."

More silence. The conversation seemed over.

At the cash register, Vic handed out his cards and asked the men to call if they heard any news about Dave Bender or his father-in-law, Gil. They were reluctant to give out their phone numbers, but Middleman, Henry Fowler, gave him his. Lefty and Righty said Vic could get a hold of them through Henry, but they did introduce themselves as Fred Van Gelder, Lefty, and Jim Keene, Righty. They all seemed to relish the notion that everything they talked about was "off the record." Vic told them it was for background only and shook their work-bitten hands in the parking lot before parting ways.

Vic sat in his Jeep for a while before starting it up. He went over the conversation again in his head. On his way back to Denver, he dictated what he could remember into his digital recorder.

# 49

From the Branding Iron, Vic drove west along State Highway 52 and turned left onto County Road 23. He drove for a while on the oiled gravel road running roughly parallel to the South Platte River before he turned west for a few miles and then south again. Vic often wandered these dirt, gravel, and blacktop roads that segmented off the sections of farmlands and ranches north of Denver.

Everything always seemed less orderly from ground level. When he flew into or out of Denver International Airport, Vic always marveled at the tidiness of civilization's squares and rectangles. Some of the dusty squares were all but filled with emerald green circles, indicating the use of the huge spindly pivot irrigation systems that rolled around fields on massive tires delivering water to the crops. Often that water came from high-volume irrigation wells, the kind the state was now shutting down.

Closer to the South Platte, the water could be taken directly from the river, provided the farmer had a senior right to use the liquid gold. River water was diverted by small dams into irrigation ditches and distributed to crops by a variety of mechanisms. Some farmers ran irrigation pipe down one end of a field. Small holes or gates in the pipe delivered water to each crop row. One of the fields had a dirt trench running along one side. Small u-shaped pipes had been placed upside down with one end in the trench and the other end at the beginning of each row. Irrigation water was then siphoned into the field, turning the shallow depressions between each crop row into mini canals filled with life-giving water.

He stopped his car by an irrigation gate, opened the windows, and listened to the water rush on by and into a cornfield. He thought about the rushing water in the irrigation canal by Rosenthal's ranch. Then he felt his shoulder slam into the control gate. He shivered. As he watched the moving water, he saw his life pass over the small spillway gate and irrigating a new era in his career. Returning to journalism at his age after such a long time did seem to be a nutty move, but he knew it was the right one.

Vic restarted the car and continued meandering through the checkerboard of farm fields and housing developments. Waist-high corn, a lot of it, marched in narrow rows down most of the planted fields. Corn and energy, he thought. Instead of growing food to feed us, they were growing crops to feed machines. If he were a farmer, he would probably do the same. If he had stuck with chemical engineering when he started out in college, he might even have been part owner of an ethanol plant today, he thought.

Not a farmer, not a chemical engineer, simply a plain old scribe, Vic was tired as hell, too tired to even think about all that he had learned that day. He found I-25 and sped home as fast as he could and crashed into his bed, leaving Baker unfed, unwatered, and bewildered. Still working the night shift, Vic set his alarm for three in the afternoon.

# 50

"Good morning, sunshine," Marsha said. "Get any sleep?"

"Not much," Vic said, collapsing in the chair at his usual spot when he worked the city desk. He set a venti Starbucks cup in front of him, a little to the right.

"Guatemalan?" Marsha said.

"Dark roast. I just say dark roast when I order, so I'm not really sure what it is."

"Other than strong," Marsha said. Vic nodded, and she said, "So, did you meet with, uh, what was his name?"

"Gil," Vic said. "Yes, I did." He took a sip from his coffee.

"And is there a story anywhere in all this?"

"I'm not sure," Vic said. "I think he was just a lonely old man. Retired farmer. His kid's in farming. Actually it's his daughter and son-in-law who took over his farm."

"What was so important that he had to see you at dawn?" Marsha said, heavy on the "you."

"I don't know. He saw my name in the paper on one of my stories, and he called me."

"Wild goose chase?" Marsha said.

"Well, no," Vic said. "I thought maybe a feature on his farming days might work, how they were different from what his kid has to face today. Something like that." Vic made it as vague as possible, vague enough so that neither Marsha nor Peggy would jot it down on the schedule, all but committing him to write something quickly.

"Oh boy," Marsha said, spinning her index finger in the air. "Another old farmer story."

"Do they actually have classes in cynicism these days in journalism schools?" Vic said. "There's not much else to teach, maybe how to do a web page." She glared at him.

"Can you work it on your own time?" she said. Vic glared back, then scrunched his eyebrows. Marsha caved. "I mean on the paper's time, but when things are slow."

"Sure. That's what I sort of had in mind."

"Keep us posted, will you?" Marsha said. Vic nodded. "In the meantime, Gary's on vacation, so I'm wondering if you could—"

"I know, a news obit," Vic said. A few years earlier, the *Sun* started running more detailed profiles on the recently departed, shedding more light on lives than what can be gleaned from the standard obituary. "You know, I actually read all of Gary's pieces. He does a great job. A real service to the community."

"Whatever," Marsha said. She tossed him a file folder. "He left a couple of leads. Pick one and run with it."

"Where's Peggy?" Vic said, leafing through the file.

"She's in a meeting with Christopher. You need her?"

"No. Just curious. Anything else right now?"

She shook her head and pointed to the file in Vic's hand.

"Okay, boss," Vic said. "You want me on the desk?" She shook her head, so he made his way back to his cubicle.

Jennifer Wilson was at her desk next to Vic's. Tall, darkish skin, long black hair with gray strands, Jennifer could have been Hispanic, but she was not, Middle Eastern, nope. She was Jennifer, attractive, happy, intelligent, and a boomer like Vic.

"Did you speak with Gil?" Jennifer said.

"I did," Vic said. "Bright and ugly this morning. Thanks for the message."

"No, he called again, about an hour ago."

Vic looked at his terminal and saw another pink post-it, this one dwelling in the lower left quadrant.

"Really? Did he say anything?"

"No, he seemed anxious to talk with you, though," Jennifer said.

"All right. I'll give him a call. Do me a favor, though, would you?" He took the pink post-it in his hand, crumpled it, and shoved it into his pocket.

"Name it."

"Don't mention this to the desk," he said, nodding toward Marsha at the other end of the room.

She grinned. "I love conspiracies. Got a hot one?"

"I don't really know," Vic said.

"Like hell you don't know, Bengston."

"Let me check it out," he said.

"This conversation never happened," she said, zipping her mouth shut like a mime.

# 51

"Betsy called," Gil said.

"Betsy?" Vic said. He did not use the paper's phone to return the call. My phone, my time, he thought.

"My daughter. Dave's wife."

"Sorry. I don't think I ever asked you her name."

"Well, it's Betsy," he said. "Named after her mother." Vic waited a moment for the coughing to stop. When Gil regained control of his breathing, he continued. "She said Dave's in a real state."

"What about?"

"She wouldn't say," Gil said. "Didn't want me to worry. Like I'm not going to worry. All I do is worry."

"I'm not sure what I can do, Gil," Vic said.

"I told her I talked to you," he said. "I thought maybe you could help."

"How?"

"With a story. Or your contacts. Maybe you can go out to Dave and Betsy's, talk to them, write something. I don't know."

Vic sensed that Gil was pushing him to cross that fuzzy line between being the reporter or being part of the story, becoming too involved, too much of an advocate. It might give the wrong people enough ammunition to get him canned. Flame out at fifty-nine, he thought, and all he wanted to do was write for the newspaper.

"I'll go see them," Vic said. "I'm not sure when I can shake loose, though."

"Don't wait too long," Gil said. "It might be too late."

"Too late for what?"

"I told you, the bank sent them papers. I can't do anything about it, financially at least."

"I hear you've got a lot of friends," Vic said. "Can they help?"

"Maybe, maybe not."

"Well, you need to check that out, Gil. I'm just a reporter down here. On probation too."

"That wasn't the way you did things last time," Gil said.

"Last time?" Vic said.

"When you used to be there," Gil said.

"I said I'd go out there," Vic said, a little perturbed. "I'm working here tonight. I'll go out tomorrow, in the afternoon."

"Remember where it is?"

"Yeah. Yeah. East of Fort Lupton. Road Twelve. I remember."

"Sign still says—" Gil said.

"Johanssan Farms," Vic said.

Gil started coughing again. "Gotta go."

"Okay, Gil, goodbye."

Vic was looking forward to catching up on his sleep, but he saw another short overnight in the sack ahead, after a long evening shift in the newsroom.

He opened the file Marsha had given him. On top was a memo written by the newsroom's main utility man, Norm Carbone, before he left on vacation. Vic skipped it and fished through the notes to find someone interesting to write about. He found one, some old guy who had died at the age of eighty-seven. The man had worked on the Williams Fork Project, which siphoned water from western Colorado over the Continental Divide for use on the state's thirsty Front Range.

"At least he had something to do with water," Vic said to his cubicle.

"You're talking to yourself again," Jennifer said from the other side of the fabric-covered wall.

"Comes with age, Jennifer."

"Tell me about it."

# 52

Dave and Betsy Bender's small single story frame house, white with black trim, sat maybe twenty or thirty yards up from the county road. Tattered gray asphalt shingles fought off the rain and snow. A red brick silo, missing its hemisphere cap, stood as a mute sentry behind the farmhouse and a bit to the right. The silo had long since fallen into disuse when the need to store grains on the farm evaporated with the increased mechanization of planting, harvesting, and shipping to market.

Machines now sped through the fields at harvest time, plucking only the needed grains, depositing them directly into trucks that headed directly to regional grain handling facilities operated by farmer co-ops, some of them allied with corporate agribusiness giants. From there, the bounty was trucked or trained to food or energy processors, depending on the grain. Parts of the plants not required by commercial agricultural interests were left in the fields to be plowed under so they could decay into the soil for the next crop.

The farms and the people who lived there working the land were left in the dust to sort out the year's economics and figure out how to pull it off again the following year, hoping the cycle would not be impeded by drought, hail, or a court order to shut off the irrigation wells. At least a drought or a crop shredding hailstorm could be attributed to the whims of nature, triggering emergency government loans to keep things going another season, to buy seed and fertilizer, keep the son in Ag school another year, make truck and tractor payments, get those braces for the daughter's teeth, or feed and shelter the family. But shutting off the wells by order of some judge who knew nothing about life on the land brought no such emergency relief. It only brought misery, foreclosure, repossession, and sometimes death.

It also brought the lawyers, hordes of them, the water lawyers who, as they emerged from their law school cocoons to fly among real humans in real life, saw the arcane specialty of water law in the West as a pathway to riches. The Benders and the Johanssons knew firsthand the value of the clear liquid that spewed skyward from the aquifers far beneath their feet. Water provided their families the ability to grow sugar beet crops season after season before the plunge in sugar prices wiped them out. But still the water was there, water from Mother Earth, water that gave their fields life, water that grew onions and potatoes for eastern markets and alfalfa hay for the region's livestock. When another energy crisis beset the country in the wake of terrorist attacks, Middle East wars, and high gasoline prices, water once again offered lucrative potential, this time to grow corn for profitable ethanol fuels, priced artificially low at the pump with taxpayer subsidies.

In the three years leading up to the court-ordered well shutoff, Dave and Betsy Bender's century-old roll top desk, which had borne the papers, the ledger books, and now the laptop computer with internet connection for the family's three-generation farming enterprise, had become engulfed in a tornado of engagement letters, court motions, depositions, orders, stays, pleadings, and invoices from the water lawyers who were systematically draining local farmers of their financial resources while those same farmers struggled with dwindling time, energy, and money to cultivate their fields. Finally, the water was cut off. Now the only things that flowed were loan demands from banks, foreclosure and repossession notices, flyers from farm and ranch auctioneers, and bankruptcy petitions. All of these items comprised the top layer of the Bender family paperwork.

While the water lawyers were mountain biking in Aspen and the Greeley judge was on a "much-needed," according to her clerk, one-month vacation in Greece, Dave Bender, sat in the hot sun on an old kitchen chair tipped back on two legs and leaned against the closed door of his large new barn. The building once housed his thundering John Deere tractor with air conditioned cab, a variety of well-maintained implements for disking, planting, and cultivating, along with a massive green combine with a corn head that could slip along twelve rows of corn with high-tech efficiency pulling each ear from the stalk, stripping each cob of its dried grain kernels and piping the grain into a closely following truck. All that was left in the barn was a workbench and a few tools. A crew from the Greeley office of Peabody Equipment Leasing had come down the week before when no one was home and repossessed the tractor, implements, and the combine.

The seat and back of the chair was covered with a shiny smooth red vinyl. Its chrome-plated steel frame reflected sunlight in all directions. Bender's mother bought six of them along with a matching plastic-topped chrome-legged kitchen table from Sears for next to nothing when Dave was a year old. Despite its age, the chair showed no signs of rust. Barely thirty-five miles away, in lower downtown Denver where "new urban" lofts ran about a million bucks each, chairs like the one Bender rested on would go for a hundred and fifty apiece because they were kitsch.

As a dust devil twirled, twisted, and danced its way across the broad farmstead driveway and equipment staging area, Bender thought he heard a car. He looked up from his reverie, thinking about the shooting of Bobbie Hague by their old friend, Jake, and looked back down at the twelve-gauge pump action shotgun resting on his lap.

Now the bank was coming for the farm.

# 53

An unassuming graded gravel strip in Weld County called County Road 12 guided Vic to the Bender-Johansson farm. A plain black mailbox, the twenty-dollar model from the Ace Hardware, guarded the left side of the driveway entrance. "Bender" was hand-painted on it in crude white lettering. On the other side of the driveway, a faded wooden sign fought with a massive rose bush for attention. The pale sign declared the property was "Johansson Farms," only someone had scratched out the final "s," something Vic thought might have been done in anger after Gil lost most of his farm property in the sugar beet crash.

Vic squinted and then stomped on his brakes, bringing his Jeep to a skidding halt. He swore he saw a shotgun or rifle across the man's lap. He picked up the small monocular he kept in the console tray and took a closer look at the man. It was a gun all right.

He considered leaving, but then pressed the button to lower the driver's side window. "Mr. Bender!" Vic called. Nothing, no movement. "Mr. Bender, could I speak with you?"

The farmer's ragged straw cowboy hat tilted up. He hesitated for a moment, adjusted his sunglasses, patted the shotgun in his lap, and then shouted, "You from the damn bank?"

"No," Vic shouted. "I'm from the *Rocky Mountain Sun*. A reporter. I wanted to talk to you about—"

The blast from the twelve-gauge sent a small flock of pigeons tearing from their perch across the top rim of the dilapidated silo. Vic jumped so high off the car seat his skull smashed into the headliner. He slammed the gearshift into reverse and pressed his foot hard on the brake, getting set to peel away. The shot was straight up into the air. As his heart crashed against his sternum, Vic thought about three things all at once: the story about the Bobbie Hague shooting, a dead lieutenant governor, and his own doctor who told him at his last annual physical that his blood pressure was on the high end of normal.

"You damn reporters! I've talked to you till I'm blue in the face. That's all you do is talk." Bender remained in his kitchen chair.

"I think I might be able help you," Vic said, thinking this feeble offering might be worth a try.

"Bullshit," Bender said, raising the gun barrel slightly.

He was right about that. This did not seem like it was going anywhere.

"I'm leaving," Vic said. He yelled it out the window. "You can work the shotgun thing out with the sheriff."

Vic rolled the Jeep backwards down the driveway, slowly.

"Wait," Bender yelled. "Wait a minute, will ya?"

Vic eased his foot off the gas, letting the Jeep come to a stop, but ready to tromp on the accelerator to get out of there.

"One more talk can't hurt at this point," Bender yelled. "Aw shit, I'm sorry. It was just to scare ya."

Bender stood up from the chair and started walking down toward Vic, but he stopped and spun around toward the house, and yelled, "Betsy." He stood there, holding the shotgun, his back to Vic. "Betsy!"

Gil's daughter, or at least Vic assumed it was Gil's daughter, pushed her way out the front screen door. Vic balanced his glasses on his nose again. He saw a full head of brunette hair, almost a forties hairdo, and a stunningly attractive face. She wore a simple flowered dress that came down a few inches past her knees, and white running shoes with white socks. She wiped her hands with a dark dishtowel. "Are you okay, Dave?"

Vic could hear her clearly. She was calm, poised, all of her the farmer's wife, and in control, or under control.

"Come get this," Bender said. "I've got to talk to this guy."

Vic held his right foot above the gas pedal.

Betsy strode down from the house and crossed the wide expanse to the barn. Casually, she tossed the dishtowel over her right shoulder, then stopped six feet away from her husband. With a quick snap of his left arm, Bender tossed the shotgun at his wife, who caught it easily with her left hand, the gun remaining vertical through its entire arc. Bender said something to her. Vic could not make it out, but she quickly pumped the shotgun four times, ejecting the remaining shells into the dirt, held the gun up breach open so Vic could see it and yelled, "It's empty." Then she cradled the shotgun in her arms as though she were a pheasant hunter about to start a sweep down a cornfield row and walked back toward the house. She and the shotgun disappeared through the screen door.

Bender turned and walked toward Vic, whose heart was frantically trying to escape from his chest and flop down onto the dusty driveway and quickly expire in the hot sun. Maybe I am getting too old for this, he thought, as he threw the car into park, cut the engine, jumped out, and moved quickly to the back, popping the hatchback and pulling out a fifteen-inch long piece of one-by-one oak that he kept in the car for protection.

"I'm awful sorry," Bender said, raising his hands up as a sign of submission and shaking his head. "I'm going nuts here. I'm truly sorry. I am. After what happened to Bobbie Hague, I don't want to take any chances." He wiped a tear from his eye. "I know that was stupid."

Vic felt his heart settle down a bit, but he decided to keep the Jeep between him and Bender for the moment. "Could we talk for a few minutes? I'm Vic Bengston, a reporter for the *Sun*."

Bender had stopped. He pulled off his hat and rubbed the back of his neck with a red handkerchief like the ones Vic's dad always carried around with him. The man before him was lean and brown, having spent much of his life outside exposed to the elements and horsing big things around the farm. Vic imagined him tossing hay bales onto wagons the way he had done one summer in high school. But he knew this guy did far more. Bender pulled off his sunglasses, folded them, and tucked them into a pocket on his faded blue denim shirt. The sleeves were cut off, revealing strong sinewy arms terminating in a pair of calloused hands that betrayed the work he did every day of his life. Thin kid leather work gloves poked out of one back pocket on his jeans. He was not wearing cowboy boots, something Vic had expected. Instead, Bender was wearing a relatively new pair of heavy-duty work boots with rounded toes, protected, no doubt, with metal on the inside.

"You're the guy Gil told us about," Bender said. "You look too old for a reporter."

"You may be right," Vic said, thinking that he was right. "Nevertheless, I am the reporter who talked with Gil."

"Had one girl out here, from TV, channel nine I think," Bender said. "Well, she come out here in her dainty high heels and skirt. Wind came up that day. She had a hell of a time keeping that skirt down. Her crew guys and I just shook our heads. Didn't bother us.

She was, what? All of twenty-four or so. Crew guys were older. Guess they'd seen it all."

With his right hand, he pointed out past Vic's Jeep, out toward the road.

"She stood out there and did her little thing after she talked to me," he said. "I didn't even see it on the TV. We get three stations out here now that the satellite's cut off. Don't know when it ran. Couple of fellows over at Lil's Café said they saw me on TV. They was hopin' something would get done, get the wells back on, but nothin' happened. I don't know. Hey, I'm really sorry about that shotgun." He stretched an empty right hand.

Vic tossed the oak club into the back of the Jeep and walked up to Bender. A thought jolted him. What if the guy had a handgun or a knife? His heart started throbbing again. I've got to call Nelson, he thought, and get a knife or something, or some kind of self-defense training. Trembling, Vic reached out with his right hand. The two clasped their hands with genuine firmness and looked at each other. Vic wondered who was the amateur and who was the pro in this dusty farm driveway in northeastern Colorado.

"Dave Bender," the farmer said, beginning the ritual of shaking out a cigarette from a pack of Camels. He offered one to Vic, who shook his head.

"Vic. Vic Bengston."

"The *Rocky Mountain Sun* hurt us bad, Vic," Bender said. "They sided with that damn Greeley judge."

"Well, I know that, but you have to understand, the editorial department doesn't actually run the news department."

"Since when? There hasn't been one sympathetic story about us farmers in the *Sun*. *Times* ran a whole series."

"Okay, but that was before I joined the *Sun* staff," Vic said, playing for time. "I'm looking into this irrigation well story and how it affects you guys. It's a feature."

"My ass," Bender said. "You want to know why the lieutenant governor was killed?"

"Other reporters are working on that, not me," Vic said, wondering why Bender even brought up the Swain murder. "It's a crime story anyway."

"The crime is what that judge did to us," Bender said. "And what that state water engineer did to us. You looked at the river? The ditch companies? The state water supplies?"

"Not yet," Vic said.

"We've got more damn water now than we've ever had. That drought's over. They didn't have to shut down those wells this year."

"You had, what, five years to buy water rights? And a bunch of you didn't do it," Vic said.

"Couldn't do it is more like it," Bender said, his voice raising an octave, flashing anger. "Couldn't!"

Vic edged closer to his car. "How hard did you try?"

"I tried about twenty-five thousand dollars' worth, all our savings," said Bender. "I know for a fact that Bobbie sunk fifty thousand into our legal fund. Everything he had. We pissed our money down a rat hole with those lawyers down there on Seventeenth Street. Ten of us put up all we had, and we got nothin' but piles of paper. I swear some of that money went into the judge's pockets too. We've lost everything, and nobody gives a damn, not even that sweet Democratic governor who claims to have grown up on a Colorado farm. After all that, what in hell could you and the *Raunchy Mountain Sun* do to help?"

"Fair question," Vic said.

"What about a fair answer?" Bender said.

"Do you think there might be a connection between your legal problems and the murder of the lieutenant governor?" Vic said, grasping at straws.

The suggested link darkened Bender, who dragged on his cigarette and held it all in. He looked out across his withering cornfield, then exhaled the smoke through his nose. The ash had grown to an inch in length, and when he spoke it flipped off into the air and flittered away with the wind.

"See that field?" Bender said, sweeping his right arm before him.

Vic could not really miss it. The two were standing at the edge of several hundred acres of stunted yellowing corn.

"Shouldn't that corn be taller?" Vic said.

"Damn right! The sixty-four gol darn dollar question," Bender said. "You're lookin' at the end of two, no really three generations of family farming in this area," Bender said.

"Who's two and who's three?"

Bender did not look at Vic when he spoke. He continued his gaze out across his dried up cornfields. "Well, my daddy and his daddy farmed out that away for a long time, but when I was away at school the sugar beet thing wiped them out, and they lost it all. Betsy's dad, though, well, he had four farms out here and some trucks. He lost everything but the one farm. That's this one, the one I'm gonna personally lose for him." Then he turned and looked directly at Vic. "That's a fine gift from a son-in-law now, isn't it?"

"I'd like to write your story," Vic said. It was really his only card to play. "Maybe some publicity could help, maybe even get the wells turned back on."

"Maybe. Maybe. Maybe. That's what we got from the damn lawyers. Maybe won't turn that field back into corn, Vic. It's too late. Maybe won't get Betsy and me to market with the grain that old Emil Rau and his kid can turn into alcohol so you can run all over the state in your flex-fuel SUVs and write stories about nothing."

He had a point, Vic thought. The garbage that passed for news these days was hardly fit to line a birdcage.

"What if I had been from the bank?" Vic said.

"I don't know, Vic. Betsy wanted me out there with the shotgun, sort of a show of force. But if you had been Ben, I don't know what I would a done."

"Ferguson?" Vic said.

"You know him?"

"No," Vic said. "Just heard his name. From the bank, right?"

"Fort Lupton Bank," Bender said. "They sent me a notice."

"Foreclosure notice?" Vic said.

"Two months, Ben said, like it was a gift," Bender said. He looked down and wiped his hands on his jeans. Then he pinched both his eyes with the thumb and forefinger of his right hand and wiped his pants again. "Eighty years. We've been out here since 1928, my family at least. But we Benders, we survived the dust bowl, the depression, grasshoppers, droughts, you name it. Eighty years. Gil started up in forty-eight. I'm losing the last of his farms. I can't even stand to face him anymore. Then Ben Ferguson, my old high school buddy, leaves a message on my cell phone. Says we can stay here another two months, like it's a grubby handout."

"I thought you farmers could rewrite your notes," Vic said. "Can't you secure some water rights, muddle through the year and then refinance?"

"We're not government insured," Bender said. "It's just a conventional farm note with the bank. Ben said that would be cheaper."

"Cheaper how?" Vic said.

"You got a mortgage?" Bender said.

"Sure, who doesn't?" Vic said.

"What's your interest rate?" Bender said.

"I don't know. Six per cent. Maybe five and three-quarters. I can't remember."

"Mine's two per cent," Bender said. "But no government

backing. Ben knocked down the rate. Saved me a bundle, or so I thought. He took a share of the crop."

"Ferguson covered himself both ways," Vic said. "With the energy boom your corn would have been worth a bundle. He'd share in that. If you crashed, he just forecloses."

"And we crashed." Bender pointed toward the west. "You see those houses way over there?" Vic nodded. "Well, Fort Lupton wants this land so it can do the same thing here. Or, so Ben and his pals can do the same thing here."

"They're not going to budge an inch, are they?" Vic said.

"No they're not," Bender said. "Hey, do you have some time?"

"For what?" Vic grew wary.

"I want to show you something," Bender said. "Jump in the pickup."

"Far from here?" Vic was not sure about this guy.

"No, over by the river," Bender said.

Down by the river, Vic thought, out of sight, out of earshot. Like Jessica Swain.

A little voice said leave. The other stronger one hinted at a story, and not some lightweight feature about farming. Bender knew something. Vic wanted to find out what. He ignored the strong voice.

"As long as it doesn't involve guns," Vic said.

Bender laughed. "I said I was sorry."

"I like to hunt birds," Vic said. "But I hate getting shot."

# 54

Bender tossed his cigarette butt into the dirt and ground it down with dusty work boots. He walked with purpose toward a new-looking Chevy Silverado pickup with a shiny metallic blue-gray finish. Vic went around to the passenger side, opened the door, and looked up into a cab big enough to hold a family of six along with a small horse.

"This is a Sherman tank," Vic said.

"Can't run a farm without one. You gettin' in?"

"Where's the elevator?"

"Climb up!"

Vic reached high with his right hand to begin his ascent. Carabineers and a rope might have helped, he thought. Maybe a piton or two. He strained to step up eighteen inches with his left leg, planted his foot, and swung himself all the way up to the summit, landing in a comfortable leather seat on the front passenger side.

"How big is this thing, the engine?" Vic said.

"Six point seven liter diesel. Turbo. V-eight. Four hundred

horses. Torque like you wouldn't believe. Burns bio-diesel."

"Bio-diesel," Vic said. "Non-OPEC. Corn."

"All American fuel," Bender said. "Douglas Motors has been calling me day and night."

Vic recognized the name Douglas. The old man, Bill Douglas was in the legislature back when Vic covered the statehouse. Douglas Motors was one of the Ford dealerships in Greeley.

"What do they want?" Vic said.

Bender growled, "They want the damn truck back."

He gunned the pickup and fishtailed out his driveway onto the road and headed west.

Vic knew this war horse was not all ego. It was a tool that carried the Bender family to all of their activities in the county. They pulled stuck equipment out of mud with it, helped neighbors, hauled hay, crops, seed, fertilizer, and horse trailers. Its massive tires hogging the narrow dirt farm and ranch roads, this jumbo truck was an essential implement that cost too much and probably lasted too few years the way he had seen them used out in the countryside. Farmers like Bender mortgaged their souls and their family legacies to keep things happening out on the land, to put food on our tables, and now fuel in our gas tanks, fuel that doesn't demand international troop mobilization or loans from Chinese banks.

"How much corn do you have to harvest just to pay for this truck?" Vic said.

"More than you can imagine," Bender said.

"Do you have a number?"

"I gotta think about it," Bender said. "Look, there's a guy has a place about the same size as mine, few miles down this road. Weird name. Sounds like Jeff, but he spells it G-E-O-F-F. Geoff Martin. Anyway, I want to show you his place."

"Does he use wells for irrigating?" Vic said.

"Yeah, he does." Bender shook his head.

"What's the matter?" Vic said.

"You know what the hell of it is?" Bender said.

"What?"

"The guy's a plastic surgeon. In Denver. Grew up on a farm. Says he missed it, so he bought this one, oh, five, six years ago."

"Okay, so he's a relative newcomer," Vic said. "That can't be all bad." Vic supposed the locals always viewed gentlemen farmers suspiciously. All of us resist change.

"Aw, it's not just that," Bender said. "Geoff plays the game. Joined the Grange, put some money into the barrel-racing rink over to Steuben's ranch. Even came out to help us paint the little announcer's hut we built for the rink, and donated the public address system. Good guy."

"So what is it?" Vic said.

"When he was in college, you know before medical school, up in Fort Collins. His roommate, I am told, was Gary Kendrick."

"Water lawyer." Vic casually tossed out the words, like he knew the guy, but did not care much about him.

"No, Bender said. "The water lawyer. The very same jackass we've been pumping our money into to get our irrigation water back. Slick little bastard, that Kendrick."

"How so?" Vic said.

"While he was taking our money, Kendrick and one of his lawyer buddies waltzed over to the doc's place last winter," Bender said. He shook another unfiltered Camel out of the shrinking pack and lit it up. "Pulled the damned wool over his medical school eyes. Don't get me wrong. I like the doc, but he's a bit too gullible for farming."

"Bring me up to speed, Dave. What happened?"

"Well, Kendrick brought this good old boy lawyer over to the doc's. He wanted to buy a section of doc's land, out there along the river." Bender blew smoke out of the corner of his mouth and waved the cigarette hand to the west, toward the South Platte River. "Hobby farm he called it, for his horses. You ever been up and down this river? North of Denver?"

"A lot," Vic said.

"What do you see, through that whole valley from Commerce City north?" It was rhetorical question. Vic waited for the answer. It came after another long drag on the Camel. "Gravel pits. All up and down the river valley."

Vic knew what Bender was talking about. When he and his folks took rides through the South Platte River Valley farm country north of Denver, the pits were evident everywhere. Some considered them scars, while others viewed them as lucrative building materials, gravel riches deposited on the plains by the erosion of the Rocky Mountains. Wet pits were abandoned, left to fill up with river water that flowed through the entire valley a few feet below the surface. Dry pits indicated areas still being worked by tangles of heavy equipment covered with flaking yellow paint and rust, conveyor belts, and screens sorting the material into different sizes and consistencies. Construction companies bought the gravel and sand to build the housing, office, and retail complexes that were rapidly replacing farm and ranch land in a frenzied effort to recreate Southern California in the middle of Colorado.

"Well, I know there are a lot of them," Vic said, to keep the conversation moving. "Some houses are going in around some of the old pits."

"Million dollar houses," Bender spat out. "They excavate the shores, build them up, plant trees, so these bastards from Denver can come up here with their little ski boats and ride around those little pits in little circles, pulling kids behind them on water skis. Aw, my daughter even does that, with one of her friends. Her old man works downtown. He's a damn lawyer too."

Vic sensed Bender was getting off track. "What about the doctor and his land?"

Bender looked blankly out across the plains toward the east, then back to the west toward the river and said, "The doc's really a good guy. He wanted no part of gravel mining. He wanted to keep that land just the way it was, in hay or some other crop."

The truck rolled to a stop on a small bluff overlooking the South Platte. Ribbons of water wove in and out of sand bars and small emerald islands. A heron stalked prey. The two men disembarked. Bender, distracted again, pointed at a stone monument about thirty feet away.

"Historical society, the ladies, put that up," Bender said. "Supposed to be the site of Fort St. Vrain, one of the first trading posts out here."

"You don't think it's accurate?"

"I think it was an easy spot for the stone. Those folks weren't that dumb. Can you imagine them hauling stuff from the river way down there, up this hill, more like a cliff, to the fort out here on the plains, exposed to the wind, rain, and Indians?"

"You have another theory?" They were drifting again. Vic decided to pull them back on course.

"There's an old homestead down there by the river," Bender said. "That's probably where the fort was, not up here."

"So where's the doc's place?" Vic said.

Bender turned around, and jerked his head toward the south. "Over there."

The southern end of a hay field below them terminated at an eight-foot chain link fence with barbed wire on the top. Two mountains of sand stood silent on the other side, but diesel trucks, bulldozers, and huge gravel processing contraptions created a din that spread throughout this part of the river valley.

"That was the doc's land?" Vic said.

"A section of it," Bender said. "The one he sold off."

"I thought he wanted his small farm."

"We all thought that," Bender said. "Even the doc thought that. The good ole boy lawyer told the doc all he wanted to do was run a few horses on it. White fences. Hay barns. A horse farm. Well, okay, we thought. We could have put it to better use, but a small horse ranch, a hobby ranch, wasn't all that bad."

"Can he just do that?" Vic said. "Buy the land, then start digging?

"Well, Kendrick and that other lawyer were pretty darn low about it. The new landowner moved a few head out there, so it looked like he was true to his word. But a month or so after he took over the property, he pulled a core-drilling rig onto the land. I knew exactly what he was doing, that bastard. Gettin' gravel samples. We got the county to stop them dead in their tracks. Guy had a gravel contract for some big box store wantin' to dig that up. They'd already been kicked out of Adams County."

"Well, they're plainly digging now," Vic said.

"Sure, they bought off the town."

"Fort Lupton?"

"Yeah," Bender said. "When the county turned 'em down, that hobby ranch lawyer went to the town council and got them to annex the land. Kendrick had a hand in that too. Heard about that sometime later."

"That happens a lot in Colorado," Vic said.

"We made 'em put in tons of erosion control, pretty much gave 'em a hard time," Bender said. "But they're diggin.'"

"How long will they be in there?" Vic said.

"Hundred years," Bender said. "Broke my Mom's heart. She grew up out here. That land was once part of our family farm, the one we lost in the sugar beet crash. The old house where mom grew up was on that section too, before we moved it up closer to the road." He pointed back up toward the paved road. "But the big old farm house, the two story job over there, the one mom raised me in, we had to sell that."

"I doubt if the gravel miners will stay down there for a century," Vic said.

"Doesn't really matter now," Bender said. "They swung back pretty hard."

"How?" Vic said.

"The wells," Bender said.

"I'm not sure what you mean," Vic said. "Damaged them? What?"

Bender looked over toward the gravel operation, then back to Vic, and said, "That little bastard lawyer turned us into the state water engineer for illegal irrigation wells. That's what was watering my corn. Would have been a hell of a year. Already had the crop sold to the ethanol co-op up near Ault."

"Your crop was already in the ground," Vic said. "Why cut the water off then?"

"Didn't make a hill's worth of difference to them," Bender said. "We never thought they'd do it to us. Even our damn state senator walked away from us. He grew up on a farm over near Platteville and should know better. They paid him off. Paid off that lame city council too."

"Who did?" Vic said. Bender seemed so sure of himself, so absolute about his accusation. Everyone says politicians are paid off. Very few come up with the proof.

"Gary Kendrick," Bender said.

"Can you prove it?" Vic said.

"I can't," Bender said. "But I know who can."

"And who would that be?" Vic said.

"Not at liberty to say," Bender said. He reached for the cigarette pack and ran through his light-up routine.

"Dave, I'm a little confused here," Vic said. "Isn't Kendrick the lawyer you're using to get the wells turned back on?"

"Got no choice with that right now," Bender said. "We're in way too deep. We're stuck with him. Bobbie's got things set up with Kendrick. We argued a bit over that. Bobbie doesn't think Kendrick's playing both sides. No one does, but me. I gotta wait, bide my time. Anyway, he's got our money, and if he's got the connections, well, I just want my damn water back on."

"Kendrick's name seems to come up an awful lot," Vic said.

"That's 'cause he's Mister Water Lawyer," Bender said. Then the farmer, battered by life far beyond his years, looked again at the land where his mother grew up, and, again, he pinched the tiny isthmus between his eyes. To the sky, to the river, and to the mountains of sand covering the old family farm, he said, "When this is over, he'll be next."

A shiver ran down Vic's spine as he pictured the remains of Jessica Swain so inelegantly tangled in the snag on the South Platte River.

"What are you saying?" Vic said. "What do you mean next?"

Bender hesitated, like he was mulling over his words. "If he's screwing us, we'll, or I'll, file a complaint about it with the court or whoever looks into that sort of thing." Somehow, Vic could not picture this man taking such a measured approach to solving a problem, or settling a dispute.

"You know, airing it out in public might help," Vic said, handing out the old public-has-the-right-to-know pitch.

"Why, so you can sell more damn papers?" Bender said, sounding a bit more vicious than Vic would have preferred. Everyone seemed to be the enemy of the media.

"We do more than sell papers, Dave," Vic said, knowing it was a half-truth. Advertising wanted the revenue. Reporters still wanted the glory. Informing the public was an added benefit, often a justification. "If you want to go public, let me know."

Bender fiercely sucked in tobacco smoke from the Camel. "They killed my mother," he said flatly.

"What?" Vic said.

Vic's short question snapped Bender out of his nicotine-induced reverie. "Well, might as well have," he said. "When they scraped the topsoil off her cow pasture and knocked down the old barn I thought she'd die right then. She raised six blue ribbon Herefords from calves down there when she was a kid. Won ribbons. A lot of memories were wiped off that land when they went in for the gravel."

"And now?" Vic said.

"She's dead now," Bender said. "Died a month ago, a week after they shut off my water. Massive heart attack. They say that doesn't happen a lot with women."

"My God, Dave, I'm sorry. I had no idea, really—"

"Aw, you didn't know."

"Honestly, I'm really sorry," Vic said. "I wouldn't have bothered you so soon. How old was she?"

Bender finished the Camel, twisted its ash on the back of his boot to make sure it was out and ground the remains into the soil.

"Seventy-three," he said, sucking in a long drag on his cigarette. "And I have to lie back for now and keep dealin' with that bastard on the wells."

"Kendrick?" Vic said.

Bender nodded.

"I thought the other lawyer turned you in."

"I'd bet my life that Kendrick was behind it," Bender said. "He drove the final nail into mother's coffin."

# 55

Vic climbed up the dimly lit narrow stairway to the offices on the third floor of the dark brown brick building on the northwest corner of Colfax Avenue and York Street. Only the first floor had changed. What was a bank decades ago was now a trendy and hip Italian bistro with a menu and a brand catering to Gen X or Gen Y or whatever Gen was tweeting and facebooking these days. He wondered if his city editor frequented the joint. Peggy probably lived around the corner, he thought, in one of the new urban condos squeezed in amongst the century old brick residences that dominated the neighborhood. At the third story Vic rested. The creaky wood floors, heavy oak office doors with frosted glass windows, spindly light fixtures, even the musty old building odor, were all the same, as though time had ceased to advance a dozen feet or so above the pavement.

When Vic spoke to Evelyn Cosgrove on the phone, she sounded tiny and old and far away, as though the decades-long battles over coal mining, wetlands, wilderness, clean water, and clean air had extracted nearly all of the life force from her. It was the same office she had when he first visited her, he a newly minted reporter for *United Press International,* she the stubborn coordinator for the Western Environmental Working Group. Only "W.E.W.G." was stenciled on the frosted glass of her office door, which was open barely a crack. The lower left edge of the "G." had flaked off. Vic pushed on the door. It creaked as it swung open enough for him to step through.

"Hello Vic," came a small voice from deep within a canyon flanked on the left by a wall of bookcases littered with volumes, papers, and dog-eared reports, and on the right by a bright west-facing window. She sat barricaded behind a massive wooden desk, beaten, worn, scratched, dented, and blanketed with more books, more papers, and more reports.

"Is that you down there Evelyn?"

"The remainder," she said. "How have you been Vic? Didn't you have kids?"

"I did. They're all grown up," Vic said.

"Grandkids?" she said.

"Two, both boys," Vic said.

"I thought something had happened to me when I saw your name in the *Sun.* Time warp, or the like."

"Back from the dead," Vic said.

"Back from corporate America," she said. "Guilty conscience?"

"No guilt," Vic said. "I followed Kurt Vonnegut's advice."

"Which was?" she said.

"It's okay to work for the Man, so long as you did nothing evil," Vic said.

"As I recall," Evelyn said. "You helped pass a tax bond issue in Mesa County that assisted the oil shale industry."

"God, that was more than twenty years ago, Evelyn, and, as I recall, it was to help the county deal with the impacts from the development."

"Which never happened," she said. "Oil shale went bust and the county with it."

"I wasn't a fortune teller," Vic said. "A little evil? Still, we knew back then that oil shale would never be developed. It never will. You know that."

"None of us are clean," Evelyn said.

"What about you?"

"I still smoke like a chimney, and I drive an SUV," she said.

"Nobody's perfect."

She handed him a stack of papers. "This is what you want."

"I'll read it all," Vic said.

"I know you will," she said. "You always were a good boy with your homework, very thorough."

"Could you net it out for me?" Vic said. "Give me the executive summary."

Evelyn sat back, removed her reading glasses, and tossed them onto the desk. She was petite, but the woman that Vic was looking at was almost microscopic. Yet she still had that powerful slow-talking, measured way about her.

"I wasn't in on any discussions with Jessie," she said. "Very hush hush. I think she thought I might leak it to the press. She knew me pretty well. But I heard things."

"What did you hear?" Vic said.

"Will it be in the paper?"

"Not sure. Right now, I'm trying to get a handle on this water right angle."

"Who are you pursuing this for, Vic? The farmers, the developers, or the politicians? Certainly not the conservationists."

She had a way of drilling down to the core of anyone's motivations.

"Like any honest journalist, Evelyn, I'm pursuing this for me," Vic said.

"Let the chips fall where they may, then," she said. "Not like the old days."

"No. Not like the old days." Back then, the chips fell more on the environmentalist side of the ledger. "I'm done with partisanship, and I'm done with advocacy."

"Fair enough," she said. "Now we know where we stand. I've become a little more cynical. You've become a little more objective, in your 'I'm-out-for-me' sort of way."

"Well, objectivity never made much sense anyway. If you agree with the story, it's objective. If you don't, then it's subjective. I'm just not afraid of anyone any more, Evelyn."

"Not even your boss?" she said.

"Hogan or Mayer?" Vic said.

"Well, Hogan. He's the publisher."

"Hell no," Vic said. "It's a fluke I even got hired. I wonder how long I can last."

"Still don't play well with others?"

"No, it's not that," Vic said. "Jury's still out for me. You'd think they'd be able to deal with a baby boomer rookie in off the street."

"Age discrimination not what it's cracked up to be?" she asked.

"I thought that was all behind us," Vic said. "Naive me."

"They've still got a few old farts down at the *Sun*," she said. "Hoffman was at the statehouse with you, wasn't he?"

"Sure. If they're in the game, the guild keeps them there, but none of that applies to new hires, believe me," Vic said.

"Then why did Hogan hire you?"

"My guess? On a whim. He never told me. Technically, I'm an editor, part of management, and not under the guild contract."

"Oh, so Hogan can fire you at whim as well," she said.

Vic nodded and smiled.

"But you don't care, do you?" she said.

"Not one twit," Vic said.

"Good," she said and hunched herself forward. "This is all about you, then."

"Damn straight," Vic said.

"Well, I still owe you. So, this is on deep background, okay?"

"Okay," Vic said. "I'll find corroborating sources."

"Jessie was about to gain control of a senior water right on the South Platte River, a very senior right," Evelyn said. "1887, I think. The ownership track is fairly convoluted, but the right was owned by a family that had farmed up near Fort Morgan. One of Jessie's relatives. A death in the family passed ownership of several farms and water rights into some sort of trust. Jessie was the trustee."

"Do you know what she was planning to do?"

"The trust was designed to protect the interests of the farms and the river system. The language was pretty vague, I'm told."

"She was pushing it, then? The language?"

"Seems so," Evelyn said. "She wanted to switch the right to cover minimum stream flow as a way to protect the lower river basin. Primarily for migratory water fowl.".

"I thought agriculture took priority," Vic said.

"Not always. I doubt if she'd be able to convert the entire water right exclusively to minimum stream flow. Even so, what she was going to do would have tied up the right for years in the water courts."

"So that would delay housing developments or even municipal use for a few years," Vic said.

"Delays everything" she said. "Fort Lupton wants to annex the farm land. That's a big new tax base once the houses are built. But without the water right sewn up, the annexation probably wouldn't go through."

"So Democrat Michaels lines up with Republican Currington on the statewide water development bond issue and they quietly work to stop Lujak's irrigation well bill for the farmers," Vic said.

"Marriage made in heaven," Evelyn said.

"Lujak is a Democrat. Whatever happened to party loyalty?" Vic said.

"No longer in fashion," she said. "Don't you read the papers?"

Vic shook his head. "I get all my news from those large type screaming emails that all my old friends forward to me every day."

"The ones that keep circulating year after year?"

"Exactly," Vic said. "Why read when you can be fed?"

"You are a naughty boy," she said. "Your old friends must love you."

"They think I'm nuts," Vic said.

"And so they should."

"You're sure about Lujak," Vic said. "He's the farmers' poster child."

"As far as I can tell," she said.

Only Lujak was in on the deal. Mister Farmer Senator was all in with Currington, Michaels, and Kendrick. Evelyn did not know that and Vic was not about to mention it to her, preferring instead to remain the central repository of all data relating to his investigation.

"Like everything, it's about the color of money," Vic said.

"Green grease," Evelyn said.

"And Kendrick plays the balancing act, running hither and yon from one interest to another," Vic said.

"Playing both sides of the fence when he can," she said, "but nobody in this government wants to challenge him on it."

"It might be tough to prove," Vic said. "Let's get back to politics for a minute. Assume Currington's financial future is tied up in the housing development."

"All right, I'll assume," she said.

"Michaels' political future is dependent on support from the likes of Currington," Vic said.

"And every municipality and developer that needs water," Evelyn said.

"Lot of green there," Vic said. "Especially for campaign war chests."

Evelyn nodded.

"Lot of motive there," Vic said.

"For what?" Evelyn said.

"To kill the lieutenant governor before she transferred the water right or tied it up for ten years," Vic said.

"You sure?" Evelyn said, scrunching her tiny face.

"Why not?" Vic said. "Currington and Michaels have a lot at stake."

"That sounds more like New Jersey than Colorado," she said.

"Didn't Al Packer eat his political foes?" Vic said. "At least the judge who sent him to jail said so."

"Good point," she said. "Politicians often eat their young. You really think these guys killed her? That's pretty horrific."

"I do have my doubts about Michaels," Vic said. "He seems a tad too ambitious, an opportunist, but not a real killer"

"Not like on TV, huh?"

"No, but Currington and Kendrick seem connected enough to have it done," Vic said, realizing if they were that connected they could have him killed too. "It is ironic though."

"What's that?" Evelyn said.

"The farmers hated Jessie Swain, but they would have been better off if she were alive and gumming up the water right transfer in courts for years, so they might have a chance to keep using that water."

"Have you run across anyone nutty enough to kill her?" Evelyn said.

"Other than Currington and Kendrick, there are a couple of farmers out there wound tight enough to do it."

"Misplaced anger," She muttered, peering up at him and grinning broadly. "Those farmers are getting screwed by their own lawyer, and they don't even know it."

# 56

"Hey, Bengston, you still remember where the statehouse is?"

Vic looked up from his city desk work and saw Mal Hoffman carrying two grande Starbucks coffees. "Vaguely."

"I assume you still drink coffee," Hoffman said, setting one of the cups in front of Vic.

"Sorry, I'm strictly double cinnamon dolce latte," Vic said.

"Bull," Hoffman said. "This was the darkest roast they had."

"Thanks," Vic said. "Statehouse. That's the place up on the hill, isn't it? What's the occasion? Those must have set you back a half a day's pay."

"You, maybe. I'm way beyond top scale."

"They started me all over again, cheapskates that they are," Vic said.

"It's all about the bottom line these days," Hoffman said.

"At least I didn't have to know how to program a web page," Vic said. "And they're paying me as an assistant managing editor."

"They probably assumed you didn't know how to turn on a computer," Hoffman said. He pulled a chair around and sat down.

"Still drink it black?" Hoffman said, nodding toward the paper cup.

"He remembers," Vic said. "How sweet."

They put in a few late nights together covering the legislature, actually a ton of nights.

"You know what they say?" Hoffman said.

"No, what do they say?"

"The one thing a newspaperman needs is a long memory," Hoffman said.

"Well, I do still retain a slight notion of where the statehouse is located," Vic said. He could see the gold capitol dome through the east facing windows. "And your memory is still aided by two sugars and cream, right?"

"Pink sugar now. Diabetes." Hoffman picked up a notebook and set his coffee down on the corner of the desk.

"When did that happen?" Vic said.

"About ten years ago," he said. "Came on slowly."

"Insulin?" Vic said.

"No, thank God," Hoffman said. "Gulp pills and watch the diet."

Vic welcomed a break from rewriting press releases and obits, but he knew Hoffman wanted something.

"So what's up?" Vic said.

"Suzanne called in sick. I need some help up at the statehouse."

"I seem to be the utility man around here," Vic said.

"Is that so bad? The go-to guy? At least you're performing a useful function while the brass gets used to you. I need someone to sit in on a senate Ag committee hearing and take some notes."

"Feedlots, pork bellies, and such?"

Hoffman opened his notebook and flipped through a few pages. "Senate Bill 305."

"That's Lujak's irrigation well bill," Vic said.

"You know it?" Hoffman sounded surprised.

"Sure. That's the one the farmers are backing, to get those irrigation wells turned back on."

"Well, sure they want to," Hoffman said. "But the cities and their developer pals are against it."

"You're expecting fireworks up there?"

"I don't think so. I'm told the meeting will be short, just to hear from the state engineer. He's supposed to tell the committee that turning about two hundred irrigation wells back on won't materially harm the South Platte River basin aquifer, at least in the short term. No vote is scheduled. All I want is something on what the engineer says. A copy of his testimony if you can get it. Good quote wouldn't hurt. It'll be a brief on the legislative page tomorrow."

"Simpson's been shutting down the wells," Vic said. "Plus, he issued a preliminary report saying the wells screwed up the river."

"Simpson is re-thinking his first report. He's acting under court orders and pressure from Governor Dowd," Hoffman said. "Dowd was acting under pressure from Swain."

"Who is now terminally dead."

"Correct. That was a nice story, by the way, on your first day back. I told Hogan picking journalism back up for you would be like getting back on a bicycle."

"Anything but this," Vic said, spreading his hands over the stacks of obit forms and press releases on the city desk. "Did you run it by the boss?"

"Hogan?" Hoffman said.

"No, the real one, over there," Vic said, nodding toward Peggy.

Peggy stopped pretending not to hear. She looked up and said, "I think I can spare the rookie for a few hours."

"Senate Committee Room 353," Hoffman said. "Two o'clock."

"Who do I know up there?" Vic said.

"No one," Hoffman said. "They're either dead or term limited out of office."

"So it's all our kids, then, running the state?" Vic said.

"Mostly. Bring back your notes. I'll give you the tour of the new press room some other time."

Vic took a long draw from his coffee. "You didn't need to bring such gifts."

"A peace offering," Hoffman said.

"For?"

"The hard time we gave you when you showed up," Hoffman said. "You've got to admit, it was pretty funny seeing you walk in the door."

"Ha ha."

"For the record, they should have left you on the Swain story," Hoffman said.

# 57

"You're legal," the state trooper minding the statehouse security screening line informed him.

"Don't tell anyone," Vic said, "I've got a reputation to uphold."

After clearing security, Vic grabbed his fountain pen, cell phone, car keys, digital recorder, Timex wrist watch, and stuffed them back into his pants pockets, all except the watch. Then he slung his small computer case over his shoulder and sauntered into the Colorado State Capitol building.

Stately oil portraits of Colorado's historic figures ignored him. Vic wondered when the last time someone got up on a ladder and dusted the frames. An agglomeration of award-winning 4-H projects occupied most of the rotunda. The displays informed visitors of such things as how corn made it into the gas tank of SUVs or the progress of winter wheat in Eastern Colorado. The broad stairway took him down to his real target, the basement cafeteria. Legislators, staffers, reporters, and lobbyists were milling about, some standing and talking, others sitting at tables covered with papers and copies of bills, others quietly reading the incredibly shrinking daily newspapers.

Vic acquired a medium dark roast coffee and scanned the area for a perch. Dwight Anderson sat at a small table jammed up next to a polished marble column. "Dwight," Vic said as he walked over. "Labor doings today?"

"Pipe fitters and carpenters. I've got a house labor committee meeting to catch. Another right to work bill. You?"

"Senate committee."

"Ag?"

"Yeah, why?"

Anderson leaned toward Vic. "I heard two guys talking about it. All I could hear was there was going to be quite a surprise."

"Well, I guess we'll see," Vic said. "Hoffman says it's supposed to be routine, take a little testimony, then lay the bill over."

"That ain't the way I heard it," the former TV reporter said, smiling. "Keep an eye out."

"I'll let you know what happens," Vic said.

Anderson got up and waddled off.

# 58

"The Senate Agriculture, Natural Resources, and Energy Committee will come to order," State Senator Gerald Robinson said while tapping the broad curved dais in front of him with a small gavel. "The clerk will call the roll."

Not all of the state was being run by children. Robinson, who chaired the committee, was a seventy-something farmer from northeastern Colorado. When Vic last covered the statehouse, Republicans controlled both houses and Robinson was a state representative and a minority member of the House Agriculture Committee. Now that Democrats controlled both houses of the legislature, he was grand pooh-bah of the Senate Ag Committee, a fairly powerful post given the influence of Colorado's agricultural industry, albeit a waning influence.

A young clerk finished her roll-call and announced, "Seven present. No absences."

"A quorum is present," Robinson said. "We have one item before us today, Senate Bill 305. Without objection, we'll dispense with the reading of the bill. Hearing none, I'd like to open up the public hearing on this measure. I think we have one witness, Mr. Simpson. Would you please stand and take the oath?"

A tall sunburned man, sandy hair thinning on top, stood up from the front row of seats and stepped forward to the witness table.

"Raise your right hand," Robinson said, standing up. Simpson complied. "Do you, Mr. Harold Simpson, swear that what you are about to say is the truth, the whole truth, and nothing but the truth?"

"I do," Simpson said.

"Please be seated," the chairman said, and Simpson sat. "Would you state your name and occupation for the record?"

"Harold Simpson, Water Engineer for the State of Colorado."

"Thank you," the chairman said. "My understanding is that you have a short statement."

"Yes sir, I do." He fumbled with a pair of reading glasses and then picked up a single sheet of paper from an open manila file folder on the table in front of him. He adjusted his reading glasses and held out the paper in front of him.

"After reviewing all the preliminary studies—"

"Excuse me, Mr. Simpson," said Robinson.

"Sir?" Robinson said.

"Uh, flip that switch on the base of the microphone in front of you, would you please," the senator said. "We'll be able to hear you better."

"All right." After more fumbling, Simpson activated the microphone, which also meant all the committee members, the audience, the recording devices, and those listening over the internet would be able to hear him as well.

Simpson began again, "After reviewing all the preliminary studies our office has undertaken with respect to the adverse impact of the use of high-volume irrigation wells on the aquifer in the

South Platte River Basin, my staff concurs with its earlier finding that the irrigation wells along the river are tied to the river system, materially affect the recharge of the river, and should remain subject to adjudication. I also concur with these findings."

Vic heard a slight commotion behind him and some man saying "I can't believe this." He recognized the voice, but remained focused, writing down everything Simpson said. It was a complete one-eighty from what Hoffman expected.

The chairman rapped the table again with his gavel. "The public hearing is closed. The bill is on the table, and I will consider a motion."

This was not right either, Vic thought. Hoffman said Simpson was going to say that turning the wells back on would not harm the river basin in the short term, an about face from his earlier ruling. Also, there was not supposed to be a vote on the bill, yet there was the legislation, naked, on the table, up for a vote, and exposed to the whims of politicians.

"I move to send Senate Bill 305 to the committee of the whole with a favorable recommendation," said Senator Barry Crandall, a Democrat from Denver.

"I second," said a Republican member.

"The clerk will call the role," the chairman said.

Sen. Karl Lujak jumped to his feet from the front audience row and shouted, "Mr. Chairman?"

Robinson rapped the gavel so hard the windows shook.

"You're out of order, Senator Lujak," he said. "We're in the middle of a vote." Lujak dropped back to his seat. Nice performance, Vic thought.

The clerk called the roll. All three Republican members voted against the bill, along with two Democrats, Crandall and chairman Robinson.

"Two ayes, five nayes," the clerk said.

"The motion fails," Robinson said. Then, without looking at Republican Senator Wilson Raines, he said, "Senator Raines."

"I move to postpone Senate Bill 305 indefinitely," said Sen. Raines.

The Second was mumbled. Vic missed who said it.

Those who voted against the bill all voted to postpone it indefinitely, which killed the measure for the current session of the legislature.

"Bastards!" It was an angry cry from the back of the hearing room. The same voice. Then, another loud rap of the gavel.

"We'll have order in this hearing room or I'll clear it," Robinson shouted.

Vic turned and saw the original odd couple stand up to leave. The stocky one was Gary Kendrick, wearing a light gray business suit, a cream-colored Stetson, and black cowboy boots. No chopper hat this time. The lean one was Dave Bender, his face red either from working the fields, his anger at the committee, or his hatred for Kendrick. Yet he was with Kendrick. Bender wore clean crisp blue jeans, a maroon golf shirt, a Rockies cap, and work boots. Bender said something to Kendrick, but Vic could not make it out.

"Dave, come on," Kendrick said, grabbing at Bender's right arm but the farmer ripped it from his grasp and marched out of the hearing room. The water lawyer pulled a cell phone from his inside coat pocket, dialed a number, waited for someone to answer, said something, then slapped the phone shut. He nodded at the committee chairman and casually walked out of the room.

"I move to adjourn," said Senator Raines.

"Second," some other committee member said.

"Mr. Chairman," said Senator Lujak.

"We have a non-debatable motion to adjourn on the table," the chairman said. "The clerk will call the roll."

Lujak even faked a flushed face.

The same five to two vote adjourned the committee meeting.

"Meeting adjourned," said the chairman, and he lightly tapped his gavel before getting up to walk out the side entrance behind the dais.

Simpson fled the hearing room. Vic caught him in the elevator, Simpson inside, Vic outside holding the door open with his right arm. It hurt his bad shoulder.

"Mr. Simpson, Vic Bengston with the *Sun*."

"No comment."

"I haven't asked a question yet," Vic said.

"It doesn't matter," Simpson said. "I have nothing to say beyond my written statement." He pressed the down button. Vic let go of the door and thought about an icepack later that evening for his shoulder.

Outside on the Fourteenth Avenue side of the capitol's circular drive, Vic saw Kendrick step into a dark sedan. It might have been Currington's car, but he could not really be sure.

Bender was nowhere to be seen.

# 59

"They what?" Hoffman said.

"They PI'd the bill," Vic said into his cell phone.

"That wasn't the deal," Hoffman said.

"You didn't tell me there was a deal."

"Well, you didn't need to know that," Hoffman said. "I was just told that Simpson was going to overturn, or partially overturn, his decision to shut down the wells."

"Who told you?" Vic said.

"A little bird," Hoffman said.

"He concurred with his original decision," Vic said. "In favor of the well shut-off."

"Apparently."

"A little bird told me there was going to be a surprise," Vic said.

"What bird?" Hoffman said.

"Another little bird," Vic said. "Actually, not so little."

"Up there five minutes and you're lining up sources," Hoffman said. "Should I be nervous?"

"Don't be. I couldn't begin to fill the impression your cheeks left on your chair at the press room poker table."

Although he would do it, Vic did not especially want to cover the statehouse, not just yet.

"What was the vote?" Hoffman said.

"Five to two. Both votes were the same. Robinson and another Democrat went with the Republicans."

"Who voted with Robinson?"

"Crandall voted against his own motion," Vic said. "Is he a farmer?"

"No." Hoffman said. "No, he's a real estate investor."

"Fixer and flipper?"

"Nope. He's commercial. Seventeenth Street. Big time. Big developments. Big money."

That fits, Vic thought.

"Lujack couldn't have been happy," Hoffman said.

Vic did not tell Hoffman he knew Lujak was play acting.

"Robinson gaveled Lujak out of order when he protested and just rammed the vote through."

"Something's wrong here," Hoffman said. "Robinson is on the wrong side of the vote. Crandall was supposed to stay with the party line. That's if they voted, and they weren't even supposed to do that."

"Isn't Robinson from Sterling?" Vic said. "It seems to me he'd be looking out for the interests of the farmers."

"Some of them. But he also represents the big farmers and corporate agriculture. Those are the boys with the serious campaign bucks." Hoffman paused. "Anything from Simpson?"

"No comment," Vic said.

"Swell," Hoffman said. "That's all that went down?"

"Basically," Vic said. "The whole thing seemed savagely choreographed."

"Was Gary Kendrick there by any chance?" Hoffman said.

"Dressed to the nines, cowboy boots that had to have been made from something illegal?"

"Probably," Hoffman said. "You know him?"

"Remember that oil shale water lawsuit a hundred years ago?" Vic said.

"Vaguely."

"I covered it. Kendrick was the winning lawyer, that time for the energy companies."

"Now he's representing the small farmers who want their wells back on," Hoffman said.

Not to mention some folks who want to keep the wells shut off, Vic thought. He also did not mention Dave Bender's outburst, or Kendrick's attempt to calm him down. Or his nod to the committee chairman.

"Kendrick didn't say anything, then, I take it," Hoffman said.

"Not a peep."

"Why don't you come back in," Hoffman said. "I'll write up a lead and show it to you. Then we'll go from there."

"You've got everything that I've got, Mal," Vic said. "I need to go home, feed the dog and get ready for a little fly fishing tomorrow."

"All right," Hoffman said. "I'll call if I have a question."

"Fine."

Vic felt like an errand boy. He did not like it.

# 60

The South Platte River north of Deckers ran clear and low. With a large looping roll cast, Vic dropped a number twenty-six mercury midge near the opposite bank about fifteen feet downstream from a small shadow. The sinking line helped drag the wet fly to the bottom where, if all went according to plan, the midge would bump its way beneath the nose of a hungry trout. As the fluorescent green line stretched out in a long sweeping curve it hesitated for a fraction of a second. Vic flicked his wrist backward, and he had one on.

"Got one," Vic said loud enough for Kirk Largent to hear. Largent edged toward the other shore to get his camera.

The two met in seventh grade, after Vic's family moved from the edge of Crystal Lake, Illinois, to the center of the small town. For years, Vic's dad eyed the two-story dark brick house three doors up from the junior high school and across the street from the high school. When he had a chance to buy it, he did, and the family abandoned their diminutive frame ranch house built for returning World War Two veterans for the commanding twenties-era brick structure in the center of town.

The friendship matured during grade school and high school, stumbled a bit in college because they attended different schools even though they were close by, and sputtered over the professional years, with Largent in Seattle practicing law and Vic in Denver committing journalism, public relations, and other wicked acts of writing. When Largent called and said he would be in Colorado Springs for a law conference, Vic set up a rendezvous at his default fishing spot on the South Platte.

All twelve inches of the brown trout broke the surface and danced back upstream. Vic slowly walked backwards toward the bank to keep pressure on the line. Pulling too hard would break the delicate thin leader that presented the bantam fly to the fish. South Platte trout were under such intense fishing pressure, only the tiniest of artificial flies worked anymore. Largent had already reached the east bank and was out of the river. Vic worked his way over to him, carefully reeling in line. After five minutes of gentle persuasion, Vic reached down with a gloved hand and carefully cradled the feisty brown under its belly. He lifted it from the water and displayed it to Largent who snapped one shot of Vic and his conquest with a small point and shoot digital camera.

"One more for the left coast," Largent said, and he took another photograph.

With his free hand, Vic pulled on a silver hemostat dangling from his fishing vest by a retractable lanyard. He locked the pliers-like tips of the forceps onto the bend of the barbless hook and gently backed the fly out of the trout's upper lip. Vic did not like the barbless hooks. He seemed to lose more trout than he landed. But it was the way of the catch-and-release era, along with using gloves for handling the fish, which results in less damage to their sensitive skin, and always returning the animals to the water. He reached down and held the captured fish in the water, nose upstream. When the gills pulsed a few times, Vic released the brown, and the trout darted off into the dappled greens, browns, and blacks of the South Platte River.

"Let's have some coffee," Largent said.

"I'm down with that," Vic said. "Then we can talk about water lawyers and conflicts of interest."

# 61

Vic lifted the Jeep's hatchback revealing a compact galley operation in the way-back. While preparing drip coffee with a small backpack stove, a titanium pot, a plastic coffee cone, and two fold-up coffee cups, Vic wondered out loud whether Gary Kendrick was committing any sort of crime or ethical breach.

"He seems to be working with a politician, his political adviser, a land developer, a handful of farmers chasing water rights, a statewide water bond issue campaign, and maybe a banker who was trying to foreclose on the farms and annex them to a nearby town," Vic said.

"He's either got a huge law firm, or multiple personalities," Largent said, laughing. He removed his glasses and carefully cleaned the thick lenses with a tissue he pulled from a small pocket on his fishing vest. "Ethically, a lawyer can represent only one person associated with a conflict or an issue. Now, that's not always the case, though, if the parties agree to have the same guy represent them, but that doesn't usually happen." He slid his clean glasses back onto his face. "Looks like a train wreck."

"Really?" Vic said, thinking about a story on Kendrick's conflicts, or something even more sensational, like the Swain murder.

"Well, if you only look at the water issue, there seems to be built-in conflict right there, especially if he's done any work for that bank. It doesn't sound like the farmers would have the same interest in the water as the developer, what was his name?"

"Currington," Vic said. "I think Kendrick is stringing the farmers along so they won't be a factor in the water development legislation," Vic said.

"And you know this, how?" Largent said.

"Sources," Vic said.

"Sources," he said and then smiled. "Close to the investigation?"

"What investigation?" My investigation, Vic thought.

"Isn't that what they say, 'sources close to the investigation,' when they really can't pin anything down?"

"Well, I don't," Vic said. He didn't want to tell Largent about his late night snooping with the night scope.

"Okay, let's say there's a verifiable source. If that's the case, the guy has a definite conflict between the farmers and the developer. That's only one."

"What are the others?" Vic said.

"Potentially, the water development program, the bond issue election, and the banker, especially if some municipality is involved. Do you have any 'sources' for that information?"

"Only that Kendrick met with Michaels at least once about irrigation well legislation," Vic said. That came from the spy mission as well.

"The first amendment might be enough to cover that," Largent said. "Maybe a violation of Colorado's lobbying regulations."

"All seems pretty thin, doesn't it?" Vic said.

"Not necessarily. Your state supreme court or whoever oversees lawyers could suspend or even disbar him. Lobbying laws might generate a fine, a slap on the hand."

"They don't disbar many lawyers in Colorado," Vic said. "Wild West. All that. Those in power tend to get away with quite a lot."

"They still shoot it out on Main Street?"

"Damn near."

"What else can you tell me about the water right?"

"All I know is that everyone seems to want it," Vic said.

"Need it, you mean," Largent said.

"Need it. Want it. Whatever. They're after it. Fort Lupton wants it for their annexations. Farmers for their crops. Currington for his development. Swain for the wildlife."

"That's where the bank comes in, and the farmers," Largent said. "Municipalities like to gobble up farmland to improve their tax bases with residential and commercial real estate. The same thing happens up in Washington State, only we've got fairly strong state laws designed to slow the conversions, or stop them altogether."

"Colorado's land use laws are toothless," Vic said.

"I'm surprised they don't do more to protect the farms," Largent said.

Vic laughed. "They only talk about family farms during election season. The legislature doesn't do much to preserve them."

"On the other hand, Colorado water laws are rock solid, and those who can manipulate them can wield immense power," Largent said. "I spent some time studying them in law school. I thought about practicing law here."

"That would have been nice," Vic said. "We could have terrorized the native cutthroats."

"I don't think so," Largent said. "We've been fishing for three hours, and you've caught one fish."

"One more than you I must point out," Vic said.

"Colorado water law favors the money because of the expense of water lawyers and engineers," Largent said. "I'm guessing the farmers don't have enough if they're up against state government and a municipality that can float bonds fairly easily if it annexes the land for development."

"One of the farmers, Dave Bender, is all but bankrupt," Vic said. "His pal, Bobbie Hague, seems to have a few more resources, but not much more. I think he's dumped a lot of cash into Kendrick's hands."

"Hague's the hothead, right, the one who got shot?" Largent said.

"Yeah," Vic said. "A few of these farmers have gotten involved with Kendrick, including Bender, but he's got a nasty grudge against the guy."

"Against Kendrick?" Largent said.

"Yeah," Vic said. "Apparently, one of Kendrick's buddies screwed his mother out of her farm not too long ago. Bender is in on the deal with Kendrick but only because of his farmer pals."

"Because he's the lawyer who can get the water right for the farms," Largent said.

"Right. If Bender gets his water back, he saves face with his wife and his father-in-law. So he just puts up with Kendrick's involvement."

"A pact with the devil?"

"You could say that," Vic said. "Will you take my case, counselor?"

Largent looked up. pushed his glasses back up on his nose, and laughed. "Okay. The picture I'm getting is that the farmers are on the low end of the totem pole, getting screwed, and Kendrick is bullshitting them to make it look as though he's going to get them their water right, but really not. That right there would get you disbarred in Washington, probably Colorado too, if you could prove it."

"How would you prove it?" Vic said.

"I don't know if his involvement with the bond issue would do much for you, except show somewhat of a conflict of interest because of multiple overlapping clients," Largent said. "It's really about the money. When he accepts fees from the farmers, he has the duty to do everything within his power to go after that water right."

"They have paid him," Vic said. "Bender told me."

"That's a start," Largent said. "If money changed hands, there's a fiduciary obligation there. So if he did anything to weaken that representation, like advising Currington, even informally, or the bank, or the municipality, on how to get the water right for their use, that's a fairly serious breach for a lawyer. That kind of a conflict gets you into trouble. It's evidence that the fees the farmers paid him were done so under false pretenses."

"Like fraud," Vic said. "That's a good story."

Largent nodded and said, "So is murder."

# 62

Vic took a sip of his coffee and pondered the possibilities. Tying Kendrick into a murder conspiracy with a couple of high-end politicians is not a bad story. Then he thought the P-word, Pulitzer. Still, he was not too sure. "Your thoughts on the murder, counselor?"

"I don't have many," Largent said. "Corporate law doesn't get me onto the criminal side of the bar all that much."

"But?" Vic said.

"But, I told you I looked long and hard at water law, as a specialty."

"And?" Vic said.

"And, all I can say is that controlling the water controls the land in states like Colorado," Largent said. "I wonder if Kendrick was trying to hedge his bets."

"How so?"

"Well, by getting his fingers into everything, maybe he thought he could come out on the winning side no matter what."

"Kendrick's already got a successful law practice," Vic said.

"How much is enough?"

"He might owe a favor to one of the parties," Largent said. "Or, maybe he's in trouble financially. Is he a partner with the developer?"

"I don't know," Vic said. "He could be. I do think Currington's in trouble."

"From that phone call?"

"Yeah."

"Not much to go on there," Largent said.

"I don't know. Currington looked pretty stressed when he was on that call, although he always looked a little stressed, or stern. Always serious."

"Or worried," Largent said.

"Possibly," Vic said.

"A hunch, then," Largent said.

"That's what my editors say, I'm a hunch guy."

"That was always my impression of you, Vic. You went with your gut."

"Gut doesn't work well in a court of law, does it?" Vic said.

"Not usually," Largent said. "I have to dot every 'i' and cross every 't' or the corporate client throws you overboard."

"I've got liable to think of," Vic said.

"Not with a public figure," Largent said.

"Well, that's only Michaels and maybe Currington. I can't go after Kendrick without dotting every 'i' and crossing every 't'."

Largent smiled. "Do you think those guys, the majority leader, the professor, the lawyer, and maybe the banker conspired to assassinate the lieutenant governor to get their hands on that water right?"

"You left out the Butler and Mr. Plum."

"No, I'm serious," Largent said, "Just the Four Horsemen."

"That would be one hell of a story," Vic said. "But I think it's too good to be true."

"History is replete with murders for politics, economics, power, and religion," Largent said.

"It seems too calculating to me," Vic said. "Don't get me wrong. I think they're all glad she's dead, but they still have quite a bit of work to do to get their hands on that water right. Now, I'm starting to have doubts about Michaels' involvement."

"Based on what?" Largent said.

Vic still did not want to reveal the night scope mission. "Sources."

"You're down to three horsemen then."

"Ferguson, the banker," Vic said. "He wins no matter what. The Benders either pay the note or he gets the farm."

"Two horseman," Largent said.

"You know, Kirk, the Sixties in me wants it to be the fat cats," Vic said, taking another sip of coffee. As high school students, the two spent hours sitting in the Largent family kitchen drinking coffee and talking with his folks, a memory burned into Vic's psyche. "Kendrick's strung out with conflicts of interest. Currington's stretched tight as a drum, financially. At least it seems he is. I still wonder about them both, though. I have my doubts. Kendrick's a hot dog, a rich one. Currington's a pretty serious family man, big reputation, you know."

"A lot to protect, but you have your doubts?"

Vic nodded.

"Hunch?"

Vic nodded again.

"So, you think it's the farmers then," Largent said, looking at his notes, cross-examining the witness.

"I do."

"Crime of passion?" Largent said.

"No way," Vic said. "Intense anger, maybe. But it had to be

planned out. Swain was known for using little or no security. She always drove herself to the capitol every day and usually to the events she attended."

"She was unguarded at the event before her death, her murder?" Largent said.

"Yeah," Vic said. "And some of those farmers are wound pretty tight."

"Bender and Hauge?" Largent said.

Vic nodded. "These folks out here are pretty independent, the guns and God thing. The Four Horsemen want money and power, usually in that order. With the farmers, though, it's family, history, and then the money."

"Money and power are compelling motives for murder," Largent said.

"I know, but these farmers are seeing their entire way of life swirling down the drain along with everything they own," Vic said, "everything they think they owe to their family legacies, everything about the family farm."

"Those are compelling motives too," Largent said.

# 63

Vic fidgeted at his desk. Restlessness and boredom bothered him because he was rarely bored, not as an adult, not ever when he was a kid growing up north of Chicago. Something else must be bugging him, he concluded.

After a half hour of futzing around with drab news releases, Vic grabbed his empty paper coffee cup and walked up to the city desk where Peggy was attacking her terminal non-stop. Statue like, she stared at the screen. Only her fingers flew across the keyboard, which made a high-speed plapping sound as she wrote, rewrote, edited, and dispatched email memos to other reporters. Vic stood next to her with his empty cup.

"Do I look like a barista?" she said, her position unchanged. Fingers continued to fly.

Vic said, "Does your lower back ever hurt?"

Her fingers stopped. She looked up at him. "All the time. Why?"

"I have this chiropractor," Vic said.

"La Dee Da."

"He asked me that question once," Vic said.

"And your answer?"

"The same. All the time."

"Did he hand you a bill and a contract for fifty appointments?"

"No," Vic said. "He asked me if I spent a lot of time staring at a computer screen, or driving a car."

"Oh, so this was after the invention of the computer, I take it."

"Yes. It was in the modern era. Remember he mentioned the automobile as well."

"Oh yeah," Peggy said. "Although the car does date back to the nineteenth century, when you were a mare lad."

He ignored her. "Well, I did both. I was running the PR firm with my partner, frozen at a computer screen all the time, like you are there. The kids were younger, so I was driving them all over town almost every day, frozen behind the wheel."

"Your kids," Peggy said. "They must have kids by now. Someone said you're a grandpop, pop."

"This is true. Let me finish my story."

"The back-cracker. Right. Proceed."

"He said those two activities sort of freeze your head and neck in the same position for a long time, and this causes two upper vertebrae to squeeze down on each other. That, in turn, causes a pain in your lower back because the nerves are connected."

"Did he use incense?"

"The doctor?"

"Yeah. Or did he chant a little bit? He didn't get out an eagle feather did he?"

"God, and I thought I was skeptical," Vic said.

"You've seen the crap that comes across this desk," she said.

"I know. Just listen."

She looked at the clock. "We've got a deadline."

"It can wait," Vic said. "The doc told me to do this every half hour or so, or when my back hurt. Now, look at me." She did not.

"Watch," Vic said, slowly turning his head from side to side. "Are you watching?"

"Yes, dear." She watched.

After a couple of reps, he then tilted his head, slowly, from side to side. "The backache is gone."

"Frog legs," Peggy said. "I bet he used frog legs."

"You're incorrigible."

"Chicken feet?"

"I give up," Vic said. "Tell me, do we have a Lexus-Nexus account?"

"We do. Log in as RMS. The password is 'scoopthetimes,' all one word."

"Cute," Vic said.

"We specialize in cute," Peggy said.

Vic entered the key words, and the Lexus-Nexus search screen popped up.

"Could you bring me a plain old black coffee? I'll pay you back." She held up her empty paper coffee cup with her left hand, wriggled it, and tossed it into the trash can, all while continuing to plap with her right hand.

"Who was your barista last year?" Vic said, closing his Lexus-Nexus screen.

"A much younger intern," Peggy said. "Remember, straight, no chaser. By the way, your year's not up."

"Sure." Vic said as he headed back toward the break room.

In the old days, reporters in need of caffeine walked down a long hallway toward the press room and into a small break area occupied by two essentials for the newspaper industry, a bulletin board filled with union notices and a pair of massive silver coffee pots maintained by the printers. Newspapers were fueled by booze, coffee, and nicotine up until the sixties and seventies when pot and coke were added to the mix. Things seemed fairly tame today, but the staples of alcohol and caffeine remained, only in the form of pricey microbrews and four-dollar designer coffee drinks. Smoking had fallen from fashion. Vic was glad he never started.

A long kitchen counter sheathed in stainless steel dominated the black, white, and gray tiled break-room. Cabinets were locked, apparently to discourage their use. There was no refrigerator, no doubt a defensive move to prevent creation of hideous science projects fed by the forgotten leftovers of busy reporters. Yet an oversized microwave stood ready to nuke anything a hungry newspaper woman or man shoved into it.

What appeared to be a scaled down retro version of Univac, the world's first computer, occupied one end of the long counter. Upon closer inspection, Vic found it to be a coffee machine. Old coffee machines delivered horrible instant coffee, even worse decaf, weak tea, passable hot chocolate, and that infamous chicken soup made from some mystery powder and hot water. Univac, on the other hand, delivered latte, espresso, flavored coffees, decaf, and, much to Vic's pleasure, plain old coffee. But at a buck instead of a quarter.

Vic fed the machine a five. It spit back four one dollar coins. He pressed the button for strong coffee. Lights blinked, and machine noises emanated from within. A tall paper cup wrapped with Colorado Rockies advertising dropped into the liquid delivery chute. Vic watched through a narrow glass viewing port as the machine ground fresh coffee beans, dumped the brown soil-like matter into a paper cone, and then flooded the ground coffee with hot water. Below the cone a thin stream of steaming dark liquid dripped into his paper cup. When it was finished, Univac beeped. He retrieved the filled cup and set it on the counter. Repeating the process for Peggy's caffeine fix, Vic marveled at this cheap Rube Goldberg entertainment.

He delivered Peggy's coffee to the city desk and, having decided on a task that would end his boredom, said, "I've got some background work to do on that farm feature. Okay?"

"We'll muddle along without you," Peggy said. "Thanks for the cup o' Joe."

Eager to see if there was anything he needed to know about Betsy Bender, nee Betsy Johansson, nee Elizabeth Johansson, Vic returned to his cubicle. He settled in, sipped his coffee, and logged back onto the paper's Lexus-Nexus site. He entered "Betsy Johansson" in the small subject box and began a search of newspaper, magazine, and wire service articles from the last ten years. Three stories appeared, all about a bank teller in Pine Bluff, Arkansas, who had been charged with embezzling three-quarters of a million from her employer. The woman would have been seventy today. He doubted if it was Gil's daughter.

Vic looked up from his screen to exercise his neck. He could see Peggy leaning back in her chair twisting her head from side to side, then tilting it this way and that. He let her do this for several minutes. Then he dialed her number on the intercom. When the phone emitted a low modulated tone, Vic said, "Backache gone?"

Peggy stopped her head twisting and looked over toward Vic. She stood up. Her intercom mike was open. She raised her arms up like a referee signaling a touchdown and shouted, "Yes!" Then she sat down again and returned to her work.

"So it is possible to teach new dogs old tricks," Vic said into the phone.

Peggy shot him the finger.

Vic hung up and turned back to his screen. He changed his search criteria to look for "Elizabeth Johansson" and widened the query to twenty-five years. Now the screen displayed a list of about thirty entries, and nothing about the Arkansas embezzler. These were all stories about Elizabeth Johanssons from around the country. One of them was a twenty-year-old piece from the *Denver*

*Times* headlined, "Colorado girl captures sharpshooting honors." He clicked on it, and up popped the text of a brief news item:

## COLORADO GIRL CAPTURES
## SHARPSHOOTING HONORS

LANDER, Wyo. (UPI) — Brighton High School senior Elizabeth "Betsy" Johansson took home first prize Saturday in the small caliber handgun competition during the Rocky Mountain Sharpshooters Championship. She scored a perfect score in her final round.

Miss Johansson, daughter of Colorado farmers Gilbert and Elizabeth Johansson of Brighton, now advances to the national championships, sponsored by the National Rifle Association, to be held next month in San Diego.

The high school senior is equally skilled in rifle marksmanship and said she hopes to make the U.S. Olympic team next year.

Vic recalled Dave Bender's angry explosion at his farm, the firing of the shotgun, and then the apology, followed by a calming down to a mild bundle of coiled up rage reigned in with nicotine. The casual way Bender's wife had snagged the gun in midair when he tossed it to her left an indelible impression on Vic, as did the way she racked the weapon fast, spraying the unspent shells into the dirt. He also remembered, or at least he thought he remembered, that the caliber of the Swain murder weapon had never been revealed by police. Since the murder was no longer his story, he figured he could not risk asking Peggy about that tidbit. Maybe Driscoll could confirm it, Vic thought. Saturday was only two days away. He and the cop had a seven-thirty a.m. tee time.

"Small caliber handgun competition," Vic said aloud, reading the phrase once again from the story on his screen. His coffee cup refused to answer, but the tiny face in the advertisement wrapped around it, a little purple dinosaur somehow chosen as the Rockies' mascot, shot him a knowing glance.

# 64

The morning dew cast a sparkly web across the practice putting green at Kennedy Golf Course. Vic was early. No sign of Driscoll. He opened the hatchback on his Jeep and balanced himself on the edge of the way-back while he put on his white New Balance golf shoes that he had received in the goodies bag at a charity golf outing the year before. Everyone else in the universe seemed to be wearing Nike's but Vic avoided the swoosh altogether. Years ago when he was flying somewhere for some client, Vic wound up on a plane next to some kid who flew in and out of third world countries looking for the cheapest labor Nike could find to make the shoes that the company then sold back in the United States for hundreds of dollars to children who could not afford them and who occasionally shot one another in order to take a pair off the victim. The kid justified the exploitation by saying a buck or two a day to work eighteen hours in rotten conditions was more than "those people" ever earned in their lives. The kid shut up when Vic told him, "Plantation owners made the same argument about their slaves."

He laced his shoes tight knowing that New Balance at least tried to manufacture some of its shoes domestically. He also knew some were made overseas, but he still felt better maintaining his personal lifetime boycott of Nike and its damned logo. A typical liberal his conservative friends called him. They were right.

"You gonna sit there all day, or are we gonna play some golf?"

Driscoll was shouting. Vic looked up from his shoes and saw him walking from the pro shop, which had been moved down next to the driving range.

"Where's your car?" Vic said.

"In the shop. CV joints. I drove Maxine's."

"How's she going to get to work?"

"Don't you worry about Maxine. She's all taken care of. You want some breakfast?" Driscoll looked at his watch. "We've got about an hour."

"Yeah, my gut's rumbling," Vic said. "What are CV joints anyway?"

"I have no idea," Driscoll said. "But new ones cost about five hundred bucks."

Vic pulled his clubs from the Jeep and closed the hatchback. The two walked down toward the clubhouse. Vic dropped his bag next to the putting green. He saw Driscoll's Wilson Pro bag on the ground about ten feet away so he picked up his bag and re-dropped it next to his golf partner's.

They walked past the starter's shack which had two foursomes all jammed in around the tiny window. Charlie was checking their IDs, greens fee receipts, handing out stubby pencils and score cards. He was too busy to look up as Driscoll and Vic walked past him as they entered the clubhouse.

"Morning, boys." It came from behind the bar.

"Morning, Grace," Driscoll said to the voice.

"Morning and, yes, two coffees, black," Vic said. To Driscoll, he said, "Let's get a table."

Grace popped up from behind the bar and said, "To go?"

"No, we're gonna eat," Driscoll said.

The two walked over to a table next to a window looking out over the ninth green. A massive flat screen replayed the 1977 British Open. The Bear was lining up his final putt on eighteen. His blond mop nearly blocked his eyes. Nicklaus drained the forty-footer for a birdie. The crowd roared, but it was for naught. Tom Watson was going to edge him out by one stroke with a tap-in birdie from two feet.

Grace got to the table a step or two behind Driscoll and Vic. She set down two coffees in tan porcelain mugs. Vic noticed her tight round behind. She was in her early forties and loved golf, but this was it for her. The LPGA never materialized. She gave lessons and ran the restaurant which made her a living and provided free golf. Vic played eighteen holes with her once. He quit playing for a year after that. It was humiliating to step back from your slice into the rough off the tee only to watch some five-foot-two petite blonde smack whitey two-hundred-eighty yards right down the middle of the fairway. Her face was pleasant, and her skin showed the toughness that years of exposure to sun and wind brought with it. Vic wondered what the skin cancer rate was among serious golfers. Probably the same as sailors, hikers, bikers, or farmers, he concluded, and made a mental note to make sure he put on his sunscreen before they teed off.

"You guys know what you want?"

"Couple of eggs, over easy, bacon, rye toast," Vic said as he sat down.

"Same," Driscoll said.

"God, you two are pushovers," she said.

"Oh yeah, we're easy," Vic said. Driscoll watched Vic watch her return to the kitchen.

"You ever ask her out?"

"Frank, I could be her father," Vic said.

"And your point is?"

"Let's change the subject."

"She looked at you," Driscoll said. "I could tell."

"Right," Vic said.

They drank coffee and caught up on the week, updating each other on family activities. Driscoll and Maxine had a son in high school pulling straight A's and a daughter coming up through middle school apparently doing the same thing. Vic filled in the blanks with his kids, oldest to youngest. Sean was steadily building his insurance agency, enjoying being a new daddy to Brent, he and Judy talking about number two. Turf, short for Thorolf, fixed computers by day, played drums with a jazz group by night, and recently built a basement audio studio in his little house to record local bands. Connor continued to amaze as he was elevated to senior network architect, whatever that was, at Beta One Healthcare, started coaching his son Devon's soccer team and was about to marry for a second time to a wonderful woman from South Korea nicknamed Johnnie. Melissa and her beau, Paul, both into photography and design, had moved into an eclectic studio-living space a block or two up 15th Street from Denver's hip "LoDo" neighborhood, she assisting a number of the city's commercial photographers and he designing hats, shirts, and other items for a local branding agency.

"And what's a branding agency?"

"We used to call them advertising agencies," Vic said. "Branding is the new buzzword amongst the creative class."

"Oh. Like crowd control means police brutality?"

"Something like that."

"I thought Melissa was half nerd," Driscoll said.

"All the Bengstons are half nerd, or part nerd," Vic said. "She's still looking for a job with some lab."

"What's her degree in?"

"Botany," Vic said.

"That's plants, right?"

"Yes, detective, that's plants," Vic said. "Nothing gets by you."

"We never sleep."

The food arrived, and both men watched Grace walk back toward the bar. Driscoll looked at Vic and raised his eyebrows. Vic shook his head.

"You're looking at her," Driscoll said.

"That won't cost anything," Vic said.

"In the end it could."

"I have a question," Vic said.

"I could see it on your forehead."

"How?"

"You wrinkle your brows slightly," Driscoll said.

"Remind me to keep not inviting you to our monthly poker game," Vic said.

"I'd wind up in a fistfight with Brisbane."

"He's still giving you a hard time?"

"Always. He chairs the council's public safety committee."

"I didn't know you had anything to do with city council," Vic said.

"I'm one of three department liaisons, so I work with them from time to time," Driscoll said.

"I could ask him something," Vic said.

"No, don't do that," Driscoll said "You don't want to get involved in that. It's bad enough you're a reporter now. Steer clear of public safety policy, will ya?"

Vic raised his hands in surrender and said, "Just offering."

"So, what's your question?" Driscoll said, nodding toward Vic's forehead. "You better get it out or that wrinkle's going to leave a permanent mark on your skull."

"It's serious, and maybe we should go off the record."

"Careful, Vic." Driscoll said. "Don't spoil my golf game."

"You've never revealed the caliber of the bullet that killed the lieutenant governor, have you?"

Driscoll hesitated. He set his knife and fork down and brought his huge black hands together in front of him. He took a deep breath and thought a moment.

"I thought you were off that story," Driscoll said. "Do you know something that I should know?"

Vic did not want to tell Driscoll about what weapon might or might not be on the Bender farm.

"No, just curious," Vic said.

"You're really taking this reporting thing seriously, aren't you?"

"Semi," Vic said.

"Still on probation, I bet," Driscoll said. Vic nodded.

"Sure, they took me off the story," Vic said. "But this is merely idle curiosity."

"Vic, if you have any information," Driscoll said.

"I don't. Just wondering. I was reading our story file and didn't see anything about the weapon."

"No, we haven't released that information, and I hope I don't see that fact in tomorrow's paper either."

"You won't, because I don't have the slightest clue," Vic said. "The desk handles the story anyway."

"It's important that we keep that confidential, Vic," Driscoll said. "It's got to stay that way."

"Understood," Vic said.

They finished eating, went Dutch on the bill as they always did thanks to anal-retentive ethics requirements imposed on public officials by a distrusting Colorado electorate and on reporters by a distrusting *Sun* management.

"She's lookin' at you, man," Driscoll said, grinning.

"Give me a break."

Charlie hooked them up with two guys in from Phoenix for a home entertainment equipment convention downtown. Except for small talk on the tees and greens, Vic and Driscoll ignored them, preferring instead to run their own mini match play tournament. Vic left all his good putts on the practice green. By the end of the fifteenth hole Driscoll was four up with three to go so the match would go to him. Vic pulled a ratty golf trophy from his bag and handed it to Driscoll who would carry it until Vic won a round. No money ever changed hands.

The two lugged their bags back to their cars, arriving at Vic's Jeep first. As Vic opened up the back hatch, Driscoll said, "Why should I tell you?"

"Tell me what?"

"About the weapon," Driscoll said.

"No reason," Vic said, sensing his friend was weakening.

"It's confidential."

"I know."

"I gotta go," Driscoll said. Vic had never seen him this nervous. "Maxine does need her ride this afternoon."

"Give her my love," Vic said. He tossed his bag into the Jeep and pulled out his street shoes.

"I'll catch you later," Driscoll said. He walked a few steps, then stopped and turned around.

"Twenty-two," Driscoll said.

"What?" Vic said.

"It was a twenty-two. Like a mob hit. That's how we're looking at it."

Vic stared at him.

Driscoll nodded slightly, raised his eyebrows. "Confidential."

"I know," Vic said. "Confidential. Curiosity."

"It killed the cat," Driscoll said. "If you know anything, I want to know it too."

"I don't know anything," Vic said. "If I hear something I'll let you know."

"You better." The tall cop turned around and walked down to his car.

Vic left his cross-trainer shoes untied, jumped into the driver's seat and took off.

He wanted to interview Betsy Bender, the small caliber sharpshooter, without her husband around.

# 65

Vic set up the interview with Betsy through Gil, who seemed more than happy to have him talk to his daughter. Vic asked the old man to join him, hoping he would decline, which he did because of a doctor's appointment. Gil told Vic he wanted to see a story about the difficulties many of the Front Range farmers faced because of fierce competition from rapidly growing cities and land developers for limited water supplies. Vic was interested in guns and how Dave and Betsy Bender used them. He also was not too excited about being told what to write, something he had been doing on his own, thank you very much, for decades.

The interview with Betsy was set for two o'clock. After eating lunch at a small Mexican café on the way, Vic drove out to the Bender Farm, or the Johansson Farm, depending on which sign was visible upon entering the driveway. It was Vic's day off. He had postponed an evening fishing expedition with grandson Devon, all to chase a hunch.

Everything was the same as it was the other day when he visited, except Dave Bender was not leaning up against the barn with a shotgun across his lap. The chrome kitchen chair was still there reflecting sunlight off all its shiny surfaces.

The small patch of grass in front of the frame house was neatly set off by rocks, all about the size of twelve-inch softballs and painted white, but they were oblong and flat, probably collected from the South Platte. The rocks corralled two sections of yard split down the center by a narrow flagstone walk. The white stones flanked the flagstones and guided visitors to a single step up to the wooden porch that spanned the entire front of the house. A broad sloping eave extended from the roof and covered the porch, providing plenty of shade from the relentless Colorado sun. The porch faced west so the afternoon sun already challenged that side of the house. Vic imagined the porch view in the morning, out across the green fields and then toward the Front Range of the Rockies illuminated by the golden light of the rising sun. Only today, nature painted the fields with a deathly dry yellow hue brought on by the lack of water.

The front door was open, guarded by a feeble wooden screen door held together by numerous coats of white paint and several dozen nails. Vic knocked. He heard slow steady footsteps from inside. Elizabeth Bender materialized behind the screen door.

"You're Victor," she said.

"Vic," he said. "And you're Elizabeth."

"Betsy, like my Mom," she said. "Come in."

Her voice was deeper than he expected. Vic tried hard not to think what he was thinking, putting her looks together with her voice. He pushed it out of his mind. It was crazy.

She opened the screen door, and Vic stepped into a modest but perfectly kept house. The polished oak floors were spotless and, unlike his house in east Denver, dustless. Tasteful rugs protected all the heavy traffic areas. Like the house, the living room furniture appeared modest but sturdy.

Betsy had stepped back as he entered the room. Vic struggled to focus on the home, the way it looked and felt. His gaze tugged back to her as his mind returned to the crazy thoughts. Her brunette hair was lush and full, softly cascading across her shoulders as though she had stepped from a forties movie moments ago. Her chiseled jaw, lean features, beautiful eyes, pouting full lips, and that voice. It was as though Lauren Bacall was standing before him wiping her hands on a dishcloth. A waist-length thin sweater revealed small firm breasts perched above a flat stomach. Her black Capri's hid nothing of her slender hips or her athletic legs. Waiting for Humphrey Bogart to step out from the kitchen, Vic's image of this woman was tempered only slightly by the very non-forties short white socks and Adidas cross-trainers on her feet. Yes, he was going nuts.

"Would you like an iced tea?"

"That would be fine," Vic said.

She turned and headed for the kitchen. The view from that angle was not disappointing either.

"I thought we'd use the dining room table," she said.

A massive hundred-year old round oak beauty with oversized claw feet dominated much of the dining area, really an extension of the kitchen. She returned carrying a polished silver tray occupied by two ice-filled glasses, a pitcher of iced tea, sugar, artificial sweetener, napkins, two spotless spoons, and six small sugar cookies.

"I love old oak tables," Vic said.

"It was my grandfather's," Betsy said as she set the full tray in the center of the table.

"Gil's father?"

"No, on my mother's side. They bought it from Sears-Roebuck, out of the catalog, along with four chairs and paid less than twenty dollars for it, At least that's the family story."

She moved effortlessly around the table, pouring two glasses of iced tea, gliding back toward the sink to dispose of the dishtowel, then back to the table. Betsy was in command of this room, and of Vic. She sat down across the table from him, tilted her head a bit, and looked straight into his eyes with her piercing green eyes. "Where shall we start?"

"Wherever you'd like," he said, sensing she was after something too, but uncertain exactly what. He was on her turf, under her spell, so she might as well direct things, he thought, in the beginning at least.

"I'd like to start with Ben Ferguson," she said.

"The banker?"

"The turncoat." She spit the words onto the table. "I grew up with him. We went to school together, were in 4-H together, and this is what he does to me and my family?"

"Dave mentioned the foreclosure." Vic wanted to keep things moving like he did on the South Platte, moving the imitation nymph pattern along the gravel bottom to lure a skittish trout from her protected feeding hole.

"Highway robbery is more like it," she said, sitting upright shooting her eyes directly at Vic's, then turning to look out the front window. "They're taking Daddy's last farm."

Vic jotted notes in his narrow spiral-bound notebook, trying to get down the direct quotes.

"How far behind are you on the mortgage payments?"

"We were behind going into this season," Betsy said. "It wasn't really a bad year last year. It just wasn't a particularly good one."

"How much did you, do you owe?"

"About one fifty on the farm and whatever Dave had tied up in the equipment, monthly payments on that stuff. I think about three or four thousand a month."

"Okay, a hundred and fifty thousand dollars on the farm?" Vic said.

She nodded.

"Total?"

"No, that's the annual note payment on the farm, the land, Daddy's land," she said. "We had a payment due at the end of last year, and we couldn't make it all."

"I thought Gil, your father, gave you this farm?"

"He did," she said. "More tea?"

"Yes, thank you."

She stood over him, pouring his second glass. She smelled sweet and clean.

"You can't run a small farm without financing," she said. Dave had to borrow to replace the big well pumps, three of them. He relined the wells and bought new irrigation equipment. Seed corn's going through the roof. He had to get that, plus we leased another quarter section with a well on it." She poured herself another glass of the translucent brown tea and returned the pitcher to its place on the tray before sitting down again. "Dave wanted to completely redo that Quonset hut out there, to honor Daddy, I guess. That was war surplus from a long time ago. Then we built the barn. That was my idea but Dave saw the value in it too. He was going to buy new equipment, and we both knew what letting that stuff sit outside year after year would do to it. If we kept it all in the barn, it would last a longer. Dave built himself a complete shop in there so he and his buddies could do all the maintenance themselves. It was a real five-year plan."

She even had that lilting rhythm in her Bacall voice, sensual sounds that resonated deep. Vic wondered if it was all an act.

"Did you use the mortgage to buy the equipment, the combine, attachments, the tractor?" Vic said.

"We took some cash out of the land in that deal with Ben for the down payment on the equipment, but those were all separate notes."

"All the equipment is gone?" Vic said.

She looked away from him again and out the front window. The Rockies, dark hazy purple, almost black, crept part way up into the sky.

"When I heard they were coming for the combine, I kicked Dave out of the house for the day. I made him go over to Bobbie's, I think. I didn't want him here when they showed up. The corn was dead by then, so it didn't really matter."

Vic wrote furiously. He wished he had brought his small digital recorder. Then she spit words again. They were harsh and jagged, not mellow and smooth like Bacall.

"He made such a fuss. Ben did. Giving us that low rate. He knew what he was doing, that bastard."

"You think he knew you were going to fail?" Vic said.

"No, but he placed one bet on black and another on red," she said. "Took part of the crop for that special low interest. That conventional loan. Only for us high school pals, he said. The little prick."

"So the black pays off with his proceeds from the crop if you have a good year, and—"

"And, he gets the farm from his bet on red if the crop fails." She stood up and sucked in a breath, choked back a sob, and ran her hand through her silky hair before walking back into the kitchen. Vic could see her shoulders shudder. After a moment, she turned back toward him. "The government let in the sugar from God knows where. The cheap sugar. It damn near killed Daddy. He had to sell all his trucks, then the farms. Three of them he lost, so he could pay off this place. Nothing but a 'we're so sorry' from High Plains Sugar Beets, 'market's changed, see you later.' After thirty years. He cleared enough to give this one to Dave and me and buy his little condo in Brighton. Mom and Daddy get by now on Social Security and what we give them."

"Gil's truck?"

"We bought it when we refinanced the farm. Cash deal, so they can't take that."

"Why did you put so much money into this, into your farm?" Vic said.

"Government again. They came out and told us something was going to happen with energy, with gas and diesel," she said.

"When was this?"

"Oh, three, four years ago," she said.

"That was well before gas prices jumped to where they're at now," Vic said. "Who told you about the energy?"

"It was a college kid from the state Ag Extension, some sort of planner for farms," Betsy said. "All book experience, no dirt under her nails. She said they got word from Washington that fuel prices would increase, and the demand for corn ethanol was going to go through the roof."

"So she said to plant corn," Vic said.

"As much as we could," Betsy said. "Price was going to triple, she said."

"That's when you borrowed from Ferguson's bank?"

"That's right. Ben Ferguson. My old friend. He told us about the new ethanol plant out by Ault. It was supposed to be built a year ago, but I think they finally finished it this spring."

"Did you plant corn last year?"

"We did, but the market went soft," she said. "No ethanol plant yet."

"And you barely broke even?"

"Except for the notes. We couldn't pay the notes. We made partial payments. That didn't bother us early on."

"It didn't bother you, all that debt?" Vic said.

"It's a farm note," she said. "We could always rewrite farm notes, hold off for a better year."

"You couldn't do that?"

"The bank wouldn't do it. Ben wouldn't do it. It was a conventional loan, he said, not a federally-backed farm loan."

"Maybe you were defrauded," Vic said. "A story might help save the farm." A little melodramatic, he thought, and then remembered why he actually came here, the Swain murder. Still, the farm story was compelling.

"No, we were greedy like everybody else," Betsy said, smiling. "We signed papers that said we understood what we were doing."

"Did you?" Vic said.

"The short answer? Yes."

"What's the long answer?"

"The long Answer? We didn't read the fine print, but we didn't really worry about it. Dave planted the hell out of the place."

"All corn," Vic said.

"Corn for all the drivers in Denver," she said. "Green fuel they called it. Corn prices shot through the roof, like that kid predicted. We would have paid off the whole note and then some with this crop."

"Then the irrigation wells were shut off," Vic said.

She froze. For a moment she was a little girl, but only for an instant. The confident Lauren Bacall returned. "Government again. State government. First, that judge sitting in Greeley in her smug little courtroom, then her lackey."

"Lackey?"

"Simpson," she said, staring at him again, eye to eye. "State Water Engineer."

"He shut off the wells?"

"Not that coward," she said. "He's too scared to step onto a farm now. No, he sent his minions. Snuck in here when we were down at 4-H with the girls. Did more than turn them off too."

"Like what," Vic said.

"They disconnected them," she said. "Pulled out something. I don't know what. Dave can tell you. They cut the power to them too. Put locks on them."

"Not a pleasant thing to come home to," Vic said. Part of him wanted to stop and talk about something else, anything else, but he felt so close to the culmination of this story he had to keep pushing. Betsy's chest heaved, and he saw her restrain herself, but Vic sensed a controlled explosion rumbling inside her. She shook her head, and that lovely hair flew all over. Then she ran both hands across the sides of her face and through the hair to tame it and settle it once again on her shoulders.

"You know what happened at Bobbie Hague's," she said in a low voice, angry, holding back tears. "Simpson's got deputies out here to shoot us down like coyotes."

"Hague pulled a gun on Simpson," Vic said. "He was lucky."

"He was provoked," she shot back at him. "Jake wouldn't kill him. We all grew up together. I think I read, or heard, he's even in trouble for that too. Someone pulls a gun on a deputy, you're supposed to put them down, not wound them."

"Jake?"

"The deputy who shot Bobbie," she said. "He grew up on Bobbie's farm. His dad was a farm worker. We all went to school together. They've got us turning on each other."

Interesting wrinkle, Vic thought, and made a note to follow up on the deputy who shot Hague.

"A couple of days after Jake shot Bobbie, we found a shut off notice stapled to the sign out there by the road."

"The Johansson Farm sign?" Vic said.

"Yeah, on Daddy's old sign," she said. "Dave found it. He went out to set the water. About a half hour later he walked back in and sat down at the table, right where you are. I asked him what was wrong."

"What did he say?" Vic said.

"They took all our water, Betsy. Then he started crying like a baby."

# 66

Betsy looked down at the table in front of her, holding back, waiting for the next question.

Vic obliged.

"Do you still target shoot?"

She raised her head slowly and peered at him.

"What does that have to do with the farm story?"

Her response sent a chill down Vic's spine. It was a tough, sincere question, tossed like the Bacall-Bogie banter in *To Have and Have Not*, the pretty good movie Howard Hawks made from Hemingway's worst book.

"Background," Vic said. "Your background."

"You have done your research."

"I try to."

The tension left the room for a moment.

"I still shoot," she said. "I like it. It relaxes me."

Vic could not lose the image of Dave tossing her the twelve-gauge, how she caught it and unloaded it without so much as a flick of hesitation. They looked like a team. "Shotguns?"

She laughed. "No. That's Dave's relaxation. He likes to hunt birds, especially in his own fields around harvest time. Do you shoot?"

"I used to hunt pheasant with my dad," Vic said.

"So you have killed things," she said. "You don't just write about killing. We've got quite a few pheasants here on the farm, you know."

"I'm sure the corn helps," Vic said.

"Not this year," Betsy said.

"Well, what do you shoot then?"

Betsy leaned back in her chair and glared at him. "Why don't you tell me?"

Vic adjusted himself in his chair, wondering who was conducting the interview. "Twenty-two. Small handgun?"

"My my," she said, leaning forward. She smiled a beautiful smile. Her silence forced Vic to speak.

"I found an old article about you when you were in high school and won the regional sharp shooting championships."

"Daddy was proud of me," she said, beaming her perfect teeth, framing them with those lips.

"How did you do in the nationals? I couldn't find any follow-up stories."

"I never went." She stood up straight to move around.

"No Olympics either?"

"No."

She stared out the front window again. Afternoon rainclouds were building over the mountains.

"Do you want to talk about it?"

"Not really."

She turned back toward him, put her right hand to her chin, and tapped those lips with her index finger. Her eyes remained unfocused.

"Lost time, lost dreams," she said. "Thanks to the government."

"The sugar company had a lot to do with it too," Vic said. "They let in all that cheap sugar."

"Government, big business. They're all the same."

"So, do you shoot competitively now?" Vic said.

"No, only for me," she said. "And Dave."

"Dave?"

"I taught him how to shoot handguns," she said. "All he ever did was hunt birds, a little deer, and elk hunting too. Long guns only. He was a real klutz with a handgun."

"How does he do now?" Vic said.

"He could part your hair at twenty-five yards."

In his head, Vic paced out the distance between him and Bender when they first encountered each other. He thought about high school football and a twenty-five yard run. That was about the distance. A chill ran down his spine when he thought about how close they were the rest of that afternoon, by the South Platte and at his mother's old farm.

"Do you go to a local shooting range for practice?" Vic said.

She laughed. "This isn't downtown Denver, Vic. We can walk right out the back door here and shoot. You'd be arrested in about ten minutes down in the city if you did that. Anyway, Dave built me a nice range out beyond the barn. A berm to put targets up against, shooting table, the whole bit. You'll have to come out some time. I'll instruct you."

"That would be nice," Vic said, picturing her arms around him helping him aim, then kicking himself internally and reminding himself, again, married women were out of bounds.

They talked for another half hour. Tense patches having been traversed, most of the conversation remained smooth and unemotional, except Betsy's eyes watered up again when she talked about her father and her husband. She seemed utterly devoted to both, despite her early coyness. Probably part of the act, Vic thought.

Betsy walked Vic through the devastation caused in her family when the sugar beet plant stopped buying crops and then closed in a span of about two months. "The farmers were blindsided. So were the plant workers. But the thing with the irrigation wells unfolded in slow motion over years. We never thought they'd turn them off."

"Why?" Vic said. "They've been after the wells for a long time."

"These water things have always been worked out in the past. The South Platte runs full even during droughts. We always had enough water for the compacts with the other states. Kansas and Nebraska never complained, until—"

"Until?"

"The environmentalists and the government ganged up on us."

"What about the businesses and the banks?" Vic said.

"Sure, but those wildlife idiots started this." She swept her right hand toward the kitchen window, which looked out over the dying corn crop.

Was it possible that her husband had not told her he suspected Kendrick of playing both sides of the fence on the water rights thing, Vic thought, or Dave's conclusion that the gravel miner's lawyer turned them into the water engineer, not the environmentalists?

"I thought the hunters and fishers teamed up with agriculture all the time," Vic said.

"Only when it suits them," Betsy said. "If push comes to shove, the farmers get shoved. Out here it's mostly the bird hunters, from Denver and God knows where else, so they can blast the ducks and geese from the sky. Upstream it's the trout. Either way, they want our water."

Vic sensed she was easing more into the subject of water, so he inched her along, at least to get her perception of what was going on. "So the duck and trout gang wanted the irrigation wells shut off?"

A spoiled child responded. "They want the water left in the river to help the duckies and the fishies." Then the frustrated adult returned to the conversation. "Didn't Dave talk to you about this? This is really his area. He was the one who was hopping mad about it."

"I don't think we even got into it," Vic said, deciding not to mention her husband's theories on who prompted the well shut-off. "We talked a bit about the water lawyers, how they seem to get their fingers into everything, and then the annexation bit."

"Oh, of his mom's old place?"

"Yeah."

"That gravel thing bothered him as much as our foreclosure," Betsy said. "Then, when Mary died—"

"Mary?"

"His mom. Dave went off the deep end."

"How deep?"

That smart Lauren Bacall looked up at him again. She suddenly realized she was talking to a reporter. "You're not going to put all this in the paper, are you?"

"Not necessarily," Vic said. "Background, remember? We can always just talk about the sensitive areas. They don't have to be in the story."

"Well, this is sensitive," she said. "I don't think it means anything, but sometimes I'm not sure."

Vic watched this beautiful competent woman wander in and out of an unsure, childlike state. He wanted her to keep talking to him. It was the talking that was most important.

"Let's say now that we're off the record," he said.

"Off the record? Like in the movies?" She smiled at him.

"Yes. This is in confidence. Just like the movies."

"*All the President's Men.*" She was still smiling.

"Yes, like *All the President's Men.*"

"That makes me Deep Throat then." She burst out with a nervous laugh. "Wouldn't you like that?"

Vic was not sure how she meant that last comment. "It's off the record. I won't use it in the story. I won't even take notes."

Betsy composed herself, back to self-assured. "I love my husband, Vic. Deeply."

"I understand that," Vic said.

"You can't understand it entirely. Dave picked me up when my family crashed. We were kids then. I, well, this isn't for the paper is it?"

Vic shook his head. "No. I said off the record."

"I tried to kill myself," she said.

"How?"

"Not with a gun, if that's what you think." She held out her arms to him, wrists up. Feint scars blemished each one. "I'm embarrassed about it now. But back then, a senior in high school, my world collapsed with the sugar beets. They took Daddy's farms and kept me out of the Olympics."

"They?"

"Bankers. Government. Tractor dealer. High Plains Sugar Beets. Everyone."

"Couldn't the community help?" Vic said.

"No. Nobody had any money. Anyway, it was the nationals we couldn't get to. I had to win them to make the team. Daddy was in meeting after meeting. He was in court, more meetings, and then everything caved in."

"Not easy, I guess, for a high school kid," Vic said.

"Not easy?" Betsy said. "Vic, shooting was my whole life. It was the one thing that was all mine, the one thing that only I could control. It was everything to me."

"Well, I'm going to need to put some of this stuff in the story, Betsy," Vic said.

"Not the suicide part, please," she said. Then a tear escaped. "It was stupid anyway. And not some of my thoughts about Dave either."

"Thoughts? From back then?"

"No, now," she said. "Sorry. Back then he stood by me. Believe me, I was a bitch after I got home from the hospital. Daddy made them put 'farm accident' on my medical records. Dave came by every day for months. He never knew what I did, and I treated him like he was a lapdog. That wasn't right."

Maybe he was a lapdog, Vic thought. "But you married him."

"After I woke up and realized what a prince he was. He saved my life."

"You were high school sweethearts?"

"Sort of," she said, getting up again to pour more iced tea, re-taking command of the oak table. "You can say that in your story. Farm kids who grew up together. Dave's two years older than me. He was in Ag school over at Fort Collins. But every day he stopped by to see me. He must have put five hundred miles a week on his old truck."

"What was happening with your father's farms?"

"Daddy was scrambling. Selling trucks, land, whatever he could. Trying to get other crops in, fast. I emptied my savings account and gave it to him. That was the money for the nationals, then the Olympics."

Betsy lost focus again. She walked over to the front window, pitcher in hand, and gazed out at the mountains. "We'll have rain in half an hour."

Vic looked out the window and saw the dark clouds. Live out here, and you can feel the weather, he thought. "What was happening with Dave's family?"

"Same thing," she said, walking back into the kitchen with the empty pitcher. "Are you going to want any more tea?"

Vic held his hands up and said, "I'm floating. I'm fine. Thanks."

"Dave had to quit school. He stayed through his sophomore year. His family lost nearly everything, all except that quarter section in his mom's name. They became tenant farmers on Dave's uncle's place. It broke his dad. Dave worked his uncle's land, to keep the family going."

"Did he ever get back to school?"

"No. After the accident, he couldn't work and do school."

"What accident?"

"Well, that's what they called it," Betsy said. "Dave's dad. They found him all tangled up in some old chains inside the barn. I don't know. But they found him in there. Hanging."

"How did Dave take that?"

"How would you?" Again with the straight in the eye look, cold and searing hot all at once.

"Not well," Vic said. "But it's not my story."

"Dave stood up to everything like a man. He had to take care of his mother. They had a small house out on his uncle's farm. Dave made the place work. But it was always marginal. Then he worked the hay meadows that his mom owned, closer to the river. About a year after his dad died, we got married. The three of us lived together in that little house. I'd come over here to help Daddy and then cook and keep house over with Dave and his mom. She did a lot too, on the farm, and she had a beautiful truck garden."

"Did you go to school?" Vic said.

"Oh, I took a few business courses at the community college," she said. "Enough so I could run the books for both farms."

"So it was kind of a two-family enterprise?" Vic said.

"Sort of. But the farms were independent."

"When did you move into this house?" Vic said.

"Right after Sarah, our oldest, was born. About twelve years ago. Mom and Daddy decided to get the little place, that condo, in town. He was already on oxygen and still trying to run the farm. He had to quit. They wanted to give us the farm and the house. More room for the family."

"Did Dave's mom move with you?"

"No. She really loved that little house on her brother's place. It was family. The farm sale to that doctor, did Dave tell you about that?"

"He did," Vic said.

"That gave her enough to live on, until, well I guess you know that too, then."

"Dave told me about her heart attack."

Betsy sat down across the table from Vic. "I like talking to you, Vic." She targeted her green eyes at his, folded her hands in front of her. "I wonder what you'll write about me."

"I'm not real sure right now," he said.

"I didn't think this would take so long."

"I'm sorry," Vic said. "I lost track of time."

"That's all right," she said, standing back up. "I did too. But I've got to go pick up the girls in Fort Lupton. Riding lessons from a friend. Free. I'd be happy to talk to you more. Maybe we can meet for lunch. The girls are both in summer school."

"Sure. That would be fine. Why don't I call you in a few days?"

"I'll call you," she said, taking command once more.

"That's fine too." Vic gave her his card. "Use the cell phone number. Not the paper's number, okay?"

"Okay." She raised her eyebrows and tilted her head so the soft hair flowed over one shoulder.

She quickly gathered up the iced tea glasses, the napkins and spoons, set everything on the tray, and whisked it all into the kitchen, leaving the ancient oak table spotless and clear.

They left the farm together in a short dusty caravan, Vic in his Jeep and Betsy leading in the Bender's big light gray diesel pickup. It was the same one Dave drove the other day when they visited the gravel pit that once was his mother's farm. The Benders must have two cars, Vic thought, or one of Dave's buddies picked him up for work. No, they probably have two cars, he concluded, for no particular reason.

The gathering rain clouds had turned the day so dark that Vic turned on his lights. Ahead of him Betsy had done the same. As they sat idling at the stop sign before turning onto the paved state highway, Vic noticed that only the passenger side taillight on the Bender truck seemed to be working. The driver's side light was dark.

"Was it Dave Bender who joined me to observe the meeting that night at Rosenthal's ranch?" Vic asked out loud, to no one in particular.

# 67

Vic turned left toward Denver and Betsy turned right toward Fort Lupton. When her truck disappeared from his rear view mirror, he pulled a fast U-turn and headed back to the Bender farm.

Heart pounding, Vic gunned his Jeep up the driveway to the frame house. He bore right, drove past the massive double door on the front of the barn, and swung around to the west side of the empty building to park. He knew this had to be quick. Fort Lupton was not that far away, and he knew it would not be long before Betsy returned unless she had other errands to run. He grabbed his small point-and-shoot digital camera, sprang from the Jeep, and jogged to the back of the sixty-foot barn, stopping at the shoreline of a rolling sea of stunted and dry yellowing corn stalks.

Out behind the barn Betsy had said, but Vic could not see anything that looked like a shooting range. He dove in, bushwhacking through the rough and uneven field, glad he had worn his lightweight hiking boots. About a quarter of a mile from the barn he spotted an irrigation well.

The heavy gauge electrical wires that emerged from an underground conduit had been severed and a junction box or switch removed from the circuit. Sunlight glinted off a new padlock on the brass valve lever, preventing anyone from opening the water line. A silver dollar sized orange plastic seal on a wire looped through the locking hole read, "Do Not Remove Under Penalty of Law. Colorado Div. Of Water Resources" on one side and "Seized Well. Do Not Operate" on the other. Vic took several photographs of the immobilized well and stuffed the camera back into his pocket so he could continue his awkward search for the shooting range.

Fifty yards from the well, his march suddenly ended when his right foot plunged into a two-foot deep hole. Vic crumpled fast, instinctively tucking his right shoulder, rolling with the fall. Only he did not roll. He fell backwards, his right shoulder slamming onto a broken corn stalk rigid enough to rip through his shirt and do who knows what to his body. Something awful was happening to his right leg. Engulfed in numbing pain, Vic finished the fall on his back. It did look like rain, he thought, as he gazed up at the dark gray clouds heavy and billowing with moisture, his eyes salty with tears, his nose overwhelmed with the crispy odor of dried cornstalks. He thought of his childhood, playing in the cornfields with Dave and Bobby and Rusty and Normie and Jeanne and Patty. Then he closed his eyes.

An annoying insect buzz in his left ear brought him around. Vic swatted at his head with his left hand. The shoulder screamed for relief, and Vic edged over to the left a bit to get off the stabbing cornstalk.

Wondering when the clouds would open up on him, Vic rested for a moment and assessed his situation, flat on his back, left leg out straight, the other one bent at the knee and in the hole. He moved a bit, but another shooting pain stopped him cold. Hands wiggled. He waved at the clouds. Arms worked. Shoulder stung. He raised his left leg and pointed the big toe at the tops of the stunted cornstalks. His right foot followed the command to move, but not before sending more agony up the leg. Knee seemed okay. Pain came from the ankle.

He hunched up on his elbows, backed out of the hole and rolled over, pushing himself up on all fours, thinking he could probably get back to the car this way. Crawl back to the irrigation well to use it to help him get up off the ground? Naw. Dad's walking stick would help. It was at Dad's house.

With no walking stick, no well mechanism to grab, Vic simply rose up to his knees, lifted his left leg, placed his left foot flat on the ground, and heaved himself skyward. He kept most of his weight on his left leg as he stood up. He hopped a few times to keep his balance, the right leg bent at the knee, his throbbing right foot off the ground. When he stopped the grasshopper dance, he carefully put weight on his right foot and ankle. Pain shot up the leg, but the foot seemed to be holding him. He gritted his teeth and really wriggled his foot this time. Everything seemed to be intact. The foot would go where he directed it to go, but not without screaming in protest. He walked and hopped and limped around until he felt confident enough to start walking back toward the barn. After two corn rows, he stopped and turned around. "In for a penny, in for a pound," he gasped, and limped deeper into the corn field to find the shooting range.

# 68

Like a minesweeper, Vic scanned ahead for more holes or uneven ground, his legs, feet, and ankles following when the pathway was visually cleared. He walked in ten-yard segments, then stopped to rest and let the throbbing in his ankle and leg subsides. On his second rest stop he looked up and saw the hill that Betsy had described. It was about fifteen feet wide, maybe about four or five feet high, cresting over the tops of the diminutive corn. At his next stop, ten more yards in, he saw chairs and a small table. Vic gradually put more weight on his right side. The pain eased slightly. Standing next to the table where target shooters placed, reloaded, maybe even cleaned guns, Vic reached down to the dirt and snatched up a half dozen small brass shells. He stuffed them into his pants pocket.

Turning toward the hill, about thirty yards away, Vic saw a small wooden post topped with a shredded piece of plywood, about a foot square. He limped downrange. As he got closer to what he presumed to be a target he could see a ragged hole through its middle, corners chipped off, and a few scraps of one or more paper targets that had been stapled to the plywood. Worried about time and Betsy's return, he walked past the target and eyeballed a straight line into the hill where bullets would have been buried. He looked back toward the target, then the hill, then back at the target again and one last time at a spot on the hill where he thought he might find spent slugs. Welcoming a rest for his ankle, Vic dropped to his knees and began digging in the dirt with his hands. A foot or so in, small metal pellets came out with the dirt and the rocks. He quickly sifted through his find, retrieved a half dozen battered projectiles and stuffed them into his pocket with the brass he had picked up by the shooting table. He pushed himself back up and limped as fast as he could back toward the barn and his car. Fat raindrops splattered on his face.

The sky opened up. By the time Vic got back to the Jeep, the rain had soaked through to his skin. He did not care. He was glad to be back inside the vehicle, thankful he had not been bashed by a classic eastern Colorado hailstorm. Vic started the car and sped around in front of the barn, down the driveway, and onto the county road, surprised but glad his right side worked so well through the spasms of pain.

He had covered about three of the seven miles back to the blacktop when Betsy's pickup flew past him. Looking at her retreating vehicle in his rear view mirror, he could see the two additional bumps that represented the heads of her daughters. His cellphone rang.

"This is Vic."

"Forget something?" It was the coy Lauren Bacall voice again.

"One of my notebooks," Vic said. "I tossed it onto the roof of the car when I left your place."

"I didn't see you toss anything up there," she said. It was matter-of-fact. Chewing the fat.

"It's a bad habit. I lost a camera lens in Wyoming doing that, my nice zippered leather calendar once, and I don't know how many cups of coffee."

"Did you find it?" Betsy said.

"I always find the cups, but never the coffee," Vic said.

She laughed. "The notebook."

"I did," he said.

"Was it soaked?" she said.

"Yeah. I've got it open here in the seat."

"Why don't you come back," she said. "We can dry off the pages so they don't get stuck together, and keep working on the story." Suddenly she was his partner.

"Can't. I'm already late for an appointment."

"You mean, there's someone else?" she cooed.

"My mom and dad," Vic said. "We have coffee dates two or three times a week."

"I won't compete with mothers, being one myself, or daddies." Betsy said.

"I'll call you," Vic said.

"No, remember?" she said. "I'll call you."

# 69

The century-old Idaho Springs Cafe wooden floor creaked as Detective Frank Driscoll walked back over to their table. Each massive hand held a cream-colored porcelain mug filled with steaming hot coffee. He set one mug in front of Vic and then nearly squashed the chair on the other side of the table as he sat down.

"One week," Driscoll said. "One week out of the year, I get my little Vail time-share getaway with the family, and I have to spend a morning with you."

"You were coming into Denver anyway," Vic said, blowing across his mug before he sipped the hot liquid.

Even though he was on vacation, Driscoll wore his trademark gray high-end suit, a crisp white shirt, and a red tie.

"Two passes I had to traverse for this. Do you realize how treacherous Vail Pass can be and how high Loveland Pass is?"

"Frank, it's July. Serious snow is four months away."

"And then having to pull off the highway and make the run down through the Springs here—"

"You always stop in Idaho Springs at Sunrise Donuts. Always."

"That's all beside the point," Driscoll said. "I'm on vacation."

"Frakes told me you were coming into the office. I thought I'd take a little drive up the canyon. Meet you here. I want to give you something."

"Oh boy," Driscoll said, spilling his third spoonful of sugar into his coffee.

"Have you ever heard of diabetes?" Vic said.

"The Greater Diabetes?" Driscoll said. "Islands off the coast of Alaska aren't they."

Vic folded his arms, leaned back, and glared at the cop.

"I know, I know," Driscoll said. "It runs in the family too. But they say the pink or blue or yellow stuff will kill you too."

"Not like diabetes will kill you," Vic said. "Start using the plastic sugar. It leads to a far more gradual and less painful death. Better still, drink it black."

"Oh, please," Driscoll said as he stirred his coffee. He shot that look at Vic, then stood up with his mug, walked over behind the lunch counter, and dumped it into the sink.

From the kitchen came, "Can I help you?"

"No, dear. It's me here goofing up with the coffee," Driscoll said. "I've got it. You keep working on our breakfast."

"My sole purposed for living," came the reply from the kitchen. "Be ready in a minute. Help yourself."

In full compliance with the owner's order, Driscoll poured himself a fresh mugful of coffee and creaked back over to their table. Clear Creek gushed clean cold water below them, right outside the window.

"Okay, which poison is best?" Driscoll eclipsed the kitchen chair again. Vic grabbed the small white sweetener caddy and fingered through the options.

"White was what you were using," Vic said. "It's off the list permanently, understand?"

"Sure, Doc."

"Yellow, I think now they say is the same as sugar, at least for diabetics," Vic said.

"I'm not diabetic yet," Driscoll said.

"Well at this rate, you will be."

"Why do they sell it then?"

"Someone said it was sugar without the calories, but I think there's a problem with it now," Vic said. "I don't know. Blue, I believe, turns your brain into Swiss cheese. I don't know what pink does. Go with that."

"The lesser of four poisons," Driscoll said.

"I use agave nectar," Vic said. "At home, for iced tea. Or honey sometimes. Agave is like honey, though. Comes from some plant."

"Aw shut up, will ya," Driscoll said, shaking his head, grabbing a pink packet. He tore it open and dumped the white powder into his coffee.

The waitress arrived with their breakfasts, both designed to clog arteries, under the theory that it was better to go with a sudden heart attack than gradually with diabetes or the fossilization of the brain. Nobody talked about strokes.

The two traded family information while they ate. Vic complained about the latest Denver police shooting, a young burglar shot in the back as he was running away down an alley. Driscoll bitched about the news coverage of a police disciplinary hearing over another shooting in which the cop was cleared.

"I still cannot believe you're working for that rag," the detective said.

Vic limped over to the counter to refill their coffee mugs.

"And the limp?" Driscoll said when Vic returned to the table.

"Injured in the line of duty," Vic said.

"Don't ask for strokes Saturday," Driscoll said, "Now, why did you drag me in here?"

Vic dug into his pocket and pulled out a baggie containing the shells and bullets from the Bender farm.

"These," he said and handed over the baggie.

Driscoll looked up at Vic. He made no move to pick up or even touch the plastic bag. "What are these, and where did they come from?"

"As you can plainly see, these are shells and bullets from a small caliber weapon."

"Like a twenty-two?" Driscoll said.

"Yes, like a twenty-two," Vic said.

"Asking questions about a case is one thing. Coming up with evidence is quite another." Driscoll saw his week away from Denver evaporating.

"They're from the Bender farm," Vic said.

"And how did they come to be in your possession?" Driscoll said.

"I took them from a shooting range the Benders have out behind their barn," Vic said.

"This is like a TV show, isn't it?" Driscoll said. He shoved a piece of sausage into his mouth and chewed it hard. "Now, you're going to ask me if I can have the lab boys, isn't that what they call them on TV, on CSI, the lab boys, or girls, take a look at them for you?"

"What do you call them?" Vic said.

"We call them techs," Driscoll said.

"Well the techs then," Vic said. "The lab techs."

"Yes, the techs," Driscoll said. "And what would I be looking for if I gave these to them?" He was now holding up the baggie with the thumb and forefinger of his right hand, twisting the package back and forth slowly. He knew the answer.

"Whether they match—"

"Don't say it," Driscoll said. "The story you're not working on because your bosses don't want you to and the murder case I'm not working on because I'm on vacation, right?"

"Uh, right," Vic said. "I'm working on a feature story, about the impact of these well shut-off orders on the farmers, and I came across these."

"Maybe I know you a little better than you think I do, Vic," Driscoll said, "because I think you're working on this, what did you call it? A feature. That's right, a feature, but it's only a cover to work the Swain case without your editor knowing about it."

"Am I that transparent?" Vic said.

"You're worse than transparent. You might as well wear a sign."

"I think my city editor might have an inkling about what I'm doing too."

"The daughter?"

"Yes," Vic said. "But don't get in the habit of calling her that. It might slip out at the wrong time."

"Well, that's what you called her," Driscoll said.

"All right, you use pink sugar, and I'll stop calling her daughter," Vic said. "Or better still, use agave."

"Done," Driscoll said.

Vic outlined the sharpshooter story from the newspaper archives, his interview with Betsy Bender, the training she gave to her husband, along with the background of both families, and the building anger and frustration within Dave Bender.

"Do you realize you're now a witness, Vic? How can you write about this case now?"

"I'm not sure," Vic said. "But the way journalism is put together these days it probably doesn't matter anymore. Ethics, standards, objectivity, everything seems to have fallen by the wayside."

"Truth seeking?" Driscoll said.

"Not that," Vic said. "Not for me. But how we get at the truth, that's what's changing."

Driscoll held up the baggie again. "I have no fricking idea how to get this into the system. I don't really know where this stuff even came from."

"I just told you," Vic said. "Plus, you're the head of the task force on this case."

"That means it's my butt if it doesn't get solved," Driscoll said.

"I'm trying to help."

"Yeah, but you don't want my detectives on your ass. I need to think about this."

"Frakes? I can handle him."

"What?" Driscoll said, getting serious, cop like, again. "You think this is one of your black and white movies? This is real life, and you just stepped smack into the middle of our case."

"In the meantime can you check these out?" Vic said. "You are the Chief of Detectives after all. I emphasize Chief."

"For the time being. You know, I've got people to answer to upstairs. This case hasn't been easy, no leads and all."

"Until now," Vic said.

"Until now," Driscoll said. "Maybe."

# 70

The front nine at Kennedy Golf Course was easy and flat, something Vic needed since he was still hobbled with a sore ankle. Driscoll returned from the mountains late the night before. They teed off at eight-thirty, an hour later than their usual time. Both men got to the course late, with no time for breakfast or practice putts. They grabbed large coffees, piled into their cart, and raced down to the first tee. The detective put his tee shot out three hundred yards straight down the middle of the fairway.

"Who are you, Tiger Woods today?" Vic said. He addressed his tiny white target, then hooked his drive into the next fairway. "You take the cart. Drop me down by the hill, and I'll walk. Or limp."

"Damn straight you will," Driscoll said. "Straight, by the way, that's the operative word out here."

"Yeah, thanks. By the way, anything on the—"

"Don't ask," Driscoll growled. "It ruined my vacation."

They were silent to the midway point on the fairway. Vic wandered off to find his errant drive. His limp had all but disappeared, but the ankle still hurt. The two met up on the green.

Driscoll parred the hole. Vic carded a bogey.

"Nice recovery shot," Driscoll said. It was. Two hundred and fifty yards with a three wood, a shot Vic hated to even attempt. He had no confidence with fairway woods.

The round was uneventful. Driscoll and Vic avoided talking about bullets, brass, shooting ranges or dead politicians, keeping it to smart-assed golf banter and politics.

"Hello boys," Grace said as they walked into the clubhouse for lunch. "Haven't seen either of you in a while."

"Driscoll here was off playing in the mountains," Vic said. "I've actually been working, harder than usual."

"Well, we've missed your sunny faces," she said. "You want the club sandwich?" Driscoll nodded.

"Sure, and two Arnie's," Vic said.

"Give me a minute," Grace said with a sparkly smile, and she headed for the kitchen.

"She's still lookin' at you, man," Driscoll said.

"Don't start," Vic said. "I need to talk to you about Swain."

"You need?"

"I need."

"I probably can't tell you much," Driscoll said.

"Have you made any headway on the water right?" Vic said.

"What water right?" Driscoll said.

"Now you're playing me," Vic said. "The one you called me about right after she was murdered."

"You know more than what you told me about water rights?" Driscoll said.

"A lot," Vic said, "And if you don't know what I know I think you're missing something big."

"You think you know something we don't know?" Driscoll said, cracking a grin, starting to laugh.

"You know, to quote our Defense Secretary, not knowing what

you don't know might be just as important as knowing what you don't know," Vic said.

"Or vice versa."

"If we don't start over, I'll be shooting iced tea and lemonade out my nose," Vic said, his eyes tearing up.

"So start over," Driscoll said.

"I have more background on the water rights thing, but I'd like something in return."

"Like what?" Driscoll said. His smile turned into a scowl.

"Like a shot at breaking this story, if you ever find out who did it," Vic said.

"We've got some leads," Driscoll said. "Nothing hard." The big cop sighed and said, "Yeah, we're not real solid on this water thing. We don't even know if it's a factor."

"Well, I think it's a factor," Vic said. He knew one of them would have to break at some point, moving ahead with telling the other what he really knew or thought he knew, trusting that the reciprocation would happen.

"We're not so sure," Driscoll said.

Sensing the cop was going to hold the line this time, probably because he had next to nothing on the water right other than a vague rumor, Vic blinked first and told him about his conversations with Evelyn on the water right trust and with Largent on conflict of interest.

"We didn't know about the trust that Swain controlled," Driscoll said. "And nobody on my team thought the, what did you call them? Oh, the Four Horsemen. We didn't give them much thought after we cleared them."

"You cleared them? All of them? Even Kendrick?" Vic's heart thumped that scared thump. He hated being wrong.

"Pretty much," Driscoll said. "We interviewed them all several times and didn't really pick much up other than they seemed to want to move forward with whatever plans they had."

"Were these dainty and very polite interviews?" Vic said.

"Yes, but to the point," Driscoll said. "They are movers and shakers, full calendars and all."

"You don't think one or more of them could have steered the farmers in the direction of, uh—"

"Murder?" Driscoll said. "Assassination? Highly improbable."

"So you've completely cleared them?" Vic said.

"That's what I said."

"I can't say I agree with you, detective."

"Doesn't matter. I'm the only cop in the room, and this cop says they're cleared."

Vic bristled. "That leaves the farmers."

"That leaves the farmers," the detective said.

"Are you focusing your efforts on them?" Vic said.

"I'll only answer that on one condition," Driscoll said.

Vic saw it coming and said, "Don't tell me."

"I will tell you," Driscoll said. "Way off the record. So far off the record I don't even want to see it in the paper."

"That's fairly useless for me," Vic said.

"Tough," Driscoll said. "I want a case that sticks to the wall."

"All right," Vic said. "But I want a leg up when it really breaks, okay?"

"Done," Driscoll said.

They did one rock, paper, scissors, which Vic lost, and then they pounded fists to seal the deal.

"We're keeping a close eye on Bender, Hague, and Winston," he said.

"Hell, I could have told you that," Vic said.

"We have a deal, a rock, paper, scissors deal."

"It's in the vault," Vic said, but he was not satisfied. "You're sure about those other guys? They've got a lot at stake. Currington's housing development. Michaels is goose-stepping to be governor, and Kendrick, well, he's too slimy for words."

"Vic, Kendrick makes more money returning phone calls than you and I make in a year. He doesn't need this. Currington might be spread a little thin financially, but he's lily white. He worked in the White House, for God's sake."

"Michaels?"

"Ambitious politician, but like most of them, a real chickenshit," Driscoll said. "His guiding light, Rosenthal, is an egghead at the University of Denver. Couldn't hurt an ant, or fight his way out of a wet paper bag.

"I thought you liked Democrats."

"They try to look after people, but beyond that, both parties have sold us down the river," Driscoll said.

"You're sure about them?"

"The Democrats?"

"The Four Horsemen," Vic said.

"Absotively."

Vic's heart settled down a little bit, but he had hoped that one or more of the four white collar boys, the plutocrats, were wrapped up in Swain's murder. He found Driscoll's certainty a real drag.

"Maybe I can get Kendrick on conflict of interest," Vic said.

"Maybe you can," Driscoll said. "But that doesn't concern me in the least."

"What if he broke a law, committed fraud?"

"Take it up with the DA," Driscoll said.

"A close eye on Dave, Bobbie, and Darryl, that's all?" Vic said. Driscoll nodded. "Anyone of them in particular?"

"For now, all of them."

"No one else?"

"No one else," Driscoll said.

"Does the water trust thing help?" Vic said.

"It does," Driscoll said. "It's a possible motive. The change in the water right would really mess the farmers up."

Grace delivered the sandwiches and Arnie Palmers. The two ate silently and watched the replay of the 1983 Masters on the big screen. Seve Ballesteros from Spain was on the 18th green, a few minutes away from his second Master's win. Crenshaw and Kite were in his dust, four strokes back.

# 71

Vic made the long tangled walk through the city room cubicle maze to the city desk where he took his usual position across the wide flat work surface from Peggy's empty chair and dark terminal. He sifted through the pile of news releases from local flacks and government public information officers. Each sheet begged for a spot in the ever-shrinking news hole. Even though Vic was really a reporter, both his editing skills and his editorial judgment were often called upon by Peggy to help her out at the city desk, where the local news for each edition was assembled.

But Vic knew he was an editor on paper only, made an acting associate managing editor to avoid union requirements. What it really meant was that he could be canned at any time for any reason. They still did not trust some gray-haired boomer who had walked in off the street to restart a journalism career he had abandoned a quarter of a century earlier. The business was cynical to the end about everything, Vic thought as he pawed through the releases, playing newspaper god and determining who would get their story into the next day's paper and who would not.

"Black, right?" It was Peggy's voice. She had materialized next to the city desk. Vic looked up at her as she set one of two venti coffee cups from Starbucks in front of him.

"Hal broken?" Vic said.

"Hal?" Peggy said.

"The robot coffee computer back there," he said, nodding toward the hallway that led to the break room.

"No. I thought I'd grab these on the way up. It's on me."

"What's the occasion?" Vic said.

"Nothing," Peggy said.

"Well, I thank you. My insomnia thanks you too."

"Coffee keeps you awake?"

"Only when I can't sleep."

She walked around to the other side of the city desk to ascend to her throne. "Anything happening?"

"No. But I've only been here about ten minutes," Vic said. The news releases were sorted into two piles.

"Okay. Well, give me the winners," Peggy said.

Vic handed her one of the piles. He tossed the other pile into the trash basket labeled "Recycle Office Paper Only" next to the desk, wondering if Peggy would fish out the discards to double check his decisions on the news releases. She did not.

"Looks quiet," she said. "You got anything going?"

"Oh, the farmer thing," Vic said. "More interviews to do."

"Are we ever going to see a story?" Peggy said. "Should we send out a photog? Get some art?"

She shot questions at him regularly, almost every day now, about the farm story. Don't log it yet, Vic told her. When, she would ask. Soon, he would say. Then she would look at him funny, like she knew something.

"This decade?"

"Within the year," Vic said.

# 72

A phone rang somewhere in the nearly empty newsroom. After six unanswered rings, the call went into a cue to be answered by an operator somewhere in the building. Vic had no idea where. The intercom beeped on the city desk, and the voice from somewhere announced, "Vic Bengston. Line three."

As Peggy leafed through Vic's news release winners' pile, he picked up the phone. "This is Vic."

"It's me," Driscoll said.

"Oh," Vic said. "Really? No, I don't think so. You know, it's in my notes. Let me transfer you back to my desk, and I'll give you the citation."

Driscoll said nothing.

"Who's that?"

"My bookie," Vic said as he hit the buttons that transferred the call to his desk. "It's my committee chair. He needs a cite I used for my paper."

"Paper?"

"My master's project. Citizen Journalism, remember?"

"Oh, that's right. You're a student too. You must be older than all your professors put together."

"Rub it in."

She grinned. "With relish."

Vic got up and headed back to his desk. Peggy tossed two more releases into her "Recycle Office Paper Only" wastebasket.

He sat down at his desk, put on a headset, and opened the small netbook computer he used for his outside writing, including all his notes on the Swain murder story. He did not want anything on the newspaper's terminal, which could be read by anyone with a password. He hit the flashing button on his phone.

"You might want to use my cell next time," Vic said.

"I can hang up too," Driscoll said in his cop voice.

"Not necessary," Vic said.

"You're a secondary anonymous tip," Driscoll said.

"Really?"

"Really," Driscoll said. "I found a way, that's all."

"What did you do?" Vic said.

"This is off the record, understand?"

"Off the record, yes," Vic said, not sure exactly what was on the record or what was off anymore.

"We got a tip about some disgruntled farmers, and something about a shooting range," Driscoll said. "That led to a search warrant."

"You went out there?" Vic said "Was Bender home?"

"Nobody was there," Driscoll said.

"So, they don't know," Vic said.

"We have to tell them, Vic," the detective said. "We left a notice."

"How polite."

"We found a shooting range, brass, and some small caliber slugs in a small hill behind a target."

"Where was your range?" Vic said.

"Same place as yours," Driscoll said. "Behind the barn, about five hundred yards into the field."

"The new barn?" Vic said.

"Yes, Vic. The new barn. We lucked out."

"How so?" Vic said.

"Like I said earlier, we got a tip," Driscoll said.

"Okay, you got a tip from me, unsolicited," Vic said.

"Definitely," Driscoll said.

"You can't just go out and get a search warrant on an anonymous tip, can you?"

"We had other information, from another witness."

"Witness to what?" Vic said. "The murder?"

"No, something else," Driscoll said.

"What something else?" Vic said. He was losing his patience now. "Come on."

"The shooting range," Driscoll said. "We re-interviewed all the witnesses again."

"All of them?"

"Yes." Then Driscoll hesitated.

"What do you mean?" Vic said.

"I mean all of them," Driscoll said. "Farmers and the politicos."

"Michaels and company?"

"Yes," Driscoll said. "Vic, I told you we cleared them. You desperately want one of those guys involved, don't you? You'd make a crappy cop. They're cleared. What more do you want?"

"Then it's only the farm boys for now?" Vic said. "That's too bad. It's fun to nail a white collar, clean finger nails, country club fellow, all that."

"Correct. We did open a few more farmer files after that breakfast meeting you had up in Fort Lupton with, what did you call them?"

"Lefty, Righty, and Middleman," Vic said.

"Sure. Those guys weren't involved in any of this water battle garbage, but they had a good idea who was," Driscoll said. "That was fairly lucky meeting on your part."

"Just call me Chance. Chance Bengston. So you talked to them again, and they told you about the shooting range?"

"Indirectly," Driscoll said.

"What does that mean?" Vic said.

"Well, they mentioned something about Dave Bender being quite the crack shot with shotguns, rifles, and hand guns. One of those old boys said his wife taught him 'out back behind the barn.' I think it was Fred Van Gelder."

"Lefty," Vic said.

"But somebody else told us about the shooting range too," Driscoll said.

Vic suspected that Gil might have called Driscoll, whose name featured prominently in all the we've-got-no-leads-yet follow-up news stories about Swain's killing. He pawed through his farmer story notebooks to locate the one with the date range that included his first meeting with Gil.

"So who called you?" Vic said. He flipped the notebook open and found "Tues." with the date scrawled next to it, followed by notes from his talk with Gil.

"Can't tell you that, pal, but it's real," Driscoll said.

"Was it recently?"

"No. we've had this one in the hopper for some time, but I cannot reveal the name."

"Tell me this," Vic said. "Could it have been three weeks ago?"

"Perhaps."

"Well, was it or not?" Vic put an edge in his voice, to see if it might work.

"Yes."

That's probably Gil then, Vic thought, relieved to know Driscoll had found another way to get to the shooting range.

"So I'm out of the story," Vic said.

"We can't put a reporter on the stand, not in this case," Driscoll said.

"Juries and the general public don't think that much of us," Vic said.

"Can you blame them?"

"We perform a public service," Vic said.

"Really?" Driscoll said. "I wouldn't take that to the bank."

"So what can you tell me about the ballistics?"

"You? Nothing."

Vic resorted to his old reporting technique, silence. It worked better if he sat across the desk from some sweating politician or bureaucrat. Everyone burned inside to talk, to let someone else know what they knew. The trick was to wait them out after the question was asked. Cops were the toughest, and Driscoll could be a stone wall, except when it came to a pressure putt.

"We're still off the record?" Driscoll said, crumbling.

"Yes," Vic said. "All I want to do is break the story when the arrest is made. We can fill in the details after that."

"Okay. The FBI lab—"

"FBI?" Vic said. "You've got the FBI working on this?"

"She was a head of state, Vic," the detective said.

"Lieutenant head of state," Vic said.

"No matter," Driscoll said. "We've thrown everything at it."

"And so you did," Vic said. "Is an arrest imminent?"

"Let's go back to the bullets," Driscoll said.

"By all means."

"All off the record, permanently."

"I'm not sure what you mean by that," Vic said. "An arrest is a public event."

"I mean," Driscoll said in his sternest of cop voices. "That nothing ever gets reported until you see something written in an official document. Or it comes out of my mouth and on the record. None of that 'Sources close to the investigation' crap, understand?"

"You know, Frank, I helped break this thing open for you," Vic said. "I'm not interested in the same public record crumbs that other lazy ass reporters will pick up off the floor at the same time."

Silence again. This time Vic squirmed in his chair.

"Look, you damn near blew this entire case when you went out there," Driscoll said.

"How so?" Vic said. "I was plainly the classic nosy reporter."

"We already had executed a search warrant when you pulled that stunt of yours, showing up with the brass and the slugs, screwing up my vacation, and my breakfast," Driscoll said.

"You said you hadn't looked for the shooting range until after I told you about it," Vic said.

"No, I said we re-interviewed a lot of people, mostly to see how much of the case, if anything, you messed up."

"So when I gave you those items, you already had searched the farm, found the shooting range, and had the same evidence?"

"Essentially."

"I broke my ankle, soiled my clothes, nearly pissed my pants, to get that stuff, and you had already been there?"

"For the record," Driscoll said, "you twisted your ankle while you were being, what did you say, a 'nosy' reporter. Like I said, you messed things up. You didn't give us anything we didn't already have."

"You cleared some suspects," Vic said.

"Yes, we cleared a few, but not because of you. We've got other leads, and I told you we've gotten some other phone calls."

It had to be Gil, Vic thought, then said, "You've been watching the farmers for quite a while, haven't you?"

"Let me put it this way. When you handed me those shells and bullets in Idaho Springs, I swear I could have killed you."

"Figuratively I hope," Vic said.

"Saturday," Driscoll said. "With a seven iron."

"That's just plain mean, Frank. The seven's my favorite club."

"Well, I didn't split your skull with it, did I?" Driscoll said.

Vic wanted to bring up Gil, to see if the old farmer had called the police, but he decided against it for now. Then he remembered when Betsy Bender accused him of having some other reason for interviewing her, something beyond the farmer's plight over shut-off irrigation wells. His palms began to sweat. "Betsy knew her husband was a suspect when I interviewed her?"

"Damn straight," Driscoll said. "We interviewed both her and her husband. Him twice."

"And she knew the police had searched her farm, found the shooting range, the shells, the slugs?" Vic said.

"Everything," the cop said.

Vic looked up at the city desk. Peggy's head was glued to her terminal screen. He rubbed the tips of his fingers over moist palms. "She offered to teach me how to shoot."

"Like she did for her husband?" Driscoll said.

"She said he took to it like a duck to water," Vic said.

"Yeah, we know," Driscoll said.

"Do you have a gun?" Vic said.

"Yes, I carry one every day," Driscoll said. "Even when we're golfing."

"The murder weapon," Vic said.

"You don't quit do you?" Driscoll said.

"It's my job," Vic said.

"And it's my job to say no comment."

"Off the record?"

"Off the record? No comment."

324 / RICHARD J. SCHNEIDER

"Do the bullets match what you found at the crime scene?" Vic said.

"No comment," Driscoll said.

The strain dripped through Vic's headset with the next round of silence.

"Are you going to arrest Dave Bender?" Vic said.

"I'll let you know if and when that happens," Driscoll said. "I'll try to give you a heads up, but I can no longer promise it."

"Just because I went out there?" Vic said.

"That and the ringing in my ears from the exceedingly loud voices directed toward me by the chief, the FBI, the CBI, and the DA."

"You told them about me?" Vic said. "The bullets?"

"Damn right I did, pal," Driscoll said. "We've got to have it all on the table so we know where the legal pitfalls are. They weren't too happy, especially the FBI, but I assured them there would be no premature story in your rag."

Vic looked up at Peggy again. She already suspected him of working the Swain story on his own time. He was not too sure how he would handle that issue. Resign maybe. Vic still could not quite see how his visit to the shooting range screwed up the case since he had no idea the cops had Bender in their sights. There was the golf, though. It might appear as though Driscoll had handed him the story. That would be bad for Driscoll, but good for Vic.

"I can't really promise that either, but I'll try," Vic said.

"Try real hard," Driscoll said. "This is the biggest case in this state since Columbine and Jon Benet. At least they were not in my jurisdiction, but this one is, and I don't want it screwed up by some boomer reporter reliving his youth."

"I suppose that's one way to describe my new career," Vic said.

"And a fairly accurate one," Driscoll said.

He might be right, Vic thought.

"You've got to be going for him soon," Vic said.

"No comment," Driscoll said. "And stay away from the Benders, Dave's pals, and the Bender farm."

"What about Betsy and the girls?" Vic said. "Are they safe?"

"Stay away. Go home, play ham radio, or do your job on the rewrite desk. I'll try to let you know when things will break."

"But you can't promise it," Vic said.

"That's right," Driscoll said, hanging up without a goodbye.

# 73

As Vic settled back into his chair at the city desk, he thought about Betsy and her two daughters. How they would take it when their husband, father, and breadwinner is arrested for yet another crime of the century in Colorado? Then he thought about Gil, the oxygen, and his frailty. The old man would probably lose another farm, the last one, and his son-in-law.

"That was one hell of a long footnote," Peggy said. She was like a statue, her face zoned in on the terminal screen, her body posing as city editor, Twenty-first Century style. Only her fingers moved, flying and plapping their way across the keyboard.

"It was complicated," Vic said

"I'll bet," she said.

"Have you been doing your exercises?" he said, thinking diversion.

"Actually I have," she said. The fingers stopped. Peggy twisted her neck around in kind of a haphazard oblong orbit.

"No. No," Vic said. "Like this." She looked at him as he slowly tilted his head to one side, stretching the vertebrae, and then to the other side. "Now watch." Vic slowly turned his head as far as it would go to the right, to the left, slowly stretching everything out. He did it three times.

"Have you ever seen Jack LaLane on TV?" Peggy said.

"I hope I don't remind you of him," Vic said. "He's ancient."

"And he could toss you around this room with one hand," she said.

"Good point," Vic said. "My kids call me the Bread Machine Guy."

"Yeah, I noticed the eyebrows too," she said.

"They grow like weeds. Something about testosterone."

Peggy shuffled through some of the papers and notes in front of her. Vic did the same.

"Look," they both said at the same time.

"That was special," Vic said. "You first."

"No, you go ahead," Peggy said.

"Well, there's a little more to this farm story than I've been letting on," Vic said.

"Is an arrest imminent?" she said matter of factly.

"Is it that evident?" he said.

"Pretty much," she said.

"I forgot," Vic said. "You're a trained observer."

"And I've been observing you," she said.

"Okay, that was my source, or one source," Vic said.

"Driscoll?"

"It would seem that way, but no," Vic said. "The Saturday golf looks too obvious."

"A good source?" she said.

"Stellar," Vic said.

"And?"

"And, she said she'll call if something breaks," Vic said.

"She, my ass," Peggy said. "Driscoll will call, when?"

"He'll call when something breaks," Vic said, giving up. "I think they're going for Dave Bender, maybe his friends."

"Wasn't he the guy who got shot?" Peggy said.

Vic wondered if she was playing dumb. If so, he could not figure out why, except it was a good way to get more information, the way some TV reporters tossed out the fake wide-eyed naive question when already they knew the answer.

"No, that was Bobbie Hague," Vic said. "One of Bender's pals. The cops are watching him too, and Darryl Winston."

"That's right," she said. "Those guys who are bent out of shape over a little water?"

"It's their whole life, Peggy," Vic said. "No water. No crop, no farm. No income. What if you were prevented from practicing journalism for whatever reason?"

"Like age?" She put on her smug little editor face.

"Sure, like age. You know, it could happen."

"I wouldn't kill for it," she said.

"Many have killed for a lot less."

She sounded like an editor, like Vic's boss, when she said, "Vic, I know what story you've been working on. So does Hogan."

"You don't know the half of it," Vic said.

"I don't know that I want to know the other half," she said.

"I've been chasing this thing down every which way from Sunday," Vic said. "I've even looked at John Michaels."

"Senate majority leader John Michaels?" she said.

"Yes."

"Whatever for?"

"Are you kidding?" Vic said. "This guy wants to be governor so bad you can smell it when you're in the same room with him."

"He'd kill for it?" Peggy said.

"Many—"

"I know, you said that. You're kidding, though, aren't you?"

"No, but he's been ruled out," Vic said.

"How'd you do that?" Peggy said.

"I'd rather not say," Vic said.

"I'd rather not know," she said. "You must be in big trouble with your cop friend."

"It's getting there," Vic said. "Might even interfere with our golf game."

"Is there more?" she said.

She stood up and stretched her lithe body and exercised her tight neck.

"Oh yeah," Vic said.

She flopped back down into her chair, rolled her head back, and said, "Better give it to me, the whole story."

Vic told her about his investigation into Michaels, Currington, and Kendrick. He mentioned the banker, Ferguson, and the mentor, Rosenthal, but left out the after-dark night scope operation.

"Kendrick seems to have his fingers in everywhere," Peggy said. "Interesting angle there. Conflict of interest."

"But not connected to the murder," Vic said.

"How can you be so sure?" Peggy said.

"The task force has cleared them all, except the farmers," Vic said.

"They were actually interviewed by the cops?"

"Yes, several times, and they were cleared," Vic said.

"That's a bummer," Peggy said. "Cop sources good?"

Vic nodded. Then he explained that while Dave Bender, Hague, and Winston were working with Kendrick to get the Swain water right, Kendrick was working with Michaels and Currington to make sure they did not get it. Peggy was not too happy.

"How in hell am I going to explain this to Hogan?"

"No need to," a voice said. It was Hogan, from a few cubicles over. He pulled all six-foot-four of himself out of the chair and leaned on the edge of the cubicle partition.

"I should fire you right now, Bengston," Hogan said, and then to Peggy, "You too, maybe."

"But?" Vic said.

"But, it looks like a ripping good yarn, or some of it does," Hogan said.

"You're damn right it is," Peggy said. "Anyway, you need cause to fire Vic."

"No I don't," Hogan said. "He's exempt, remember?"

"Well if you fire him, I'll quit," Peggy said.

Wearing a fake grin, Vic looked at Peggy. "You do like me."

"You bastard," she fired back at Vic. "You left me hanging out to dry on this."

"I did all this on my own time," Vic said. "What's the problem?" He knew the answer.

"You either work for the paper or you don't," Peggy said. "There's no line between job and non-job in the news business. We give you all the resources, and then you use them to your own personal ends," Peggy said.

"What about my resources?" Vic said. "My sources? My knowledge? I know this town, this state for that matter, like the back of my hand."

"He's got a point, Peggy," Hogan said. "That's why I hired him."

"You stay out of this," she said, then realized who she said it to. "Sorry."

"That's okay," Hogan said, both hands raised in surrender. "You've got a point too." Then to Vic, he said, "You did this all on your own time?" Vic nodded. He knew what was coming. "And at any time did you ID yourself as a reporter for this paper?"

Vic scrunched up his mouth and nodded again.

"You were on the job, then, regardless of whether it was your time or not," Hogan said. "Read your employment contract."

"Well, I wasn't freelancing," Vic said. "Anything I came up with would have gone to the *Sun*."

Hogan looked at Peggy and said, "I think we can all agree on that, can't we?"

This time Peggy nodded and said, "I didn't mean to imply he was doing it for someone else."

Hogan looked at Vic.

"I had no such plans," Vic said. "I just—"

"Just what?" said Peggy.

"Well, I did it, that way at least, because I wasn't assigned to the story, couldn't get assigned to the story, so I chased down some leads on my own."

Face flushed, Peggy spun on Vic. "I couldn't—"

"That's okay, Peggy," Hogan said. "Vic, I told her to keep you off the story. She actually thought you should have stayed with it from the start."

"So, I am on probation," Vic said.

"Wouldn't you have done something like that in your business?" Hogan said.

"Have you ever been in business?" Vic said. "I mean beyond the newspaper business. Have you ever started a business, gone out and gotten clients, and then did the work from the ground up?"

Vic knew most journalists had no real life work experience. Instead, they lived life vicariously through their stories about real people meeting payrolls, fighting wars, getting jobs done, sending kids through school, getting killed or injured, living the high life or struggling to make ends meet. Reporters often understood life only in theory, one step removed from the genuine article. Vic had built both a statewide government agency and a real business. Real life.

"No," Hogan said. "I came up through the ranks from the

editorial side, like Peggy here. Reporter, assistant city editor, city editor, managing editor, editor."

"Then publisher," Vic said.

"Editor and publisher," Hogan said. "Sure, but I run the place."

"That you do," Vic said, a bit uneasy over his critical assessment of the newsroom fantasy land. "But to answer your question, I don't think I've ever put anyone on probation per se. If I needed someone for a job, I put them right on the project."

"What if he or she screwed up?" Hogan said.

"Fix the problem. If it was a contractor, maybe never use him or her again," Vic said.

"That's sort of like probation," Hogan said.

Sensing he was on a slippery slope to losing this argument, Vic changed the subject.

"I felt I had to prove myself," Vic said.

"To us or to you?" Peggy said.

"Both, maybe."

"Well, so far, I could fire you right now, no questions asked, for failing to keep your city editor informed of what you were doing," Hogan said.

"Aside from that minor infraction, how would you assess the work for the paper thus far?"

Hogan turned to his city editor. "Peggy?"

"Exemplary."

"That's what I thought you'd say," Hogan said. Then he looked back at Vic. "I've read every word you've written for the paper, Vic, and she's right. I even liked the South Platte fly fishing story."

"I worked the Swain story on my own time, mostly," Vic said. "It was for the *Sun*, no other publication."

"I know," Hogan said. "I never doubted that. I know someone else who wanted to prove herself once."

"I wasn't going to bring that up," Peggy said.

"No matter, I will," Hogan said. "This was, what, a year or so after you joined the staff?"

Peggy nodded.

Hogan continued. "She was covering the statehouse. That was your beat once, wasn't it, Vic? Well, she had to cover the legislative session, but on her own time she went over about five years' worth of bills, lobbyist financial reports, and legislators' disclosure statements. She uncovered some interesting links. One night I found her sound asleep at her desk and saw some of her notes."

"You read my notes?" Peggy said.

"They were on your desk, upside down," Hogan said. "Of course I read them."

Vic liked that. He used to do the same thing, always surprised how much he could read upside down while documents were lying on someone's desk. Hogan might have been a fairly decent reporter, he thought.

"Doesn't matter, Peg," Hogan said. "We finally put two and two together here and got you some help up at the statehouse, so you could wrap up your story. How many legislators had to resign?"

"Seven representatives and five senators," she said. It was her red badge of courage.

"I remember that story," Vic said, feigning absent-mindedness, because he re-read the entire series once he found out Peggy would be his immediate boss. "I knew two of those guys you took down. They were tough. It was a good series."

"Indeed it was," Hogan said. "Helped Peggy with her Nieman Fellowship application, so I wound up losing her for a year while she went to Harvard. As I recall from your file, Vic, the *Sun* lost you for a year when you trotted off to Knight Journalism Fellowship at Stanford."

"It was nine months," Vic said. "The Energy Affairs fellowship was only two quarters."

"Even so, you two 'Fellows' make a good team," Hogan said.

Vic and Peggy looked at each other. Then Peggy burst out laughing. "May and November," she said.

"September, please," Vic said.

"Code names?" Hogan did not get the joke.

"Yet another slap at my advanced state," Vic said.

Then Hogan got serious. "Is there going to be an arrest in the Swain case?"

"Vic thinks Dave Bender," Peggy said. "Maybe others."

"Are you sure about that?" Hogan was anxious to spread it across page one. "Can we go with it?"

"No and no," Vic said.

"I thought you had a handle on this story?" Hogan said.

"I did, or I thought I did. I mean I thought it was pure politics, until—"

"Until what?" Hogan said.

"Until he trespassed on the Bender farm and took some evidence," Peggy said.

"No way." Hogan's voice had departed from its usual even monotone.

"He had a hunch," Peggy said. "Looks like it was a good one."

"What did you do?" Hogan said.

"I found some bullets," Vic said to Hogan. "They turned out to match the ones found in the lieutenant governor's head. I'm sorry, not a match. They were the same type and caliber, twenty-twos."

"What, you're a cop now?" Hogan said. "I don't know if I've ever had a reporter cross the line as many times as you have. Going back to the farm had must have been trespassing. Tampering with evidence is an interesting infraction."

"That wasn't evidence tampering," Vic said. "I had no idea Bender and his pals were under investigation. The cops already had bullets and shells from the range. I didn't know it at the time. That was what I call good reporting."

"Except for the trespassing part," Peggy said.

"You'd better give me a list of names of the people you've checked out on this thing," Hogan said, feeling a bit out in left field. "I don't want to be blind-sided."

"Well, they're not that important, not now," Vic said. "They're really just minor characters. You know the big names, and Driscoll says they're all in the clear. But if you like, I'll put together a list."

"I would like that," Hogan said.

Vic decided he would not bother with the list, at least until Hogan followed up a couple of times.

"Vic," Hogan said, pausing a bit. "Why did you go looking for the shooting range?"

"Well, I wasn't acting on police information if that's what you think," Vic said. "After I interviewed Bender's wife, I thought more and more about how she trained her husband to shoot, and how much he liked it."

"You had a hunch," Hogan said. "You're a hunch guy."

"Yeah, I'm a hunch guy," Vic said. Sometimes it got him into trouble. "I knew it was a twenty-two that had killed Swain."

"Knew how?" Hogan asked.

"I just knew, okay?" Vic said.

"That sounds like golf talk," Peggy said.

"Don't go there," Vic said. "I can't go there. I have many sources." Sure you do, Vic said to himself.

"You went back to the farm knowing Betsy would be gone," Hogan said.

"Yes, and I found the shells and slugs."

"Then gave them to the cops," Hogan said. "I'll bet they were delighted."

"Not overly," Vic said. "They had already searched the place. I didn't know that when I went there. Driscoll already had shells and slugs. I didn't know that until today. I think the cops scrambled to make sure their legal path to the search and the evidence was iron clad."

"And make sure you didn't screw it up when you pulled your little trespass and search stunt, right?" Hogan said.

"Probably," Vic said.

"When you interviewed Betsy Bender, did you know her husband was a suspect?" Hogan said. "By the cops, I mean."

"No. I didn't realize that until after I talked to Driscoll today."

"But Betsy knew Dave was a suspect when you interviewed her, didn't she?" Peggy said.

"Yes, she did," Vic said. "And she sure played it cool with me."

"Most of this is off the record?" Hogan said. "The Driscoll material I mean."

Vic nodded and said, "But I'm losing track of what's what."

"Bingo," Hogan said. "You know Vic, you seem to think you're about a half a step ahead of the police when, in fact, you're about a half step behind them."

"Not bad for working a story on your own dime, though, isn't it chief?" Peggy said.

Vic looked at his city editor and kept his mouth shut.

"Not bad at all," Hogan said. "I'm sure the *Times* is way out in the weeds on this one. So, Vic, do we know or will we know when an arrest will be made?"

"They're supposed to call," Peggy said.

"Call?" Hogan said.

"Vic said he'd get a heads up," Peggy said.

"A heads up," Hogan said. He seemed to be in repeat mode.

Vic hoped he would get a heads up. Driscoll was pissed at him too.

# 74

"Let's get ready for a page one splash," Hogan said. "We'll need some more help. What about Mal? Who's at the cop shop?"

Was the story slipping away from him once again, Vic asked himself as he sat down in his familiar slot at the city desk. Hogan walked around the other side of the sprawling desk and sat down at another empty city desk slot.

"A page one splash?" Vic said. "What is this, a performance of *The Front Page*?"

"Fred's covering police," Peggy said. "I'll call Mal to work the statehouse angle."

"That's good," Hogan said as he logged onto a terminal. "Where are our web producers? Out skateboarding?"

"Jennifer?" Peggy said. "Hardly the skateboarding type. I think they took and early dinner, probably at the press club." She punched in numbers on her desk phone. Vic heard her talking to Mal, the statehouse reporter who took over the story after day one. Then she said to Hogan, "Malcom and Joseph are working the website now." She was a taskmaster.

"Who wrote *The Front Page*, anyway?" Hogan said. "Ring Lardner?"

"Who's he?" Peggy said.

"Sports writer, short story writer, satirist, influenced Hemingway," Vic said. "You never read Ring Lardner in high school English?" She pulled back both corners of her mouth and raised her eyebrows. To Hogan, Vic said, "No, Ben Hecht and Charles MacArthur wrote the play."

"I thought it was a movie," Hogan said.

"Several times," Vic said. "Bartlett Cormack adapted the play for the 1931 movie. Pat O'Brien played Hildy Johnson, then Charles Lederer re-adapted it for Howard Hawks and flipped genders. Rosalind Russel played Hildy opposite Cary Grant's Walter Burns. That was 1940. In the early seventies Billy Wilder wrote another screenplay, and he directed Jack Lemmon as Hildy and Walter Matthau as the editor, Burns. That was after they teamed up for The Odd Couple. There have been a few other versions of *The Front Page* made for television, even a series that ran for a couple of seasons in forty-nine and fifty."

While talking, Vic had been shuffling papers on the desk in front of him. He looked up and saw everyone near the city desk standing motionless, silent, and staring at him.

"What?" Vic said. "I like old movies."

"Should we be taking notes?" Peggy said. "Will there be a test?" Vic waved a hand at her.

"Whatever," Hogan said, "You want to work here or at your desk, Vic?"

"Work on what?"

"The main story, man," the publisher said. "It's all yours. We're here to help you."

"And beat the crap out of the *Times*," Peggy said. Her hand was over the phone. She said to Hogan, "Mal says he can be here in a half hour. That okay?" Hogan nodded.

"You know, I have no idea when they're going for the arrest," Vic said.

"That's all right," Hogan said. "Let's get ready for it, though."

The sparring behind them, the team flexed its muscles to work the arrest, which was the best breaking news story since the Swain murder itself. Vic spent the next hour writing the bottom of the crime story, covering details of the lieutenant governor's killing, the investigation to date, and how many of the leads went nowhere. He included a few speculative paragraphs on the shooting range where the cops would have found the spent shells near the shooting line and the bullets buried in the berm behind the target area. The shooting range information was attributed to police sources, which he knew would anger Driscoll, but Vic did not care. He sent the work electronically to both Peggy and Hogan, both of whom added their tweaks.

The phone rang. Vic heard Peggy say, "City desk." Then a pause. "Vic?" He turned toward her.

"It's Gil Johansson," she said.

"I'd better take this at my desk," Vic said.

Hogan looked up. "Private?"

"My notes are back there," Vic said. He ran to his cubicle. His phone was beeping by the time he got there. "This is Vic."

"Mr. Bengston?"

"Yes. Gil?"

"I need to see you."

"I'm awfully busy right now," Vic said. "Can we talk over the phone?"

"No, I won't do that," he said, then coughed for a few seconds and said, "I'm sorry." Vic heard the sucking whoosh of the oxygen over the phone.

"Where are you?"

"Up at the Branding Iron, in Fort Lupton."

Vic's heart pounded. That was a half-hour drive on a good night.

"I can send someone—"

"No. I won't talk to anyone but you, damn it." He coughed again. "Face to face. Man to man."

Vic looked back at the city desk, the activity, everyone workng, and the story slipping further away. He envisioned a swarming city room with him absent, up in the sticks when the call from Driscoll came in.

"It's about my son-in-law," Gil said.

"Did the police talk to you?"

"Yeah, but I didn't really have much to say about Dave anyway."

That seemed odd to Vic who was convinced Gil was tipping off the police as well as him.

"What did they say to you?" Vic said. "The police."

"Not a real lot. They said they were checking on some vandalism. Oh, some cars that were scratched up or something like that. State engineer's cars."

"They wanted to talk to you about scratches on cars?" Vic said. "You've got to be kidding me."

"Seemed pretty silly," the old man said. He coughed. A whoosh from the oxygen. "Well, they asked me about Dave and Bobbie Hague."

"What did they ask about Hague?"

"Oh, wondered how long Dave knew him and the like. I got to thinking then." He stopped. This time he was not coughing. "I told you, I don't want to talk to you over the phone. It's harder than hell." Then another oxygen whoosh, and a cough.

"Hang on Gil. I'm putting you on hold for a minute."

Vic threw the handset onto his desk. It hit with a bang loud enough to raise the heads from the city desk. He walked back up toward the editors.

"He wants me to come up to Fort Lupton to talk to him," Vic said.

"What about?" Peggy said. Hogan looked at him, then sighed.

"He won't say over the phone. He did say it was about Dave Bender, but he wants to talk in person."

"Great timing," Peggy said. "I'll have Marsha work the desk with me. Jennifer can play cleanup, and Lashawn will watch the bozos over on the website when they get back."

"Wait a minute," Vic said. "That's a half hour from here."

"If it's the byline, Vic, don't worry about that," Hogan said. "Isn't he sort of a critical source on this story?"

"It's not the byline," Vic said. But it was. Hogan had him on this one. "Yes, he's critical. I don't think I can get him to talk over the phone, though."

"Then go up there," Peggy said. "Take Jones with you."

Vic turned and walked back to his desk. If something happened tonight, he thought, at least he would be in the neighborhood with a photographer in tow. He picked up the handset and pressed the blinking hold button.

"Gil?"

The reply was more coughing. "Yeah, I'm still here."

"I'm on my way," Vic said. "Now, you'll stay there won't you?"

"I'll wait," he said. "They haven't even brought me the menu yet."

# 75

The drive up U.S. Highway 85 was broken mostly by sailboat banter with Jones. Vic called the desk twice to check in. On the second call, Peggy told him to relax and that she would call if anything significant happened. He would have preferred to go alone and savor the late day sun spilling over the Rockies while gliding northward through the one-time agricultural area now being gobbled up by thirsty housing developments. Still, Vic was glad to have a photographer along. The paper could get some art, possibly a somber shot of the aging northern Colorado farmer struggling to retain what was left of his dignity, while his farms had fallen to the sharp, heavy blades of bulldozers, earth movers, and the tonnage of bank paperwork.

Exactly thirty minutes after Vic had left downtown Denver, he pulled into the parking lot of the Branding Iron Restaurant in Fort Lupton. He parked between two pickups, Gil's black long bed and the other a rusted but functional old Chevy that probably belonged to one of the area's Mexican farm workers.

Vic turned to Jones and said, "Would you mind waiting here for a bit? I want to check out the old man first, before we start popping photos, okay?"

"You got it," Jones said. "But I'd like to get something before we lose the sun."

"Get the restaurant," Vic said. "I've done a couple of interviews here for the story, one with some farmers who filled in a few holes. Now Gil."

"That's cool. Let me know when I can get the old guy, though."

"Will do," Vic said. He got out of the car and walked into the restaurant thinking Jones seemed to be placated, which apparently did not take all that much.

# 76

Bent, wrinkled, and sucking on oxygen, Gil sat alone in a long booth next to the window. The sun danced on the rim of the mountains to the west, washing the sky with a brilliant orange while the shadows in town grew to their longest of the day before fading into varied shades of twilight gray. The old man gazed out the expansive plate glass windows at the passing cars and trucks heading to homes built on land that once produced sugar beets, cabbage, and onions. Half of the vehicles had their lights on.

"Gil," Vic said as he slid into the booth across from the retired farmer.

"Mr. Bengston," Gil said.

"Vic, remember?"

Gil nodded and adjusted the clear plastic cannula in his nose as the small portable oxygen unit expelled a brief gasp. "Thanks for coming." He extended a shaky hand. Vic shook it and still found the handshake firm, like the first day they met.

"How is everybody, Gil?"

"Everybody?"

"Your wife. Daughter. The girls. Dave."

"Oh," he said. Vic detected slight relief on Gil's part. "They're fine. Fine. Well, no. Not really. Well, I'm not sure."

"What's going on?"

"I think Dave and Bobbie Hague, maybe Darryl, they're going to do something, something stupid."

"Like what?"

"That's what I'm not sure about," Gil said.

"What makes you think this?"

"Oh, I was at the farm last night to bring the girls back to Betsy, and those guys were out in Dave's barn cooking something up."

"What did you see?"

"I sent the girls into the house, and I walked out toward the barn," Gil said. "It was dark. Dave's yard light was off, or burnt out, I don't know."

Vic eased a notebook from his hip pocket and a fountain pen from his shirt pocket. Carefully, he unscrewed the top from the pen and pushed it onto the bottom until it snapped into place. He scrawled a few notes.

"They was in there doing something at Dave's workbench. I heard heated conversation. Water this. Water that. Lose the farm. Lost the tractor. I looked in the window and saw Hague really sticking his face into Dave's. Couldn't really make out what they were saying." He tapped one of his hearing aids and shook his head. "Battery went dead."

"What else did you see?"

"I saw guns, couple of them, on the bench. Dave's twelve gauge and a small target pistol."

Vic's cell phone rang. Gil stopped his story. It was Driscoll. Why now, Vic thought. Then to Gil, "Would you excuse me for a minute? I've got to take this."

Gil nodded and returned to staring at the traffic outside.

Vic hurried toward the front of the restaurant and pushed through the heavy door leading to the parking lot. He leaned against a five-foot wagon wheel cemented into the ground near the front entrance.

Vic hit the green answer button and said, "Bengston."

"We're going," Driscoll said.

"When?"

"Soon."

"To the farm? For Dave?"

"Yes on both counts. No. Sorry. To Hague's farm. That's where they are."

"Keep your cell phone with you," Vic said.

"I usually do," Driscoll said, "but why?"

"Just in case. Make sure you have it, okay?"

"Worried little hen, aren't you?"

"They've got guns."

"They?"

"Hague and Bender for sure," Vic said. "Maybe others."

"Really? Now who told you that?"

"A little bird," Vic said.

"A hunch bird maybe?"

"No, a real bird," Vic said. "I'm serious."

"So are we," Driscoll said. "We already knew about that. How did you hear about it?"

"An old bird," Vic said.

# 77

"Will you call me when you make an arrest?" Vic said.

"If I can," Driscoll said.

"Come on, Frank. I've sat on a ton of crap for you. We haven't even run a story saying you've got a suspect."

"Look. I know. I know. But it might get hairy out there. It's gonna take us an hour to get organized and move our asses up there, if we're lucky. Gotta make all the jurisdictions happy, you know. If I can call you I will. That's all I can promise."

"All right," Vic said, looking back inside the restaurant. A young waitress was standing next to Gil. They were talking. Then Gil reached out with his right hand and patted her behind. She swatted the old man's hand away.

"Be careful out there," Vic said into the phone.

"How touching," Driscoll said.

"You're my partner in the tournament this weekend up at the Dunes, remember? I'd like a chance to win even though you stink."

"I'll remember that," Driscoll said. "I've got to go."

Driscoll was gone. Vic flipped his phone shut and stuck it in his shirt pocket while he stepped back into the restaurant. The young waitress walked up to him. She looked all of seventeen, if that.

"You want to order, hon?"

"Coffee, black" Vic said. "I'll get it at the counter and take it back." She turned and grabbed a tan porcelain mug from one of the counter place settings and dispensed hot brown liquid from the massive coffee urn behind the counter. Vic dropped a five on the counter and tapped it so the waitress saw it. Raising her eyebrows, she mouthed, "Change?", and Vic shook his head.

Taking his coffee, he stepped back outside and waved Jones in from the car. The photographer came running with a pair of Nikon digital single lens reflex cameras swinging madly from his neck. Jones wore the obligatory Dan Rather khaki journalist's vest to carry batteries, extra lenses, and memory chips, Vic supposed, since thirty-five millimeter film was but a wispy memory of days gone by.

"Art time?" Jones said.

"Yeah," Vic said. "Sit at the counter. Get a coffee, a roll, whatever. Shoot what you can. Turn the fake camera shutter sound off too."

"You got it," Jones said.

"Get what you can," Vic said. "I'll ask Gil about a photo and wave you over. But even if I don't, when I get up to leave, you walk over there and get a good shot of Gil, so we have it, okay?"

"You got it."

Jones definitely was a "you got it" guy, Vic thought as he walked back over to Gil's booth. He sat down and placed his coffee mug in front of him.

Gil took a bite of Mother's Meatloaf, as it was billed in the menu. He chewed, swallowed, and adjusted his oxygen line all at once. Then he looked at Vic and said, "Let's get right to it."

"Okay, let's," Vic said. "Do you think Dave was involved?"

"With the murder? The lieutenant governor?"

"Yes," Vic said.

Gil shook his head. "Not that night."

"What about Hague?" Vic said.

"Well, he's the hot head," Gil said, hesitating. "Pulled the gun on the water engineer, now didn't he? Got shot." Vic nodded and made a note. "I just don't know what to think about Bobbie."

"You're sure about Dave?" Vic said.

Gil nodded, scoffing up another helping of meatloaf, this time with a dollop of mashed potatoes splattered with brown gravy. "He's in over his head."

"How can you be so sure?" Vic said.

"That night, the night she was killed," Gil said. "We was all together. The girls and I, Dave, and my Betsy."

"Are you sure, Gil? It's important, you know."

"I know it is," Gil said. He took a drink of water. "We rented a movie. One of those toy movies. *Toy Story*. Kids loved it. You know, Betsy and I even liked it."

"Did you tell this to the police?"

"They never asked me, Vic," Gil said. "That's why I'm telling you. Those others, they weren't with us. It was just family. Bobbie's got the short fuse. Police should go after him."

"So you and the kids, Betsy and Dave, you were all together. For how long?"

"All night. We had dinner early, actually right here. Drove up from Brighton. It's not that far. Food's worth it. Then we got the movie and went back to our place, which is pretty small, you know. We all relaxed in the living room and watched the movie. The girls fell asleep, so we carried them, well Dave carried them, into the spare bedroom and let them sleep. He sacked out on the couch."

"A fold out couch?"

"No, a regular one."

"Well, where did your daughter sleep?" Vic said.

Gil hesitated. "She wasn't there."

Vic sat up and straightened his back. He glanced over at Jones who was kibitzing with the waitress but keeping an eye on him and Gil. Vic raised his head a bit and nodded slightly toward Gil. The photographer grabbed one of the cameras dangling from his neck, excused himself from the girl and began edging around to get a shot of Gil.

"I thought you said Betsy was there," Vic said.

"My Betsy," Gil said. "My wife. Not my daughter."

"Where was Betsy, your daughter, then?" Vic said.

Gil adjusted his oxygen line again. He looked out the window at the darkening mountains and took some deep breaths. Then he pinched both his eyes with his thumb and forefinger, sliding the digits across his closed lids, and bringing them together at the bridge of his nose. Moisture seeped from beneath each closed eye.

"Betsy said it was a girl's night out, over to Greeley," Gil said, his voice shaky. "Eileen told me. She told me yesterday. Betsy's friend. They didn't go to Greeley. They went downtown, to Denver, down to one of them hotels, I forget which one. It was a big party. Those eco-nuts. Wildlife. That wildlife group she did all those ads for."

"She?" Vic said.

"Swain," Gil said. "The lieutenant governor."

Vic sat up even straighter, his heart pounding even harder.

"Gil?" Vic said.

"God Almighty, I don't even want to think about it," Gil said, forcing back more tears, sucking hard on his oxygen, his chest heaving. "Eileen said, well, they was together and then Betsy gave her a hundred dollars to go take a cab home. Said she had something to take care of."

"What time was this?" Vic said.

"Nine-thirty," Gil said. "Least that's what Eileen told me."

"Was Eileen there?" Vic said.

"No, she said she left," Gil said. "Betsy told her not to tell, no one. Not even Dave. They just had a girl's night out in Greeley, that's all."

"Why did Eileen tell you?" Vic said.

"She said she was scared," Gil said.

"That doesn't mean—"

"Eileen said, well, before she left, she saw Betsy talking to Swain. Not arguing. Just talking, and holding hands, you know, the way women do."

"Holy shit," Vic said.

Gil gently placed his knife and fork on the table next to his meatloaf plate and looked up at Vic. A salty flood burst over their spillways and streamed down through the canyons and stubble forest of a face that had spent nearly seventy years out in the hot dry sun of eastern Colorado.

# 78

"Just a minute, Gil," Vic said. "I've got to call somebody." Gil said nothing. Vic walked briskly through the restaurant again and out into the parking lot. He dialed Driscoll.

"This is Driscoll. Leave a message." Then the beep.

"It's Betsy, Frank," Vic said. "Not Dave. God, he wasn't even there. Who the hell missed that? I've got someone who saw her with the lieutenant governor that night. Watch it! She can shoot. Call me."

He dialed the city desk.

"City desk," Peggy said.

"It's Vic."

"And?"

"They're going tonight. Soon."

"For Dave Bender?"

"Yeah, but he's not the one," Vic said.

"Who is, Bobbie Hague?"

"It's Bender's wife, Betsy. Gil's daughter."

"The sharpshooter?" Peggy said. "You're kidding, right?"

"No I'm not," Vic said. "I just talked with Gil. He said he was with Dave and the grandkids the night Swain was killed. All night. Cops don't have a clue."

"Where was she?"

"Gil said she was downtown with a friend, Eileen something. I'll find out from Gil. Anyway, he said she was at the wildlife fund dinner. That's where the lieutenant governor was right before she was killed. This Eileen told Gil he saw Betsy with Swain."

"Holy shit," Peggy said.

"That's exactly what I said."

"All right, what can you tell me right now?" Peggy said.

Vic told her about Driscoll's call, his promise to call him back, and what Gil told him about that night.

"Why didn't Gil tell this to the police," Peggy said. "Or did he?"

"I don't think he did. Gil said he just found out. I don't think the cops have even talked to Bender yet. Somebody's feeding info to the cops."

"Gil?" Peggy said.

"Probably," Vic said. "The old guy thought Bender was hooked up with Hague and some others in something, but he didn't really know what. He may have passed that along because they're the ones that Driscoll and the task force are targeting."

"How did Gil tell you about his daughter?" Peggy said.

"It just poured out," Vic said. "God, the guy was in tears. He's a wreck."

"Keep calling Driscoll," she said. "Have Jones shoot the old man. We need some art. Then get over to the Bender farm. Stay in touch. And stay safe."

Vic brushed his left hand over his heart, then looked up and saw Jones come out the door and head toward him.

"I'm done," Jones said.

"Saddle up," Vic said. "We need to get out to the farm, and I've got to get a hold of Driscoll. Let me go say good bye to the old man."

"You got it," Jones said.

Vic tried Driscoll again. No answer. He went back inside, and walked over to Gil, who was dabbing his eyes with a napkin.

"Gil, I've got to go," Vic said. "Are you going to be all right?"

"I'll be okay," Gil said.

"What's Eileen's last name?" Vic said.

"Collins. Eileen Collins. Lives in Ault."

"Should I call you a cab, Gil?" Vic said, not even sure if there were cabs in Fort Lupton. "Do you have a friend I can call?"

"No, I'll be fine," he said. A cough, then, "The girls are over at our house. They're staying with us for a while."

"Is Dave there?" Vic said.

"I don't know where he is. I talked to him a little while ago, but he said he had to go out. My Betsy's there."

"You don't know where he might have gone?" Vic said.

"Probably Bobbie Hague's. I don't know."

"I've got Hague's number," Vic said. "I'll call over there."

"But the girls are going to stay with us," Gil said, issuing a stern final command decision as patriarch of a family farming institution that had been ground down into nothing but dusty memories by market collapses, land swindlers, water thieves, banks, and, now, a sensational murder.

# 79

"Hague Farms."

"Bobbie?"

"Who's this?"

"It's Vic Bengston. I need to talk to Dave Bender." A hand went over the phone. Muffled rustling. Vic thought he heard, "You want to talk to him?" Then more rustling and another voice.

"I can't talk right now," Bender said, his voice dead and distant.

"Where's your wife?"

"Not your business."

Vic knew he could not reveal the impending arrest. He also knew he had to tell Driscoll where Bender was. "Just curious."

"That's why you called? Just curious?" Bender hung up.

That went well, Vic thought. They could have been at Hague's drinking beer and watching a football game, or arming themselves to hold off a posse. He dialed Driscoll. Again, no answer. Vic left another message, "Frank, I just spoke with Dave Bender. He's with Bobbie Hague at Hague's place." Miles from where the murderer was, Vic thought.

"Where are we going?" It was Jones, hollering out the passenger window. He was at the wheel of the paper's SUV, which was idling and ready to go. Vic closed his phone, walked over to the car and got in.

"The Bender farm," Vic said. "Watch for cop cars. East through town."

"I know," Jones said. "Turn right on twenty-seven then left in a few miles on twelve. It's in the GPS."

"Yeah," Vic said. He buckled his seat belt and dialed Driscoll. The message. Then he dialed the city desk.

"What?" The wonders of caller ID.

"I got Bender on the phone," Vic said. "He's at Hague's, but he wouldn't talk. He hung up on me."

"Don't let it hurt your feelings," Peggy said. "You didn't tell him about—"

"No, I can't say anything about the arrest," Vic said. "I can't get Driscoll, though. We're headed to the Bender farm."

"All right," she said. "Who was at Hague's besides Dave and Bobbie?"

"Don't know," Vic said. "Darryl, I assume, but that's a guess. The old man said the girls are at his place in Brighton."

"Keep at it, and call me with anything new. Anything."

"Right, chief." Vic slapped his phone closed.

"Chief?" Jones said, looking straight ahead so he could keep an eye on the darkening roads. "Daily Planet?"

"You got it, Jimmy," Vic said.

"And you're Clark Kent?"

"Well, I'm not Superman," Vic said. "So be careful. We both break."

# 80

Jones sped through the darkness of eastern Colorado. Vic tried Driscoll again with no luck. When they turned onto County Road 12, Jones spotted a flashing light coming down from the north and said, "Cop."

"Find a spot to move over and let them pass," Vic said. "Stop if you need to. Get your press card out."

Jones fumbled for his wallet and then tossed it onto the dash. Vic grabbed it.

"It's under the drivers' license," Jones said. Vic pulled out Jones' press card and put it in a small tray on the console between their seats. He stuffed Jones' wallet into another storage slot and pulled his own press card out of his shirt pocket.

"I don't think I ever used mine in the old days," Vic said.

"We have to use them all the time," Jones said, "especially since nine-eleven." He looked up into the mirror again. "They're getting closer." He pulled into a cut that led to a farm field and stopped. The patrol car flew by at a dusty sixty, red lights, and no siren. It was a Weld County Sheriff's car. Vic turned around and saw another set of flashing lights.

"Hold it," Vic said. "There's another one coming. Don't pull out yet."

The second car pulled into the cut right behind Jones and Vic. Jones hit the down button on his window, grabbed his press card, and held it out so whoever was in the car behind them could see the credential.

"Vic, is that you?" It was Driscoll.

"There's a *Sun* logo on the back of the car," Jones said. Then the photographer waived his card up and down. "Here, give me yours." Vic handed his card to him and Jones put it in his hand with his own. He waived them both.

"Stay put," Driscoll said. Vic could see him inching up toward the driver's window from behind. He shined a flashlight on the cards. "Stay where you are, guys. Don't move, okay?" Then he shined the light through the windows of the car to see what all was in it. Vic assumed Driscoll had a gun in his other hand, down by his leg.

Finally, the detective peered in through Jones' window and grinned. "Beats the excitement of a three hundred yard drive doesn't it?"

"I'm too old for this, Frank," Vic said.

"Like hell," he said. "You're lovin' it, son."

"I am," Vic said, his heart thumping.

"I got your message," Driscoll said. The big detective sighed with resignation. "Some asshole, I won't say who, cleared the sharpshooter. Thanks for the call."

"You know him?" Jones said to Vic. "What are you? A reporter or a cop?"

"A reporter. Driscoll and I play golf. That's all." Then to Driscoll, Vic said, "Dave Bender is over at Hague's."

"I know," Driscoll said. "Our other team picked them up. They were watching The Great American Race. With pizza and beer. Their friend Darryl was with them. All pussycats."

Another car, this one unmarked, flew by.

"The girls are at their grandfather's condo in Brighton," Vic said. "We want to come in with you."

"Well, you can't, not into the farm," Driscoll said. "Follow me, and I'll show you where you can park. You'll have to stay there."

"Better than nothing," Jones said when Driscoll went back to his car.

"I'll show you better than 'better than nothing,'" Vic said.

# 81

Driscoll got back into his car, front passenger side, a silver Colorado State Patrol car, a Chevy Camaro, one of the zippy models state troopers muscled around in. Vic could not see who was driving. A man and a woman were in the back seat, but he could not make them out either. Jones pulled in behind Driscoll's car and followed it down the dark road.

"More coming," Jones said, glancing up at the rear view mirror. "I see two."

"There's an S-curve up ahead," Vic said. He was going on vague memory. "Pull over up ahead when the road makes a sharp turn to the left. I think there's an access road for a big irrigation ditch. Bear to the right on the curve, then turn to the right. Drive a bit, and cut your lights. But stop first."

"Yeah, I really don't want to run this puppy into an irrigation ditch," Jones said.

"No, you don't," Vic said, a chill running down his back as he recalled the frigid waters of the canal near Rosenthal's.

"You sure about this?" Jones said.

"No."

"Thought so."

"Up there," Vic said. "See it?"

"You got it."

It was more like going straight ahead, then a shade to the right. A path opened up that led to a stand of giant cottonwood trees. Jones nosed the vehicle in, stopped it about a foot short of a massive tree trunk, cut the ignition, and hit the light switch, plunging them into darkness. Vic turned around and saw the two other squad cars silently fly on by, lights flashing.

"God, I used to do stuff like this when I was in high school," Vic said.

"Like what?"

"Ditching cops."

"In cars?"

"Yes, in cars," Vic said. "Our dads' big Detroit cars, with massive V8s."

"I had a friend who did that once," Jones said.

"You never did, I take it," Vic said.

"Hell no," Jones said. "He went to jail, actually reform school, for six months. Eluding police."

"That would describe what we did," Vic said.

"Well, cops take it seriously now," Jones said. "They get pretty torqued if you don't follow orders."

"For us, those are advisory opinions only," Vic said. "We need to see how this thing plays out. Let's go."

Both men jumped from the car. Jones ran around back, opened the hatch, and grabbed two cameras, which he slung around his neck.

"Wait a minute," Jones said. He opened a nylon camera case, pulled out a long lens, and stuffed it into a large pocket on the inside of his vest. "Do you have a flashlight?"

"No," Vic said.

"Here, take this in case you need it." Jones handed him a small metal flashlight.

"Don't you need one?"

"I've got two," Jones said.

"Aren't we prepared?" Vic said, heavy on the "we."

"And aren't we nuts?" Jones said with the same emphasis.

"I think this road follows the ditch all the way to the Bender farm driveway," Vic said.

"You think?"

"Well, I only saw it during the day when I was out here with Betsy Bender," Vic said. "I think it goes all the way."

"Great," Jones said, then stopped. "You interviewed her? The murderer?"

"Alleged," Vic said.

"You actually were with her?" Jones said. "I didn't see any story, or art."

"No, it's all still in my notes, Steve," Vic said. "Background for a feature."

"Did the desk know you interviewed her?" Jones said.

"Kind of," Vic said.

"Kind of?"

"It was off the books, on my own time," Vic said.

"We never really talked about anything like this in J-school," Jones said. "You're sort of a rogue reporter."

"Whatever," Vic said. "I never could imagine what they filled the four years with in journalism school anyway."

"What's your degree in?" Jones said.

"Poli Sci," Vic said. "Bachelors and Masters."

"You mean you could be teaching in some comfy community college instead of tromping around out here in the dark?" Jones said.

"Yes," Vic said, "but this is so much more exhilarating."

"You got that right," Jones said.

The access road along the ditch ended a few hundred yards from the Bender farm when it took a sharp turn to the north, passed through a culvert beneath the road and vanished into the night. Jones and Vic used the road to get across the canal. Then they dropped off the graded gravel surface and bushwhacked their way up to the edge of the Bender cornfield. Dry dead cornstalks clattered in the night breeze.

"We can see most of the farmyard from here," Jones said.

"Not very well," Vic said. "You see that tree over by the driveway? That's a better spot."

"What if there's gunplay?" Jones said.

"Gunplay? You've been watching old *Gunsmoke* episodes again."

"No, really," Jones said. "I don't want to get shot."

"You won't get shot," Vic said.

"How do you know?"

"I don't," Vic said. "Hold that thought. I've got to call the desk."

"Now?"

"Yes, now." They could see all the cars parked down near where the Bender driveway cut into the county road. Shadows of cops milled about in the dark. Vic dialed the direct city desk number.

"Garfield. City desk." It was a boy's voice. Garfield, the sports writer.

"Who's this?" Vic said.

"Who's this?"

"Bengston," Vic said. "Where's Peggy?"

"She's tied up," Garfield said. "You have something?"

"Untie her," Vic said. "Give me Peggy."

"She's on the other li—"

"Please, give me Peggy and cut the crap. Get her off the other line." A click started a pre-recorded ad pitching a subscription to the *Rocky Mountain Sun*, now only fifty dollars a year. In five years, it'll probably be gone, Vic thought.

"Vic. What?"

"We're here, Peggy, at the arrest."

"We've got the lead ready to go," she said. "When did they get her?"

"Hold it," Vic said.

"They haven't arrested her?"

"Not yet," Vic said. "We're getting closer, but we're kind of on our own out here in the dark."

"Nothing new for you, Vic," Peggy said.

"I can't talk much longer," Vic said. "We're almost up to the cops."

"Leave the cell phone on and in your pocket," Peggy said. She's really thinking, Vic thought. "Where's Dave Bender?"

"In custody. They arrested him at Hague's, the two of them along with Darryl. They were watching TV."

"Some conspiracy," Peggy said.

"They might have been clueless, Peggy."

"Typical men," she said. "Lot of hot air. Women have to finish the job."

"Peggy," Vic said, a bit too fatherly. "Swain was murdered."

"Yeah, well. Call me when you know Betsy is in custody, okay? Then we'll move the story on the net."

"All right," Vic said.

"Vic?"

"Yes?"

"Be careful out there."

"You watch *NYPD Blue* too?"

"They don't make TV like that anymore," she said. "Leave your phone on. Don't hang it up."

"I won't." Vic ripped open the Velcro-sealed flap on his shirt pocket right over his heart, slipped in the open phone, and then resealed the flap.

"Hold it!" It was Driscoll, from the direction of the milling cops. "Bengston?"

"You got me," Vic said, he and Jones walking toward the group. "Dead to rights."

"He's all right," Driscoll said to the other officers. "Well, he's not all right. He's with us, though."

"Isn't he that damn reporter?" a cop said.

"Defective genes," Driscoll said. "Bengston, get over here. Bring your little friend."

It was Driscoll in front of a cop crowd, Vic thought. Not the Driscoll out on the golf course. Pecking order, he figured.

"It's Vic Bengston," Driscoll said, "an aging reporter with the *Rocky Mountain Sun*, and photographer Steve Jones."

"We can't screw around with this, Frank." It was the woman.

"Right," Frank said.

"Is this the one who told you about Betsy?" She had a deprecating voice.

"Yes it is," Driscoll said. "The sharpshooter the FBI cleared."

"Frank," Vic said. "Detective Driscoll. We need to see what happens here."

"You stay back here, both of you," the woman commanded. She looked at Driscoll and shook her head.

Driscoll took charge again.

"This is Agent Kerry Elwood, with the FBI," Frank said. "Deputy Jake Gonzales with the Weld County Sheriff. We've got two other deputies, over there, two more uniforms from Denver over there, and this is Detective Martin Garza from the CBI."

"This isn't a cocktail party, Frank," Elwood said.

"Look, Kerry," Driscoll said. His tone was not pleasant. "You're here as a favor to your boss. Don't push it."

"No SWAT?" Vic said.

Driscoll spun on him. "For what?"

"She's a sharpshooter, Frank," Vic said.

"So am I."

The cops worked out a plan to approach the house, which sat dark, quiet, and a hundred yards away. Bengston and Jones were told to stay right where they were, by the cars, so the "adults," as Garza called the team, could do their jobs.

"We should be able to see all this from the barn," Vic said so only Jones could hear. "Right near the front door over there."

"Well, I can't do all that much, at least until they get things under control," Jones said. "And didn't they say to stay here?"

"What's your point?"

Jones had no answer.

As soon as the big boys and the big girl left, the little boys from the newspaper started walking slowly over toward the barn, which was as dark as everything else on the farm. The yard light on the front of the barn was off. Maybe the cops had cut the power, Vic thought, like they did on TV.

The moonlit police team silently fanned out in front of the farmhouse, slowly approaching it. Two went around back. Vic could see shadowy arms, hands, and weapons pointed skyward, ready to draw down and fire, or not fire, in the flick of time given officers to make life and death decisions.

"Is that Driscoll on the porch?" Vic was whispering.

"I think so," Jones said. "But Gonzales is as tall as he is."

"No hat, Steve," Vic said.

"Sorry. I forgot we're in the sticks. Mandatory cowboy hats. There's Gonzales, over there." The moon caught the wide brim of the deputy's hat.

"I had a hat like that once," Vic said. "A Stetson. The CU chapter of Delta Sigma Chi gave it to me."

"What for?" Jones said.

"Uh, Top Hat Award, Colorado Journalist of the Year."

"Is there any award you haven't won?"

"The Pulitzer," Vic said.

"I'm not impressed." It was Lauren Bacall, from the dark cavern of the barn. Jones almost jumped into Vic's arms, while Vic's heart struggled against his ribcage wanting out, now.

"Get in here," Betsy commanded. "I've got a gun. A real big one."

# 82

The massive barn door was slid open about three or four feet. Vic stepped into the darkness. His heart followed along under protest.

"You too, or I'll shoot him right here," she said. Jones followed Vic in.

"Right there, in the doorway," Betsy said. "I've already killed a lieutenant governor. A couple of reporters can't be that much worse."

"Technically, I'm only a photographer," Jones said.

"For a rag that could have cared less whether we lived or died out here," she said.

"I was working on your story," Vic said.

"I haven't seen a thing in the paper," she said. "We do get it each morning. I usually feed it to the pigs."

Pigs make noise, Vic thought. "You don't have any pigs."

"Oh, that's right," she said with a brutal sarcastic bite. "We had to sell them to buy shoes for my little girls."

Since this was likely to be the last story he would ever be on, Vic decided to start reporting, hoping his cell phone was still on and working, and that Peggy was on the other end taking notes, perhaps even calling Driscoll.

"Why the pigs?" Vic said.

"You should know the answer to that. The money was gone. The wells were cut off. The bank was camped on our front porch measuring the windows for new curtains. Ferguson wouldn't lend us a dime once we'd lost the crop. How's that, Mr. Reporter?"

"And you blamed the lieutenant governor for all this?" Vic said.

Jones edged a little to the right.

"I said don't move," she barked. Jones froze.

"I can drop either one of you little bastards anywhere along that door. You know I can shoot, Vic, that I'm still in practice, don't you?"

"I think so," Vic said.

"You know so," Betsy said. "You checked out the range, didn't you?"

She suspected him back then, Vic thought, when he drove past her on the road that day of the interview.

"Sure I did," Vic said.

"And you picked up some brass. Probably a slug or two."

"I might have," Vic said.

"Well, I'm not holding one of those pea-shooters now," Betsy said. "This one makes nice big holes."

"You mean like the pea-shooter you used on Jessica Swain?"

"Or maybe the one the police think David used on her?" Betsy said. "The gun I taught him how to use?"

"You already said you killed Swain," Vic said. Jones jabbed Vic in the ribs with a 'shut up' poke.

"True," she said. "With my very own hands."

The same hands that served him iced tea and wiped themselves on that dainty dishcloth. The same hands that somewhere off in the dark recesses of the barn were pointing a serious weapon at him and Jones.

"Just stand still, Steve," Vic said. They were about three feet inside of the barn door and silhouetted by the feint light from outside. "Getting shot would put a serious crimp in my golf game." His throbbing heart must have broken at least one rib by now, he thought.

"Why didn't you sell that gun to buy shoes for your girls?" Vic said.

"Pigs sell fast up here, Vic," she said. "Rarely do we sell our guns. Second Amendment, you know?"

"Killing Swain was some sort of political statement?" Vic said.

"No, it was a personal statement," she said. "That bitch was selling us down the river."

"That was a pun, Betsy," Vic said. Silence. Then he dove into the deep end. "How did you do it? Get to her?"

"It was easy, Vic, almost too easy. No security at that silly hotel, and none for the lieutenant governor, not even a driver. Plus we women carry big handbags these days, great big ones. Plenty of room for a small pistol."

"A Coach purse?" said Jones, motionless but lips still operable.

"Funny," she said. More silence. Nothing from outside either. What in hell was Driscoll doing, Vic wondered.

"When one woman walks up to another, it doesn't really take much," Betsy said. "We don't need to dance around like you boys do. We're so trusting. We walk straight in. I shake the hand, then hold the hand with both of mine, shed a little tear, and express joy over how all the precious wildlife would be protected. Then I tell her I was a breast cancer survivor like her. All of a sudden we're lifelong buddies."

"Were you?" Vic said.

"What, Vic?"

"Were you a cancer victim?" Vic said.

"No, Vic, they're both still there," Betsy said. "Intact."

"They?" Vic said.

"I saw you looking at them," she said. "When we were together at my house, you looking at them, thinking about them."

He was. He thought about them several times since then, and how she was married, and how he would never do that again.

"And what did you buddies do?" Vic said.

"We strolled out onto the patio," she said.

"That little one? Next to that street-level parking lot? Opens onto Fourteenth Street?"

"That's right," Betsy said. "Simple. I locked my arm into hers and stuck the barrel into her belly. We strolled over to my car and got in."

"Was anyone with you in the car?" Vic said.

"Jessica Swain was with me," Betsy said.

"Besides you two," Vic said.

"You mean like Dave?"

"Sure, like Dave, Bobbie Hague. Anyone," Vic said.

"No. I took her down all by myself. I knew how to get her in. Twist her arm, grab her hand a special way, and crack her on the head. That was all it took."

Another fact left out of the picture, Vic thought. There must have been another wound if Betsy hit her with the gun. Cops held it back. Driscoll held it back.

"Then what?" Vic said.

"Then we drove to the river."

"Where?"

"You know where. Everybody knows where."

"Why to the river?" Vic said.

"Because that was the water we needed. I wanted her to see it and feel it for the very last time."

"But you used the wells," Vic said, thinking, Peggy, are you there on the other end, taking notes? Calling the cops?

"That didn't matter," she said, spitting out the words. "The water engineer said they were one and the same. The river water and the well water. I wanted her to see our water, our life blood, and I wanted to mix hers with it."

"Did you shoot her?" Vic said.

She hesitated. In the silence, Vic heard muffled movements behind him. Then she said, "Yes, I shot her. I was glad I shot her. Right in the back of her head."

"Glad?" Vic said.

"She never worked a day in her life," Betsy said, "not on the land, with her hands, with her body. Her father was a damn lawyer. His father was probably a lawyer. She was a lawyer. People like her, people who never worked a farm, ruined it all for me and my family. Who knocked the hell out of the sugar beet market? Not farmers. Some jerks in Washington who decided to let cheap sugar into the country. Some executive at some giant Ag company. They never saw Daddy work the farm, keep everything going, help out the other farmers. I was supposed to go to the Olympics. They cut that right out of me, forever. Farmers didn't do that. And now that state water engineer, another one who never turned an honest shovel of dirt for a crop, goes and shuts off the wells, shuts off the blood to our farm, to what's left of my Daddy's farm, and they wreck another family. Then the bank, that Ben Ferguson, some boyhood friend. He grabs the paper on the farm. The tractor dealer takes our tools. None of them ever worked a real lick in their lives. They come in and take and take and take from us. They take our food, but if we miss one payment they take everything. Swain was all of them. She was all those people who reach into our wallets with their soft pink hands and steal our money, and snuff out our way of life. I killed her because she was all of them."

Something flew over Vic's head and into the barn, followed by a loud explosion, then a blinding flash. In that fraction of a second, his ears ringing from the blast, he caught a fleeting glimpse of a once beautiful face now twisted with anger and rage. And he saw the gun in her hand.

# 83

The heart attack hit him like Bears linebacker Dick Butkus blitzing through the Packers' offense at full gallop. Vic's chest seized into a searing knot of pain. Breathing stopped. A lightning bolt shot down his left arm to the tips of his fingers. Dropping to his knees, Vic saw Betsy's feet, encased in dusty brown western boots. He thought of his daughter, her beautiful face, and hoped she would take care of his aging parents. Images of her, Mom and Dad, his three sons, their children, his little sister, and Erin, all marched before him like an ill-timed PowerPoint presentation. "I will miss them," he gasped as the dusty cement of the barn floor heaved up and smashed him in the face.

# 84

"Well, it's about time. We were wondering if you'd ever wake up."

The voice came from darkness. Vic heard a steady beeping sound. It was not his ham radio. He opened his eyes. Institutional ceiling tiles stared down at him. A flat screen television on the wall displayed a NASCAR race with no sound. He started to move, but his left arm tugged him back and a shooting pain tore through his chest.

"Hold on there, buckaroo. You can't go to the races just yet." She had a friendly face with rosy cheeks, fronting a round head with tight curly brown hair gripping its top. Vic thought of Nancy, the cartoon character.

"Can I talk?" Vic said.

"Sounds like it," said Nancy the nurse, followed by a high pitched beeping. She reached above him to adjust something and obscured his view of the race with a colorful smock splattered with gleeful Disney characters. Goofy, Vic's favorite, smiled at him from the nurse's belly. The beeping stopped, and she pulled back.

"I survived?" He thought of Grandpa Al, who made it through his first heart attack, but not his second. Vic's throat hurt like hell. So did his head, his arm, and his chest. He thought a moment. He could not move his left arm. It was in a cast or something.

"Where's Mom and Dad," Vic said. "My daughter, sons. Grandkids. Can I call?"

"I sent them all home a little while ago. I'll let them know."

It was a familiar voice. Vic thought some more, focused again. "Frank?"

"Yes, dear," Driscoll said.

"Where are we?"

"The knife and gun club," Driscoll said.

"Denver Health? Trauma center? I survived?"

"Yes you did, so relax," Nurse Nancy said, then admonished Driscoll. "Detective, please. We're trying to upgrade our image here."

"It's not your image, it's the clientele," Driscoll said. "Look at this one right here."

"Good point," she said. "He looked pretty seedy when they rolled him in last night. God, look at that nose."

"You're as cynical as he is," Vic said, barely a whisper. Everything hurt.

"Yes we are," she said. "This ER sees everything Denver has to offer."

"I'm surprised I'm alive," Vic said, seeing his brief encore career in journalism coming to a rapid close as he spent the next six months recovering from a heart attack, if he was even able to recover at all.

Yet something did not seem quite right.

"Betsy?" Vic said.

"Girl friend?" Nurse Nancy said.

"Perp," Driscoll said.

"You were quite lucky," the nurse said. "Her bullet missed the artery altogether."

"Her what?" Vic said.

"Her bullet, chum," Driscoll said. "Take a look at this."

The detective pulled a small plastic evidence bag from his coat pocket and held it up so Vic could see it. The cell phone inside the bag looked like someone had taken a mallet to it after getting the bill for extra minutes. It looked vaguely familiar.

"Mine?"

"It was," Driscoll said.

"What happened to it?"

"It caught the bullet, asshole," Driscoll said. He tossed the mangled phone onto the bed and flopped down into a chair between the bed and the window. A stack of papers, magazines and files on the table next to the chair indicated Driscoll had engaged in some sort of a vigil. Or maybe Vic's family did.

"This bullet stuff again," Vic said. Nothing registered in his foggy mind.

"She shot you, bubba," Driscoll said. "That lovely woman, or at least lovely until she murdered our lieutenant governor, shot you. That's how much you meant to her."

"I had a heart attack," Vic said. "I felt it coming on for a long time."

Both Nurse Nancy and Driscoll laughed.

"Sorry to disappoint you," she said, laughing more. "The bullet cracked your sternum and went right through your humerus."

"It's not funny," Vic said.

"It was the humerus," Nurse Nancy said. "Broke your upper arm bone. Your H-U-M-E-R-U-S."

"She can't spell either," Vic said.

"You were damn lucky," Driscoll said. "The phone deflected the bullet."

"Maybe all those outrageous cell phone charges were worth it," Vic said. "What happened to, uh, wasn't someone with me?"

"Jones, your photographer," Driscoll said.

"Yeah, is he, it's Steve. Is he okay?"

"He sure is," Driscoll said. "And he finally put that Nikon to good use."

"Oh?"

"Yeah. After he flashed his strobe in her face, he clobbered her with the camera," Driscoll said. "A real roundhouse. Dropped her like a sack of potatoes, right onto the floor."

The night before spilled back into Vic's memory.

"Flashed his strobe?" Vic said.

"Said he saw it on some TV show," Driscoll said. "With Charles Bronson."

"*Man With A Camera*," Vic said. "Bronson ran around New York with a Speed Graphic or his tiny little thirty-five millimeter camera. Whenever he got in a jam, he flashed the guy who was after him."

The cop laughed. "Flashed him? Open raincoat, all that?"

"No. With bulbs. Flash bulbs. You remember those."

"Bulbs. Strobe. Doesn't matter. The flash probably saved your life."

"Does that mean I have to look out for him the rest of his life?" Vic said. "Or, does he have to look out for me?"

"I forget how that works," Driscoll said. "Buy him a new camera. We've got the one he used."

"The paper can do that. I'll just send him a thank you card."

"You're such a dweeb," Driscoll said.

"I know. How did you know we were in the barn?"

"Well, we saw the house was empty," Driscoll said. "Then we heard you and you-know-who."

"All the way out in the barn?"

"You were like a pair of banshees," Driscoll said.

"What are banshees, anyway?" Vic said.

"Got me," Driscoll said. "But I know they're noisy."

Vic remembered he had left the phone on.

"I'll be back in a bit," Nurse Nancy said. "I want to get a doc now that you're awake." She swooshed into the hallway.

"The paper," Vic said. "Do you have a paper?"

"Well, I've got a morning fish-wrap if that's what you mean," Driscoll said.

"You don't fish."

"But if I did, I'd wrap them in this." Driscoll said, holding up the *Sun* so Vic could see it.

It was not a typical front page, usually dominated by a large photo, a big headline, some small subheads referring to inside stories and no copy. This front page was topped by the *Rocky's* masthead, and beneath it, a giant bold headline reading "Arrest in Lt. Gov. Murder." Two columns of copy split the front page below the headline. On the left, a headline "Swain Murder Timeline" topped a series of short briefs and headshots of Swain and Betsy Bender. The meaty story was positioned in the right-hand column, the sweet spot of any newspaper page. It began with a summary headline and a byline that surprised Vic.

### ARREST IN SWAIN MURDER
#### Police name farmer's wife in
#### slaying of Lt Gov. Jessica Swain
*Rocky Mountain Sun Staff*

FORT LUPTON – Acting on information provided by a *Rocky Mountain Sun* investigation, police arrested the wife of a northern Colorado farmer in the execution-style slaying of Colorado Lieutenant Governor Jessica Swain.

Elizabeth L. Bender, 39, of Brighton, was arrested late Tuesday night after a confrontation during which *Sun* reporter Vic Bengston was shot and wounded. Police acted on Bengston's tip leading to the arrest, police said.

*Sun* photographer Steve Jones was credited with disarming Bender by hitting her with one of his cameras.

Bengston, 59, was reported in good condition at Denver Health, where he was taken by Flight for Life.

A special multi-jurisdictional police task force also arrested three other men, including Bender's husband, David Bender, 40, a Weld County farmer, on suspicion of conspiracy in the murder. The other two suspects, also farmers in the area, are Robert Hague, 41, of Gilcrest, and Darryl Winston, 38, of Milliken.

During the confrontation with Bengston and Jones, Elizabeth Bender admitted involvement in the lieutenant governor's murder. Bengston had an open cell phone in his shirt pocket. The conversation was recorded by the *Sun*.

"Admitted involvement in the killing?" Vic said. "She told me how she did it, Frank. They didn't even go with the sharpshooter angle."

"We want it all tied up properly if there's a trial," Driscoll said. "Anyway, this was all resolved with calls from the governor, the DA, and the attorney general to your publisher."

"Hogan?"

"Yeah, Hogan."

"He probably caved quickly," Vic said.

"Actually, it was the paper's lawyer and the CEO back in Scranton who threw in the towel," Driscoll said. "Hogan wanted to print the confession transcript verbatim."

Good for him, Vic thought. "Well, there's one for truth, justice, and the American way," he said. "Where's Betsy?"

"About two doors away," Driscoll said. "Under armed guard, and, no, you can't see her or talk to her."

"Frankie says?"

"Frankie says."

"You think the boys were involved?" Vic said.

"Off the record?"

"Yes, okay. Off the record. Am I working here?"

"Not a chance," Driscoll said. "They couldn't find their corn cribs with both hands."

"What's going to happen to Betsy?" Vic said.

"Well, the docs say she'll be ready to go today. A bump on the head and a few stitches. She'll be arraigned in the morning. But she's already lawyered up and you won't believe who with."

"I'm too sore to figure things out for myself," Vic said.

"Geller and Sanchez."

"That doesn't surprise me," Vic said. "Actually that does surprise me. Mitch likes the high profile cases, but those guys still want to be paid."

"Someone retained them," Driscoll said. "We're not quite sure who. Swain was not loved by all you know."

"Mitch Geller," Vic said, staring out the window. "And Lucas Sanchez. You know I worked with Luke when I was at the *Sun* the first time. Streetwise kid on the way up."

"Well, he's at the top of the defense game out here now, along with Geller," Driscoll said.

"They'll turn this into a three-ring circus," Vic said.

"They'll rake you over the coals," Driscoll said. "You're a key witness, now. I suppose the tournament this weekend is out," Driscoll said.

"Well, my dad had a one-armed friend who played a fair game," Vic said.

"Good point," Driscoll said. "The cast might actually help yours. Rest up and call your family. They were here all night, even the grandkids. Call your desk. Stay away from my prisoner." He gathered up his files. Then he walked over to the bed and grabbed the destroyed cell phone. "I'm going to need this."

"What for?" Vic said.

"Evidence, Vic. You helped break this case. I'll give you that, but now you're a witness in the Swain murder. You're also a victim in an attempted murder." Driscoll held up the cell phone. "This is evidence for the latter. Most vexing. You're a reporter involved in both crimes. I don't know if we'll ever get it all sorted out. Anyway, I've got to take this."

"Will I get it back?" Vic said. "Momento."

"Maybe. Someday. Anyway, I've got to go fight crime."

"The caped crusader," Vic said.

"And you're Crusader Rabbit," Driscoll said on his way out the door.

# 85

A half-hour later, Nurse Nancy walked in with a tray of food. Vic was on the phone.

"Mom, you and Dad please take it easy," Vic said. "I'm sorry for putting you through this. No, no. I'm okay. I've talked to the kids. Connor's going to call you later. He'll pick you up and bring you back down. Really, I'm okay. You guys go take a nap."

"It never stops does it?" said Nurse Nancy, now in a plain green nurse's outfit and holding a tray.

"What happened to Goofy and Mickey, and all their friends?"

"Some drunk barfed on me," she said, as she set the tray on the rolling table and eased it over toward Vic.

"What's that?"

"That is food, something you need. Eat as much as you can. The broth is usually pretty good."

"Mom would tell me to eat too," Vic said.

"Always being the kid, the child," she said. "Always explaining yourself to your parents. I do the same thing."

"Like a kid trapped in a grown up body?" Vic said.

Nurse Nancy looked at him. "Ten years old? That's about how old I feel when I'm looking out through these eyes."

Vic thought a moment. "Yeah, ten's about right. How can ten year olds do what we do?"

"We fake it," she said. "We're all just ten year olds inside with a lifetime of experience on the outside."

Nancy the philosopher-nurse whisked back out the door. Vic still had not caught her real name from her badge. The night nurse's name was still up on the white board across from his bed. Some guy named Fred. The phone rang.

"Hello," Vic said.

"Well, glad to hear your voice," Peggy said, full of concern.

"Peggy," Vic said.

"Update me," she said in her city editor voice.

"On me or the story?"

"Both will do," she said. "You first."

"Broken arm. Smashed cell phone. Busted nose."

"Did you have that replacement insurance?"

"I think they're letting the arm grow back together all by itself. No replacement. They got off easy."

"The cell phone," she said.

"I guess," Vic said. "I don't know if bullet damage is covered."

"I'd like to be there when you turn it in for a claim," she said, laughing. It was a nervous laugh. He cleared his throat and spoke in as normal and even a voice as he could, a reassuring voice, a father's voice, a ten-year old father.

"I think maybe I'll keep it," Vic said. "It's like the marshal's badge that deflected the bad guy's bullet at the end of the movie. The cops have the phone right now, though. Evidence."

"You saw the story?"

"By the *Rocky Mountain Sun* Staff?"

"Vic, you're in the story now," Peggy said. "We can't run you in the byline too. You can't even cover it anymore now that you're hip deep in it."

"I know, I know."

"But Hogan is on cloud nine," Peggy said. "He wants you to, we want you to write a first-personer, a series, on the whole thing, the entire investigation, start to finish. We might have you blog during the trial."

"Could be a book," Vic said. "But there are some things I can't write about, Peggy. I did a few—"

"We'll work those out," she said. "It could be a real shot in the arm for the paper."

"So I've gone from washed up old fart to shot in the arm," Vic said.

There was a pause. "Pretty much."

"I was actually shot in the arm," Vic said.

"Does it hurt?" she said.

"Only when I write."

Vic told her about the lawyers involved and how the media circus was likely to play out. Peggy was ecstatic about Sanchez's prior connection to the paper. After spending four years in college learning whatever it was they taught in journalism school, she turned out to be a real hard news editor.

# 86

"The Senate will come to order!"

Democratic State Senator Bennet Howell III, now majority leader, rapped his desk hard with the heavy gavel from the front of the senate chambers. Rowdy members quieted slightly. A few made their way to their small desks.

"The clerk will call the roll."

As a young male clerk droned on to see who was present, Howell conferred with two other state senators standing next to him. They were actually planning the annual House versus Senate charity softball game, scheduled for the following week at Coors Field.

By late January, nearly nine months following the Swain murder, the Colorado Legislature found itself dominated by a controversial proposal to revise state water law. The bill would make it easier for businesses and cities to get their hands on water used for farm and ranch irrigation.

Land developers and municipal government officials designed the bill to take advantage of the statewide water development bond issue narrowly approved by Colorado voters the previous fall. The close bond issue election was made even tighter when the *Rocky Mountain Sun* broke a series of stories about water lawyer Gary Kendrick, his conflicts of interest, and his behind-the-scenes involvement with the bond issue election.

To get the water bill passed, Howell engineered a compromise that neutered the state water engineer and handed the governor the power to override water court decisions if the governor declares any dispute over water rights to be a "matter of state interest." It was a bone tossed to the environmental, wildlife, and agricultural interests, and they knew it.

While it was called The Great Water Compromise, it came too late for a number of Colorado farmers who lost their irrigation well water, then their crops, and finally their farms the year before, but the politicians at the statehouse were all puffed up and pleased with themselves.

Most political observers agreed that the compromise did not really mean all that much since few, if any, governors would buck land developers for the sake of a few fish, or ducks, or even cornfields.

"Thirty-five present, none absent," the clerk said.

Lieutenant Governor John Michaels stood quietly in the back of the senate chambers as the lawmakers began their day's work. His chief political adviser, law professor Randal Rosenthal, stood next to him. Governor Dowd had appointed local car dealer Joe Rohlas to fill the state senate seat vacated by Michaels, who was sworn in as lieutenant governor one week after Vic was shot by Betsy Bender.

"Introduction of bills," Howell said.

"Senate Bill 201 by Senator Lujak" the clerk said. "A bill concerning the management of agricultural irrigation wells in the South Platte River basin and making an appropriation therefore."

"Committee on Agriculture," Howell said.

"God, the man won't give up," Michaels said quietly to

Rosenthal, who nodded. "Dead on arrival. And he's still faking it."

While the senate conducted additional inconsequential business, Democrats Michaels and Rosenthal pushed their way through the heavy wooden double doors into the senate lobby where they were greeted with warm handshakes by former White House advisor, and now Colorado land developer, Eugene Currington. The three men exchanged pleasantries and then walked off toward the lieutenant governor's office.

# 87

Late July crops in the remaining agricultural fields north of Denver burst with nature's promise of abundance, assured only by irrigation water collected in western Colorado and siphoned over the Continental Divide to the eastern part of the state. A few more fields that had produced tons of onions or cabbages a year earlier lay fallow, occupied only by giant commercial real estate signs declaring the land's availability for industrial, commercial, or residential development. Millions of gallons of water once used to grow food would now be used to water the lawns and flush the toilets of the ever-expanding strip city running north and south for a hundred and fifty miles along Colorado's eastern Front Range of the Rocky Mountains.

As Vic made the turn onto Riverdale Road from 104th Avenue, Dad said, "Did you ever stop at that dairy?"

"No," Vic said. "I'd like to some time. It's more than a hundred years old."

"It'd be a nice story, Vic," Mom said from her passenger side spot in the back seat. Dad rode shotgun. On the floor between his puffy feet, a small portable oxygen tank gasped every so often. Vic thought of Gil whenever he heard it. Mom gazed out the window mentally collecting scenes to paint in watercolors, oils, or acrylics.

"With gas prices down, I'll bet there's not as much corn planted this year," Dad said.

"I don't know," Vic said. "Those ethanol plants still need corn to keep them running. They mix some ethanol in with the gas during the winter out here to knock down the pollution, thin out the brown cloud."

"Gas prices are bound to go up again," Mom said.

The ride up Riverdale Drive went like that, talk about farms and crops and water and gas. The blacktop road hugged the western edge of the broad South Platte River valley as it meandered northeast of Denver. Battalions of tract houses had moved in from the west, halted in their conquering march only by the small ridge overlooking the farm fields and gravel pits in the river bottom flats to the east. Vic wondered if this fertile soil might someday morph into housing developments. Probably not, he thought, thanks to nature. If the Denver area ever experienced a three hundred year flood this entire valley would be filled with water. That prospect alone might be just enough to keep the Curringtons of the world at bay. It certainly would not be state government policy. Those in charge believe that owners of land in Colorado can do about anything they want to with it.

Their route took them north past the Adams County Fairgrounds, the two county-owned golf courses, beneath the E-470 tollway owned by some Italian industrialist, past the yellow farm house Mom always liked, to State Highway 7 where they turned east toward Brighton, the Adams County seat.

They crossed U.S. Highway 85, cruised into town, and turned north onto a street that took them through one of Brighton's older neighborhoods with big trees, two-story frame and brick homes, tidy yards with abundant vegetable gardens.

"There's a nice one," Mom said. "They must like zucchinis. They're everywhere."

"There's some corn in that one," Dad said. "We'll have to get some sweet corn for dinner."

"I think some Olathe corn is in," Mom said. "Let's stop at the Safeway on the way home, unless we see a stand."

Vic turned south off Longs Peak Street onto 12th Avenue, taking them along the eastern edge of Bjaa Park, a small recreation oasis that occupied about three-fourths of a block in old Brighton. Toward the southern end of the park, near the gazebo, Vic noticed two young girls running and playing. An old couple sat almost motionless at a nearby shaded picnic table. A clear plastic hose ran from a silver and green oxygen bottle on a wheel pull-cart to Gil Johansson's head. The old man adjusted the cannula, repositioning it in his nose and draping the two lines over his ears, movements that had become familiar to Vic because his father did it all the time. Gil and his wife, Betsy, sat across from each other and watched their granddaughters play. Vic pulled over to the curb.

"That's them," Vic said.

"Who?" said Dad.

"Gil, Betsy, the girls."

"From your story?" Mom said. "I thought she was in the hospital."

"Betsy, Gil's wife," Vic said. "The Mother. Or, grandmother. I think they got custody of the girls."

"Do you want to go see them?" Mom said.

"No, they need to be left alone," Vic said.

"Where is their mother again?" Dad said.

"In Pueblo," Vic said. "At the state hospital."

"Is there going to be a trial?" Dad said.

"That's hard to say," Vic said. "But I doubt it."

Geller and Sanchez had done their magic, getting Betsy Bender declared mentally unfit to stand trial. They angled for an insanity plea, something that rarely happened in Colorado. The lawyers even brought up one of Colorado's more infamous failed assassins, John Hinkley Jr., who was consigned to a lifetime of mental care after being found not guilty by reason of insanity for wounding President Ronald Reagan and three others with a cheap six-shot twenty-two-caliber Saturday night special. The two Denver lawyers convinced a "soft-on-crime" judge, as one of the local right-wing yak radio gabsters called him, to send Betsy to Pueblo for observation. That was nearly a year ago. Maybe there would be a trial. Maybe there would not.

"Where's their father?" Mom said.

"I heard he sees the girls on weekends," Vic said.

"Is he in jail?" Dad said.

"No," Vic said. "He and his farmer buddies didn't really do anything."

"Didn't that Bobbie something shoot at someone?" Mom said.

"Bobbie Hague?" Vic said. "No, but he pulled a gun on the water engineer, and a deputy shot him. Injured him. Didn't kill him."

"Winged him," Dad said. Then he laughed between oxygen puffs.

"The deputy who shot Hague grew up with him," Vic said. "The sheriff reprimanded him for not going for the kill."

"Lucky for Hague," Dad said.

"Hague got probation for pulling the gun," Vic said.

"I still think they put Betsy up to it," Mom said.

"The cops couldn't prove a thing," Vic said. "If anyone put them up to it, it was the water lawyer, Kendrick."

"Oh, the one you won the ribbon for," Mom said, like it was a Boy Scout merit badge.

"It was the Pulitzer Prize, Mom," Vic said.

"I'm so proud of you," she said.

Vic and his Dad looked at each other. Dad raised his eyebrows and smiled.

"Did anything ever happen to him, the lawyer?" Mom said. "I mean after you wrote all those stories about him."

"Disbarred and pleaded guilty to one count of misappropriation of client funds," Vic said. "Six months' probation."

"I think he was in on it," Mom said. "The murder."

The girls ran from the monkey bars over to their grandparents, who had set out a lunch or some snacks.

"Where is their dad that he can see them on weekends?" Mom said.

"Not that far away," Vic said. "He lives in a little house on Bobbie Hague's farm. He works for Hague, farming. That's what he knows."

"They have extra houses," Mom said. "That's nice."

"I think it's more like a shack they used to use for migrant workers," Vic said.

"What about the water?" Dad said. "Didn't this Hague have the same problem?"

"Hague and some other farmers put up all their savings and borrowed against their farms to help with the legal work and to buy some water rights," Vic said. "They got quite a bit of their money back from Kendrick after he was disbarred. When the cities won that statewide water bond issue election, a few of them actually worked out deals with nearby farmers to share the water. The deals stay in place until, or if, they build storage reservoirs with the bond issue money. Then they have to renegotiate them. I think Hague got a well or two turned back on."

"Could we go past the farm?" Mom said. She felt sorry for the small farmers squeezed out of their agrarian lifestyles.

"The Bender farm?" Vic said. "Or the Johansson farm?"

"They're one in the same," Mom said

"Just checking," Vic said. "To see if you actually read my stories."

"Did I pass?" Mom said.

"With flying colors," Vic said.

"Where they caught her," Mom said, then, choking up a bit, "where she shot you."

"I'll bet there's nothing there," Dad said.

"Nothing farm-wise or just nothing at all?" Vic said.

"No crops," Dad said.

"I think you'll be right about that, Dad," Vic said.

They drove north from Brighton, mostly in silence, and east out the county road from Fort Lupton toward the Bender-Johansson farm.

All three gazed at the mid-summer fields with a variety of greens pushing up through the soil, the scattered housing developments in all directions, and the occasional oil well.

"That one's pumping," Dad would say as the giant grasshopper pump bobbed up and down on a stripper well.

Vic pointed to a group of massive cottonwood trees next to an irrigation ditch and said, "That's where we parked the car. Steve Jones and I walked down that little road to the farm."

"I could kill you," Mom said.

"Someone almost did," Vic said.

"Oh, you know what I mean."

He did. The whole thing shook up his entire family, the newspaper, and him. Vic put his right hand over his heart, then rubbed his left shoulder.

As he rolled the Jeep Grand Cherokee around the corner and let it come to a stop in the road cut that once served as the driveway to the farm, Vic's mother let out a low gasp.

"Oh my God," she said.

"See, no crops," Dad said.

"You're right about that," Vic said. "I guess I'm buying the coffee." His father laughed again, a cherished sound to Vic.

The farm lacked more than crops. The farm lacked everything. The dueling Bender and Johansson signs were gone. So was the small frame house where Betsy Bender served Vic iced tea and told him about her shooting range. The silo was not there. Nor was the Quonset hut, nor the barn. Nothing was there, no green, no crops, no buildings, no cars, no hint that three generations of a family had bent to the earth to grow food for those who demanded to be fed. Only the brown dusty soil remained. Three massive yellow earth movers were parked where Dave Bender had sat in the sun on his mother's chrome kitchen chair, leaning up against his barn with a shotgun laid across his lap, waiting for the bank to come and confiscate his final scrap of family heritage. One thing remained, a massive sign declaring:

# VALLEY FARMS
3-5 Acre Rural Estates
From the Mid 600s

## South Platte Land and Cattle Company
Eugene T. Currington, President

### Financing provided by
Fort Lupton Bank & Trust
Benjamin A. Ferguson, President

# 88

Vic stepped from his front door and set a freshly brewed French press coffee down next to the stack of newspapers on the small round table that occupied one corner of his porch. The crisp Labor Day morning air was expected to warm up to the high sixties by afternoon. He sat down and began his morning ritual, kneading the left shoulder with the right hand, pumping the left arm, working the elbow a few times to loosen it up. His ortho doc said there would always be some residual pain and stiffness in the shoulder and elbow.

Newspapers would consume the morning, first the *Sun*, then the *Denver Times*, and finally the *New York Times*. Vic scheduled the afternoon with grandson Devon to begin work a short wave radio kit. The boy had already successfully completed the AM radio project, took it to school for show-and-tell, and now kept the radio next to his bed at home. On Tuesday, it would be back to work and his next investigative target. Vic took a sip of coffee and pulled the *Sun* from its yellow plastic delivery bag. The front page displayed a large photo of the news room and a single story.

## ROCKY MOUNTAIN SUN FOR SALE
### State's oldest paper on the block
*Associated Press*

SCRANTON, PA – Scranton Media, parent company of the Pulitzer Prize-winning *Rocky Mountain Sun*, announced Tuesday that the 149-year-old paper, Denver's oldest, was up for sale.

In the past decade, the *Sun* has won five Pulitzer Prizes, the most recent one by reporter Vic Bengston who received the award for community service for a series of investigative articles that led to the disbarment and criminal prosecution of one of Colorado's most prominent water lawyers.

A spokesperson for Scranton Media said the company would take offers for the daily newspaper until October 1. If no acceptable offers are made, the newspaper would be liquidated, the company said.

The *Sun*, founded in 1859 by Jonathon Renfrow, has been owned by Scranton Media since 1926 and has published under a joint operating agreement with rival daily paper, the *Denver Times*, since 2001.

"No one buys daily newspapers anymore," Vic said into his coffee. He looked up and waved at his neighbor, who was across the street walking her micro dog, a real yapper that looked like a dust mop. "They just shut them down."

# Afterword

*By Dave Elsner*
*St. Charles, Illinois 2012*

Richard J. Schneider, author. Sounds impressive, but I prefer "My pal, Dickie," and I really can say "Pal" as I've known him since we were kids. If my calculations are correct, we're going on sixty years. As I reflect back on Dickie and all the things we did together, including the trouble we caused, completion of his first novel comes as no surprise. Dickie always seemed to be ahead of the curve. Perhaps it was his upbringing as his folks seemed to always be a few steps ahead of other families on Everett Avenue: first to own a color TV, first to have a boy & girl dance party and in second grade no less! I was one of the "Lucky Couples" shot with a Polaroid Land Camera (another first). Girls wore dresses and boys wore sport coats and ties. Plus, Dickie and I were able to make use of the dance lessons for which his and my parents had signed us up. You could tell by the awkward position I was in with my dance partner, Jeanne Tatman, that I'd rather be playing Army in the vacant lot next door.

In our summertime campouts, we'd bivouac in Dickie's back yard cooking hot dogs and roasting marshmallows over a campfire built in his sandbox, in sleeping bags under the stars, roughing it, cracking jokes, telling stories and laughing hysterically until our stomachs hurt and Kool-Aid bubbled out our noses. In the morning, we'd stoke up the embers and cook one of his signature dishes, Scrambled Pancakes, which came to Dickie not so much by design as by accident. He was also quite a wordsmith and had picked up on some lingo we all thought were dirty words or, at least as dirty as he could conjure up, which was the insult of all insults to call another guy. It was "Ya Naked Lady." He bravely, or perhaps foolishly, used this against the neighborhood bully and got popped in the eye for his verbal talent. He was known even in early years as one to speak his mind and not back down.

Suddenly, I fast forward to Richard J. Schneider, the author. While much has happened over the years, we have remained friends and stayed in contact. I've watched as Dickie has grown, matured and moved into his comfort zone of a creative, persuasive and imaginative person: writing, marketing, developing business plans and strategies, using his photojournalistic skills, also, as a self-employed consultant and a champion of environmental causes. And, finally, into authoring his first novel, *WATER.*

I believe he has been on this road since childhood to achieve this, and he has now arrived. All the adventures, experiences, hardships, and joy that he has experienced along the way were preparing him. Now, here it is, *WATER.* So what makes a good read? Research, Research, Research. And the ability to take this research and craft a story that is timely, credible and that comes from spending many years residing in Colorado and witnessing, first hand, the politics of water rights. This has enabled Dickie to create believable characters like Vic Bengston. And, yes, I can see some of my pal in this central character, and some of me for that matter. I was absorbed by Dickie's first book and look forward to more books in the Vic Bengston series. Thanks for allowing me the privilege of writing an afterword to your first effort. Doing this has helped me to travel back in time to unearth many fond memories of the times we spent together. The next time I drink a glass of water or eat vegetables or fruit grown in the rich soil of Colorado, I'll think of you.

All My Best and Good Luck!

# Acknowledgements

This is my first novel, a perceived unconquerable summit for most of my professional life, until a number of people helped me scale its heights. I would like to thank them.

I will begin with my mother, Jeanne Schneider, who encouraged me throughout the entire process, served as a sounding board as I read passages during our many breaks together at various coffee shops, and helped resolve a particularly onerous plot point.

My father, Richard R. Schneider, who passed away in 2005, had a love for photography and for words. The scenes I describe are photographs put to words. I strive to keep them like Dad's black and white photos, crisp, lean, to the point. He was an incurable reader of mysteries, a few of which I picked up and read. I was hooked for the rest of my life.

Here's the first book, Pop. More to come.

A word about my late uncle, Casey Schneider, my Dad's and Uncle Bill's younger brother, who died too early. Casey wrote all his life, short stories, essays, poems about the Chicago Cubs, country and western songs, a novel, and whacky fill-in-the-blank Rotten Ralph cards. Casey, who was more like my big brother as I grew up, was a bit of a rake. But he always kept writing, all his life, and he had fun with it. I will be doing the same.

Others who provided invaluable support, editorial comments, encouragement, inspiration, focus, prodding and help (knowingly and unknowingly), in no particular order, include Kathie Schneider

Golden, Kevin Schneider, Kim Schneider, Kathy Gleason, Judy Stephen, Trygve Schneider, Liam Schneider, Clarissa Schneider, Craig Wasilewski, Bill and Caron Schneider, Michele Schneider Conlan, Willard Schneider (Uncle Bill) who finally put his World War Two stories into print, my late Aunt Marie Schneider who encouraged all forms of art, my late uncle Casey Schneider, my Auntie Midge Black who always sent me books for gifts, Candace Black Schaefer, Verlyn Schaefer, Robert Himber, John and Robin Lindsey, Ila Pyatt, Elissa Tivona, Paul Rohrer, Cathy Moore, The Real Bob Scott, Jim Czupor, Nick Del Calzo, the late Mike Golden, Marge Golden, Maureen Golden Campbell, Rick Campbell, John Golden, the late Charlie Golden, Pat McNulty, Bob and Ellen Sieh, Ted Bailey, Dale Rau, Joyce Bernard Masters, Kenny Albrecht, The Kitchen Sink, The Class of 65 CLCHS; some important high school teachers, namely, Dale Whiteside, Mrs. Wright, Mr. Rippl; college professors Marilyn Moats Kennedy and Thad Tecza; the Rocky Mountain Lake Rowing Club; the Everett Avenue Gang: Jeanne, Norm, Linda, Patty, Bobby, and Rusty; and the pal I have known the longest on Earth, Dave Elsner. The grandkids: Darin, Brysen, Alec, and Justin. You know, if I missed someone, I apologize. There will be more books.

The fictional character Vic Bengston is an amateur radio operator, as am I. Two amateurs, or "hams," in particular, provided inspiration to keep on trucking, Ron Kienzle, KZ7P, an avid mystery reader, and Jane Woedening, AA0ZR, a long-time writer, whose memoir, *Way Up There*, should be read by men and women, young and old. It is a modern day *Waldon*. My call sign, by the way, is AB0CD.

Last, a word about the Independent Authors Movement — Indies, as we are called. The publishing industry is changing radically, and by the minute. *WATER* is an Indie project, launched by the artist. Changes in technology — primarily, eBooks, eReader devices, the internet, and Print-On-Demand technology — result in more titles available to readers. Traditional publishers are narrowing their publishing scope more and more to guarantee future profitability, often closing doors to good writers. This means more and more Indie launches like *Vic Bengston Investigations.* The work of many Indie authors are on a par, and sometimes better, than those marketed by traditional publishers. Music already has gone this route, and film and television are not far behind. So, support your local Indie.

— *Richard J. Schneider, Denver, Colorado 2012*

*Richard J. Schneider is a former journalist, scriptwriter and video producer. He co-founded and ran a creative services company in Colorado for many years. His journalism, scriptwriting, and producing have won many awards. For more information, visit: www.richardjshneider.com.*

www.ingramcontent.com/pod-product-compliance
Lightning Source LLC
Chambersburg PA
CBHW051312250626
47155CB00007B/2293